Paradise on the Plains

Happy Fathers Day.
with lots of Love,
marjorie

Paradise on the Plains

By
Keith A. Cook

A Leathers Publishing Production
4500 College Blvd.
Leawood, KS 66211
Phone: 1 / 888 / 888-7696

ISBN: 1-890622-61-3

Library of Congress Catalog Card No. 98-75677

A Leathers Publishing Production
4500 College Blvd.
Leawood, KS 66211
Phone: 1 / 888 / 888-7696

THE GARDEN

TIMES WERE GOOD in the 1920s. Pete and Effie Pisanmoan had decided to move from the Bar P ranch south of Wallace, Kan., to the county seat, Sharon Springs. It was more of social conformity; it just seemed right. When their son, Piedmond, came home from World War I, married the Union Pacific section foreman's daughter, Pete and Effie decided it was time to turn over the reins, let the young folks run the ranch. Pete and Effie put on their town clothes, loaded up the buggy with a couple of grips and a trunk, hitched up the horse and told Pied and his new wife to "Have a nice stay."

Pete did not own an automobile; his comment was, "They's not practical fer the ranch; saddle horse belongs on a ranch. A automobile jest sits till we go ta town fer grub an' that's only about onct a month. Too much of an investmint." Effie just nodded. Not much was said on the trip; Pete was the talker and Effie was the listener. About the time they crossed the Smokey Hill River east of Sharon Springs, Pete said, "We'll stay at the West Hotel fer a coupla days. I'll go up to the barber shop an' jest listen, keep m' ear peeled. There'll be a house we kin buy somewhere's. You kin wash the dishes, clean rooms fer our bed and board, Effie ol' girl." Effie just nodded, gritted her teeth.

Pete got a shave every day; it took him just over a week to hear what he needed. He heard about a house. George Peebles was bumped to Oakley; he was the third trick operator at the Union Pacific Depot. Pete heard he wanted $1,200 for a two-bedroom house.

Pete took a stroll up to the Peeble's residence. Effie was too busy washing dishes, cleaning rooms. Pete was meticulous in his appraisal of property. He commented, "Way too high on the price, Missus Peebles. Looks ta me like one good blow outta the north come winter an' this shack would fold like a card table. Why, you an' the young'ns ain't atall safe. Condemnation, that's what I'd do, condemn this shack a shambles." Pearl Peebles was in tears when Pete left and walked down the street, sucking on a toothpick, smiling. He tipped his Triple X Stetson to his future neighbor, Penelope Pinchlips, went down to the hotel and informed Effie he'd found the perfect domicile; it was a dandy.

"You jest keep awashin' them dishes, ol' girl. It's a nice place." Effie nodded, twitched an attempted smile.

Third trick operator gets off work at eight a.m. It took Pete three mornings walking home with Mr. Peebles to get the house for what he deemed "Fair market value. Mr. Peebles, bin in real estate all m' life." Pete bought the house furnished, pots, pans, potholders, pastry brush and the chamber pot for $950, cash.

"I'll get a warranty deed drawed up, close the deal come Saturday; you folks git moved out and come Sunday, Effie, thet's m' wife, we'll take possession. She's sick of livin' the life of luxury down at the West Hotel."

Surprisingly, Effie did kind of like the house. It had a big kitchen stove. Furniture was better than they'd had on the Bar P, and she'd now have some neighbors to visit with. No more rattlesnakes in the hen house, no more daughter-in-law who couldn't find her way to the mail box and was always in the way.

It was a day or so when Pete said, "Godalmighty, Effie, ol' girl, I missed one thing when I bought this here place. They's not a nuff room for a big garden. Why, you'd wither away, need our fresh air and fresh vegetables and this glorious western Kansas sunshine."

Effie bit her lip, just nodded. Pete did not see her clenched fists behind her back.

Pete walked to the window, looked to the south and remarked, "Wonder who owns them three vacant lots? Think I'll jest mosey over to Penelope Pinchlip's house; those lots would make us a dandy garden. Must be hunnert-foot front, maybe two-hunnert foot deep. Jest the right size for a garden."

Pete put on his Triple X Stetson, stuck a fresh toothpick in his mouth and said, "Wish me luck, ol' girl."

Effie kind of wished Mr. Peebles had left a Winchester with

the place.

Pete eyeballed the vacant lots as he strolled by. Had it all mentally planted. He knew just where everything was to be planted: peas, carrots, pole beans, sweet corn, turnips, beets, watermelon and cantaloupe. Two rows of parsnips. Penelope Pinchlips and Daphne Damptowel were sitting on the front porch swing, having a nice chat.

"Mornin', ladies." Pete tipped his Triple X and wiggled his toothpick, had a twinkle in his eye. "I'm Pete Pisanmoan, yer new neighbor, bought out the Peebles, makin' a neighborly call. M' wife Effie, she's kinda shy, bin down on the ranch too long. What's yer name there, girlie?"

"I am Daphne Damptowel; I live two doors down on the corner, a dear and devoted friend of Miss Pinchlips. We are both very active in Women's Suffrage. We women will be voting this fall for the very first time. May I inquire if your wife is registered to vote, Mr. Pisanmoan?"

That was more conversation than Effie said in a week; it kind of surprised Pete. "She ain't registered. Miss Pinchlips, could ya tell me who owns them vacant lots between our properties? I bin thinkin' 'bout makin' garden, nice size one."

"Why, Mr. Pisanmoan, I own those fine lots. A garden is a marvelous idea. I could have all my vegetables free and have rental income on the lots at the same time." She smiled demurely at Pete. Pete could see this was small town materialism; there was that smugness, that intellectual intolerance for the outsider.

Penelope had just given Pete a zinger. He thought to himself that this ain't Effie I'm a-dealin' with. He needed a snappy reply. "It was my intentions to make this a one-crop operation, Miss Pinchlips. Which is ya partial to, watermelons or cantaloupes?"

Penelope batted her brown eyes; she had always been a coy one with the men. "Why, I just dearly love cantaloupe."

Pete rolled his toothpick, "Had watermelons in mind, Miss Pinchlips, them Dixie Queens grow right well in this country."

Penelope admired the ripost; she had gotten trapped on that one. Pete just might become a formidable foe, one who could mentally joust.

Pete asked, "How much are yer property taxes, Miss Pinchlips?"

"They Are $6.80 per annum, Mr. Pisanmoan. Why do you ask about my taxes when we are discussing making garden?" (The taxes were really $3.40; Penelope was volleying for the watermelon twist of fate, double up on Pete and his toothpick.)

"Well, now, I kinda thought we'd draw us up a tidy little lease on those lots. I'd have a good deal of what we call sweat equity in them lots. Let's say I draw up a lease at five dollars a year as consideration, and all the watermelons you can eat. I don't want one takin' advantage of an honest man. 'Course, it bein' your land, we'd use yer windmill for the water ta irrigate. Wind's free, ya know, Miss Pinchlips. I'd prefer the lease was to run to three years. Lotsa sweat in a garden, ya know." Pete smiled.

"Let us make the rent $7.50," said Penelope. "That will just pay my taxes. I agree to the use of my windmill, and you trapped me on that watermelon. I shall eat the watermelon, but I do want my $7.50 now, Mr. Pisanmoan; I might change my mind or lease it to another party. Daphne has been talking about the purchase of some goats. They would keep the weeds down; a couple of nannies would provide us with healthful milk."

Daphne smiled, kind of a snotty sort of a smile, nodded affirmatively. Pete knew he had a toughie, kind of like a slick cattle buyer that came out of Denver. Ranchers in Wallace County named him Slither, hard to get a fair price for your calves.

Pete pushed back the Triple X, "Now, that's not atall fair, Miss Pinchlips. I'd figured on payin' the lease money when the crop comes in, when I commence sellin' those watermelons for 'bout a penny a pound. Good watermelons bring as high as twenty cents. Thet's the way I figure all m' financial transactions."

"Why, I am appalled, Mr. Pisanmoan." Penelope clutched at her throat as if she were being financially strangled. "You expect me to let you use my valuable land, pump my water and not get paid until the crop comes in? What if you should get hailed out? Suppose you should become ill and not work your garden properly? You just might swallow that filthy toothpick and choke to death. No, I must have my money up front when we sign that tidy little lease." She gave the swing a little nudge, commenced swinging.

"I guess I'll jest have to pay up front; it ain't the way we deal in agriculture. I may just put in a row or two of something special since I kind of snookered you on thet watermelon. You partial to parsnips, Miss Pinchlips?"

"That is quite gentlemanly of you, Mr. Pisanmoan. Let me see — no, I am not partial to parsnips. I do crave carrots. Peas are pure pleasure; beets are beautiful but I just **abhor** sweet corn."

"Now thet I know yer prefcrences, I'll git thet lease ready and go borrow $7.50 from the bank. See ya in a coupla days. Was a real pleasure ta meetcha, Miss Damptowel. Don't buy any goats."

Both Pete and Penelope felt their first encounter a Mexican stand-off. Pete rolled his toothpick over to the other side of his mouth and smiled. He was calculating the amount of sweet corn seed he needed to purchase for that garden. The next day the town drayman drove up in his wagon, had a walking plow in the back, pulled it off on the vacant lots and drove up to the Pisanmoan house and knocked on the door.

A woman answered; she kind of stood back in the kitchen. "Whatcha want?" Effie was shy around strangers; only company she ever had come calling down on the Bar P was the Raleigh man.

The man informed Effie, "I delivered a walkin' plow, Mrs Pisanmoan, traded it for your buggy. Pete said the buggy was in the shed. I'll pick it up now, that all right?"

Effie was not of the loquacious sort. She merely said, "Yep." She would improve her communications ability when she became acquainted with Penelope and Daphne; they would educate her.

Pete hitched the horse to the plow, and no one ever plowed a straighter or neater furrow. He had Effie hoe down the big clumps of sod. "When ya git that done, we'll hand rake 'er, Effie. Make 'er real nice an' smooth. We'll sell them roastin' ears fer two cents apiece. Plant just two hills of watermelons. Honest man lives up ta his agreements."Effie hit a rather large clod a mighty wallop with the hoe. She pretended it was Pete's head; it was about as hard. While Effie was busting clods, Pete took a little walk, mostly up and down alleys. Two blocks from home he found what he was looking for, a nice big chicken house. He opened the gate, cast his experienced eye under the roosts and smiled. He knocked on the summer kitchen door; a man came to the door.

"Howdy, neighbor. I'm Pete Pisanmoan, jest moved up from down south of Wallace. Me an' the missus need work. Clean out yer hen house fer five dollars, haul the manure away. Them hens lay better in a clean environment. Put in nice clean nests if'n ya git the straw."

The man looked Pete over, trying to figure out where he was getting slickered, "I been looking for somebody like you. I'm from Missouri, gotta show me your work. I'll give you three dollars, Mr. Pisanmoan; Missouri is full of the likes of you — all talk and no work."

"Spit and shake on 'er, mister. You throw in thet broken-handled shovel, a nice fat hen and the three dollars. Me. and the missus will commence our hen house cleanin' tamorra mornin'. They's nuthin' we like better than cleanin' a hen house." The men spit and shook; Pete picked out a nice fat hen for the Pisanmoan pot and walked home with a fine white Leghorn in one hand, a broken shovel in the other. It had been a good day for Pete; he smiled and twitched his toothpick, yep, a fine day.

"Thet was one fine meal of chicken an' dumplin's, Effie. Jest fer thet, ya gets yer choice of jobs. Ya kin shovel the wheelbarry full of chicken manure or ya kin wheel it down ta the garden and kind of spread it around, take yer choice."

"Shovel."

"Good choice, Effie ol' girl. I got jest the shovel for ya. I saw a wheelbarry in a shed today, I'll jest borry it. Folks weren't ta home when I knocked on the door."

The Pisanmoans got an early start. There was a whole lot of chicken manure under those roosts. Pete calculated it would take all of three days hauling. Along about nine that morning he ran into a young fellow; maybe he could speed things up, get a little help. "Howdy, there, Lars. I haven't seen ya for a month a Sundays. Watcha bin doin'?"

"Heard you moved to town, Pete. I ain't doin' nothin". I got laid off down at the coal chute, just couldn't seem to satisfy them Union Pacific folks on firing a stationary boiler."

Pete could see help had arrived when Lars showed up. "How'd ya like ta pick up a quick an' easy dollar, Lars? I gotta little job cleanin' a henhouse. Ya got a wheelbarry at home?"

"Sure, I could use a dollar. Pa's got a wheelbarrow. You want me to help ya wheel chicken manure; it's light stuff, dusty though; not many folks like chicken manure."

"Here's the skinny on the dollar, Lars. You havta wheel two loads ta my one. I've got me a condition, a herny, have to take it kind of easy. You understand now, Lars, if I haul ten loads a day, you gotta haul twenty. Is it a deal, Lars?"

"Sounds fair ta me, Pete. Where ya haulin' this stuff?"

"Vacant lots on the north side of Penelope Pinchlip's house. You go git yer pa's wheelbarry an' go to Evilsizer's chicken coop. M' missus will load ya, be nice if you had sideboards. Jest walk mighty brisk like, dump the manure on the lot. Kinda kick it around a little so's ta spread it out, make it kinda even like."

Penelope Pinchlips had been uptown that morning, been to the Clip and Curl, had a new permanent. Her brunette curls just bounced when she walked. She stopped to show Daphne her curly locks and started home just as Pete rounded the corner by Dollarhide's house pushing a big load of chicken manure. She stopped and watched, wondered what that addlepated man was doing.

Pete dumped his load of manure. But it wasn't all manure. A cloud of white feathers drifted southward and skyward; the fluffy down floated in the Kansas breeze. Down settled in the bouncy brunette curls.

"Mr. Pisanmoan! Just what are you doing to my property? You have feathers in my spirea bushes, all over my front porch! I have never witnessed such a mess!"

Pete gave the last load a few good kicks to spread it around; feathers flew.

"M' dear Miss Pinchlips. I done tested yer soil yesterday

after I finished plowin'. Yer soil is shy in nitrogen and in iron. Fair ta middlin' test in zinc and potash, needs a boost in maganese sulfate and the sulphur departments. I'm goin' ta a great deal of expense an' effort ta improve yer propity. Even hired help, paid with m' own money to haul this here manure. Why, here comes Lars trottin' down the street now; he's got a nice fresh load. Yer propity will become more valuable with a dose of prime fertilizer. Now, as to them feathers, if I was you, I'd select 'em an' put 'em in a sack, make a fine down-filled piller. Down piller would make yer curly locks last longer. Now don't ya expect me to be a-chargin' ya fer the soil advice. I gotta go; Lars is two up on me now." Pete wiggled his toothpick and left Penelope Pinchlips muttering.

Penelope stomped her foot on the front porch; feathers flew. She muttered to herself, he wouldn't know manganese sulfate from a Model T Ford!

It was not until the sweet corn sprouted that the feud commenced. "I distinctly told you, Mr. Pisanmoan, that I abhorred sweet corn!"

Pete acted astounded, "My dear Miss Pinchlips, I musta misunderstood. I thought ya said ya **adored** sweet corn. Now ain't thet a shame. Ya gotta accept m' humble apologies." Pete rolled the toothpick over to the other side of his mouth, tilted back his Triple X, "I did plant some very nice watermelon; thet is in that there lease. I bought some new leathers fer yer windmill, gotta go home and git 'em. Good day ta ya." Pete went home, a satisfied man. He liked them zingers.

The next morning when Pete went to see how the irrigation water was running down the corn rows, there was no water! The mill had been shut off; Penelope had shut off Pete's water. He came to a conclusion. "Looks like a little game a hard ball. Penelope has done violated the lease; I could record that lease and cloud her title to the propity, pick me up three nice lots." Pete changed his mind, decided to go uptown for a few items.

Later, when he came home for dinner, he yelled in the kitchen door: "Effie, come see what I bought ya."

Effie was surprised. The last time the old penny-pincher bought her anything was for her birthday two years ago, a dime's worth of horehound candy. "You bought me a new shovel. Why didn't ya do that afore I shoveled all the chicken manure with that broken-handled blister-maker one?"

"I got an apology ta make, Effie ol' girl. I didn't make a thorough inspection of this propity we both hold title to. Half yours, ya know. Thet outhouse hole is jest 'bout plumb full. Now I could git a sack 'o slack lime an' dump 'er in, but they's no gittin' 'round it, thet hole's 'bout full. I'll take the busted shovel an' do the irrigatin' on the corn crop; you kin dig us a new hole. I'll git Lars ta hep me move the outhouse over when ya git the hole dug. Now if ya'd like a change a view, you kin face it south. Kinda pleasant out there a-lookin' towards Penelope's, watchin' thet corn crop grow.

"What you got in the sack, Pete?"

"I bought us a couple a pork chops and some gardenin' supplies. Pied and Flo was in town. They was driving a new Model T. Pied said the calf crop looked good, thanked us fer brandin' all them calves. He's sure gonna be in fer a surprise when thet brand inspector tells the cattle buyer ta make the check out ta us. Them calves are all a-wearing the -P. Did ya notice the shovel, Effie? Thet there handle is genuine hickory, a real beauty."

After supper and along about sundown, Pete ambled down to the mill, picking pork chop meat out of his teeth. The mill was running, water was flowing down the rows. He noticed the kitchen curtain part, not much, just a tad. That was his intention; Penelope was watching him. Pete checked the mill. He looked it over clear up to the mill head, then walked home, tongued his toothpick over, spit a little pork chop out and smiled.

Pete and Effie were reading *Capper's Farmer* by kerosene lamp light.

"Where you goin', Pete? Too early for bed."

"Gotta stretch m' legs. Won't be gone long."

Pete went out to the coal shed, got a tube. He'd already cut off the end. He was primed and ready to slip quietly down the alley to the windmill. He used the tube on the long handle that shut the windmill on and off. He eased back in the darkness about fifty feet and waited, waited almost an hour. Then the back door was eased open; lamplight fell on the path to the mill.

Pete saw Penelope had on her night clothes, including a night cap to protect her bouncy curls, little pink slippers with little pink bows. She reached up and grasped the mill handle to shut it off, and then Pete heard a tight little shriek. He smiled; the little pink slippers were swinging in the air. Then there was a yelp. One hand came loose, another yelp even louder and a hasty, hand-wringing little trot to the back door; the door slammed!

Pete mused, belt dressin' will do 'er ever time.

(Belt dressing was 100% pure rosin. It was used on the belts of threshing machines to keep them from coming off the pulleys. It was extremely sticky!)

Pete didn't see Penelope for several weeks. No problems with the windmill, and my, how that corn did grow. It was thigh high on the 4th of July. He did note that Effie seemed to be in Penelope's house almost every morning. He thought it good for her to have a neighbor like that, although he detected her talking more now that they had moved to town. She seemed to be talking back more to him, too; she'd turned his crank a time or two.

Effie and Daphne helped Penelope remove the bandages. The palms of her hands were healing nicely Effie had used Bag Balm dressing. It says right on the famous green can, "For chapped teats, superficial scratches, abrasions, windburn and sunburn." The two neighbor ladies had been doing the house-work. All three women were quite agitated, perturbed and just plain mad. They were working on a plan, attack on Pete. No military maneuver had ever been planned more carefully. Pete was tending his sweet corn. He purchased Effie a good used pick at a farm sale; it seemed slow going on the outhouse hole what with adobe and Penelope's sore palms. The slack lime effect was wearing off.

No one in Sharon Springs could believe the corn crop Pete Pisanmoan had growing. People would drive by in the evening to admire it. Pete took a rocking chair down and visited with the drive-bys, told them all about his soil analysis, irrigation techniques, and whatever they wanted to know.

"Yesiree, three ears ta the stalk. Golden Bantam. Tassels as long as a pony's tail. Two cents an ear. Must be ten thousand ears in that there patch. About two more weeks, folks! Save yer money fer m' sweet corn."

People kinda liked Pete. Some said he was a born peddler; some said he was a real hustler; others said he's just an old cob.

It was about the first of August when Pete discovered the deed. One morning he walked down to the garden, glanced up, the mill was running, and then he saw them — about thirty corn stalks, pulled up and thrown right there on the ground. He had expected retaliation, but not this! This was beyond vandalism, bordered on a misdemeanor, felonious assault on a corn field. Pete picked the ears of corn from the stalks. He got 87 and sold 80 that evening to some of the drive-bys. He and Effie ate seven ears. Good corn. Sweet and tender. Pete built a shock out of the stalks, and as he was carrying a couple of stalks to the shock, he looked down. Right there on the ground next to a white Leghorn feather was a little pink silk bow.

Pete rolled his toothpick over to the side of his mouth and smiled. Pete now had evidence. He eyeballed Penelope's house, considering it as adequate for his financial loss, pain and suffering. Damages were considerable in Pete's mind. He would have to delay the lawsuit.

The word was out in town, Pete Pisanmoan's sweet corn was ready. Ed Ward came down and wrote an article for the local *Western Times,* right there on the front page. Free advertising — sales were brisk. Effie was carrying a tote sack, snapping ears. Pete was taking the ears and sorting them according to size. The longer ears would bring three cents apiece. "If'n ya want 'em husked, it's only a penny more." No takers, it was worth a try.

One evening Pete came in from a trip to the outhouse. There had been an increase in these trips for both Pete and Effie. They'd been eating a lot of sweet corn, Pete called them "nubbins."

"I see ya got 'bout another foot ta go on that hole, Effie. We got to move that outhouse pretty soon. Flies are plumb irritatin'."

Pete was reading the *Denver Post,* saw a small but interesting article: "U.S. Post Office Dept. rules children may not be sent by parcel post." Pete wondered how one did that. Stick stamps on a kid's forehead? He figured it was cheaper than a ticket. He walked over to the window and looked at the mill. It was pumping nice and steady. Not much to irrigate now but the watermelons. He had decided this was the night to strike. Along about nine Pete told Effie he had to make a trip outside. "Must be the sweet corn."

Pete had cut a four-inch piece of tin the width of the well rod, drilled a hole in it. The hole fit over a bolt on the well rod guide. He slipped the tin over the bolt, put a nut on and bolted the tin so it rubbed on the well rod as it pumped up and down. Pete had to move fast if this worked the way he had planned. Penelope would be bouncing out that back door quick as a provoked panther. She would be plenty piqued. Oh, how the idea worked! Far better than Pete ever anticipated. It sounded just like a kid running his fingernail on a slate blackboard at the schoolhouse. Every time the rod went up, it screeched. Same when it came down.

Out the back door came Penelope, her little pink slippers slapping on the board walk. She was sure it was not the proper time of year for tom cats. Then she realized it was the windmill. She reached up for the rod to shut off the mill, gasped and pulled back her pink and nicely healed pink palms. Pete had cured her of turning off the mill at night. The tin was too high for Penelope to reach, and she couldn't see what was making the noise anyway. Penelope went into the house and slammed the door. She knew that Pete Pisanmoan was prowling around out there in the dark. She had only one thought, "If only that man knew what we have planned for him!"

By midnight, Penelope could not stand the screeching any longer. She put on her robe and little pink slippers and went down to Daphne's house. Along about four a.m. Pete got up and went down and removed the tin screecher. Effie heard him come back to bed; she thought it was too much sweet corn.

The sweet corn was all sold, and Pete started shocking the corn stalks. "I'll git us three, maybe four dollars for them stalks. Make good fodder. They's a good wagon load o' stalks, Effie ol' girl."

Penelope was nervous. She didn't know when the screecher would strike again. She was short on sleep, short on temper, and she was short one little pink bow on her lovely slippers.

When Effie came for her morning glass of Koenig's Nerve Tonic, Penelope had already been hitting the tonic pretty hard. It had become a morning ritual for the three women, having a small shot of nerve tonic just about made their day.

"You just must finish that outhouse hole quickly, Effie! I don't know when he is going to strike again. I jump at every sound all night long. Just cannot get any sleep. I am becoming a nervous wreck!"

"Penelope, I'll finish that there hole today. Pete will have to git Lars to hep him move the outhouse tomorrow. You kin buy the chocolate laxative. I'll bake them cupcakes with the dark chocolate frostin' tomorrow. They's freedom down in the bottom of that outhouse hole, girlies." The three of them smiled; all seemed in a giggling mood. It was the nerve tonic. They were positive their plan was perfect.

When Pete came home with the mail, Effie told him, "That hole is done. You kin move the outhouse, but I got me a condition."

"I know you got a condition, which one is it this time, Effie ol' girl?"

"I want you to face 'er south. You said we was halvers on this here propity. I want to go halvers on the outhouse. East half is mine, west half yours. It's a two-holer, you stay offen my half; sometimes you dribble too much."

"Fair 'nuff, Effie, good condition. Catalogue goes smack dab in the middle. Ya always knowed I was a fair an' reasonable man in all my dealin's. It's folks like me thet has made this country great. Fine outstandin' citizens."

Effie considered saying the Pledge of Allegiance or singing the National Anthem after that load Pete had just unloaded on her.

Penelope had formulated the plan; it was a peach of a plan. "Ladies, time is the critical part of this escapade. Pete eating all that sweet corn has affected our time; we do not know the condition of his bowels and its movements. The laxative bottle says it takes a minimum of two hours for full force and effect for proper relief. How many of those cupcakes does he generally gorge, Effie?"

"He kin stuff six or more, Penelope. If I load 'em good with the frosting, I'm guessing in about an hour he'll be prancin' for the privy. I have a concern; if'n he's got them cramps read bad, he might not hit the west half. Guess it's just the chance we have to take, girls." Effie was becoming downright chatty.

Penelope was the coordinator. "Daphne, did you get that two by four with the nails pounded in at each end? Is it ready?"

"Yes, that door on the outhouse is two feet, four inches wide. I have a two by four, four feet long. Pop Gailey at the lumber yard said to use sixteen-penny nails. I have the nails all pounded so they just barely protrude through the other side. I have placed them, two hammers, one for you, Penelope, and one for me in back of the privy. As soon as he hits, we shall both rush around and bang that board across that door! We shall have Pete properly penned in the privy. I am so excited! Do you have your things ready, Penelope?"

Penelope was ready, "I have the pan and the large taper candle in the pan of water. The twine is tied through the holes to lower it to the bottom of the hole. We'll just drop the twine and leave the pan on Effie's side. What is the loss of one little old pan in a crapper-caper like this anyway? Have another shot of nerve medicine."

Then Penelope asked, "Effie, it is up to you to get those cupcakes down Pete. Daphne and I shall light the candle and lower the pan before dark. You have to keep Pete occupied, not nosing around. We will then hide behind the outhouse. We must wait for Pete to unload good so he will be unable to put out the candle from above. Then you come to the door with the cup and the spoon. Now, does everyone understand everything? We certainly do not want any slip-ups. Our very sanity depends on our success!"

Effie's cupcakes were quite successful. Delicious and topped with a fine chocolate frosting, Pete downed five in just a short time. He looked at Effie, "How's come ya ain't eatin' a cupcake, Effie ol' girl? These are larrupin' good!"

"Just don't seem to have a hankerin' tonight, Pete. You go ahead and enjoy them. Makes me proud to have someone enjoy my cooking. Here, have another one; they are best when they's nice an' fresh." She handed a plate to Pete, ol' Pistol Pete.

Pete was reading *The Denver Post,* sitting in his easy chair with his prize Navajo all-wool saddle blanket covering the holes in the upholstery. He kind of eased over on one cheek. Effie saw the movement and twitched a slight smile.

Pete remarked, "Says here Jack Dempsey holds onto his heavyweight crown. Knocked out Billy Misek in the third round up at Benton Harbor, Michigan. Golly-darn, m' stomick feels kinda like Dempsey hit me a good one. Got a dose o' somethin', stomick cramps."

Pete had no more than said this and out the back door he went. Pete was reaching for his overall suspender strap so there was no delay when he hit the west half. There was a dandy explosion.

Penelope and Daphne were patient but nervous. They couldn't pounce yet. They were not about to spoil this plan. They heard Pete mutter, "What's this *Capper's Farmer* doin' over on Effie's half? Covers up the hole; she might get a cramp, too, and she would make a mess. She ain't atall happy 'bout a little dribble from me."

Penelope nodded her head, and around the outhouse the two women went, Daphne on one side, Penelope on the other. They hammered that two-by-four across the door quickly and quietly went back to the rear of the outhouse.

Effie had been watching from the kitchen door. When the nails were pounded home, she poured a half a cup of coal oil and got a teaspoon, headed for the privy where Pete was penned.

"Hey! What in tarnation is a-goin' on? Who done nailed the door on this here outhouse?"

Effie was now outside the door. She flipped a spoonful of coal oil on the door; crack in the door was close to Pete's sweating head.

"I smell coal oil! Who's out there with coal oil? Ya could burn this here outhouse down with me in it if'n ya ain't careful!"

Effie stood by the door and answered Pete's question. "We done come to a partin' of the trail, Pete partner. You old penny-pincher. I have done had it! You been skatin' on thin ice for a long time. Take a look down on the east half; that's my half. You see that candle burnin' down there in that pan of coal oil? It's decision time, Pete. When that there candle burns down to that half a gallon of coal oil in that pan, I'll be one happy widder

woman. No evidence, just a few of yer onery bones, maybe some suspinder buttons offen your overhalls. No one ever checks a outhouse fire. Folks might inquire about you, and I would say you just disappeared, or I might say you went back to Ioway." Effie flipped another spoonful of coal oil in the crack of the door. She wished Pete's undivided attention.

"Why, Effie ol' girl, whatever did I do ta deserve this kind o' inhumane treatment? Ya got some kind a compromise, woman, a second chance afore ya light off this outhouse! We oughta palaver over this problem. Remember thet new hickory-handle shovel I bought ya? Thet candle sure does seem ta be burnin' right brisk-like, Effie."

Effie just flipped on another spoonful of coal oil. "Got some conditions, Pete. You agree to every one of 'em, you being so humane, an honest man an' all. Maybe I'll put out that candle. You put up a argument, and I'll toddle back to the house and watch the cremation begin. Now are you ready for the conditions, Petey Pet, or do I take a walk?"

"I'm a watchin' this here candle, Effie ol' girl. Pronounce them conditions an' don't stall around too long!"

Pete heard three distinct giggles; he thought he was going to have another cramp.

"Here are the conditions, and I'll say 'em real slow so's you don't have any misunderstandin'. No more shovelin' chicken manure. No more diggin' outhouse holes. No more brandin' calves, plowin', making garden. I want a life of leisure. I want a lady to come in and clean the house once a week. She can do the washin' and ironin'. I want $500 and I'm goin' to Denver and have a clothes shopping trip. Take Penelope with me for advice, you pay all her expenses. I want my hair done up at the Clip and Curl once a week. I'm gonna learn to play contract bridge. Here's one that will tie your knot, get out of the house by nine every mornin' except Sunday and don't come home 'til five. Leave Penelope's windmill alone. That's about it, Petey Pet. I might think of something later, so this here conversation ain't closed. What's your answer, Pete?" Effie flipped two spoonsful of coal oil on the door this time.

"Agreed, Effie ol' girl. I'm eyeballin' thet there candle. It's gittin' powerful close ta thet coal oil! Pry off thet board on the door an' let me git some fresh air; them cramps kinda fouled the air."

"I got me some witnesses to this here visit, Pete. I'll git a hammer and see if I can pry that board off. Now you keep your eye on that candle. There's still quite a possibility I jest might become a widder woman, lots of peace and quiet."

Penelope handed the hammer around the corner to Effie. Effie wasn't making much of an effort, "Can't seem to loose the nails, Pete. How's the candle holdin' out? It may take us an hour or so."

"Jest 'bout an inch ta go, Effie. Git thet damned shovel, thet new shovel I bought ya, the one with the pretty hickory handle. Try the shovel ta pry 'er loose. Hurry an' get the shovel!"

"Pete, I just can't recollect where I put that shovel. I'll just mosey over and look around the coal shed. You keep a good watch on that candle. I'd like to be a little distance when she blows anyways. I'll be back directly, Pete. You think mighty hard on them conditions."

Pete was puckering up, trying to get a wad of phlegm to ptuiy down on that candle flame. His mouth was just too dry. He was also too frightened. The candle burned down to the coal oil and just went "pfft." Pete had been trying to shoulder his way out of the outhouse when the candle went "pfft." Then Pete had another attack. The new laundress would have some foul underwear her first day of employment.

Effie found the shovel. She pried off the two-by-four.

Pete walked out into the evening and straight to the house. He took kind of little mincy steps. All he said was, "You'ns tricked me, Effie, but it was a good 'un. I won't back out on m' word. I'm an honest man, Effie ol' girl."

Later that night the corn fodder shocks went up in flames, cause of the fire unknown. The next morning when Pete was looking over the ashes and around the garden, he found the other little pink bow. Pete rolled his toothpick, smiled.

* * * * *

Urban Population Exceeds Rural in U.S.

Sept. 30 — How can you keep them down on the farm? A new census report shows the urban population exceeds the rural in the United States. And Chicago, New York and other cities are growing 7.5 times faster than rural areas.

The cities teem with young people dissatisfied with small-town life. Theater, motion picture houses and good paying jobs are not found back home. New immigrants, Italians, Greeks and Poles also prefer the intimacy of urban life.

Yet the unforeseen growth poses problems: housing shortages, lack of sewage treatment and spread of disease. Crime festers in the cracks of the decaying tenements. And where can food for the urban millions come from? From the farmer still down home on the farm.

— Des Moines Register
Sept. 30, 1920

Germany Flooding America with Drugs
Nov. 18 — Dr. Carleton Simon of the New York Police Narcotic Division has revealed that synthetic

cocaine, heroine and other habit-forming drugs, manufactured in Germany, are being smuggled into this country. As a result, the United States government has put 150 more agents in his district.

Germany developed a synthetic method of producing drugs when it was cut off from its normal supply of raw materials during the war. Such drugs include novocain, aminol, pyrdanadon, veronal, sulfonal and eucain. These are smuggled in frequently by way of South America. Simon advocates tougher congressional penalties for drug smuggling and said that it should be considered a form of treason. He also said that in his experience very little drug addiction was caused by doctors' prescriptions.

— New York Times, 1921

America's Unknown Soldier Comes Home
November 11, 1921

Nov. 11 — America's own hero, the unknown soldier, lies in state in the vast rotunda of the nation's Capitol, three years after the end of the war. For days now, they have come, the old and the young, the blacks and the whites, even those who are badly crippled, to pay homage to the man — or perhaps he was little more than a boy — who died in France. The simple black coffin bearing his remains rests on the spot where only the nation's assassinated presidents, Lincoln, Garfield and McKinley, have slept in death.

As cannon boomed down river, the body arrived at the Washington Navy Yard earlier this week aboard the gray cruiser Olympia and was taken to the Capitol. Since then, hundreds of thousands of Americans and foreign diplomats have filed by the flag-draped coffin. The widow was attired in black, including a black veil. Among the wreaths is one sent by King George of England, bearing the words, "An unknown, and yet well known, was dying, and behold, we live." One could not help but notice the widow with a black lace handker-

chief wipe back a tear under the veil as she filed past the bier in turn with the other lookers on.

▲ ▲ ▲ ▲ ▲ ▲

THE SALESMAN
1921-29

SOME INDIVIDUALS ARE FORTUNATE, they were born to suit the times, historically correct to that individual's abilities and capabilities, and then they were born with the perception to see that change was sometimes good. Thus it was with Pete Pisanmoan when he left the Bar P ranch and moved to town in 1920. He knew that change was coming, he'd seen electric lights, he had heard a radio, and he observed that the automobile was replacing the family trotting horse and buggy. Tractors were becoming more visible on what farming operations he'd seen east of Wallace, Kan. As far east as he'd been was Ellis, bought a bull, but he had observed the change in agriculture.

The details of Pete's being cast out of his own home by his wife and wonderful helpmate, Effie, and her friends is chronicled elsewhere. He had given his promise under duress; he was keeping his word; he was on an adult curfew. Where was he to go? Pete had only one place to go and try to contemplate his next venture. That was Borst's Barber Shop. Pete retained that theory that one sit around the local barber shop long enough in a small town, one will get an idea and that idea will make money.

Pete was an affable sort, well liked but known to be a mighty good horse trader. One has heard the saying, "Horse of a different color." Pete had dyed a few himself, not often, it was not uncommon among horse traders and horse thieves. Pete had slickered a few strangers, never a friend nor a neighbor.

Volney Borst liked Pete. Good conversationalist. He was knowledgeable about most things, politics, religion and women, but Pete's best attribute was he was a good listener. Every morning Pete left home before 9 a.m., went to Borst's Barber Shop, got his shave and sat and read the *Topeka Daily Capitol*.

It was common during this time in history for the local

businessmen to have their morning shave. Henry Williams, president of the Citizen's State Bank. Del and Ward Lutz of the local Ford Motor Car Agency. Charlie Koons of the hardware store and local mortician. Doctors Carter and Nelson. All these men were the movers and shakers of the local community. Business, banking, life and death were represented, a railroad conductor on lay-over could be an informational source; he was from another locale, widened Pete's horizons.

Pete just sat and listened — rolled his toothpick from one side of his mouth to the other. He had a habit of jiggling it when he wished to emphasize an important point. It always distracted the person he was addressing; it was a planned maneuver, one might say hypnosis via the toothpick.

It took just a little over a week for Pete to listen for the idea. It was just a chance comment by one of the Lutz Brothers. "I just don't know what we're going to do with all those used Model T Fords. Our valiant soldier boys are buying all new cars with their Kansas bonus money, we've had good crops and prices for the last few years, everyone is prosperous. We just can't get shet of those used cars!"

Volney nodded in sympathy, he didn't even own a car. Pete's toothpick went straight up, got tangled in the hair in his nose. There was the idea! Open up a used car lot. Get those Fords off the Lutz Brothers' hands!

Few people around Wallace or Sharon Springs knew that Pete Pisanmoan was worth considerable in the monetary department. He didn't tell Effie much either, best if Effie walked the path of pecuniary innocence.

When Effie and Pete left the —P and told Piedmont Pisanmoan to "have a nice stay," little did Pied know that Pete had slapped a very large Federal Land Bank loan on their ranch of prime grassland. The proceeds of that loan were sitting in a savings account in Denver at the Colorado National Bank. Pied would be in for a bolt from the blue from the bank when he was notified that a payment was due.

Pete knew for this venture that location was the most important decision. He walked up Main Street. He had his Triple X Stetson tilted over on one side, kind of cocky-like. Hell, he already looked like a used car salesman. Pete lacked the shifty eyes and the slap-em-on-the-back approach, but he was 100% in the appearance department.

Pete found the location; he'd never paid any attention to this vacant lot before. It was right next to the new Township Hall and almost directly across the street from the Lutz Motor Car Co. He casually walked over the frontage, seemed almost like the same size as the garden, and he noticed a large pile of new bricks piled on the back of the lot. He checked the bricks, chips out of the corners but not bad. He decided these clinkers would be just fine to build a free sales office. That would be a first-class sales office; only Don Duphorne had a brick office; abstract and insurance was his business.

Pete was methodical in his approach to this business location. He was not about to get caught again with a full outhouse. He wandered around to the front of the Township Hall. If one had been watching, they would know he was looking for something and he found it. Right at the base of one of the pedestal light fixtures that lit up the entrance, an electrical outlet. Pete knew he could plug into that outlet and get free electricity. Let the City foot the bill for his electricity. His next question was who owned the lots?

Pete was a satisfied man. He had the material for his sales office. Free electricity, he'd lease this weed patch for about ten dollars a year. He rolled his toothpick over to the other side of his mouth and smiled, headed for the courthouse to seek the ownership of those lots.

"What! I'm a saddle-sore sonofabitch from Salina. You say Penelope Pinchlips owns them three lots. I ain't turned a tug muscle since I moved ta Sharon thet I ain't run up against ol' Persimmon Penelope Pinchlips. I admit she has improved some since they passed prohibition."

"How much is them lots taxes, girlie? $15.50, much obliged, sis."

Pete thought he had 'er on the downhill until he found out who owned those lots. This was going to take some thought. Parsimonious Penelope Pinchlips was a pesky participant in any business deal. Pete thought of it. Those two pink bows when she burned his fodder. "Blackmail, that's it, I'll black-mail 'er. I still got those two bows hid out."

"I told you not to show up around home 'til five. Whatcha want, Pete?" Effie wasn't near as docile as she used to be.

"Need m' grip, pack a few duds, Effie. I'm headed fer Denver on a business trip. Be gone maybe a week or two. Here's ten bucks ta tide ya over. If ya run a little short, ya can always work down at the West Hotel. Ben said ya was fair-ta-middlin' hep. Might want to wait on tables, git a tip or two." Pete gave Effie a good pinch, rolled his toothpick over to the other side of his mouth. "Ya always had a nice bottom, Effie ol' girl. Bye."

Pete had just enough time to stop in at Gert and Myrt's Variety Store before catching Union Pacific Train No. 123 westbound.

"We have a new type of notebook, Pete. It is called a spiral, has a nice blue cover, it is just ten cents." Gert liked Pete; she had worked at Mollie's Cafe when Pete used to come to the county seat to pay his taxes, and he had given her a pinch, too.

"I'll take it, Gert. Say, that reminds me. Did you know they was a bunch o' loco weed a-growin' up there on them lots jest south of the Township Hall. Someone oughta tell the city fathers 'bout thet. Next thing ya know the kids will be rollin' that loco weed and a-smokin' it. Those lots need a good hoein' and weedin' out. Seems to me the owner outta pay fer it. Thanks, Gert."

Pete heard 123 whistling from the east. Plenty of time. He rolled his toothpick over to the other side of his mouth and smiled. Them lots will be all nice an' tidy when I git back. Ol' Penelope Pinchlips will git a bill from the city. Pete smiled.

Pete Pisanmoan was no dummy. He fully realized he did not know one damned thing about the automobile business. In fact, he didn't even know how to drive. He knew it took a lot of perspiration, patience and perseverance to perpetuate a prosperous business. Pete was going to Denver to learn the used car business. He was not about to tell Effie about his plans; she'd hot-foot it right down to Penelope's house and ruin his plans.

Pete made no hesitation at taking a seat in the chair car; he headed directly for the smoker. What he needed was information. A smoker was similar to a barber shop. Keep his ears peeled and it would pay off. Pete didn't smoke, chewed a little. He took out his pen knife, cut a small quid of Horse Shoe, tilted back his Triple X Stetson and said, "Howdy, boys."

His friendliness eased any hesitating on the other occupants to continue their discussion, and someone inquired as to Pete's destination. They knew he was a rancher and a country boy. All seemed eager to assist this country boy on his venture to Denver. The cheapest place to sleep was the Salvation Army Center, two bits a night. Meals aren't bad, soup's a dime. One can get a bath once a week up at the Y.M.C.A.; that's on E. 16th Ave. There's a barber college down on 18th St. You can get a shave free the first time, but it's better to tip the guy a nickel. Been known to cut a feller up a little the second time you go in. Buy street car tokens, three for a dime. Always ask for a transfer, even if you don't use it. You can always sell it that day for a penny. The used car lots are located mostly on Lawrence and Curtis Streets.

By the time Pete stepped off the train, looked at the inside of the Denver Union Station in awe and walked out into the busy streets of Denver, he had all the information he needed for survival in the big city. MIZPAH, the big sign read out front.

Pete rented a locker at the Salvation Army for his grip, took a walk. This was his first day of auto sales school. He stopped at Truthful Tommie Tidwell's. Tommie hadn't told the truth for so long he could lie with an honest countenance. Pete picked up a pointer, honesty. Then he met "Big Bill Beal, Always an Honest Deal." As it has been said, "It takes one to know one." Pete knew them; every one was a liar and rapscallion. He found his professor the second day. His mentor, a real professional. Just the man he wanted. The sign on the lot read, "If you're down on your luck, see good ol' Buck." Buck Brockway would trade for anything — a stud horse for a Studebaker, a ton of coal for a Cole, a Star for a moon or a Packard for a pachyderm. Pete hit good ol' Buck for a sales job. Buck knew one when he saw one, too. He could see Pete was a natural for selling used cars.

"Yer hired, Pete. There's no salary; you work on straight commish. I give you ten dollars a car, fifteen if we finance it at 22% interest. You git half of the profit on all trade-ins and pay all the loss if we lose. How's that sweetie of a deal suit you, country boy?"

"I got 'er, Buck. Spit and shake; honest boys like us need a good handshake when we seals a deal." They shook, went eyeball to eyeball and laughed; they both knew they were lying. Pete twitched the toothpick.

Buck looked at Pete, "Say, you're mighty good with that toothpick, but it gits dirty, might offend our customers. Go over on Larimer St. and git a gold one at a hock shop. We'll work out some signals with that toothpick. We'll git the yazoos right up the kazoo. You and me will make a great auto sales team."

Pete began making notes in the blue spiral notebook. He wrote the amount of the sale, the trade-in, make of car and year of manufacture. Few realize it now, but right there in a Christian Science Reading Room, Pete Pisanmoan from the small town of Sharon Springs, Kansas, started the automobile blue book, the bible for all used car salesmen to this very day. He had every sale and type of car, how much he made; it was all right there in that Blue Book. Few recall those cars today that were listed; here are a few I found in that old spiral blue book: Apperson, Auburn, Cadillac, Chandler, Chevrolet, Chrysler, Cleveland, Cole, Dodge, Duesenberg, Durant, Essex, Franklin, Kissel Kar, La Salle, Locomobile, Hubmobile, Marmon, Metze, Moline Knight, Moon, Nash, Packard, Oldsmobile, Rauch and Lang Electric, Star, Velie, Stanley Steamer, Studebaker, Whippit, Wills St. Claire and the Winton. That Blue Book was sort of a diary, and back on the last page it showed how much Pete made in the month he worked for ol' Buck. $392, and that ain't bad for a country boy in the big city.

Pete walked into the office, "I'm a-quittin', Buck. Gonna go home to m' Effie back in Sharon Springs. You done taught me everything I need ta know ta start a used car business. I'm gonna go home and skin me some Jayhawkers, not serious skinnin' but jest 'nuff to git a laugh or two and make 'em come back."

"Pete, I sure do hate to have you quit me. You was the best I ever had, and you was sure good at takin' back that loan paper on them cars. How ya gonna collect on them loans in Kansas, Pete?"

"I done peddled thet paper for a 10% discount ta Big Bill Beal, he paid me cash. Makin' money on these used cars is like shootin' ducks on the set. When I git my lot all set up, I'll send ya an invite on a penny post card, have ya come down an' see the Paradise on the Plains."

The two men shook hands; they had become friends. Pete rolled his gold toothpick over to one side, flipped it up and down twice. That had been just one of their signals. Buck laughed and Pete headed for the Union Station, got a ticket on Union Pacific Train No. 22 eastbound. He had a dried-up cheese sandwich, no high-priced meal in the diner for Pete. This time he did not venture into the smoker; he was just sitting and mapping his strategy, pondering about Penelope Pinchlips. He now knew how to sell used cars, but he had to palaver and have a pow-wow with Penelope about property— those three vacant lots. Never once did Pete even consider purchasing those lots from Penelope. That tied up cash; his goal was to get them free of rent and free of weeds, especially loco. There wasn't any loco.

When Pete got off the train, it was dark. The usual curious and busybodies were there to meet the train, who got off, where had they been and why did they go where they did? Questions like, "Where ya been, Pete? We was wonderin' about you," and the comment, "Effie's working over at the West, waitin' tables."

Pete rolled his gold toothpick over to one side of his mouth and smiled. It was a pure pity that Effie had ta go ta work. Pete had planned it that way; maybe Effie had forgotten the coal oil in the outhouse, not Pete.

"Bin up ta Wyomin' buyin' cattle. Bought twenty load of ratty-assed heifers for a feller back in Ioway. I'm a commission livestock buyer now, see ya, boys."

That sandwich hadn't lasted very long. Pete stopped in at the West Hotel. New waitress, Effie was not in sight. Pete told her, "Give me the pork chop special, sis. Go heavy on the gravy and throw on a couple extra biskits."

When the waitress brought Pete his bill, he said, "Jest charge it to m' wife, Effie. She's a good ol' girl. Tell her thet her precious Pete is back in town. Sell ya a autymobile some day."

Pete left the waitress a nickel tip and went home.

Effie washed dishes until ten. She was provoked plenty! Pete left the lamp burning down real low, barely a glimmer of light, save on kerosene. Effie was surprised to have Pete leave a light for her. She slid into bed and kind of cozied over to Pete's side. Pete didn't move a single muscle. Effie grunted, banged her pillow and went to sleep, one tired dishwasher.

The next morning Effie heard Pete get up and decided to make his breakfast. Pete had a question, "How come you ain't workin' down at the West this mornin', Effie?" I figured ya was on permanent."

"Quit last night right after I paid for your supper. That weren't the deal, Pete. I bin takin' English lessons, joined the Eastern Stars, got in that fine organization on my brother bein' a Mason over at Hoxie. Penelope says she is gonna make me a blue stocking. That saw-buck you left didn't last long with all them dues and schoolin'. I had to go to work at the West. I stopped at the bank; they said you had no account. I told them they was right. You don't account for much."

"I kin plainly see ya been takin' those English lessons. Be teachin' school real soon. Why, yer a regular pedagogic." Pete smiled; he really blew that word by her and her English lessons.

"Whatcha been doin', Pete? You was gone over a month. You said you'd be gone 'bout a week. You could have at least wrote me a penny post card, even Penelope asked 'bout you. Yer a real tightwad, Pete."

"I was real busy, Effie. Ya know those three lots we leased from Penelope for our garden last year. Gave her three years rent money right up front, and she went and burned my fodder crop! I'm gonna make a first-class junk yard on them three lots. Plan ta purchase old autymobiles, tear 'em down and sell parts. Why, they's a fortune in spare parts fer autymobiles. I'm agonna cobble up a buildin' with a bunch of tin ta keep m' parts dry — put in some bins and watch the money roll in. I'm a-hittin' this idee hammer and tong, and I mean they's gonna be a lot of hammerin'. Mornin' 'til night, hammerin', takin' off nuts and bolts. Burn any old tires and tubes. Reminds me, thanks for burnin' the bacon and eggs, now I really know I'm ta home. I'll be headin' uptown fer m' shave. Want ta look real nice when I tell Penelope about the junk yard."

Pete put the gold toothpick in his mouth, put on his Triple X at a jaunty angle and went uptown. He wanted to see if those vacant lots by the Township Hall had been all cleaned up in his absence. They were as clean as a baby's butt, not a weed. Pete smiled; Penelope had paid.

When Pete left to inspect the lots, Effie waited, watched until Pete got around the corner, went down to Penelope's. Effie just could not wait to tell Penelope about the proposed junk yard.

When Penelope heard the story, she really came unglued. After taking a slug of nerve tonic, she merely sat petrified in her overstuffed chair. "He cannot possibly be serious. One cannot put a junk yard in a residential area! My beautiful home would depreciate to absolutely nothing! I must find a copy of that lease, go to Goodland and see my attorney, Sylvester Fixum. He'll put a stop to this junk-yard nonsense!"

Effie added another small note to the Pinchlip problem. "I plumb forgot to tell you, Pete told me something about a dog — a German Shepherd I think he said it was, he's gittin' it trained as a night guard dog for his tin parts buildin'. Guard them spare parts. He said it was taught to bark at the slightest noise, said it was plumb dangerous." Penelope paled at the thought.

Pete walked into the Lutz Ford Motor Car Co. He wanted to view the used car inventory. Wanted to talk to Ward and Del. "Ward, how many used cars ya got parked around this here place? Like to peruse the inventory with a possible purchase in mind."

Ward looked at Del; Pete recalled that same look on the faces of used car salesmen on Lawrence St. in Denver. "We have twenty — various makes and models, most have low mileage. I'm sure we can find one that would fulfill a man of your means, Pete."

Pete could fool a lot of people about his financial condition, but prior to changing banks he had had a bank account in Wallace with the Lutz brothers. They knew Pete was far from busted. Ward figured that Pete didn't know an automobile from a roll of barbed wire until they began the so-called perusal of the merchandise. Ward was giving Pete the full load with Del topping it off about the qualities of every automobile they had parked in the garage, on the street, wherever they could find a parking place. Pete was buying the sales pitch, and the brothers wondered how, where and when Pete had learned so much about automobiles. They knew he'd been away, but the word was he was a cattle buyer, working for some commission outfit in Denver. "See any you liked, Pete, some fine merchandise there, good transportation."

Pete tilted back his Triple X, rolled his gold toothpick over to the other side of his mouth, twinkle in his eye. "Tell ya what ya do, boys. You have yerselves a pow-wow. Then put a real sharp point on thet pencil an' give me a price on all twenty-two of them pieces of good transportation. You boys got a ton of cash just a-sitting there doin' nothin' but drippin' oil outta crankcases. I'll strip them suckers out an' open up a used parts store — kind of like a junk yard. We kin go inta kahoots with each other. I got a figure in mind on what ya got in your mind. Give ya three days ta git a figure, I'll pay ya all cash."

The Lutz Brothers had been given something provocative to consider; this just might be the deal of the year, sell twenty-two used cars at one time. They watched Pete as he walked over to Citizen's State Bank; they thought he might be going to get a loan.

"Mornin', Jesse. Henry Williams in the store?"

The bank president just hated it when Pete called his fine financial institution a store, felt it degrading to be a banker and be compared with just an ordinary shopkeeper. Bankers are a cut above a butcher or a barber, there is an air of professionalism about a banker.

"Yes, Henry is in the bank; he's in his office. If you wish to transact some business, I may be of some assistance, Pete."

"Jesse, you couldn't loan me a dime. I want ta talk to Henry. I need $10,000 at 5% interest, due in twenty years. Did ya hear thet, Henry?"

Of course, Henry heard the comment about the junk yard. He walked out of his office, hand extended, shook hands with Pete. Maybe Pete was going to deposit his commission check.

"What was that I heard about you opening up a junk yard, Pete?" This had surprised Henry; he had mortgages on a number of junky places but not on a junk yard.

"Henry, let's go in ta yer private office, palaver a little. I got a coupla questions I need ta have answered, and ya bein' in the money store business an' all I figured ya was the feller to see.

Let me take a gander at one of yer chattel mortgage forms; I'm thinking 'bout the purchase of a used autymobile."

Henry reached in one of his desk drawers, gave Pete a blank form. Pete read the main line; that's the line that has the interest on the loan. "Guess ya never heard a usury. Godalmighty, ya gittin' 22%! This here bank must be a mint! Poor old farmer or rancher, milks cows twice a day seven days a week. The missus has a bunch a hens, gathers the eggs, then they come ta town in their autymobile, bring five gallon o' cream, couple crates o' eggs, then bring the money up here to this money store just so's they kin drive a lousy autymobile ta town. You cut the interest rate 5% an' the folks would buy more. Merchants would prosper. Ya oughta call this the Citizen's House of Pure Greed. Adios,Henry. I'll jest keep this chattel mortgage paper, kind of a souvenir."

When Pete had shut the door to the bank, Henry remarked, "He always was kind of an odd-wad, Jesse. Fought that income tax, Federal Reserve banking system and said prohibition was an insult to the rights of men. He just might have an idea on that junk yard though."

Pete kept that copy of the chattel mortgage. It would come in handy. He'd had something in mind since he sold that paper to Big Bill Beal. It was to be called PETE PISANMOAN'S PERSONAL PURCHASE PLAN. He'd stay a full 5% under the bank on any automobile he sold.

Now was the time to visit his good friend and neighbor, Penelope Pinchlips. He figured Effie had her well informed by now, tipped his Triple X forward, didn't want anyone to see the gleam in his eyes. Made him look kind of shifty-like, resembled a used car dealer or a junk yard owner that sold used car parts. He debated in his mind every move — should he knock on the door loudly, or maybe just a little tappity-tap-tap? As soon as he rounded the corner, he saw the curtains move; he knew Penelope was watching, Pete tappity-tap-tapped. Penelope had regained her composure better than Pete had anticipated.

"Howdy ta ya, Miss Pinchlips. Ya are entirely kerrect. We ain't had us a nice chat since ya torched off my fodder. M' lawyer up in Denver calls thet first-degree arson. He's got them two little pink silk bows offen yer slippers as pure and simple evidence, just wanted to mention thet in passin'. His name is Simon Beatum. Ya got a copy of thet there lease? I got ya paid for another two year; been thinkin' 'bout a little business right next door on them lots. Somethin' new to the area, create a lot of traffic on our street, lot of dust in the air, but it shure is a profitable venture. Why, I jest might even be agreeable ta give ya another five dollars a year on the rent monies if'n it was as successful as I expect. Got this idee up in Wyomin'."

"Just what kind of business did you have in mind, Mr. Pisanmoan? You recall we discussed a garden last year, and all you put in was a large crop of corn. You do realize this is a residential area, not zoned for business?"

"Now I kind of expected ya to bring thet point up in our discussion so I checked up at the Town Clerk's office. I told him you had previously considered running a herd of goats on them lots. Thet's what ya said, Miss Pinchlips, goats. Came right straight from the horse's mouth. You said goats. Yesiree, I planted corn, had a bountiful crop thanks to all thet chicken manure thet improved yer land. Town Clerk says there are no zoning laws on the books, folks have a family cow right there in their back yard, you planned on runnin' goats." Pete kind of wiggled his gold toothpick at Penelope; he noted a vein on her forehead standing out.

Pete continued, "My intentions is honorable and should be mighty profitable. I fully intend to have me a first-class junk yard right there on them three lots. Why, I got me a police dog a-trainin' right now up in Denver — guard dog. They got a old box car that I can move up here on some telegraph poles, kind of roll it up here. Nothin' permanent, mind ya, I could use it fer an office an' keep the more valuable parts in bins in the boxcar."

Penelope was fiddling with her brooch that was attached to a necklace; Pete could tell she was nervous. "You really are serious about the venture, aren't you, Mr. Pisanmoan! When I first heard of your intentions, I considered it so ludicrous I fully dismissed the idea. Now I can see you are quite serious."

"Oh, my, yes. I really am serious, Miss Pinchlips. I had me a little visit with m' attorney when I was in Denver. Simon says, 'attempted murder, at least manslaughter.' Thet's what he says, when you, Effie and thet Daphne Damptowel was gonna torch off the outhouse with me nailed in it. He's got the paper all writ up; he called it a brief. I told him not to be too brief 'cause we was discussin' money and quite a bunch o' money."

When the word money was mentioned, Pete noticed a slight tic at the corner of Penelope's mouth. "My goodness, Miss Pinchlips, ya is 'bout as pale as one of them white Leghorn feathers I hauled in fer the garden. Seems like I struck a sour note in yer happy day."

"You are without a doubt the most despicable human being I have ever encountered. I am going to have someone drive me to Goodland tomorrow and discuss this with my own attorney!" Penelope thought Pete was blowing a lot of smoke, but one never knows about Pete Pisanmoan.

"Why, thet's a good idee. I'll even let ya drive one of m' cars. I jest bought twenty-two junkers from the Lutz Brothers. The ones that won't run, got John Craven towin' down here with his team. We ought ta start parkin' 'em tomarraw, junkin' 'em out in a couple o' days. Now, I gotta another deal thet ya might like, but I'll take m' leave now, ya think on this, Miss Pinchlips. If'n ya want ta hear m' other deal, I'll be down at Borst's Barber Shop 'til five. Remember thet was one of them diplomatic conditions Effie laid on me when I was nailed up in the outhouse.; I'm holdin' up my end of the bargain. You think on it, might save ya a trip over to Goodland. Bye." Pete doffed his Triple X and shut the door. Penelope felt that little tic by her mouth again.

Volney Borst looked up from the newspaper he was reading. "By golly, Pete, you are sure one busy man. First I heard you had been to Wyoming buying cattle for some farmers back in Iowa. Then another source said you bought out Lutz Brother Motor Co., and then I heard you were opening up a junk yard. You make it hard to run a barber shop with so much news floating around."

"I don't rightly know what I'm a-gonna do, Volney. I jest delivered a zinger of an idea to a party — have ta wait an' see. Give me the want ads of thet *Topeka Daily Capitol.*" Pete wanted the used auto section and noted the prices of used cars in Topeka, seemed comparable to Denver. No one showed up at the barber shop seeking Pete; he went home at five, see Effie ol' girl.

"What kind of mischief ya been up to today, Pete?"

"Effie, I bin one busy boy. Bought me a busted box car from the Union Pacific down at the rip-track. Made a deal on twenty-two junker autymobiles from the Lutz Brothers. Gittin' a eight by sixteen sign made up showin' m' new auto junk yard. I stopped ta have a friendly chat with Persimmon Pinchlips; she was downright hostile. Not a neighborly type atall. I always bin a good neighbor, straight arrow so's ta speak. I see ya burnt the biskits agin, they's nice and black on the bottom."

Effie had done it on purpose; she still had a slight cough from cleaning the hen house.

Pete was sitting in his easy chair reading the *Capper's Farmer* when he heard a tap-tap on the front door. He smiled, rolled the gold toothpick over to the other side of his mouth. He didn't move a muscle. Effie couldn't see his face, the paper covered it. She got up and answered the door.

"Why, Penelope! What are you a'doing out this time of night? You don't generally go out this late unless it is Star night."

"I came to ask your husband a question, Effie dear."

Pete put down the paper, looked over the top of his Woolworth reading glasses and squinted at Penelope. "Welcome ta our humble house, Miss Pinchlips. I reckon the last time ya was on my' propity was the night of the terrible fodder fire, or was it the night I was nailed up in the outhouse, you bein' the one thet did the nailin'. What's yer question, neighbor?"

"Do you perchance have a copy of our lease? I seem to have misplaced mine."

"Need ta take it ta yer attorney over at Goodland, don't ya? Sorry, but my copy is up in Denver at Simon's office. Simon says don't be passin' it around; he mentioned somethin' like prima facie evidence. I gotta warn ya, Miss Pinchlips, 'bout a problem. Don't ya dare go out a-prowlin' at night when I git m' guard dog at the junk yard. He's taught ta attack anything thet moves. He's gonna be a dangerous devil. Ya might want ta visit a tad afore ya go on a trip to Goodland. Save ya a lotta time.

Now ya have a good night's sleep, might be yer last when thet dog gets here."

Penelope didn't sleep a wink. Pete Pisanmoan was a formidable foe. How well she recalled her hands when they got stuck on that belt dressing. He probably does have a dog getting trained up in Denver, a really mean bitch of a dog. I'd be a prisoner in my own home! I never know when that man is telling the truth; he can flip that toothpick around like a drum major with a baton, and wouldn't you just know it, I'm out of nerve tonic!

Not much was said at breakfast the next morning. Effie did remark, "Ya got a real mean streak in ya, Pete."

"Yep, Effie, you got it, kinda resembles your'n. As I recollect, you and them two pieces o' fluff had it all planned fer me ta be a human skyrocket right outta thet outhouse. Ya kinda lost yer touch with the flapjacks. Not near as good as they used ta be down on the Bar P. Bye."

Pete wanted to whistle a merry tune as he walked by Penelope's house — hard to whistle with a gold toothpick. He did stop and admire the lots, nodded his head several times; he knew Penelope was watching. Pete turned the corner, and one would think he was headed uptown. Not this time, he doubled back and hid behind Wandling's outhouse, wanted to see the progress of his plan. There was a feeling of pomposity to Pete's peculiar personality. Progress was good. It took less than five minutes for Penelope to come out of her front door; down the walk came Effie from the north, Daphne from the south. Pete couldn't hear, didn't need to. The arms were waving, Effie was wringing her apron, twisting and turning it, and Penelope, her hair was all wispy, wind blowing it all around her pale and tired face. She was a real feminine mess, frenetic. Pete tongued his gold toothpick over to the other side of his mouth and went uptown.

Pete had some business calls to make uptown. First to Borst's Barber Shop. "Mornin', Volney. If'n anyone stops in lookin' fer me taday, tell 'em I went ta Denver on 123 ta pick up a dog."

"Golly, Pete, you going into the dog-raising business, too?"

"Yep, Volney. Vicious guard dogs, gotta go."

Volney came to the conclusion that Sharon Springs, Kansas, had been kind of a dull town prior to the immigration of one Pete Pisanmoan.

About the time Pete came out of the barber shop, John was driving up Main Street with the dray wagon, had a load from the depot. "Hold up a minute, John. I got a job comin' up fer ya. Gonna need 'bout six loads of cinders from down at the roundhouse. I figure cinders 'll cover up drippin' oil spots 'bout as good as anything. How much for six loads and put some sideboards on thet piddly-assed wagon?"

John Craven was aware of Pete's ways; he pushed his hat back and eyeballed Pete. "Here's the way I charge fer cinders, Pete. One dollar a load when I use the piddly-assed wagon, one-fifty with sideboards that are a real butt buster, and an extry two dollars for smart-asses like you. Sound about right, Pete?"

"Tell ya what I'm agonna do, John. I'll give ya ten dollars fer six loads, spread. Ya heard thet word, spread. I'll let ya know when I want 'em. Is it a deal?"

"Deal," and John clucked to his team and went on his rounds.

Next stop, Pete walked over to the Standard Oil depot. In those days it was common for the company to put the name of the local agent on a sign. Standard Oil Company, Jack Chisum, Prop.

"So you think you're gonna need a drum of heavyweight oil, Pete. Bet it's to loosen all them nuts and bolts when you open up that new junk yard."

"Now how'd ya ever guess thet, Jack? I hardly git back from Wyoming afore every body an' soul in this here gossipy town has got me in the junk-yard business. I think I only mentioned thet jest onct. News sure travels fast. Yep, thet's just what I want it for, ta loosen nuts, an' a little dab wouldn't hurt ya either." Pete just smiled; Jack knew Pete was joshing him.

Jack had a suggestion, "Penetrating oil would make it a lot easier, more expensive but you'd save on labor costs."

"Heavyweight oil is cheaper, and free advice ain't worth nothin'. For junk yard profits a feller needs ta watch ever penny." Pete needed the oil for some leakers; he'd seen them at

Lutz Brothers; they had some leakers.

Pete went to Mollie's Cafe for dinner, listened to the conversations, didn't say much. Several inquired about the junk-yard business; Pete was non-committal. He just smiled and walked out and viewed Main Street. He looked over toward Koons Hardware, and there was Penelope Pinchlips in her black dress, new hemline, new style, just below the knee about two inches. Pete thought she'd look right nice if she was carrying a broom. Nope, she was carrying a parasol and waving it at Pete. He couldn't understand a word, but she sure was yelling. Pete thought it a pity to see Penelope so upset, he smiled.

"Your threats have worn me down, Mr. Pisanmoan. I must know your intentions before I travel to Goodland. You mention a lawsuit, foolish judgments and a ferocious guard dog have discombobulated my entire personality."

Pete was sympathetic, he still recalled the coal oil. "Miss Pinchlips, thet was not m' intent a'tall. Here, let me take yer arm an' let's us walk up and set a spell on the steps of the Township Hall. You'll soon learn that Pete Pisanmoan is a pretty princely sort of a fella, a real pedigree." Pete put his hand on Penelope's elbow, he could feel the tenseness, Pete smiled. "Here we are, Miss Pinchlips. Now ya jest settle down there on them there steps, gaze out at this lovely town an' its real estate. Notice them three lots right there next door; I checked over ta the Court House. I understand ya owns all them lots."

"Why, that is correct, Mr. Pisanmoan. No one has shown any interest in those lots since my dear dead daddy took them as a down payment on a team of horses quite some time ago. Just what might be your interest in those lots?"

"I got ya a propysition, Miss P. Ya gotta pay close 'tention to it. Deals like this one come jest onct in a lifetime."

"Proceed, Mr. Pisanmoan. I predict this proposition of yours will be what the young people now call a dipsy-doozy." Penelope was not quite as nervous now that she saw some interest in her real estate, an asset that produced nothing but property taxes.

"I think yer mentality kin handle this deal. I'll run 'er by ya jest onct. First, I got a quit-claim deed all made up by my lawyer. Got it right here in m' pocket. Simon says it should read inta perpetuity. That means forever and a day. I would stake no claim on them three lots by yer house. Cancel the lease, the assault with a deadly weapon; thet was the hammer ya nailed the door shut with me in the outhouse. Ya committed arson on m' fine fodder crop, and the frostin' on the cake —" Pete let her hang out ta dry, Penelope leaned forward, anxious for the frosting. "I'll send a telegram ta thet dog trainer ta stop shipment on thet hundert and fifty pounds of pure fangs, fur, fury an' ferociousness. Ya deed me them three lots right over there; I'll give ya a $20 gold piece, an' now ya got exactly five minutes ta make up yer mind. I'll just meander over there, check an' see if'n I kin find any loco weed. Bad stuff, thet loco."

Penelope Pinchlips realized she had just been propositioned by a professional. Pete just poked along, tonguing his toothpick, expecting a prudent reply. It came much sooner than he expected. It took precisely thirty-seven seconds for Penelope to reach her decision. "You have a deal, Mr. Pisanmoan. We shall promptly go over to the courthouse, notarize your signature and record that quit-claim deed. We will have a warranty deed drawn up for the three lots; I shall deed them over to you and they will be recorded. I assume you do have a $20 gold piece, as I recall you had to take out a loan at the bank just to lease those lots for a garden."

Pete had prevailed, "Sounds fine ta me. I'll give ya yer money when thet Recorder puts the book and page number on thet there deed." The business was transacted. Pete now owned the three lots right there on Main Street, prime commercial property.

As they walked out into the hall from the Clerk and Recorder's office, Penelope made a remark. "I am going up to the County Judge's chambers for a little business."

Pete had a questioning look on his face, "Why, Miss Pinchlips, I thought we was all done with our business?"

"Not quite, Mr. Pisanmoan. I am on my way to get a restraining order on you personally. If you ever set foot on any of my properties again, I shall seek a large sum in judicial recourse!"

Pete was really quite proud of his prime property, and

there was never a more innovative used car dealer than Pete Pisanmoan. One was what he named "Pete's Pen of Pigs." Always had three or four junkers that he held the price at $20. High school boys would buy them and fix them up. He had a ramp built up about three feet high. He would drive up a "Special" on the ramp; this was "Pete's Pick of the Week." He had a copy of the Citizen's State Bank chattel mortgage framed, put it on the wall of his brick sales office. Then his finance was named "Pete's Personal Finance Plan." That was a real success, the butter and egg money was coming in on Saturday to Pete, bank never financed another automobile. Even new car buyers came to Pete for financing. When he got several thousand dollars ahead, he sent a postal money order to the Colorado National Bank.

Pete began to get uneasy about the economy, things were just too good. He sold out in August of 1929 for cash. Pete Pisanmoan was a man of his time, few could see what was coming. Then the crash of 1929; Pete had a bundle of cash. Pete saw panic, someone named the economic problems a "Depression." The era was aptly named; meanwhile Pete had a picnic, and he was prosperous only no one knew it. Pete told Effie, "We'll jest have ta be frugal."

Effie wondered how they could be any more frugal. Tightwad Pete!

* * * * *

Station Wagons Are for Play, Not Work

October 23 — In a decision bound to interest many car owners, the New York State Appellate Court has ruled that the "station wagon" is not a commercial truck but a passenger car and thus entitled to lower license plate rates. Such owners will save, and the state will lose thousands of dollars next year when the difference between the two will reach six dollars a plate.

The case was brought by George Zabriskie, who argued that these large automobiles are not commercial vehicles but are used "for transporting people and for bringing packages from stores and carrying baggage to and from the railroad station."

— Kansas City Star, Oct. 23, 1922

Lizzie Borden Dies a Peaceful Death
June 2, 1927

"Lizzie Borden took an ax and gave her mother forty whacks. When she saw what she had done, she gave her father forty-one!"

That was a popular rhyme in the '20s after Lizzie (Miss Lisbeth A. Borden) was acquitted of murdering her father and stepmother in Fall River, Mass. Their mutilated bodies were found Aug. 4, 1892, after Lizzie had rushed into the house of a neighbor and reported her father dead. Lizzie was subsequently arrested, and her trial was one of the most celebrated in New England. Andres J. Borden was rich. The prosecution argued that Lizzie believed her stepmother might get a large share of the fortune, and killed her parents to ensure that she and her sister would inherit it all. Lizzie denied everything, and the ax was never found. Today, a virtual recluse, she died at age 68.

— Chronicle of the 20th Century

When Pete had worked with good ol' Buck, it became his habit to paw around in the various concealed places in a trade-in automobile. By simply removing the back seat in a touring car, he was assured of at least fifty cents. Often it exceeded this. He had a considerable inventory of ladies' lingerie, broken packets of condoms, an occasional jacknife, combs of various shapes and sizes. A sack of hairpins. Once he chanced on an ax under the seat of a La Salle; he said nothing to good ol' Buck, but was sure it was covered with blood. Was it possible that this ax was the long missing piece of evidence sought in the Lizzie Border murder trial at Fall River, Mass.? Stranger things have happened!

THE POLITICIAN
Late 1929

PETE WAS IN THE BARBER SHOP reading the newspaper. "Jest what I thought, Volney. Ya can't legislate morality. Says right here in the *Topeka Daily Capitol* that alcoholism is a soarin'. Metropolitan Life Insurance Company has reported thet deaths from alcoholism among its policyholders last year was six times the rate of jest ten year ago. I told thet Penelope Pinchlips a long time ago thet it was a peculiar law, she's a puritanical prudish ol' prune." Pete twitched his gold toothpick, emphasis.

Volney was sitting in the barber chair, observing the traffic on Sharon Springs Main Street. "Pete, you haven't turned a tap since you sold the used car business last August. You have all that money in cash from Hubcap Hubbel; it's just laying up there in the Citizen's State Bank. A man of your quick wit and great intelligence needs to put your brain to work. Might putrify your fine personality. Pete, did you ever think about going into politics?"

"Yer suckin' a lot of wind, Volney, regardin' thet Citizen's State Bank. The only thing I take out of thet bank is a calendar onct a year. No one knows where thet money is, not even m' wonderful hepmate, Effie. She has spint prodigious time an' effort a-tryin' to locate the mother lode. I profess I haven't given a single thought ta politics. Just how might I profit from a venture inta politics, Volney?"

"A politician needs a record, something solid so the people can make a decision when they are in the voting booth. First, you ran that used car lot for almost ten years. I never once heard a bad word about you. Everyone knew you were a liar and a cheat. They were expecting it when they went on the premises. You never let them down. That's what people like in a politician, they want consistency and confidence of incredibility. They were confident you'd lie and cheat 'em, and you were consistent. You also have a lot of good common sense, only one in Wallace County that saw the stock market crash coming. You are some kind of a prodigy, Pete Pisanmoan, yes, sir, a real live prophesier."

Pete sat there in the barber shop and pondered. He pondered about politics; yes, politics was a possibility. Pete could see the future being pretty bleak. He glanced down at the *Topeka Daily Capitol* on his lap and noted this article:

> *"Hoover has formed a high-powered council of business and banking leaders to advise and assist him. Their chief job, said the President, will be to 'keep the country's business on an even keel.'"*

Pete snorted, mused to himself, "The whole bunch Hoover had helping him couldn't plug up the leaks in a canoe, let alone the sinking ship of state. Bankers ain't got no sense!" Pete knew the stock market crash was not Hoover's fault, the subsequent depression was not Hoover's fault, but he got the blame.

"How's that boy of yours doing down on the —P, Pete? These cattle prices make it pretty tough to hang on to the ranch."

"Well, Volney, I'm a-payin' the propity taxes on the place. Piedmont don't know it; he's bin makin' the payments ta the Federal Lank Bank up until last year. I told him not ta be concerned. We'll throw the Homestead Act an' the Soldier's and Sailor's Relief Act at them government agents. M' lawyer up in Denver has already filed the papers. Simon Fixum says they'll never foreclose. I do pretty much what Simon says." Pete tongued his gold toothpick over to the other side of his mouth, put on his Triple X Stetson and went to the door. "See ya, Volney. Think I'll be goin' ta Denver, maybe go into politics."

Pete had just given a howdy to Fred Cox when around the corner of the Strand Theater came Penelope Pinchlips. Pete anticipated a snotty snub.

"Oh, Mr. Pisanmoan, so good to see you. Hold up for a moment, please. I have a problem I wish to discuss with you."

Penelope hadn't spoken to him for almost six years, why now? Penelope and Effie were now fast friends. Penelope hated Pete and that was fine with him, but she did admire his business astuteness. Pete was a pistol when it came to business.

"Mr. Pisanmoan, you are quite well-read on current business and political problems. My dear dead daddy left me two sections of prime wheat land down in Harrison Township, Sections 22 and 23. I have a cash offer for this 1,280 acres at $35 an acre and am considering accepting the offer. Would you mind giving me your prudent opinion of this pressing problem?"

"Why, not a-tall, Miss Pinchlips. I reckon I kin prognosticate 'bout as well as the next feller. Why, just this mornin' I read in the *Topeka Daily Capitol* where our President, Mr. Hoover, is surroundin' hisself with some high-powered intellectuals from business an' banking to solve our nation's financial problems. Why, there ain't nuthin' like a good banker ta solve one's problems, Miss Pinchlips. Now if it was me, I'd hold out fer $50 an acre. Not a dime less, Miss Pinchlips. These land values are gonna go up when them bankers an' intellectuals git things all screwed down nice and snug. Powerful policies and politicians."

Penelope gave Pete a limpid smile, "Thank you, Mr. Pisanmoan, for that provocative information. I feel so reassured. If our President follows a prudent pattern of political passion, we shall all avoid poverty. Good morning, Mr. Pisanmoan."

Penelope turned to leave when Pete asked, "You did say them was Sections 22 and 23, didn't you, Miss Pinchlips?"

"Yes, that is correct, Mr. Pisanmoan."

Pete tipped his Triple X, rolled his gold toothpick over to the other side of his mouth and headed up Main Street for the courthouse. Pete was on a mission; he noted that Hubcap still had most of the inventory when he'd sold him the used car lot. Pete went to the Treasurer's Office.

"Howdy, Pete, how kin I help you? My feet are killin' me. Arthritis, I can't hardly walk no more. This has got to be m' last term as Wallace County Treasurer."

"I need to check on some taxes, Otis. Look at Sections 22 an' 23 down in Harrison Township. Who owns them two sections?"

"What I really need is a deputy treasurer. These damned tax books weigh 'bout fifty pounds." Otis flopped the book on the counter and began thumbing through the pages, "Um, let's us see, Sections 22 and 23? Why, Penelope Pinchlips owns them two sections. Old Palmer and Phoebe left Penelope a pile a property, didn't they? Taxes are two years in arrears. Say, Pete, a fella was in here just the other day inquirin' about them very two sections. He didn't ask about the back taxes though."

"How much to pick up those two year a back taxes, Otis? Penelope Pinchlips m' neighbor; I jest might pay them taxes."

Otis replied, "They's both the same, Pete. Mineral rights an' all, $42 a year. Looks like $168 would bring 'em right up to date. Just one more year an' I kin sell them to you on a Treasurer's Deed. You do know she can redeem 'em."

Pete wrote out a check; it was a Colorado National Bank check.

"Thanks for the check, Pete. Don't collect many taxes any more; folks ain't got the money."

It had been a profitable trip to the courthouse for Pete. Several thoughts occurred to Pete on that walk home. Otis was just about physically unable to perform the duties of a Treasurer. He needed assistance, Otis needed a deputy, Pete was the man. What better way to learn about being a treasurer than working in the office? Let Otis rest his arthritic feet, walk around in his carpet slippers, put his feet up on a desk, keep them elevated. Thet way Otis could create a little sympathy from the plebeians for the difficult task of being their county treasurer. His other thought was it was a time for a change in his politics. Pete was a Republican, and Pete knew the Republicans would get their butts stomped come the election of 1932. "I've got to discreetly become a Democrat, but not 'til after I've got me a deputy position."

Effie was at a meeting of the Sharon Springs Sensation and Sensibility Club. Pete sliced a coupla slices of bread, slapped a piece of cheese in the middle, grabbed an apple and sat down in his easy chair, pondered this idea of politics. He came to one conclusion; this paying up of delinquent taxes was not all that bad as an investment. It pays 7% interest if they redeem them; if not, one gets a treasurer's deed. "I'd own me some propity." He heard the paper boy hit the front of the house with the *Denver Post;* thet Meyer boy never could hit a porch. Pete mused as he picked up the *Post,* "Think I'll go ta Denver an' have a chat with Simon, see what Simon says about politics.

The headline on the *Denver Post* that evening:
> *"Stiff New U.S. Tariff Is Signed Into Law*
> *President Hoover has signed the Smoot-Hawley*
> *tariff bill, ushering in a new era of protectionism."*

Pete finished reading the article, shook his head at the idiots in Washington. "Why, they's a-layin' golden aigs, if'n one kin jest see it. They say it will stimulate the economy. Thet there bill will kill the economy! I got ta git ta Denver."

Pete was down in the cellar getting his grip when he heard Effie pound across the living-room floor. Pete recalled the sound of a shod horse walking across the wooden bridge over Eagle Tail River. He could even hear Effie grunt when she untied her shoes. Pete knew it was all those social events Effie was attending that was stretching the elastic. She was Starpoint in the Eastern Star. She told Pete they were the most important part of that secret fraternal organization. She also told Pete she was the very top star.

Pete smiled, he refrained, "Probably the biggest one, too."

Effie was surprised when Pete came up from the cellar. "Just where you headed now, Pete? I had in mind wallpaperin' the pantry."

Pete knew she was jest dreamin', paperin' the pantry. "Here's twenty. The way ya look, you'll probably pant over a pile a pastry at one of them meetin's yer always attendin'. Ya ever heard o' poverty? Git used to thet word, Effie ol' girl. This country is goin' to be one pile o' poverty and pretty pronto."

Effie took the twenty before Pete could change his mind. "Penelope told me you gave her some real estate advice today, Pete. Said you was profound an' profuse with the professional information. Said you was full of it. I had to agree."

"I jest passed a few thoughts," Pete said. "First time Penelope has spoken ta me since I purchased the used car lot, and thet was over six year ago."

"Whatcha going to do in Denver, Pete? You got some floozy up there I don't know about?"

"No floozy, be nice if I did. I got me a new idee, Effie. Ya know how thet adobe dirt gits when it's wet? Put a little straw, and ya kin form it inta bricks. Them bricks are harder than the hubs o' hell. Heard of a Mex, Pedro Perez from Pueblo, he builds ovens ta bake them bricks. Kind of got in mind a partnership with Pedro. We'll call it Pete and Pedro's Adobe Brick Plant; has a nice ring ta hit, don't it, Effie? We'll start with outhouses with them bricks, send out a crew of Mexicans and build outhouses." Pete kind of rolled the gold toothpick, see if Effie was listening.

"Where are you plannin' on puttin' this here brick plant, Pete?" Effie was paying attention; that's about all Pete aroused.

"Why, right next door on them three lots thet Penelope Pinchlips owns. I'd be close ta work thataway, come home fer lunch. Them three lots is pure adobe. We found thet out when we planted thet crop of sweet corn. If'n it hadn't been for thet pile of chicken manure I personally hauled and spread on them lots, we'd of had nuthin'. I kind of had in mind a mine-type operation. Everything would be underground 'ceptin' the kilns. Ya see, Effie, we use a mold, make it out of used lumber. Make a bunch of rectangles. Ya pour in adobe mud, mix it with straw and then git the Mexicans to barefoot it around; they is stompin' in the squares, kinda like hop-scotch. With them Mexicans hoppin', it mixes the straw in with the mud, tightens 'em up thataway. Then ya shove the molds in a oven fer 'bout two hour, take 'em out and, Effie ol' girl, ya got yerself a bunch a bricks. Pedro, he gits the stompers and some freejoles, 'bout ten gallon muscatel. The womenfolks, they take a team an' wagon and go out an' gather cowchips fer fuel. Ain't hardly no overhead, make a pile a money."

Effie bought it, Pete could see she was convinced. "I thought you signed a quit-claim deed to Penelope on them three lots, Pete. She got some kind of a courthouse order that you was never to set foot on any of her properties again, forever!"

"I am truly surprised at ya, Effie. Why, jest taday Penelope Pinchlips asked fer some advice, an' I done checked up at the court house. Statute of Limitations done run out on thet; nothin' says I can't buy thet propity from Penelope. Why, I'd even pay her cash; she gives me a warranty deed and we commence ta makin' bricks. Little Mexican kids runnin' around peein' on her spirea bushes, pitchin' cow chips in the kiln. Why, I would not do a thing to provoke m' neighbor, Penelope

Pinchlips."

Pete threw a few things in his grip and was ready for his trip to Denver. Picked up the evening paper, noticed in the sports section, Babe Ruth was making $160,000 a year. More than the President; Ruth says he had a better year than the President. Pete agreed. The folks in Washington and Ruth were both entertaining.

"I'll have breakfast at the West in the mornin', Effie. Ever since they came out with them corn flakes, ya seem ta think thet's the answer ta breakfast. Yer a little short in the breakfast department. Ya jest stay in bid, but don't tell thet Penelope 'bout the abobe an' this money-making idee. When Pedro and his crew gits them stompers moved inta them tents an' us a burnin' them cow chips, Penelope jest might raise the price on them three lots."

Just as Pete had planned, Effie was down on Penelope's front porch about the time Pete planted his foot on the depot platform ready to board Union Pacific Train No. 123, westbound for Denver. He went to the smoker, talked politics and about hard times. Pete was pretty pitiful with his pronouncements on poverty. Some of the boys in the smoker considered taking up a collection for Pete. Pete liked Denver, the business, the hustle and bustle. Everyone was trying to hustle someone; most avoided Pete. They knew one when they saw one. Pete renewed old friendships with various used car dealers; he had kept in touch over the years. Why, he even had loaned good ol' Buck some money at various times.

Four of the good ol' boys went out for lunch at Pell's Fish House one day; it was a happy reunion for the used car sales people. They ordered; Big Bill Beal told the waitress to put the meals on one ticket. Not a one of those used car dealers would pick up that ticket; they acted like it was a stolen car, hot merchandise.

It was around three in the afternoon when Pete finally reached for his Triple X and walked out on Welton St. "Got ta stretch m' legs a mite, boys." Pete had had a free meal, had a set of salt and pepper shakers in his suit coat pocket, a gift for Effie. "She's a good ol' girl." Pete never did know who paid the check.

"Surely you must be jesting, Effie, my dear. I realize I have not spoken to your husband for over six years, but I had not the slightest inkling he was still perturbed about the potty purge we pulled on him. I have considered selling those three lots recently, as I have need for some cash for other properties I possess. I had in mind a nice round figure of $500 a lot. That sum would certainly ease the pressure of my various financial pursuits and investment problems."

"Well, I just wanted to warn you, Penelope, Pete's a persistent person, and he sure don't ever forget when someone has provoked him. I don't doubt for a minute he's got that Pedro and a bunch of tamale-eaters lined up to parade around in the muck a-makin' adobe bricks. We had us a sod chicken house down on the —P, it's still standin'. It was cool in the summer, warm in the winter. Hens would peck away at them walls fer grit, even when there was snow on the ground. Pete must have a good idea on that there adobe brick. What with these hard times, it makes a good deal of sense to find cheap materials to build."

Meanwhile up in Denver, Pete was in the office of Simon Fixum.

Simon considered Pete a good brick, too, one of the few clients that paid his bill. "So you are considering entering the arena of politics, Pete? I've been your attorney for well over twenty years; saw you pull a lot of pranks, never once been in court. You are getting a mite older, you should slow down. I do agree, politics might just be your ploy. Now, let us consider you purchasing tax titles. We have to skirt around putting those tax titles in a personal name. I would suggest from an income tax and estate tax situation we create a corporation. We do not wish to be promiscuous with our purchases. We'll have one-hundred shares at one dollar a share. You will own ninety-eight, give one share to Effie and one share to Piedmont. Make Effie president, Piedmont the vice, and you will be secretary-treasurer. We give you that office so you are the only one that signs a check, but to cover our tracks you put me on the signature card at the bank. I'll sign the checks, we'll incorporate in the State of Delaware; no one will ever check to see who the stockholders are way back in Delaware. What should we name the corporation, you have any ideas, Pete?"

"No problem a-tall, Simon. I wanta name 'er Tightwad Tax

Title and Trust Company, Incorporated. That's a pip of a name!"

"Pete, that is a titillating title. We'll have no trouble incorporating under that name. There will be none other like it. Now I would suggest you go over to the Colorado National Bank and put $5,000 in the bank account under that name, bring back the signature card for me to sign. Don't buy any back taxes yet. Don't be in a hurry on the delinquents. Wait until you hear from me for final approval. You need to learn a little about being a treasurer before you commence politicking and purchasing. I have a suggestion; are there any county seats in towns on your way back to Sharon Springs?"

"They's two, Hugo and Cheyenne Wells, both of them is in Colorado." Pete knew the county seats. Why, he might even pick up some delinquent taxes in Colorado.

Simon Fixum gave Pete some instructions: "You stop at those two towns. Go to the courthouse, visit with the county treasurer. Most small town politicians will tell you their life history and everyone's business in the whole county if you just pump them, Pete. You are mighty good at that, throw a few pundits at them; they'll be glad to tell you all the problems of the office. You aren't in the office for the money, you want to possess land, get land cheap. Now there's one other thing, Pete. Get some personal liability insurance with an errors and omissions clause, just in case someone checks on the Tightwad Tax Title and Trust Company, Incorporated. You have any trouble, I'll see that it is Effie and Piedmont that get it in the neck. Say, perchance did you save the list of all the sales you made when you had the used car lot? I have an idea."

"Nope, I sold that there list for a thousand dollars cash to ol' Hubcap. He felt it was a tad high; I tol' him them names was a pure gold mine, repeat customers." Pete kind of smirked.

"How many cars has Hubcap sold since the stock market crash, Pete?"

"Far as I know, one. He claims I sold him a dead horse. He don't pay them taxes an' I get m' lots back, may open a brick yard."

Simon told Pete, "You go see Hubcap. See if you can buy back that list. Why, Pete, you have a wealth of friends in

Wallace County on that list, important political friends. I'll send you a bill for the formation of the corporation and our conference."

Pete followed Simon's advice; he stopped in Hugo, Colorado. Spent several days at the courthouse and visited the treasurer. Lincoln County had a deputy, so did Cheyenne County in Cheyenne Wells. Pete decided it would not be hard to talk the Wallace County Commissioners into hiring a deputy. There was sympathy for Otis and his arthritis, the three commissioners were all Republicans. Pete was confident he was to be the new deputy.

Most people misunderstood Pete Pisanmoan; some even pitied poor Pete, thought it was pure greed that made him do the things he did; that was not the case at all. Pete loved the challenge of wit, trying to outwit an adversary, whether it be leasing three vacant lots for a garden or selling used cars. The end result was wit; wit produced profit. Politics was not Pete's ploy. His intentions were not to piddle around in the game of politics; his plan was a procedure to ensure and produce victory. He was going to be the Wallace County Treasurer election time.

On Pete's return trip on the train from Denver and during his stops at Hugo and Cheyenne Wells, there was considerable conversation about the lack of moisture in the spring of 1930. Another big D was creeping into everyday conversations; this one was Drought. Pete added two others that seemed appropriate, Despair and Desperation. Pete had a newer Ford Model A, coupe. He took a drive out south of Sharon Springs, wanted to see Sections 22 and 23. The ride was interesting, good road on the west and south side of Section 22. There had been a section line road on 23, but it seemed abandoned. Penelope had leased both sections on shares; the wheat looked fair, needed moisture. If it rained, Penelope would get her ownership third of the crop and be able to pay the taxes. Pete could see that with a few choice purchases, he could isolate Section 23; there would be no ingress or egress.

"That's what Simon says, I got me an island of wheat, and no one can get to it without trespassin'." Pete rolled his gold toothpick over to the other side of his mouth and smiled. Kind of putzed slowly back to town. Tomorrow was the weekly commissioners' meeting, and although they didn't realize it at the time they were about to hire a deputy county treasurer.

"Well, boys, I think ol' Pete here has presented a pretty good case for hirin' him as a deputy. Pete's been here in Wallace County since '02, he's a lad from pioneer stock. A good Republican and a taxpayer. I heard he paid a neighbor's taxes just the other day out of the goodness of his heart. He knows everyone in the county, and for just fifty dollars a month I don't see how we can go wrong. Let's us put 'er to a vote." The commissioners voted. "Pete, welcome to the public trough."

Pete just smiled, flicked the gold toothpick. He'd won.

Hubcap Hubbel was perturbed, "What do you mean you'll give me a penny a name for that list of sales you made, Pete? I paid you $1,000 for that blue sky. Why, that list ain't worth nothin'. I ain't made a single solitary sale from that list!"

"Well, then, Hubcap, a penny ain't a bit outta line. It is all in salesmanship; ya gotta cast the bread upon the waters; ya thought them folks was jest gonna come in an' slip ya a coupla hunnert, drive off — don't work thataway. All I wanted to do with thet there list was ta sind them all a penny postal card with m' thank-yous for their business and announce ya as the new owner. That's what we in the field of business calls public relations, a gesture. I guess business is so good for ya, ya don't need any hep, Hubcap."

"Well, hell, Pete. Why didn't ya say so? I sure would appreciate that. Might pep things up, provoke a little prosperity around here. Guess you know the city came along and put in an electric meter for me last week. They said they didn't know you'd been runnin' all the lights off the Township Hall. It was no wonder your overhead was so low when I examined your books. You are really a peach, Pete. Go ahead and take the list, no charge. Feller doesn't have friends like you very often."

Now you see, if one knows the angles, he gets something for free. Pete knew all the angles; he worked the plebeians.

The smoke screen Pete had put out worked. Of course, he had no intention of starting an adobe brick plant, although it might have worked except no one had any money to buy adobe bricks.

"How'd you and that Mex, Pedro Perez, get along on baking them bricks, Pete? I found out on the Q.T. that Penelope was interested in sellin' them three lots. She wants five hundred each; seemed kinda high to me, but you been in real estate all yer life." Effie kind of smirked; she could give a zinger once in a while, too.

"Effie, ol' girl, me an' the Mex is in the process of negotiations with Simon, an' Simon says not to do a thing until we complete the complicated negotiations. Penelope's proud of them lots; I'll just casually mention thet price to the county assessor. Judas jest might want ta raise them taxes a tad on Penelope. I'm agonna go to work come Monday up at the courthouse. Been appointed deputy county treasurer. Goin' to hunker down at the public trough, git me a snoot-full o' easy pickin's."

"Why, Petey Pet, I didn't know you was goin' into politics. My star will burn just a little brighter at the Easterner Stars now that you got honest an' steady work. I never was too proud of that used car business. I heard you wasn't too successful at it neither."

Pete just tongued his gold toothpick over to the other side of his mouth, gave Effie a little smile. That's just what a fellow needed from his helpmate, a real confidence builder. Effie didn't know it, but that used car lot was a pure mint. Pete's account at the Colorado National Bank had grown considerably. When he sold out, the chattel mortgages were sold at a 5% discount to good ol' Buck. It was a timely sale; Buck got chattels on automobiles he could not repossess, and with the depression he just used the chattels to start the fire in the sales office one morning. "That Pete, he was a pistol."

Pete picked up the *Denver Post*. Headlines read:

"Hoover Seeks Aid to Combat Depression

Hoover states that the nation must prevent hunger and cold for those in real trouble. President Hoover has announced he has named a committee to draw plans for combating unemployment. The President's action came amidst definite signs of a deepening depression in the United States."

There was more in the article. Pete leaned back in the Navajo saddle blanket on his chair and ruminated on the newspaper article; There was that first big "D," that awful word the public knew but hated to hear. That word was Depression!

Otis Armbuster was really pleased with his new help. "I never seen the likes of you, Pete. You caught on to this here treasurer's job in no time a-tall. You are a natural for a County Treasurer. I rub my feet with Ben-Gay and put on two pair of wool socks. If I put 'em up on the steam radiator, why, they don't seem to hurt hardly a-tall. I see you was down there at the Assessor's Office; what was you talking about anyway?"

"We been discussin' a coupla things, Otis. There are some people that are mighty proud of their property. We are goin' ta raise their taxes. County needs more revenue. If it wasn't fer the Union Pacific, we'd be in one terrible mess financially. I came up with another idea. Judas jest about jumped outta his Justins when I gave him this one. We're commencin' ta tax cemetery lots where folks have bought 'em ahead of their expiration time. We figure 'bout a dollar a year would be a justifiable figure. Judas says this is a first in any county in the U.S. of A., and it was me thet thought of it, Otis. Judas says I'm a proverbial power of potential tax idees. Pummel the people without prejudice, thet's what Judas said."

"What's your plan on collectin' this tax, Pete? There must be six or seven cemeteries in the county."

"Grave digger collects. Tells the family no hole until the county death tax is paid. The sexton can wheedle a buck out of a bereaved family. I always knowed they was a way to tax the dead. After I'm through with this here county, I'll have a tax on groceries. Yessiree, Otis, I'll git a tax on what we eat!"

"Yer a natural, yessiree, Pete, a natural treasurer. You'll have this county runnin' in the black in no time a-tall. Say, rub a little more of that Ben-Gay on my elbow. Seems to be progressing from my feet to all my joints. I've been in a lotta joints in my day, but these is the worst."

Pete's progress was slow. He observed the land adjacent to Section 23. In 1931 he paid taxes on the west half of 24 and southwest quarter of 25. He had a little map in his deputy desk, had it hid under his Bible. Simon had said it was all right to start paying taxes. Tightwad Tax Title and Trust was now in operation.

Otis never saw the actual check and the signature on the check, just noticed the receipt was made out to some strange outfit. "Wonder who this Tightwad Tax Title and Trust is, Pete. See that name crop up once in a while on some back taxes?"

"Don't know who they are, Otis. I jest make the receipt out to T.T.T. & T." Pete rolled his gold toothpick over to the other side of his mouth. Penelope Pinchlips' taxes were past due. It hadn't rained.

Pete was reading the *Denver Post* that evening; headline and the story read:

"Jobless Reach Over Four Million: Aid Sought

With unemployment continuing to soar, Pres. Hoover has urged Congress to provide up to $150,000,000 for public works to create jobs. The President's message had no sooner reached the Capitol than an avalanche of bills to help the jobless began pouring into both Senate and House hoppers."

Pete could see the handwriting; it was hopeless for Hoover. Tomorrow Pete was going to become a Democrat. That was the way the wind was blowing, and Pete was well aware of political wind. The next day he waited until the County Clerk went to lunch and went in and visited with the deputy, Sadie Sobles. Sadie changed her affiliation at the same time. She had planned to run for County Clerk against the incumbent. What Pete said had made good sense to her; she was aware of the wind, too. This was the year of the Democrat, the Paradise on the Plains had had enough conservatism.

Pete had to prepare for his campaign for the 1932 election. He knew he needed the women's vote; his only hope was Effie, his chances there bordered on slim and none. Effie had been pleased with the gift of the salt and pepper shakers, although she had difficulty understanding why they had salt and pepper in them. Pete needed the Easterner Stars, the Women's Club, the Garden Club, the Ladies Aid; hell, he needed a lot of aid. He realized Penelope Pinchlips and Daphne Damptowel were going to be real nuts to crack. He had an idee, pay Penelope's taxes on those three lots. Pete would perform a philanthropic deed, buy a vote.

Everyone in Sharon Springs and Wallace County knew Otis Armbuster would have to retire due to his arthritis and fully expected Pete Pisanmoan to announce his candidacy for County Treasurer on the Republican slate. They held the Republican caucus. Pete was not in attendance; tales began to wag. Penrod Penrose finally stood up at the caucus and said, "I'll run; if I win I'll keep Pete on as my deputy. He's done a fine job. Pete can kind of teach me the ropes of the office.

Pete needed some printing done. He went to see the editor of the *Western Times*. "Swede, I writ me up some copy for an advertisement and fer some cards ta pass out ta all the voters. Are ya ready, I consider m'self an expert in the field a politics."

Swede nodded and smirked. "I'll spend just two dollars; here's m' copy: Pete Pisanmoan for County Treasurer. Vote Democrat! Vote for Pete Pisanmoan; his determined dedication for deadbeat delinquents will keep yer taxes down!"

"That's it, Pete? No more superlatives."

"Thet's it — run 'er just the way I writ 'er, Swede. Folksy is the way ta touch the heart an' souls of our fine citizenry. I need 'bout a thousand little cards printed with the same copy. I'm agonna talk to every citizen in Wallace County, show

Penrod how to campaign with the populace."

Sadie Sobles slapped Pete on the back when he came to the Courthouse the morning of July 3, 1932. "You was right, Pete. Franklin Delano Roosevelt got nominated for President. Why, he even promised us a 'New Deal,' and this ain't jacks or better to open either. We're gonna give it to 'em, Pete. You're a peach, Pete."

"You jest wait, Sadie, on November 8 you'll be the new County Clerk. I'll be the new County Treasurer. I jest knew we'd ride on someone's coattails, and anyone named Roosevelt has mighty fancy coattails. I'll hep ya all I can, Sadie, but I need the women's vote jest as bad as you need the men's. Betwixt us I think we kin pull this here deal off."

It didn't rain, the wind commenced to blow. It blew from the west, put a load of Colorado topsoil on Wallace County, but Wallace County sent an equal load of her topsoil on further east. It blew from the south; Oklahoma placed a large load of red topsoil on Wallace County. Wheat farmers didn't even get their seed back at harvest time. Meanwhile, Pete picked up the south half of Section 14. Pete got about one million Russian thistles and an equal number of cockle-burs, no wheat. Good crop of sand-burrs.

"Oh, Mr. Pisanmoan, I do wish to speak to you for just a moment."

Pete knew it was Penelope; he thought now was the time to shake hands, call a truce, let bygones be bygones, get a vote, get all her friends' votes. Politicians do that; they get chapped lips from kissing odd places just for a vote. Pete smiled, rolled his gold toothpick over to the other side of his mouth. He would call for an armistice.

Penelope P. placed her finger right on Pete's chest and began to harangue; she began several generations back in the Pisanmoan family tree.

Pete heard words he'd never heard at the barber shop, even at the pool hall. Why, not even from a disgruntled used car buyer.

Penelope finally stopped for a breath of air, and Pete smiled down on her red and angry face; a fellow might say Penelope was mighty pissed.

"Why, Miss Pinchlips, it looks ta me like I can't plan on gittin' yer vote come November. I kinda thought you'd feel kindly towards me since I been a-paying yer propity taxes the past coupla year. Ya jest might consider yer own little happy home an' them three lots next door ta me. Jest one more year an' I'll be a-servin' what Simon says is a eviction notice fer non-payment of taxes." Pete delighted in zingers like that. Pete tipped his Triple X, smiled down on Penelope.

Penelope just gasped! Otis had told her T.T.T. & T. had been paying her property taxes!

"Don't you dare walk away from me when I'm speaking to you, Pete Pisanmoan! It was your prodigious advice that made me turn down $35 an acre for some fine wheat ground I own. Someone told me that land was blowing away. I couldn't get $5 an acre for it now. You did that dastardly deed on purpose. I just know you did! I could be sitting on a nice little financial nest egg of about $45,000 now if I hadn't followed your prejudicial perjurious advice. I am seriously considering going to Goodland and consulting with my attorney, Sylvester Beatum. A lawsuit just may be in the offing. Just a warning, Mr. Pisanmoan."

"Now, Miss Pinchlips, I am what ya call a patient an' prudent fella, but you are beginnin' to put a crimp in m' patience. You best be a-thinkin' 'bout me not gittin' provoked and puttin' ya body and parcel out on the street fer non-payment of property taxes. Remember m' slogan fer m' election of Treasurer of Wallace County: 'Determined dedication for deadbeat delinquents,' and it seems ta me yer about the best an' biggest deadbeat I know. Good day ta ya, ma'am."

Penelope stamped her little foot. She knew that Pete was quite serious, and Penelope was in a pickle.

Otis, too, jumped party lines. Pete pulled a fast one on the public. "If I git elected, I'll make ya m' deputy, Otis. Pay ya the same as I bin a-gittin', fifty dollars a month, and I'll be there ta rub yer joints with that there Ben-Gay." It was similar to a pork barrel proposition, but it worked.

Otis told everyone he could that Pete would make a fine treasurer even if he was now a Democrat. "He used to be a Republican, didn't he? Better than one of them Independents.

Pete ain't no fence straddler, he's on one side or the other! He's been my deputy, knows the office, experienced person, and he's as honest as they come, that's what Pete is."

Penrod Penrose kind of pussy-footed around Wallace County. He attended some of the women's club meetings, the Sharon Springs Sensation and Sensibility Club. He had to agree with Pete; there was not a nickel's worth of sense in the entire bunch. He was cozying up to the women's vote.

Pete was out there in the country talking to the farmers and ranchers. He told them, "I'll git us out of this here mess in Wallace County. Ya put yer X behind Pete Pisanmoan's name come November 8!" Pete went to farm sales; most of them were foreclosures, and he bought the northwest quarter of Section 26. Pete paid a dollar an acre more than the Federal Land Bank, and Pete made a lot of friends with that magnanimous gesture. Pete informed folks that that $360 heped get thet family out of the county, git them off the welfare rolls and to California; little did they know the reason.

Pete almost bought a Jersey milk cow for Effie. While he was out in the neighborhood, he observed Penelope's two sections. They were covered with Russian thistles and cockleburs. Pete was not alarmed; they made a good cover crop, hold the top soil. Land would not blow, but those thistles were hell on fences.

Pete knew it was going to be close, not many Democrats in Wallace County. The final precinct, Stockholm, didn't come in until way past two a.m. Pete Pisanmoan 604 votes, Penrod Penrose 544. Sadie Sobles was the new County Clerk. Judas Knight was retained as Assessor. Pete felt the failure of the Citizen's State Bank the previous March had helped, and F.D.R. was going to "restore this country to prosperity." Pete smiled; he knew F.D.R. was whistling in the dark, but he was as good as Hoover, even used most of Hoover's ideas, just put a different name or initial. There were now eleven million jobless. The next D was desperation.

"You have a piece of grey hair hanging on the end of your toothpick, Pete. How's it feel to be a big-time politician? A County Treasurer, mighty important job."

Pete was really quite proud of his venture into politics. "I owe my election to honesty and integrity. The success of m' campaign can be measured by the quality of the people thet was a-runnin'. The public knows when they have a politician."

Volney snorted, quickly turned the barber chair so Pete was unable to see him smiling in the mirror.

"You know who I'm a-goin' after the very first thing? That Union Pacific Railroad. I got Sadie Sobles to typerwrite me a letter this very mornin'. I told thet U.P. I wanted their check for all their property taxes on m' desk when I came ta

work January 2 of each year, or I was gonna burn a bridge a day until thet money arrived. I'm a carryin' out m' political pledge ta my mandate from the voters. 'Determined Dedication for Deadbeat Delinquents.' How's thet sound to ya, Volney?"

"I have been telling my customers you'd make one terrific treasurer. You're the best tergiversator I have ever seen, Pete. I'd kind of go easy on the Union Pacific, Pete. That's the hand that pours slop in your trough; that railroad is your prime tax provider, Pete."

Pete slowly nodded, tongued his gold toothpick over to the other side of his mouth, but he didn't smile. Maybe he'd made a typical Pisanmoan puerility; the letter was in the mail.

Pete informed the County Commissioners that they should

get the W.P.A. and C.C.C. boys working on the county roads. "Save the county a bunch a money. We could give ourselves a raise if the federal government is goin' provide the money and the manpower." The Commissioners all agreed. One remarked that Pete, he's a pistol of a politician. We'd oughta send him to Congress. He thinks like a Congressman, works harder than any Congressman, and when he stands up to talk to those politicians, they'd take notice of a fellow Kansan. Commissioners all nodded their assent as to the attributes of Pete Pisanmoan.

The dust blew; in March 1933 there were now 14 million out of work; a number of the railroaders employed by the Union Pacific were permanent extra-board. Then Pete received a letter from the Accounting Office, Union Pacific Railroad, Omaha, Nebraska. The letter was a little blunt for Pete's tender eyes and ears; the letter more or less read if you torch a trestle, you're in for terrible trouble and tragedy. Pete got the hint, but he was in a good mood; he paid the taxes on the east half of Section 26; he was getting close to his goal. He'd have Penelope Pinchlips penned in on Section 23. Pete rubbed some Ben-Gay on Otis' shoulders. Otis rarely got up and waited on a taxpayer, sat there in his stockin' feet with both of them on the steam radiator. He visited a lot, sort of a public relations man.

There was just a skiff of snow that winter; wheat didn't look a-tall good.

Prohibition came to a jubilant end in '33. Pete didn't drink, but he had sold several automobiles to bootleggers. They always paid Pete cash and bought the best he had on the lot. Roosevelt devalued the dollar sixty cents, raised the price of gold to $35 an ounce. Pete knew someone made a pile of profit on that little proclamation. It was a $2.8-billion profit; the Federal Reserve, the U.S. Treasury and a few already wealthy insiders got rich. It was supposed to stabilize the market. It didn't.

Pete just about had it on the downhill; tugs were kinda slack. He was getting close to isolating Section 23. T.T.T.&T. still had a considerable sum in the Colorado National Bank. That bank hadn't gone broke.

Otis told Pete to rub a little more Ben-Gay on his neck. Otis sighed, it felt better. He'd have put his neck on the steam radiator, but it was too uncomfortable.

Pete tipped back his Triple X and looked up. There stood a man at the Wallace County Treasurer's counter. This was not just your ordinary sort of a sod-buster. This man had on a Five X Stetson, creased Fort Worth bull-dogger style. Had a little fur collar on his top coat, silk necktie. The whitest shirt Pete had ever seen. Points on his shirt collar were like little knives. This guy was starched; Pete wondered if his underwear was starched. Pete had seen a few of these kind in Denver, mostly bankers and those that hung out over at the Mining Exchange Building.

"Yes, sir, kin I hep ya? I'm Pete Pisanmoan, Wallace County Treasurer."

Pete stuck out his hand; the stranger gave Pete a good hearty shake, smiled. Pete rolled his gold toothpick over to the other side of his mouth, smiled.

"Name's Sylvester Beatum, attorney at law from over at Goodland; here's my card. I am Prosecuting Attorney representing Sherman, Wallace and Greeley Counties. Mr. Pisanmoan, I have a local client, a Miss Penelope Pinchlips. She has been corresponding with me regarding some of your activities. Seems you and Miss Pinchlips go back quite a few years, have had some difficulty over crops, vacant lots, windmills. Yes, considerable trouble between you two. This time I feel you have what we barristers call your ass in a crack, Mr. Pisanmoan. I intend to squeeze that a tad, make you squeal just a little."

"Why, Mr. Sylvester Beatum, Penelope Pinchlips has mentioned you on numerous occasions. I'm mighty glad to make yer acquaintance. Speakin' of m' posterior, jest what seems to be yer problem, yer shorts creepin' up on ya?" Pete smiled.

"Mr. Pisanmoan, are you perchance familiar with the term, 'conflict of interest?' "

"Well, now, Sylvester, I've done had a lotta conflicts in m' life, an' a lot of 'em have been downright interestin'. Please proceed with this here conflictin' problem."

"You have been purchasing delinquent taxes prior to advertising them in the legal county newspaper. You have been operating a corporation called Tightwad Tax Title and Trust while being a public and elected official of Wallace County. I have been down in the Recorder's office, have an idea of your intentions. Intentions are difficult to prove in a court of law, but you are what we call a fraud, Mr. Pisanmoan, and I fully intend to prosecute, but I do have one way to let you off the hook and ease your ass out of that crack. Do you wish to hear my proposition?"

Pete rolled his toothpick over to the other side of his mouth; he didn't smile. "Proceed with yer solution to the possibility of fraud against the fine citizens of Wallace County. I personally think yer skatin' on the ragged edge of circumstantial evidence, hearsay, gossip, and I'll throw in defamation of m' fine character. I just may have to consult m' attorney, Mr. Simon Fixum, up in Denver. I always do what Simon says."

"Think this one over, Mr. Pisanmoan. I have a certified check for all of Miss Pinchlips' back taxes. That would include Sections 22 and 23, her home and the three lots north of her domicile. The check is made out to T.T.T.& T. It includes interest to your corporation for the past years at the legal rate of 7%. The check is from a trust that Palmer and Phoebe Pinchlips set up for their two daughters, Penelope and Prunella. I assure the check is good. You will merely sign a quit-claim deed for these properties and I will not prosecute your ass, Mr. Pisanmoan."

"Place that there check on the counter, and the deed. I got one of them new Sheaffer fountain pens; she's fully loaded with Scripto blue. Where do I sign, Sylvester?"

Pete Pisanmoan ran for County Treasurer just one more time, got elected to another term. Then it commenced to rain, and Pete had some prime wheat land, 1,280 acres of wheat land. Pete had Penelope for a neighbor in town and out in Harrison Township, but that's another story.

Some of the news of the times:

Hoover Seeks Aid to Combat Depression
Oct. 23 — Saying that the nation must 'prevent hunger and cold' for those in real trouble, Pres. Hoover

has announced that he has named a committee to draw plans for combating unemployment. The President's action came amidst definite signs of deepening depression in the United States.

In naming the cabinet-level panel to devise ways to create jobs, the President called on state governors and private industry to cooperate in solving the growing problem. It would appear that the President is leaning toward creation of an organization patterned after that which he, as head of President Harding's unemployment conference, was a joint venture of public and private agencies working to spur industry and accelerate public works. It was credit with a curve upward toward prosperity."

—*Rocky Mountain News, December 1930*

Tammany Boss Piles Up Millions!

Nov. 30 — George W. Olvany had an income of more than $2 million during the four and one-half years he served as Tammany Hall leader. The financial status of the former Tammany boss was disclosed by a legislative committee that is probing possible diversion of New York's unemployment relief funds to campaign uses by the Democratic machine once headed by Olvany, a Madison Ave. lawyer.

— *New York Times, July 27, 1932*

▲▲▲▲▲▲

In a historic Dorothea Lange photograph, a homeless Okla-homa family walks a long, hard road during Dust Bowl days.

PETE THE FARMER
1934

VOLNEY BORST SNIPPED a few hairs on Pete Pisanmoan's neck, turned the chair around so Pete could view the tonsorial job in the mirror. "I heard they had the state auditors up at the courthouse, Pete. Otis told me you passed with every penny accounted for, and I didn't think you could do it, Pete."

Volney was sitting in the barber chair, observing the traffic on Sharon Springs Main Street. Pete ran the palm of his hand along his temple. "Trim m' eyebrows a tad, Volney. Effie says I kinda resemble thet John L. Lewis. Notice how m' hair seems ta be grayin' nicely at m' temples. Gives me a distinguished look, makes me look like a County Treasurer. I'll tell ya one thing — if it wasn't fer Otis and his arthritis, I'd be in a fix. He sits there an' does them books with two pair a socks on his feet, I'm up at the counter, I do the public relations, I related real good ta the public." Pete tilted his head to the side and admired what he saw in the mirror. "Yessiree, ya recalls the slogan I had when I ran in '32, 'The success of the office would be measured by the quality of its people.' Right there's the answer ta m' success. It's me an' Otis, Volney. I go out an' collect them taxes, Otis writes 'em up in what he calls the double-entry. I haven't the slightest idee what he means, but the auditor says we're hunky-dory. I see where thet guy Hitler over in Germany has told Uncle Sam ta take a big jump offen a short bridge on 'bout a half-a-billion dollars o' debt. Ol' F.D.R., he send me over there ta Germany, I'd collect that there pile a money plenty pronto, they call it reparations."

"You going to announce you're running for re-election pretty soon, Pete? Most folks that come in the shop think you did about as well as they expected. They didn't think you showed any favoritism, seemed to cheat 'em all about equal."

"I bin a-watchin' Otis's feet an' joints. That's the clue, rub him good with Ben-Gay. We are a team, Volney — Otis at the desk and me at the counter relatin' to the public. Good will and all that there stuff. I'll toss m' Triple X in the circle, kind of fond of thet public trough. I got me a new idee on raisin' taxes. I got ta scuffin' around out there on some of m' tax title land. I thought the Russian thistles would keep thet land from a-blowin'; it hepped a little. Road tacks and sand-burrs were better, and you know what, when I got to scuffin' around I found some grass comin' back. I named this land 'Go Back.' Hit's a-goin' back ta grass, Volney. I figure a penny an acre increase on a section. Thet's $6.40 more on each an' ever section in Wallace County. Ever little dab heps."

There it is right there in Wallace County, Kansas, a county politician, the County Treasurer named land that was re-seeding itself "back." It was a slow, very slow process, but that is where the name of "Go Back" land came from — it was Pete Pisanmoan in 1934.

Volney remarked, "I heard there's no roots on those thistles. When they mature in the fall, wind just blows them away. They pile up in the fence rows, break the posts and the barbed wire."

"Yer absolutely kerrect, Volney. Those thistles are ruinin' all the fences. There's blow-dirt in the fences so bad I haven't seen a fence sometimes fer miles. We just busted up too much sod. Pure greed, pure and simple greed, thet's what we done to land, we raped the land. Governmint was partly ta blame, they give ya 160 acres and tell ya to be a farmer. Young feller fresh outta K. State been assigned to our county; he's called a conservation agent. If'n I'd a known they was a-lookin' fer someone conservative, I'd been right up there at the head of the line. This kid says we gotta let our land lay fallow, save our moisture fer a year. Let the wheat stubble hold the land, keep it from a-blowin'. Personally, I think this kid is kerrect."

"When I started in the barber trade, it was a good and honest way to make a living, Pete. Not any more. You and a couple of other gentlemen still come in for a shave every other day. Used to have that wall over there full of shaving mugs. King Gillette and the depression ruined my shaving business. People are leaving the county about as fast as they came in back in the homestead days. Last Saturday I took in just $7.50.

I used to run $40 on a good Saturday. These are tough times, Pete."

Pete admired himself in the mirror, put on his Triple X Stetson, tongued his gold toothpick over to the other side of his mouth and remarked, "Ol' Hubcap gave 'er up yesterday. Guess his jim-dandy motto didn't pan out ta well, 'Hubcap Hubbell sells cars with no trouble.' He had thet used car lot fer over two year, sold just four cars in two year. I used to sell sometimes four, maybe five a week. Made a good livin' in the used car business. Guess I'll go by the post office and then up to the courthouse, give Otis a dose a Ben-Gay on his joints. Effie hates thet smell; I rub a dab behind m' ear when I go home, do it fer m' Effie."

Pete smiled as he shut the door to the barber shop. Volney shook his head, "He's an ornery but likeable old cuss."

There was some Treasurer's office mail, a letter to Pete from the City of Sharon Springs, office of the City Clerk. Pete was more concerned with Otis. Pete stuffed the letter in his hip pocket and headed for the courthouse. Otis had his feet up on his desk, carpet slippers on. Pete inquired, "Where's it a-hurtin' taday, Otis? I'll git the Ben-Gay, good dose always seems ta do wonders fer yer joints."

"Seems like it's in m' ankles today, Pete. Gosh, Pete, you are a kindly man. You sure do have a lot of patience. You buy most of that ointment out of your own pocket. People say they can smell you a-comin' a block away. I did notice you seem to always put a dab on your neck just a-fore you go home at night. Is your neck hurtin' you a little, Pete."

"Naw, Otis, it's fer m' Effie. She jest loves the smell of Ben-Gay. Kind of has a aphrodisiac effect on 'er. She says it jest makes her a-tingle all over." Effie's education had improved some since she had joined the Sharon Springs Sensation and Sensibility Club. Pete just knew she was a sensation; when she walked across the room of their house it jiggled. Effie jiggled when she walked, had lots of interesting little jiggles.

When Pete got home, he picked up the *Denver Post* that was on the front porch. Pete noted Al Capone was now locked up in Alcatraz. He lit the kerosene lamp; there was no electricity in the Pisanmoan residence. Effie had pleaded with Pete for some electricity. She told him about all the labor-saving conveniences she'd have. "I am unable to hold our club meetings in my own home 'cause yer just too tight to install electricity. I heard all about you sponging off the city when you had that used car lot. Plugging into the Township Hall. I am so ashamed of you; you are such a tightwad, Pistol Pete!"

Pete just smiled, didn't reply. He'd heard that song and dance about electricity before. They didn't have it down on the Bar P, why have it just because one moved to the big city. When Pete sat down, he heard something crinkle in his hip pocket; it was the letter from the city clerk. Pete cut the envelope open with his Buck knife. It read:

"Dear Mr. Pisanmoan:

It has come to our attention via a complaint from one of your neighbors that you still have not attached your residence to the City of Sharon Springs sanitary sewer. You were properly notified of this matter in 1928 according to our records. Six years seems ample time for you to cease using outdoor facilities. Pursuant to Municipal Code No. 475, State of Kansas, Revised 1929, Amended 1931, Sub-section C, Paragraph 4, you are hereby notified to cease and desist the use of your outhouse."

Sincerely,
s / Lester P. Pester
City Clerk, Town of Sharon Springs, Kansas

There was a short postscript in Lester's handwriting: "Come on, hook up to the damned sewer, you can afford it! L.P.P."

Pete re-folded the letter, put it on the lamp stand by his easy chair. He knew he had to comply with the city code. After all, he was one of the county's elected officials, but he was attempting to figure out a way to cobble up some kind of a cheap way to get around spending much money. He had become accustomed to the indoor facilities at the courthouse. He thought, "If thet Judas finds out I have indoor plumbing, he'll raise m' taxes. Outhouse is filling up. Effie dug thet there hole the first year we moved here — why, thet was 1920 or was it '21? I do recollect I bought her a new hickory-handled shovel. Another disturbing thought hit Pete; he'd have to put in a water line, too! More expense, he might be able to get Effie ta carry water from Penelope Pinchlips ta flush the toilet. Why, thet's who turned me in, it was thet Penelope Pinchlips, and probably Effie sicked her on to the idee." Pete's toothpick stood straight up; Pete was plenty perturbed at both Penelope and Effie.

Pete heard Effie plod up on the porch. She plopped down on a straight-back chair; they only had one overstuffed easy chair. Effie had plopped and now she puffed; he smiled. "See you got a letter, Pete. Do you want me to read it to you?" Effie had a way about her, she could be downright mean at times.

"Letter from the city. We got to hook up to the sewer. This is Lester Pester's last warnin'. I bin thinkin' 'bout gettin' ya a new shovel, Effie ol' girl. Ya could commence ta dig the water and sewer lines whilest I was cobblin' us up a bathroom. Build kind of a lean-to on the back porch. Havta put in some kind a heat, don't want the pipes ta freeze. Probably a kerosene lamp would be nuff."

"You and that joint ointment you rub on poor Otis and his feet. You smell like a spavined horse, and speaking of horses, you better find someone else to dig your ditches. This ol' girl has done dug her last ditch. We've lived in this shack since '20, that's 14 miserable years. What'd you pay for this dump, Pete? Seems to me it was $950, and that included all this fine furniture, pots and pans, includin' that tea kettle that has a spool for a handle on the lid. That figures out to about $68 dollars a year to live in this dump. You are a real tightwad, Pete!"

Pete leaned forward in his overstuffed chair, Navajo saddle blanket for a cover over a spring in the cushion that was in a precarious place, pointed at Effie and shook his finger. "Don't ya fergit all them taxes I've paid on this fine domicile! Lots a taxes, and we painted the house back in '29. As I recollect Pearly White was the color, I know, there's a dab in a bucket out in the garage."

Pete expected contrition, Effie passed. "Well, I've been in a lot of fine homes in our fair city, and this is the biggest dump in town. The ladies all laugh when it comes my turn to be hostess of the Sensation and Sensibility Club. A lot of gigglin' and tee-hees when my name comes up. I have to co-hostess with Penelope at her house. Penelope told me one of the ladies, and I won't mention any names, said that she would like to slum it for an afternoon, see just how the other half lived. Now, that's downright embarrassin', penny-pincher Pete."

"No, Effie ol' girl, they's two sides ta this here cow chip. It ain't bin easy on me neither. I bin a-tailin'-up Piedmont, buyin' tax titles fer investmint purposes an' assurin' yer financial future. We been lucky I got that treasurer's job. We jest might have had ta go on relief."

"Oh pshaw, Pete! You got a pile hid somewhere. I'll find it someday. Right now you'd best be thinkin' 'bout a new house. I got me a name for it, saw it in a magazine when I was at the Clip and Curl. What do you think of the name, Casa Del Sol? Ain't that got a lot of class!"

"You'll be playin' a lot ol' sol all right, trying to find m' pile. I think I got a deck a cards somewheres. Seems ta me I found a deck in a back seat on a car I took in on a trade. Kept track of all thet stuff I found in the back seat of m' autymobiles in nine years. Came to $4.76, two jack knives, a pair o' pliers and one little item of women's unmentionables."

"I shall explain the name of the house we're gonna build. That's Spanish, a house in the sun. I found that the most descriptive name of the house I wanna build, especially here in western Kansas."

"Ya know something, Effie, yer a real pain in the patoot. A positively giant of a pain, but I'll say one thing, you have been an easy-keeper. Ya never wanted much, although I kinda pampered ya, buyin' you new shovels, and as I recollect I bought ya a new manure fork when we was down on the Bar P. Ya recollect them salt and pepper shakers I bought ya in Denver? Yep, kinda pampered ya. Remember those good ol' days down on the Bar P? Ya had a nice svelt figure then — muscles. Ya was hard as nails, Effie ol' girl. Calluses on yer hands, yessiree, ya was a sight ta behold. Sweat, gawd, you could sweat jest like a man. I got a lotta pleasant memories of them times when we was young. Ya could run an over-shot stacker, stack hay as good as anyone I ever saw. Saved me havin' ta hire a man on the Bar P. Ya know, I am gittin' kind o' excited 'bout a new house. Wonder if Penelope would sell them three lots? Maybe we'd buy us a new teakettle."

Effie was positively titillated; she almost gave Pete a kiss on the neck, right where Pete had placed a little dab a Ben-Gay. Her pucker perished, she squeezed Pete's hand, tears were in her eyes. Pete thought she was displaying emotional gratitude; it was false, it was the odor of the Ben-Gay made Effie's eyes puddle. "I'll get us some supper on, Pete. Let's me and you talk about the Casa Del Sol. I have some fresh pork chops, biscuits and gravy; them's your favorites."

After dinner Pete was sitting in his easy chair, toothpicking pork chop out of his teeth, contemplating the Casa, what would it cost. He remarked, "I kinda had in mind a nice little two-bedroom cottage sort of a house, Effie. One thet would be easy fer ya to keep. Just a small livin' room, big kitchen with lotsa cupboards so's ya could cook more ta home and, of course, just one bath. Even have electricity, nuthin' expensive, mind ya, nice but practical. What I'd term kinda on the cozy side. Yep, real cozy an' comfortable. Gravity furnace in the basement, have the coal bin close to the furnace so you wouldn't have so far ta walk with a scoop shovel a coal. We'd git us one a them topsey stoves fer hot water, have a good Saturday night bath. Cozy but classy, yep, those are m' suggestions."

Effie snorted at the suggestions. "Pete, yer a real pistol. Yer such a practical man, yer about a mile from what I have in mind for our Casa Del Sol. It will have a living room with a fireplace. Formal dining room and a breakfast nook. Kitchen, a laundry room, three bedrooms as we'll have more guests and not just one bath, two baths. I have in mind a brick home, and we'll need a double garage; I'm plannin' on learning ta drive. You have a new Terryplane; I have in mind a La Salle."

Pete was pawing around in the crotch of his pants; he'd dropped his gold toothpick when Effie hit the La Salle automobile item. "I suppose ya had in mind servants' quarters in the basemint. Ya need a butler an' a maid fer thet castle in the sunshine. Why, m' votin' friends will be thinkin' I have been dippin' inta the public monies ta build this sunnyshine house. Maybe they's a solution between the two of us. What ya want an' what I kin pay fer. Ask thet Penelope Pinchlips what she wants fer them three lots. Maybe, jest maybe, we kin build this house so's ya could be close ta thet prune face. I'll plant me a persimmon tree, sweeten her perky personality. Ya kin plant a prune tree fer her, Effie. She'd like thet." Pete wondered if Effie caught on.

Effie thought on that one. "I'll just do that for my friend and neighbor, plant a prune tree at my Casa Del Sol, a blue plum."

After breakfast the next morning Pete made a surprising statement, "I'm goin' up town, buy me a tractor, got ta git ta farmin'." On his walk uptown he considered the absurdity of the idea, "A three-bedroom house, brick, a LaSalle autymobile. I'll kill this whole idee pretty badly!"

"So you want a tractor with lugs, big lugs. I got just what you need, a Rumley. I can get you a Wallis with or without rubber tires. Easier riding on rubber, but if you want lugs, I'll sell you lugs. I ain't made a sale in a month, and that was for five foot of a used section of a harrow. I don't have a tractor in stock; it takes about a week or two to come down from Denver. I do need a deposit on it, say $100. I prefer cash. How's that sound, Pete?"

"Need a plow ta go with thet tractor, Jake. How many bottoms will thet Wallis baby pull, lug 'n all?"

"Good tractor, pulls four bottoms. You got to adjust the coulter a tad. The economy fourteen-incher is the one I recommend for this sandy soil. The moldboard is carburized steel and is special heat treated. Covers, pulverizes and scours real nice." When Jake mentioned economy-size, that was the one that Pete purchased. Pete was partial to economy, pleased with his purchase.

"How much fer the pair?"

"Cash price to you, Pete, for the pair, $1,195. I got a condition; you give me $100 cash down now, $1,000 on delivery. If you can get Judas to lower my assessments, I'd pay less personal property taxes. The implement business is a mite tough with the depression, drought and dust. Judas taxed me on my stock last year. I had an old lister out there that was taxed for more than it was worth."

Sagacity was one of Pete's better attributes; he caught on real quick.

"I'll have me a chat with m' friend an' fellow political associate, Judas, our fine Wallace County Assessor. Judas has never betrayed me, Jake. Yer taxes will be a heap less next year. Spit and shake on 'er; I'm most anxious ta get ta plowin'."

From the implement dealership Pete's next stop was the City Hall. "I got yer letter, Lester. Jest how much time do I have afore ya shut down m' livin' facilities? Effie an' I have done decided ta build us a cozy little cottage, jest fer two, kinda on the honeymoonish side," Pete winked at Lester.

"Pete, it is the intent that we here at City Hall are most interested in; intent is the key word. If there is intent, we tend to be lenient. When you come in for your building permit, we'll know you are then intending to build. Legally there is no specific time limit on intent."

Pete knew Lester was full of dephlogistic gas; he'd been at the City Hall too long, but there was one part of that gas attack that alerted Pete. "Whatcha mean 'bout a buildin' permit? What do I need permission ta build a house fer anyways?" Pete twitched his toothpick up and down, menacing manner, eyes kind of glazed over. "Sounds like a tax ta me, pure and simple, a tax." Pete collected taxes; he did not spend his own monies for taxes.

Lester had heard this song before, "It is not a tax, Pete. Consider it a privilege, a right. Why, it may even be considered a part of our liberty. The money derived from the building permit helps to keep our fine City of Sharon Springs solvent. There is also a tap fee for the sewer and a tap fee for potable water. When you tap these fine facilities, we charge for that privilege, too, Pete. It keeps up our bond payments that way."

Pete was not about to buy this, "Ya ever heard the word extortion, Lester? Thet's jest what this is on them permits and tap fees. Liberty, my liver! I'll jest make a little deal with ya, Lester. Ya fergit those tap fees, and I'll tell Judas not to assess the city on them sewer and water mains. They is a taxable item since they is income producin'. I personally checked thet item with m' attorney; he says to tax 'em."

Lester knew Pete was blowing a lot of wind, but he did have a point. "You put it very succinctly, Pete. You have a certain dash to your threats. They do sound very realistic. We have a deal, no permit fee, no tap fees and you keep it under your Triple X."

Pete smiled, "Spit an' shake on 'er, Lester. Extortion an' blackmail is wonderful, ain't they? Say, I see ya got a plat of the Sharon Springs cemetery up there on the wall. I was a pall-bearer fer John Lingerlong a month or so ago. I noticed some of the plots around John's hole; show me jest where is the Pinchlips plots."

"Palmer was quite specific on their plots, Pete. First it is Palmer, then Phoebe and Prunella; finally, Penelope is on the end. Large headstone covers all four of the Pinchlips. Palmer was a prodigious planner."

Pete inquired, "Them two plots next ta Penelope sold?"

"No, they are available. Are you planning a possible purchase, Pete?"

"How much ya want for them two lots, Lester?"

"Five dollars for each plot, Pete. Recall you were the one that put an annual tax on these cemetery lots. Effie will have to pay a pretty penny when you perish and meet St. Peter at the pearlies. You're such an ornery ol' cuss it'll be awhile before she has to pay."

Pete smiled, rolled the gold toothpick over a time or two. He thought of the possibility of two zingers right there: Penelope, if he could get the lot he wanted, and Effie, if he could live to be about a hunnert. "I'll just buy them two lots, Lester. Specify m' plot right next ta Penelope. We been neighbors fer nigh onto fifteen year, me a-layin' right next ta Penelope inta perpetuity would be mighty nice, yessiree, perhaps pleasant. Make up the deed to them two lots; we'll perform the deed right now."

Lester got out the cemetery deed book and began writing. Made a note in indelible ink on the cemetery plot on one wall of the office, wrote Pete Pisanmoan-Effie Pisanmoan. While Lester was performing his clerical duties, Pete was looking over the plat of the City of Sharon Springs. "I see them three lots jest south of m' house is still zoned agricultural. Now if them lots is still zoned agricultural, how come a feller has to hook on ta the sewer?"

Lester didn't fall for it; they had already spit and shook. "The lots are still grandfathered in, Pete. From that year you had that fine crop of sweet corn. I always wondered why Penelope didn't request a change of zoning, simple protection for her fine home. Taxes are cheaper on agricultural zoning." The word that taxes were cheaper impressed Pete, good site for a new home. Pete paid Lester ten dollars for the two cemetery plots.

"See ya, Lester. Ya recollect we spit and shook on them fees." Tipped his Triple X at a jaunty angle and headed up Main Street to the courthouse. There's a certain air to a person of importance; Pete had developed that air. He was a County Treasurer, a local politician, respected in his community, admired for his diligence and perseverance as County Treasurer.

"Where you been, Pete? I need a dose a Ben-Gay. I got it in my knees today. My socks don't reach up to my knees. I've been wonderin' if an electric heater hid under my desk would help with my ankles and knees?" The combination of Ben-Gay ointment and an electric heater ought to be recalled by anyone paying their taxes at the County Treasurer's Office.

"Otis, ol' friend. I jest bought me a tractor and a plow. Goin' ta start farmin' down on the tax title ground. The T.T.T.& T. ground is about ta go inta wheat. Goin' ta summer fallow some of it. Me an' thet conservative kid is gonna give 'er a try. I bought two cemetery plots, preparin' fer perdition. Ya know, a electric heater might jest do the trick. Ya betcha, I'll git ya one. Got to make them ankles and knees hold out fer one more term. I'm a-gonna run one more time and I need ya, Otis. Ya is the nuts an' bolts of this here office, I'm jest kind of a front man. I have ta go down and see Judas a minute, need ta tell him somethin' 'bout assessments, he needs a little help. I'll be right back."

It had been the Pisanmoan family policy for some time to diversify their activities when wishing to perform some dastardly deed on an unsuspecting victim. It had started when the Pisanmoan family had settled in Missouri, way back in 1837. Each generation became more adept at deception and devilment, and the delinquency continues to this date in that state. Pete's method was one that had previously proven provocative. He was preparing Penelope Pinchlips for a psychiatric phenomenon, a frontal and two flank attacks — her not knowing the main reason, but suspicious of all three, and perennially guessing wrong. Pete's policy was to get Penelope in a predicament, a perverse perversion, in a promiscuous pickle.

Pete went to Koons Hardware. Koons handled electric heaters, but Charlie Koons was also the local mortician, Koons Funeral Home. Charlie sold electric heaters, and he also sold headstones for the dead, dearly loved, distinguished and departed. "I need a headstone fer me an' ol' Effie, Charlie. Nothin' fancy, mind ya, cheap grade of stone."

"Pete, I just knew you would want an economical slab of stone; I have a catalogue right here in the drawer. White limestone is the most economical. Folks in eastern Kansas make their houses, churches, fence posts, headstones out of limestone. Now here's one that is three feet wide, two feet high, very impressive, and it's only $52.50 including the lettering. I get $5 to set it in concrete on the plot. How do you want it to read? I'll put the birthdates right here on the order. Chiseling in the date of demise later is no trouble. I just wait until there's about a day's work and notify a fellow in Ellis. The departed don't care much about that date anyway." Charlie chuckled, Pete grinned.

"Thet $52.50 one looks fine ta me, Charlie. Here's the dates of birth. Mine's '81 and Effie's is '83. Ya know where the Pinchlips plot is up there on the hill?"

"Sure do. Palmer paid for the entire family. Palmer Pinchlips was a planner and a fine provider."

"I purchased the two plots right next ta the Pinchlips plot. I want thet economical headstone ta read with m' name right next ta Penelope. She's bin m' neighbor fer a long time. We'll jest rest an' neighbor up there on the hill inta perpetuity. I want thet stone put up just as soon as ya kin, be kind of a surprise fer m' Effie, a present so's ta speak. Now, I need a electric heater, a small one so's I kin put it under Otis's desk, keep his knees an' ankles warm, toasty-like."

"I have a nice one here — deluxe model — has a little fan

on it. Would circulate the heat around, spiffy little number, and it is only $3.95. Now here's a smaller one, no fan, more economical and it's $1.98."

"I'm partial ta the $1.98 jobbie. Otis kin kick his feet around a little, circulate the heat. I'll take thet one, Charlie."

"I thought you'd take the smaller one. I'll get that order out for the headstone in today's mail. Lots of folks up there on the hill with no headstones. Times are mighty tough, Pete. I'll have a run on headstones when we get out of this depression, and everyone will want it up by Decoration Day."

Not many days does one purchase his cemetery plot, the family headstone and an electric heater without a fan. Pete had parted with about all the money his frugal mind could handle; he headed for home.

"Didja talk ta P.P. about the three lots, Effie?"

"How come you aren't up at the treasurer's office? Yes, she seems quite proud of her property but would dearly love to have us for her neighbors. She has in mind a nice round figure of $900, Pete."

Pete snorted at the price, "I kind of had in mind a nice square figure of $400. Have a thought though, Effie. We tell Penelope we'll pass up this golden opportunity ta build this here sunny-side-up house o' yers on her high-priced lots. We'll tear this one down, lotsa good material in this one. Then we'll build right here on our own propity. If'n she should come ta her senses, git off thet preposterous price, take $400. I'd fer sure want a codicil in the contract thet the zonin' stays the same. Taxes are a heap cheaper on agricultural land than on residential."

Effie looked at Pete, puzzled, "What's a codicil, Pete?"

"Legal term, Effie ol' girl, ya wouldn't understand it. Simon says be sure an' put a codicil in every contract; big word like thet make Penelope consider a contract more serious like."

"Pete, just where would we live whilest we was tearing down this house and building the Casa? You ever think of that?"

"Thet's no problem a-tall. I kinda had in mind a tent. Put it out close ta the facilities. We could cook over a camp fire, make ya 'preciate thet sunny house when we git 'er completed.

Probably take not longer than say, six or seven months. Course ya could go back ta work part-time fer Ben down at the West Hotel like ya did when we moved up here from the —P. Maybe ya could move yer things down to P.P.'s an' bunk with her. You two could toss a lot of fan-tads. I'd live up in the furnace room at the courthouse, sleep on a army cot. I might pick up a few extry bucks firin' the furnace at night. Thet tent would be kinda fun, Effie ol' girl. We could squat out there, roast us some wienies over an open fire, have some marshymallows. Be kind of like the pioneers — even act like a tribe o' Indians, have us a rain dance, we shure do need a heap a rain. Why, maybe even build us a teepee instead of a tent. Lay out there on the ground an' look up at the stars. Too bad the buffalo is all gone, hang a haunch up there in the teepee. Sounds sorta romantic, ya like thet idee, Effie ol' girl?"

Effie was not about to buy any of this; she never knew when Pete was serious. "You kin take your codicil and teepee, and I'll take my haunch and move in with P.P. I'll approach her tomorrow, tell her you offer $400, and I suggest you start a-looking for a cot for yer codicil." Pete enjoyed giving Effie a zinger now and then. It was called prostituted procrastination.

When Pete came to the office, Otis had a question. "Are we goin' to change horses in the middle of the stream, Pete? Change back to being a Republican? I need to know just where my party loyalty lies prior to your announcin' your candidacy."

"Stay Democrat this term, Otis. Seems we have made a right favorable impression on the voting populace. Some says we're downright popular. Now thet's unusual fer a tax collector. F.D.R.'s coattails were fine in '32. We'll stay hitched to him in '36. When I toss m' Triple X in the ring, I'm a-gonna put yer name right under mine on all m' extensive advertisin', kinda like a president does ta a vice. Ya is one popular fella and yer a big hep."

Unbeknownst to Effie, Pete really did give a lot of thought to the Casa Del Sol, especially the amount of money it was going to cost. "Effie, I bin thinkin' 'bout this here sunshine house. If ya want ta name it Mex, why don't I go ahead and work on a plan makin' the Casa outta adobe bricks. When I frame the interior walls, we'll use the good lumber offen this house. Lumber in this fine residence is all cured out, won't be a crack in the plaster from any crooked 2x4's. Ya recollect how warm thet chicken house was down on the Bar P in the winter time, cool in the summer? I was workin' on thet adobe block idee sometime ago; negotiations fell through with thet Mex over at Pueblo. I might take the Terryplane and toddle over around La Junta, see if I kin find a Mex or two. Been considerin' a guy over ta Goodland ta build, name's Lute Slack. Good man, I hear, lotsa pep, works fer a pittance and really produces. Put yer pueblo up in jig time."

Effie seemed emphatic, "We'll build the house out of brick." That was all Effie said.

Pete failed to smile. Twitched both his toothpick and felt a slight twitch in his hip billfold pocket.

People were not exactly breaking down the door at the Treasurer's office to pay their taxes; Pete and Otis had sufficient time to ponder their problems. "Otis, I need a tad a hep. I bin thinkin' 'bout a deal. Tell me the return on a $950 investment if I was ta git, say $15 a month on thet amount."

"What do you mean, Pete? I don't understand."

"All right, Otis, jest suppose I was ta rent thet lovely home me an' Effie been livin' in, call it a invistment, rental propity. I paid $950 fer it, I'd rent 'er furnished and all fer $15 a month. What kind of a return would thet be?"

Otis sat there, odor of heat and Ben-Gay coming from under his desk. He licked the end of his pencil, rubbed his feet together. Otis was really concentrating, made several erasures. "Why, Pete, that's 19% return on your investment on an annual basis. That's some kind of a return! Why, it's better than Ford or General Motors stock on cars which they ain't selling. You'd havta deduct your property taxes, and then don't fergit you got to put in them facilities. It might put you in a higher income tax bracket though, Pete. How much tax did you pay last year?"

"Nuthin', takin' heavy depreciation on m' fences on the T.T.T.& T. ground. They's all covered up with dirt, them was all 5 wire fence, too." Pete smiled, so did Otis. Range fence was always 3 wire, not 5.

Otis said, "You are in the proper bracket; that's the same

one I'm in, the one where you pay no taxes. Remember though, Lester Pester is goin' to be tough on them facilities. They are gonna cost you a couple of hundred, and as to them fences, you ain't got a fence on the entire 1,280 acres of cockle-burs, thistles, sand-burrs an' blow dirt."

Up went the toothpick, "Ya think the governmint is goin' ta drive out there an' dig down an' check m' fences? Nosiree, but they will check on income propity. I'm gonna fix up our domestic domicile an' rent her out — pots an' pans, everything furnished. I might even git $20 a month. I'm considerin' lettin' the party thet rents the domicile pay fer some of his rent with sweat. Dig the ditches fer the sewer an' water, might even give 'em two months free rent fer thet little dab a work."

Otis just smiled, thought to himself, Pete's a pistol.

When Pete got home that evening, Effie had some news. "Penelope has done arrived at a price on them lots, Pete."

"Just what was her arrival price, Effie? Probably too much for us poor folk. She's done forgotten all them kindnesses an' benevolences I have done to her."

"She split it right down the middle, Pete, $450, and she said there was no problem on that codicil. She told me she's had two or three of them in the past, and they didn't hurt a bit."

Pete tongued his gold tooth pick over to the other side of his mouth, smiled. "Tell ya what we'll do, Effie, I'll git m' friend an' political associate, Sadie Sobles, the Wallace County Clerk, ta make up a deed. She'll put the codicil in, I'll bring it home and give Penelope her $450. She jest signs the deed, and we'll do some necessary land levelin' on them lots. Now jest hang onto yer girdle, ol' girl, we're gonna go ahead with the facilities on this fine home, but I'm gonna do 'em as inexpensive as I kin."

Effie wasn't surprised at the decision. "What you mean is as cheap as you can, don't ya, Pete?"

"Economical sounds better. I'm gonna rent this here house out fully furnished. Pots, pans, linens, the entire she-bang. Why, there ain't another rental income propity like 'er in the city."

"You sure do have that right, Pete. There ain't another one like this dump. You plan to provide electricity for the renters?"

"Nope, I'll throw in a gallon a coal oil a month with the rent.

Make 'er quaint-like, probably some school teacher 'll fall fer thet word. Now fer the whiz-banger for thet Mex castle ya got planned. I'll buy them three lots, git all nice and leveled fer construction ta commence. I'm gonna put maybe $5,000 in the new People's State Bank, put it in yer name. That's fer the house, all the furnishin's, no tap fees ta Lester. Them's five big ones, Effie ol' girl. This here is a depression, and you have done depleted the last of m' autymobile money profits, five big ones, and if'n you go over, you'll just have to borry or go get a job down at the West. My very first suggestion is fer ya to git ta Denver, consult with a architect. I'm fixin' ta start plowin' down in Harrison Township on some land I picked up in back taxes. This is election year, have to get out on the campaign trail, call on all m' fine friends out there in the sand-burrs and blow dirt. I haven't got time fer a house with all thet sunshine. We move out of this fine home, an' I start gittin' rental income an' thet reminds me, I want a high damage deposit from any renter; I don't want nuthin' damaged or demolished or destructed. No pets!"

Effie was taking all this in with a grain or a pile, either one seemed appropriate. "If I was you, I'd throw a big insurance policy on this dump and then hope one of them quaint renters burned 'er down, Pete."

"Effie, you are thinkin' just what I had in mind. Simon calls it arson. It's kind of like the candle-in-a-pan-a-coal-oil method. I shure know ya know about thet method. I'm gonna go up ta the courthouse, git us a deed drawed up."

Pete had all sorts of plans for that house, and he wasn't thinking about the Casa Del Sol. "Sadie, I want ya ta put thet deed in the name a Pete Pisanmoan only. Leave Effie offen this one, no joint tenancy. She's on all my T.T.T. & T. ground and the Bar P down at Wallace. I'll take thet deed down ta Penelope an' be back directly, git it properly recorded."

Penelope answered her door on the first gentle tap. She seemed surprised, she wasn't. She'd seen Pete round the corner before he ever saw the curtain move. "Why, hello there, Mr. Pisanmoan. I understood that dear Effie was to make the purchase of my lovely lots; she's such a lovely philomath. Oh my goodness, I see you have the money in cash, how thoughtful of you." She kind of squeaked when she saw the cash.

"I jest knew y'd like the cash, Miss Pinchlips. Makes it easy ta by-pass the government boys thet-away. Kinda put 'er down in the toe of yer sock, jest use the cash when yer a little short. Now ya notice thet codicil is in the warranty deed; it reflects thet ya are sellin' this here land ta me as agricultural zoned. I have cheaper taxes thet-away. That keeps Lester Pester happy at the city hall."

"So that is what a codicil is, I was confused. I thought it was similar to a bunion or a planters wart. I do note you are putting the title in your name only, Mr. Pisanmoan. Haven't you considered including your wonderful helpmate as part owner?"

"Now don't ya go a-worryin' none 'bout Effie. I got me a fine trust, jest like yer dear dead daddy had fer ya an' yer sis. Effie is well taken care in m' trust, jest sign right there where Sadie Sobles made thet little pencil X. I thank ya, Miss Pinchlips. I expect Effie will be startin' on her hacienda right soon." Pete tipped his Triple X and hot-footed it back to the courthouse. He recorded the deed and then set out on another mission.

"Thet tractor in yet, Jake? I'm most anxious ta get ta plowin'. I purchased some prime agricultural ground this mornin'. Ya got a disc an' a harry I could borry fer a short time? Need ta kind a level the land, pulverize 'er ta a fine powder."

"It'll blow something fierce if ya pulverize 'er, Pete. Yer tractor is down on the depot loading dock right now. Came in last night, I got to gas 'er up, check the oil, grease the zerks and check the adjustments on the coulters. She'll be ready as soon as you bring in that $1,000. I would prefer it in cash."

Pete was observant to this cash proposition. "I'll go git the cash, give Otis a rub-down, give him a double dose this time. Seems like every body and soul wants cash nowadays, must have somethin' ta do with them income taxes. I'll be back after dinner, and don't fergit ta loan me thet disc and harry."

Otis seemed to be having one of his better days; electric heater was considerable help along with the double pair of socks and a double dose of Ben-Gay. "I can hold down the fort, Pete. You got that deed recorded; go and try out that new tractor and plow. I know you want everything just right before you go down on the T.T.T. & T. ground. You not being used to a tractor, got ta get the feel of her. Kind of like a new woman, check out the crank, get a feel of the throttle and clutch, see how she pulls."

Jake had driven the Wallis up to the implement shop from the depot. "Pete, if I was you I'd stand up on that tractor till I plowed a couple a rounds. That's a real ball-buster, and these streets with them lugs and rims on the front wheels make steering a hard job. Them flanges are hell to turn. All you got to do is lower this here handle to the notch you want for depth. The furtherest back is the deepest. That's where you get the fourteen-inch depth. Better pull her in first gear 'til you get the hang of her, Pete. Another thing, I think it would be better if you'd plow round and round instead of forth and back; then you plow out the corners when you finish up, not so much turning thataway."

Pete was receptive to any information he could get. When one spends that much money, it is no time to horse around. "I'm gonna sock 'er down as deep as she'll go. I want ta see how this here rig handles. Me an' thet new conservative agent up at the courthouse are gonna try an' experimint on about 80 acres o' prime blow dirt. He has a theory; he's heavy on theories. He says we kin raise a wheat crop in a drought. Personally, I think he's got a loose lug, but I ain't afraid ta try somethin' new."

Pete throttled the tractor down to low; the lugs were rattling his entire body, bouncing his toothpick up and down. He pulled his Triple X down tight on top of his ears. Pete was smiling; this was really a delightful experience. He pulled the outfit onto the three lots, north side, right next to the Pisanmoan property.

Effie was attending a meeting of the Literary Society that day. Pete was sorry she was not there for the groundbreaking ceremonies for the Casa Del Sol. Pete stopped, got off the tractor and went back and lowered the plow lever to the last notch. He wanted to sock 'er down as deep as she'd go. When he got back on the tractor, he pulled the throttle down to full speed, eased the clutch out and commenced to plow. Pete went east, then south to the property line, then west right by Penelope's front door. Pete was glancing over his shoulder watching the plow scour, see how those coulters were doing.

They were just perfect in the pulverizing department. It would be a beautiful, level piece of ground when he got it all disked and harrowed. He'd have that conservation agent come down later with his transit.

Pete soon discovered a handy trait that was common to all Wallis tractors. Pull the throttle down quickly and then pop it right back up to idle, that tractor would backfire like a cannon. Pete tried it on the third round. He was now able to sit on the seat. It wasn't so rough now that he had a couple of rounds plowed. Right-front-wheel flange was down in the furrow.

Pete popped the Wallis; out popped Penelope from the front door of the Pinchlips residence. Penelope had on a pink sunbonnet, and her complexion had the same hue. Pete pretended not to notice; he just kept plowing, observing those coulters. On the fourth round he tipped his Triple X to Penelope as he passed by, smiled and tongued his toothpick over to the other side of his mouth. Got dirt in his mouth. Those lugs were throwing dirt up as high as the crown on his Triple X. On the fifth round he acknowledged that Penelope wished to speak with him, stopped and popped the throttle a couple of times.

Penelope put her hands to her ears. Her complexion seemed redder now.

"Howdy, Miss Pinchlips!" Pete had to holler due to the noise of the tractor. "How ya like m' new tractor an' plow? I'm a levelin' m' ground fer Effie. Want the ground nice an' level when she commences ta build her hacienda. Ya got some kinda problem with m' propity, Miss Pinchlips?"

Penelope spit out a little piece of sod, "I did not realize you were going to disturb the contours of these lovely lots, Mr. Pisanmoan. That was never mentioned in any of our discussions regarding your purchase. It is my personal observation you are making a profaned, premeditated effort to prostitute this plot."

"Now, Miss Pinchlips. I never onct thought I would havta run over here an' discuss any problem you might have with my personal property. I seen the gleam in your glance when ya took thet $450 in cash; ya was one happy personality then. I am makin' a slight adjustment ta the contours. The way I plan the drainage on these lots is they will slope directly towards yer

basemint winders. I'll havta use a transit to make sure; now jest as soon as I finish plowin', I plan ta disc 'er nice an' smooth an' then pulverize this here dirt ta a fine powder with a harry. Good afternoon ta ya, Miss Pinchlips." Pete popped the Wallis and commenced to plowing. Penelope couldn't see him smiling as his back was to her; he was headed north, plow was scouring nicely.

That evening Effie remarked, "I suppose you know that land you leveled is goin' to blow somethin' awful. It does look nice though, Pete. You did a right smart job a plowin'. Penelope says she has dirt all over her house. Must have been those lugs on that machine you purchased. Me and Penelope are going to Denver, get that architect started on the Casa. Do you take a dip in that Ben-Gay? You smell like a walkin' pharmacy, but I have to admit it does help clear up m' sinuses, there's so much dust in the air."

When Pete completed his work on the three Casa Del Sol lots, the dirt had the consistency of Swan's Down Cake Flour. Pete smiled, Pete was a satisfied man; add one more zinger to the Pinchlips file, he was mentally keeping track. But it was not all a bed of roses. Pete kind of dragged into the implement office. This time it was Jake that smiled.

"Them lugs on that sucker are real butt-busters, Jake. Steerin' thet horse is like herdin' a elephant. Get me some rubber tires, they gotta be better."

"Take a couple of days to git 'em here, couple of days to change 'em over, an' a couple a hundred in advance, and I prefers cash in advance."

"Do 'er, Jake. Thet dirt sticks ta m' Ben-Gay somethin' awful. Thanks fer loanin' me them implements. They worked jest perfect fer my agriculture experimint. I am now inta the serious part of my agricultural enterprises. Git thet young conservative out to m' ground, produce a bountiful crop o' winter wheat."

Effie and Penelope left the following day for Denver to search for a "suitable architect." That is what Penelope said. Pete called it "Effie's hut in the sun." Pete offered to take the two women down to the depot in his Terryplane. Penelope refused, pouted and walked, dodged the Russian thistles that rolled down the streets of Sharon Springs in 1934. Effie pensively rode in the back seat, had a peacock feather in her hat; she acted like Pete was the chauffeur and she was Lady Astor. Pete just smiled, rolled his gold toothpick over to the other side of his mouth.

When Effie got out of the Terryplane and slammed the door, Pete was kind of disappointed. He was sure he'd get a little peck on the neck; he'd purposely placed a dab of Ben-Gay earlier that morning. Effie was elusive of necks, jiggled into the depot to purchase her ticket. Penelope was coming around the corner of the West Hotel when Pete was going in to get a decent breakfast.

"Nice weather this mornin', Miss Pinchlips. Watch out fer thet thistle, snag yer silk socks, and hang onta yer hat."

Penelope's nose rose, pace quickened.

Pete smiled; them two women gave Pete a whole bunch of happy days.

It was now time for serious agricultural endeavors. Pete and the new Wallace County Conservation Agent, Lyle Lovelace, were standing on the corner of Pete's best blow-dirt ground. Pete was pointing, waving his arms, describing. "Now here's what I propose ta do on this northwest quarter of 23, Lyle. Pure an' simple, this is a experimint. This quarter is a-blowin' the least of all m' land, soil seems a mite heavier. I'm a gonna make twenty rounds an' then skip what would amount ta another twenty rounds. Ya got thet, college boy? Plow twenty, skip twenty, plow twenty and then another skipper?"

Lyle Lovelace knew he had himself a dandy student. "Yes, sir, Mr. Pisanmoan. I understand. I'm here in Wallace County to assist the farmer, college graduate, K. State; I have a wealth of knowledge in agriculture."

"Well, now, Lyle buddy boy, squeeze this inta thet treasure trove a knowledge. I farm them twenty rounds, we'll have us a prodigious crop of wheat. The stubble holds the ground from a-blowin'. Next year I farm the twenty rounds thet's been layin' there asleep. Reverse 'er ever year. I drempt thet one up tryin' ta figure out how ta hold this blow dirt. I calls it strip farmin'."

There it is right there in a little county in western Kansas during the worst drought in history, the beginning of the disastrous dust bowl, a county treasurer and farmer developed what has been known since as strip farming, a wonderful way to preserve the soil. A true soil conservationist! F.D.R., the Secretary of Agriculture, Henry Wallace nor the Soil Conservation Service hadn't a thing to do with strip farming, it was Pete Pisanmoan.

Seemed like Effie was kind of a damper on Pete's plans. She remarked, "Penelope is complaining, too much dust from your lots, Pete. She says she had at least a half an inch of dirt on her winder sills after that last big blow." Effie didn't see Pete smile.

"I've done had to wait fer over a week fer Jake ta git me some rubber tires on m' new Wallis tractor. I'll take care o' our friend and neighbor, Penelope, right soon. Hate ta have her bothered with all thet dirt. I jest had no intention of causin' her any difficulties; neighbors like Penelope is hard ta find. I'll jest plant a good stand a Sweet Stalk Kaffir on them three lots. We get jest a touch a rain an' the crop will hold the soil, no more dirt on her winder sills."

Effie took the bait, "That is thoughty of you, Pete."

Pete rolled his toothpick over to the other side of his mouth, smiled. A neighbor like Penelope, what more could a feller ask for. Pete put on his Triple X and headed for Jake's place.

"I need ta borry a grain drill fer 'bout an hour, Jake. I wanta seed a little plot of ground ta Sweet Stalk. I bought a hunnert pounds a seed. I'm a-gonna sock a crop on this piece of prime ground, right next door to Penelope Pinchlips. It's zoned agricultural, yessiree, bountiful crop of Sweet Stalk Kaffir."

Jake was aware there was more to this than met the eye. "Sure, loan ya that Case. It's only a seven-footer, but since it's just for those lots, it won't take long. Your tractor is ready. Them rubber tires make 'er look real spiffy. I think you may need some wheel weights when you get to workin' out on your farm ground. Set that drill for forty pounds a seed to the acre. If we should get lucky and get a rain, you'll raise a jungle of Sweet Stalk, Pete."

Penelope peered out the dusty pane of her north living room window. "What is that lunatic doing now? Why, he is planting something. Whatever it is, I propose an omen. Why, I can barely see him for all the dust, and I just washed and stretched my lovely curtains for the second time this week." Pete knew Penelope was peering out; he waited until the second round and popped the Wallis. Penelope promptly pulled down the shades!

Most say it didn't; records show it did rain occasionally during the drought of the '30s in western Kansas. Wallace County received five inches in that three years. Pete had barely pulled into Jake's and unhooked the drill when a little shower scooted through. He got just a little over a quarter of an inch of rain; it settled the dust good. Just about a week later little green sprouts of Sweet Stalk Kaffir popped up out of the flour powder, and darned if they didn't get another half inch of rain; crop seemed to thrive. Penelope began to think Pete was all right. She missed two weeks of having to wash her curtains, enjoyed the sight of some greenery on the lots.

Fondis F. Freeloader was the local insurer for Wallace County. He had policies that covered everything: hail, lightning, livestock, life, fire, casualty, tornado, hurricane, typhoon, earthquake, volcanic eruptions and flood. Didn't sell much flood and he had crop insurance. Fondis had a real feel for insurance; insurance was his game. When he collected a premium, he was elated, hard to deal with on a claim. He always had an adjuster come out from the main office in Topeka. Usually the claim was denied, but people that had paid their hard-earned money never seemed to blame it on

Fondis; the adjuster took the blame. That was the scheme, still is. If the claim was approved, they each took a quarter and gave the policyholder half. Fondis always paid in cash, laid that cash right on the kitchen table along with a release, had his Sheaffer fountain pen right on top. Policyholder see that cash, and he couldn't wait to sign the release, worked every time.

Fondis F. wasn't sure he heard Pete correctly, "You say you have a houseful of antiques. Rarities, one-of-a-kind items that are simply irreplaceable? You say they are all expensive. Just where did you get this detailed information, Pete?" Fondis F. felt like he was being frigged by Sharon's finest. Pete, he was a pistol. If one is an insurance agent, he knows when he's being frigged, seemed like the shoe was on the other foot this time.

"Me an' Effie had thet new conservative agent up ta the house fer dinner. Lyle Lovelace says he's never seen anythin' quite like the way me an' Effie live. Says he could take a lot of our stuff and put 'er in a institute back in Washington, D.C. Thet's where the really big trough is, Fondis, the really big 'un. Something like the Smithsonian, I think he said. He said we was using things he said hardly existed any more, could only be found in a dump. He said our house was a veritable museum. Yep, I wanta increase the insurance on our fine antique household ta exactly $5,000. Now thet's fer house, contents, outhouse, the whole shebang. Ya sell protection, I want protection, Fondis."

"I can put a policy on your fine properties, Pete. Have to put the policy with the Good and Bad News Insurance Co. Fine firm out of Ogallala, Nebraska. They recently moved their main office from Cut Bank, Montana. Now let me see, premium is $35 a year, Pete."

"They sounds kinda like they was on the shady side of this insurance business. I'll jest havta trust ya, Fondis F. Comes a opportunity fer a claim an' I shall run a check on this here company, see what m' lawyer, Simon, says. I always do what Simon says. If'n he says ya ran a ringer in on me, Simon either sues or shoots. Me, I'm partial ta lawsuits; I ain't never got any money outta dead insurance agents."

Fondis had heard of Pete's methods and threats before; he took this one seriously. He did insure with the Good and Bad

News Insurance Company, but he also ran a co-insurance with a company that has an umbrella over all the clients and agents. Seemed like the wise thing to do what with all those valuable antiques, rarities and artifacts. Insurance agents ranked right up there with bankers, lawyers, congressmen and accountants with Pete Pisanmoan.

Effie returned from her trip to Denver. She was anxious to tell Pete, "I got me a set of plans for the Casa Del Sol, got a bill for $50. I checked at the bank, no money in an account for me and the Casa, Pete. What'd you do, go out and buy another poppity-pop-pop tractor? Penelope says that machine is a menace. About one more pop outta you, Pete, and she's gonna sue fer disturbin' the peace."

Pete was working on another money-maker, had too much on his mind to worry about Penelope Pinchlips and law suits. "I got me a idee, Effie. Lyle Lovelace gave it ta me. If a college boy says we got a veritable gold mine o' artifacts in this here domicile, I think we should open it up fer a museum. Put a sign up at Lacey's Cottage Court, put some signs out on Highway 40, invite the tourists from back east that is drivin' through this Paradise on the Plains, the dust, dirt, Russian thistles and jack rabbits ta come and visit the Pisanmoan Museum. Ya could kinda dress up like the '90s, look kinda poverty stricken, greet the folks at the door. We'd charge a dime fer the tour. Here's the kicker; we solve the problem of the sanitation with Lester easy-like. I kin run the sewer from the side street, not go out ta the main in front. Won't disturb the tourists a-parkin' thet-away. We put in hopper-type stool out in a nice little house in back, charge them tourists ten cents ta use the facilities. 'Nother thing, ya could serve lemonade fer five cents a glass; maybe we could sell salty pop corn and double up on the lemonade sales. That's the way we pay fer the facilities, not a dime outta our pockets! We is sittin' on a proverbial gold mine, Effie ol' girl."

"I was telling Penelope just the other day about some of your idees, Pete. It was right after you popped that Wallis at her that we both wished it had been real coal oil in that outhouse. We'd both be out of Lansing by now on good behavior, and you'd be restin' peacefully up on the hill north a town;

all they would have buried was a cinder. You can forget that hopper idee; just hop down to the People's State and deposit some money for the Casa."

"I jest don't understand why ya always put a damper on m' idees, Effie. I've got a million of 'em; they just jump outta m' brain; they is always money-makers. What I need is some hep and cooperation, a confidence in my schemes. Ya say ya need $50 fer the architect. I'll put a hundred in the bank. Give ya a little cushion fer yer hut in the sun. Ya jest wait, Effie ol' girl, when my conservative methods of farmin' come ta fruition I'll have wheat flowin' inta the elevator like gold." (That word fruition, they hadn't used that word at the Sharon Springs Literary Society meetings. Effie had to look it up in the Webster's. Pete, he was truly a Colt 45.)

"The Union Pacific will have ta run an extry freight train. They'll call it the 'Pisanmoan Grain Special.' Give me that set of plans. I'm gonna visit with Lester Pester up at City Hall, show him m' intentions. Thet reminds me, Effie, soon have a surprise fer ya up on the hill."

Pete was formulating a plan, one that would get the city off his back on the facilities, the Casa Del Sol held way back and Pete would hold back a sizable share of the $5,000 he had mentioned to Effie. So far he was out $100, and that seemed about right.

Pete had a mission, "Mornin', Lester. Here's the set a plans fer m' buildin' permission. I want ya ta properly record an' stamp them as ta the Pisanmoan intention to construct a fine residence in our fair city. Next, I want a receipt showin' the date and the time of this here intention and thet them tappity-tap-tap fees is all paid in full on them three lots I purchased from Prune Face Penelope Pinchlips. I want everythin' above board — don't want the Pisanmoan name besmirched, it might hinder m' political career, keep everythin' legal like."

Lester had a zinger for Pete. "There you are, Pete, a proper and legal receipt. The plans are properly stamped. Tap fees show they are paid in full. I recall we spit and shook on that deal. However, there is an ordinance from the city. I'll read it to you, may cause you some inconvenience."

Lester reached under the counter, picked up a rather large

book. Pete noticed on the front cover in gold letters: "Municipal Code of the City of Sharon Springs, Kansas. Incorporated." Now Lester was in his own special realm of political knowledge; every rinky-dink town has a Lester Pester. Pete was kind of nonchalanting it, Triple X tipped back, lock of grey hair down on his forehead, pleased with himself. He had all those permits, and they hadn't cost him a dime.

"Ah, here it is: Number 1794, Sub-section B, Paragraph 3. It reads as follows, listen closely to this, Pete. 'Permission is hereby granted to the contractor, be it owner or subcontractor that a temporary sanitary facility may be constructed on the construction site, provided no other such structure exists on the permitee's personal property. In that event, the permitee must use only one of the sanitary facilities, and that one shall be on the site of the subject building permit.' Do you understand that, Pete?"

"Yep, no problem a-tall. One crapper fer the Pisanmoan household, and thet one has ta be on them three vacant lots thet is zoned agricultural. I see no problem with thet ordinance, Lester. We'll build us a new outhouse on the lots, right out there close ta the street, want the neighbors to have a good view, think 'Ill face the door towards the street. I kin sit there readin' the *Topeka Daily Capitol*, wave at the cars as they drive by. We'll abide by the law; we'll discontinue ta use the one on our present propity pervided I don't decide to proceed ta install a hopper-type out back. Yessiree, good ordinance, Lester. I thank ya fer the permit. Effie kin now proceed with her hut in the sun with absolute knowledge of complyin' with all them ordinances and sub-sections."

Lester didn't smile, his zinger had failed.

Pete pushed the lock of greying hair back under his Triple X and told Lester he was headed for the lumber yard. He wanted to see Pop Gailey. Pete didn't piddle around at the lumber yard.

"Pop, I want ya to build me a two-holer. Put 'er on skids so's I kin move 'er around the job sites and the neighborhood. Put a big tow hook on 'er so's I kin hook m' Wallis ta the honey chamber. I kin kind of play hoppity-scotch around m' lots. Fix it so's I kin slide a five-gallon bucket under each hole, pour in some bleach an' used motor oil. Why, I got me a chemical toilet."

There it is, folks, right there in Sharon Springs, Kansas, in the year of our Lord, 1934, a county treasurer, farmer, contractor and entrepreneur, invented the portable chemical toilet. Small improvements have been made over the next sixty years, but the basic idea remains the same. There was not a whiff, not even a poof of odor. Few people are aware of the origin of this invention, but it is true. Pete Pisanmoan failed to file for a patent on the "Pisanmoan Portable Potty."

"You want half-moons, Pete?"

"You betcha, Pop. Half-moons, put a screen over 'em. Keeps out the flies. Put a strong spring on the door, make sure she slams good when she closes. I git me a late call occasionally. I want all the neighbors to be aware of City Ordinance Number 1794, Sub-section B, Paragraph 3. Folks 'll give ol' Lester a call about the time I slam the door twict, once when I go in, an' then m' exit. How soon kin I come down on m' Wallis tractor and drag 'er ta m' job site?"

"I'll need about three days, Pete. You want the seat sanded real nice, put a coat of spar varnish on the seat? Paint the outside?"

"Why, nuthin's too good fer m' Effie. Sand 'er real nice and varnish the seat, put a nice slick sheen on 'er, put two coats a barn red paint. I'm really partial ta red; thet sucker will stand out like a wart on a goat's butt. How much fer this here jobbie?"

"Labor and material, twenty bucks. I'll throw in the two five-gallon buckets. Fix a little plate that the buckets can slide over. I'll put a hinged flap on the back so's one can just reach in and pull out the buckets when they are full." Pete thought this a fine idea; he'd just throw the contents out on the street. With all that motor oil it would keep the dust down when the folks drove by, get a better view.

It was truly an eventful summer for all of the City of Sharon Springs. The neighbors, the drive-bys, that summer of 1934. Pete and Effie were law-abiding citizens. Pete pulled the red outhouse up to the lots, popped the Wallis just for his good friend and neighbor, Penelope. Effie understood that they no longer had their own outhouse; she had two choices, the red job outside or go to Penelope's for an insider, but the Casa Del Sol was worth the effort for Effie. Pete was not as fortunate. He had the back yard after dark, the slammer or a quick hop in the Terraplane and hit for the courthouse. Pete wore out a pair of rear Firestones that summer. Mornings were an event for the neighbors, Effie with her old green chenille robe, hair net, house slippers flapping on the sidewalk and trotting to Penelope's, or if she was on "short time," she used the red jobbie. Many thought it almost as hilarious to see Pete burning up his Firestones on the Terraplane heading for the court-house. Unless one has lived in a small town, one cannot realize the entertainment the two Pisanmoans were giving to the neighborhood, and it was free.

There was another game going on, one had to be alert and have a keen eye to watch this entertainment. It was a chess game between Penelope and Pete. The game was not played with pawns or knights or bishops; it was played with the placement of their trash burn-barrels. It quit raining after that half-incher; the Sweet Stalk Kaffir got up about three feet tall and commenced to wilt; then it turned brown. No green leaves, no heads on the stalks, just a bunch of withered leaves. When the wind was out of the north, Pete would go out and wet his finger, hold it up to test the wind. Slide his trash barrel so it was close to the Sweet Stalk, pretend to strike a match on the seat of his pants and then he'd wave to Penelope. He knew she was watching; she was always watching Pete. When the wind was out of the south, Penelope would go out and check the windmill and move her trash barrel in to just the proper location to take out the Sweet Stalk and the Pisanmoan residential museum. She didn't light hers either. Pete wanted her to light it off; he'd collect on that insurance money and pay for the Casa Del Sol. Pete smiled.

Not a word from Goodland. Mr. Slackjaw didn't answer Effie's letters.

Finally Penelope said, "I shall correspond with my attorney, Mr. Sylvester Beatum; we'll find out about this Mr. Slackjaw. I wouldn't trust anyone your husband recommended anyway. We must get rid of that red monstrosity that is on our residential street. I planted some Heavenly Blue Morning Glories around it. I thought that would subdue that red caboose, make it less noticeable. Do you know what that husband of yours did? He poured bleach and used motor oil on those pretty little shoots of flowers. I'll try some hollyhocks next time."

"Golly, Effie, I'm mighty sorry Slackjaw moved." Pete smiled; he could nest on that $5,000 a little longer. "Guess you'll just havta find someone else ta build your hot house. I gotta git ta farmin', goin' down ta the T.T.T.& T. ground taday. Commence plowin'. Lyle is comin' down fer me later. Soon as I git the ground plowed, I'm gonna start politickin', run fer another term. I'll be leavin' early an' stayin' late. Might jest git me a pup tent. Stay out there on the prairie. Peaceful and quiet out there with the thistles blowin', jack rabbits thumpin' and humpin' all night long. Shure makes one 'preciate Mother Nature. Speakin' a nature, ya want I should move the red jobbie up here closer ta home; ya might 'preciate it if'n ya was to git a short call some night."

Effie just sighed. "Be real nice to have some peace and quiet in this dump. You just take yer time plowin' and politickin'. Peace and tranquility, that's what me and Penelope both need. She said an odd thing the other day, I didn't quite understand. She said you kinda took a small bite out of her psyche ever day. She said she was concerned about her sanity; that's the very word she said, 'sanity.' "

Pete took the better part of the day to grease up, fill the Wallis with gas and drive the outfit down to the T.T.T.& T. ground. When he began plowing, he didn't sock 'er down like on the lots next door to Penelope. He was now into the serious business of trying to make a wheat crop with new farming methods, unproven methods. He figured he could not beat Mother Nature, but he thought they might have a tie. He was determined to save some of the drought-stricken land, namely his.

Lyle Lovelace, Wallace County Conservation Agent, got to the plowing site about five, had two five-gallon cans of Standard White Crown, a grease gun and a five-pound can of grease. "You'll ruin the Terraplane hauling all this stuff, Pete. See what the bank got when they foreclosed on Hubcap Hubbell. Why not get a cheap Model A?"

"Nope, Lyle m' boy. I'm gonna buy me a Model A truck, need it ta haul m' grain next July when we start combinin', haul thet wheat ta town." Pete was full of optimism; everything Pete planned had a purpose, the possibility of profit, and Pete had prospered plenty with his many endeavors and venture capital.

Lyle walked out over the first strip of twenty rounds, knelt down on the soil, let the dirt run through his fingers, looked west towards the setting sun, not a cloud in the sky. Dust devils were playing tag across the horizon. "Plenty of clods, Pete. There's some inert matter, some roots of weeds that will help. Maybe it won't blow much when we drill wheat this fall. We'll probably have to 'dust it in.' "

There it is, folks, right there in a little county in western Kansas in 1934, a young conservation agent fresh out of Kansas State University coined a new agricultural phrase for raising wheat in dry western Kansas. If it didn't rain, one "dusted 'er in," then one prayed for rain or a wet snow.

"You decided what brand of wheat seed you're going to plant, Pete?"

"Not gonna be Turkey Red. I'm gonna try forty acres of Cheyenne and maybe forty of Kiowa. This is what we call one noble expiriment. We'll watch them two kinds a seed, Lyle m' boy — watch the protein content when I hit thet elevator with the first load. I wonder if'n I should buy me a twelve-footer or a sixteen-footer combine. When m' crop is ready, I don't want ta shilly-shally around, git 'er in the bin. It don't count fer nuthin' out here in the field, git 'er in the bin, Lyle m' boy." Pete rolled the toothpick over to the other side of his mouth, and smiled.

Lyle Lovelace smiled. "Optimistic and ornery old cuss, likeable, too."

That fall Pete drilled his wheat just as he had told Lyle. He campaigned in his Model A truck, had some high sideboards put on it so he could haul more wheat. He had a sign painter paint on sideboards:

PETE PISANMOAN FOR COUNTY TREASURER
Otis Armbuster for Deputy Treasurer

Pete spent more time talking about his new farming methods than he did politicking. Folks liked that. It took their minds off of the problem of paying their taxes with money they didn't have and just why did the well go dry? The country folks like to have a farmer for a county treasurer, seems like they had a friend at the courthouse. The County Commissioners just stopped and put their card in the mail box; Pete he visited the depressed, the drouthed-out, the downtrodden and desperate. Pete ran uncontested; not a single Republican in Wallace County had the guts to run.

The Denver Post headlines, November 7, 1934: "New Deal Wins Big Test at the Polls. The Democrats score big gains in Tuesday's election, underlining the public's support for President Roosevelt and his New Deal."

Pete bought a big tube of Ben-Gay, and when he got to the office, he told the Assessor to raise the taxes on all "go back" a penny an acre for 1935. Judas got the blame for the raise; he was a Republican. It all started way back then in the offices of the Assessor and the Treasurer, and it ain't changed a bit in over a half a century. If one thinks about it, they should have lowered the taxes; the "go-back" ground was not blowing as bad, but then we had the "New Deal," the "Fair Deal," "The Great Society" and a "New Frontier." Nothing has changed, except loss of freedoms.

It was Lyle Lovelace who ran up the stairs to the County Treasurer's office. "Quick, come look out to the west, Pete! You, too, Otis, I've never seen anything quite like it!"

It was a huge cloud of dust, maybe 15,000 feet high. It just rolled and boiled around at the top. There didn't seem to be much wind; the sun was completely obscured. It was 2:05 p.m. Cars drove with their headlights on. People were frightened; no one had ever witnessed weather phenomenon before; everyone was frightened.

The Denver Post dated April 11, 1935, headline: **"U.S. Hit by Dust Storm!"** The story continued:

"Increasingly severe dust storms are hanging like a black scourge over half of the United States, destroying millions of dollars worth of wheat crops, forcing untold numbers of people to flee from their farms as from a plague, and completely paralyzing all activity in some districts.

"The brunt of the storm fell on western Kansas, eastern Colorado, Wyoming, western Oklahoma, nearly all of Texas and parts of New Mexico. Breathing was not only difficult but dangerous. While human beings could protect themselves with masks, all livestock suffered in misery. Dust pneumonia is rapidly increasing among children. And the crop damage is staggering in the 'nation's breadbasket.'

"Little relief is in sight, as dust piles up inside houses. Schools and business are closed. Traffic is stopped and bereaved families are unable to bury their dead. In Texas, even the birds are afraid to fly."

Pete tongued his toothpick over to the other side of his mouth; he didn't smile. A steely glint came to his eyes. "Guess there goes m' Kiowa and Cheyenne seed wheat. We'll fergit the sixteen-footer Massey-Harris combine, Lyle m' boy. We'll try 'er agin next year."

Now, ain't that just like a farmer, next year! It's always, "Next year."

Farm Relief Bill Is Passed in the Senate

April 28 — A bill to aid America's struggling farmers passed the Senate today and now awaits action by the House. The measure provides for alternative ways to raise farm values, such as guaranteeing the cost of production, refinancing farm mortgages at interest rates of four and one-half percent, withdrawing from production sufficient acreage so as to cut production of agricultural commodities to actual domestic needs and stabilizing farm prices generally equal to those of 1909-1914. The Senate also included in the farm relief bill a provision, sought by Pres. Roosevelt to help fight inflation in a variety of ways. The President could increase Federal Reserve credits by up to $3 billion, issue Treasury notes to buy back government securities and devalue the gold content of

*the dollar by up to fifty percent. Although the bill is one
of the most important passed during the new Roosevelt
administration, much of the Senate debate focused on
a proposal, opposed by the President and finally de-
feated, to add to the measure a bonus for war veterans.
Watching intently from the galleries were many of the
veterans who had marched on Washington last year to
demand a war bonus."*
—*Cleveland Plain Dealer, April 28, 1933*

One should recall the Soil Bank. A few years later the
Conservation Reserve Program.

Roosevelt Devalues Dollar to 60 Cents

*Jan. 31 — President Roosevelt issued a proclama-
tion today devaluing the dollar to 59.6 cents and setting
the price for gold at $35 an ounce. Acting under author-
ity given him by recent action of Congress, the President
said the moves were needed to protect the nation's
foreign trade from the effect of the depreciated curren-
cies in other countries.*

*The proclamation took title for the government to all
gold certificates, creating a dollar profit of about $2.6
billion for the U.S. Treasury. Of this sum, $2 billion will
be used to stabilize the dollar on the international
exchange and support the government bond market if
necessary.*

P. 428, Chronicle of the 20 Century

*"The guiding principle is that the obvious is never
the obvious if it's too obvious, or is it?"*
— *A Confused Republican*

An economist in Vienna, Austria, summed up the change
in monetary system in the United States with this statement:
"Government is the only institution that can take a

valuable commodity such as paper and make it worth-
less simply by applying ink."

— Ludwig Von Mises

The United States never returned to the gold standard as
F.D.R. promised; from then on the value of the dollar continually eroded.

*Grit blows across drought-stricken fields on a farm in Cimarron
County, Oklahoma, Rothstein captured bleak scene in the spring,
the season when, in good times, the rain falls and the crops begin
to grow.*

THE PISANMOAN PLOT
1935

"YOU ARE THE ONE CUSTOMER I have to look forward to on a Monday, Wednesday and Friday, Pete. If you'd quit getting a shave, I'd just about putrify in this lonely barber shop. I see you are perusing the *Topeka Daily Capitol*. You think that new Social Security bill will alleviate the depression? F.D.R. thinks so."

"Volney, it won't hep a bit, jest another little deduction ta take outta the poor folks' paychecks — them thet's workin'. I doubt I ever see a penny of thet social sickness. Thet's jest what our economical trouble is, the whole country is ill with bills. Now you take them there railroaders, they's the ones. They got the best retirement of anyone. They's a bunch of them boys on the extry-board. Used ta run thet local ever day, now they run it onct a week. When thet Union Pacific pays their taxes, we folks up there at the county trough, we breathe a sigh a relief."

"The missus and I took a little walk over by your new house Sunday after church. I will say it's kind of slow on the progress department, Pete."

Pete looked at Volney, chuckled, tongued his gold toothpick so it kind of wiggled up and down. "Ta m' way of reckonin' it's 'bout on schedule. I planned 'er thataway; powerful purpose in m' plannin', Volney. Nice crop of sunnyflowers on thet hut in the sun. They got the foundation poured, put the sub-floor on, and then the Casa Del Sol done wilted. Too many opinions as ta the design, too many changes. Thet set a plans thet architect has so many changes on 'em it looks like a Monkey-Ward catalogue. I git a real kick outta them three women, thet's the cause of it all — three women all with three different idees. I have done plugged the progress on the Casa Del Sol."

Volney smiled in the mirror at Pete as he stropped the razor. "Tell me, Pete, how'd you go about plugging the progress? Give me a plausible reason that would give you such pleasure, Pete."

"I kin see a hair on the right side o' m' neck, snip 'er off. I'd tell ya, save the price of a haircut an' ya'd git a story. I don't see the customers exactly bustin' down the door fer haircuts."

"All right, tell me the story, Pete. You are without a doubt the biggest penny-pincher on this planet. Give you a free haircut."

"Goes back a year or so, Volney. I told Effie I'd build her a nice cozy little cottage. Coupla bedrooms, bathroom, all the indoor facilities. New furniture and utensils, kind of a little love nest. Well, it weren't good 'nuff fer Effie; she has desires of greatness and grandness. Gifted with greed, thet's what ground the Casa to a halt, pure and simple greed. I told Effie $5,000 fer the whole she-bang, thet was it, $5,000. Now, I got the name of thet architect up in Denver, an' I had Sadie Sobles write me a letter on her L.C. Smith to m' attorney, Simon Fixum. I told Simon ta have some chin music with thet architect. Most people do what Simon says when he gives 'em the treatment. Quit snippin' with them scissors and let me see jest a little hair fallin', Volney. Go over and take a look at the size o' m' Triple X on the hat rack."

Volney had to scrape some of the oil and dirt off the little ribbon that designates the size, "Says seven and a half, that's a pretty good-sized hat. Hat band seems kind of soft."

"Ya got it, Volney. I wears a seven. The rest of thet hat band is m' personal financial information. Kept track of ever' penny spent on thet hacienda. It started out with $50 to thet architect, $50 ta Effie fer cushion money, train fare ta Denver, stamps, I kept track of all the postage spint forth an' back with thet architect. I charged Effie fer levelin' those lots with m' plow, charged by the hour. Paid a heap fer thet Sweet Stalk Kafir seed. Then I bought a portable facility. Pop Gailey charged me $20 fer it. The amount spint on thet hut in the sun commenced ta mount up." Pete looked in the mirror. "Take just a tad off over m' ears, makes me look more perfessional thataway."

"What's the total in the Casa account by now, Pete?"

"Effie don't know it, but it's floatin' around the $500 mark an' risin'. Effie got some fool idee that I was a-gonna put five big 'uns in the People's State, a blank check so's ta speak. Not me, not Pete Pisanmoan, I watch my money closer than thet."

Volney smiled, snipped a couple of wild ones at the base of Pete's neck, pricked him a little just so he'd know he was getting his money's worth.

Pete remarked, "Thet foundation out in the sunnyflowers and dried-up Sweet Stalk is designed fer a cozy little two-bedroom jobbie. Cozy, comfortable, convenient and cheap. The contents will not conflict with the design. They'll be cheap, too. Trouble was, I had competition. Conflicts of interest. Odds were agin me, Volney."

"How could the odds be against you? You had the check-book."

"Put a little Lucky Tiger on m' hair, Volney. I wanta look slick and smell good when I meet the public up at the court-house. Here's the way them odds were stacked agin me. Effie, Penelope and thet Daphne, now there's three precocious, predatory personalities. Them three is proficient and provoca-tive competition. Effie shows me them plans, I make a com-ment like I think the stairs oughtta go over here ta the basemint. She then makes a little note, talks it over with Daphne, she agrees, but then Prune Face Penelope, she likes them stairs where they is. She does thet ta spite me. Then they argue fer a coupla days, git on the train and hot foot it ta Denver. Another change, the architect's fee goes up, but it gets all three of them personages outta m' hair. Thet looks real nice, Volney; Lucky Tiger smells good. 'Nother thing, I tell Simon ta pay the architect $5 per call. It's kind of a psychiatrist meetin'. Simon wrote me the architect is developin' a slight twitch but seems ta go away after them three quail leave the big city."

Volney had another remark, "Lester Pester said he's kind of tired of your stalling him on the facilities to your own domicile."

Pete smiled; he had Lester Pester just where he wanted him, kind of like the back of his neck, had him by the short hair.

"I did have one problem, Volney. Lost m' water-hauler. She's bin haulin' water from Penelope's windmill fer, I guess close ta fifteen years. I jest put a barrel in the back a m' grain truck and haul 'er home from the courthouse. Opened up the spigot last Saturday night after thet water had set out there all day; I had me a shower, nice warm water, sun warmed it up right nice."

Volney whipped the cloth off Pete, shook it and put a little powder on his brush and brushed off Pete's neck and shoulders. "That story was worth a haircut, Pete. Now get up to the courthouse and plunder the public."

Pete was in a pensive mood on his walk up to the courthouse. He had Effie and her fellow advisors in a pickle, kind of a puddle of trouble. Pete was considering running one more time for County Treasurer. He had a problem, not with Effie but with himself. He was considering returning to the Republican Party. The New Deal was beginning to play on his conscience, too many programs, too much socialism, too many initials floating around Washington. There was the A.A.A., C.C.C., W.P.A., S.E.C., N.L.R.B., N.R.A., P.W.A., R.E.A., E.R.A., C.W.A., T.V.A., that's just a few. Was it possible morality was rearing its head in a small town politician? Moral principles can never be compromised; they can only be abandoned, thought Pete. (That's pretty deep for Pete.)

When Pete walked into the treasurer's office, it was obvious another term for Deputy Otis Armbuster was out of the question. Otis was having a terrible day. No amount of Ben-Gay, aspirin or electric heat was making it easier for Otis.

"Howdy, Pete. You know somethin'? I think it's a-gonna rain. M' joints tell me we're gonna git some moisture. Say, that Lucky Tiger sure smells good, see you got a haircut."

"Ya in a lotta pain this mornin', Otis? I'll rub ya good with some Ben-Gay. We jest gotta see if we kin finish this here term. It's a cinch ya don't need ta go ta a drier climate, even if'n it don't rain purty soon them two nice wet snows last winter was a true Godsend. I'm a-gonna leave a little early this afternoon. Gonna drive out ta the T.T.T. & T. ground, see if'n there's anything left. Jest might take Effie fer a little ride, give 'er a drivin' lesson." A driving lesson was far from what Pete had in mind. His next step was to knock that La Salle idea clean out of Wallace County. As far as Pete was concerned, it would do Effie good to take shanks ponies to the Sharon Springs Easterner Stars and the Sensation and Sensibility Club meetings; she needed exercise.

Pete hadn't even made it to the back door when, "I made it quite clear over fifteen years ago, Pete. You was to stay outta the house till five. Do you recollect that?"

This wasn't exactly a marriage made in Heaven, but Pete said, "Effie ol' girl, ya are really a tough ol' hippo. I came home ta take ya fer a little ride in the Terryplane, go out and view the T.T.T. & T. ground. I was even considerin' givin' ya a drivin' lesson prior ta yer purchase of thet La Salle. I'll even let ya sit up front fer a change. Ya been sittin' in the back seat fer so long, now ya kin holler a lot closer on how I was ta drive up in the front, ya bein' so handy with descriptive directions." Pete smiled.

It didn't take much kindness for Effie to reconsider how lucky she was to have Pete for a husband, thoughtful and all. Those driving lessons were the inducement to cordiality. "You just wait up, Pete. I'll get my hat and driving gloves and I'll be ready!"

"Where'd ya git the preposterous idee ya needed gloves ta drive a La Salle?" Pete had never heard of driving gloves except when women drove trotting horses to town years ago, and no women in the Pisanmoan family had ever had a pair of gloves.

Effie put a hat pin in her latest millinery special, "Saw an advertisement in a magazine up at the Clip and Curl. These gloves are not just deer hide; they is fawn and so nice and soft. They cost $8."

Pete made a mental note of the amount and charged it to the "hut in the sun." Pete hadn't decided how much to charge for his driving lessons, but one can be assured there was a figure up there in the Triple X right alongside all that postage.

Pete was quite explicit, "First thing I want ya ta do, Effie ol' girl, and this will be the toughest —"

Effie gave Pete a smile, "What's that, Petey Pet?"

"Keep yer flap shut an' listen to ever word I say. I am a real perfessional driver. Some say I should be a-drivin' at the Indy, me and Sir Malcolm Campbell." Effie started to make some kind of caustic comment. Pete merely held up a finger; Effie shut her flap. Pete looked out the window so Effie couldn't see him smile. They walked out to the Terraplane.

"A autymobile is a major purchase; one needs ta check

these out. I have been a-checkin' up at the Cowles Motor Car Company regardin' a La Salle. They tell me the autymobile has a delicate clutch. Know what thet means, Effie?"

"Golly, no, Pete. I ain't had a delicate clutch for a long time. I didn't know one had to make love to a La Salle. Proceed, Pete, should I take off my fawn-colored gloves?"

"Now watch this, Effie. This here is the switch. Turn on the key and then press down on this here pedal. Thet's the starter. As soon as she fires, take yer big hoof off'n the starter or you'll ruin the Bendix. Move yer knobby knee, I can't put 'er in gear. Now mind ya, thet La Salle with the tender clutch means ya havta double clutch — push yer left foot in, pull down on the gear shift, ya got 'er in low gear. Terryplane has a clutch hard as a rock. Down here by m' foot, Effie, now thet's the clutch pedal. Effie, yer still a-lookin' at the starter. Now, pull down on the gear shift, let out on the clutch nice an' easy-like an' away she goes. Now double clutch 'er an' then shove this here handle up ta second gear. Double clutchin' is twict; saves on the pinion gears. Ya got thet, Effie? Go easy like on thet La Salle, tender clutch."

Effie sighed, "My goodness, that does seem complicated. I'll just sit here and watch yer professional ways. This thing don't ker-pow like that Wallis tractor, does it, Pete?" Effie was perturbed.

"Naw, no trouble with a Terryplane, thet's just what ya call a pecularity of a Wallis tractor. Gotta be awful keerful with a La Salle, been known ta blow up when ya gas 'em up. Seems ta have spark trouble." Pete was laying a lot of groundwork.

Effie did keep her flap shut, eyes bugged out a little. She was watching Pete intently. Pete was going through all kinds of professional gyrations and motions. It was an impressive sight. Pete double-clutching, shifting gears, revving up the Terraplane; then he'd hit the brake pedal for emphasis. It was an excellent demonstration for Effie. Her driving gloves were getting damp in the palms.

Pete glanced out the window, smiled. "Now, Effie ol' girl, we is comin' ta a good patch a blow dirt offen Sid Sawyer's quarter. Be keerful drivin' through blow dirt. It's mighty treacherous. It kin pull the steerin' wheel right outta yer hands. Don't grip the steerin' wheel in them spokes; thet wheel will whirl on ya, it could break both yer thumbs."

"My goodness, I didn't know driving was such a hazardous undertaking. I don't think I'll do much country driving. Perhaps just down to the Bar P to see Piedmont and the little tykes. How long before you think I can get my hands on that wheel, Pete?"

"Depends a lot on yer mental abilities ta absorb all the complications and intricacies of a motorized vehicle. In yer case I 'spect about a month of absorption fer each lesson. Six observation lessons and you'll git a chance at the wheel. May let ya drive the Model A grain truck, haul water up an' down the alley from Penelope's, pedestrians be a heap safer thetaway."

Effie looked at Pete in dismay, "Yer sayin' six months ta observe ya double-clutchin' before I get my fawn gloves on the wheel. You think I'm kind of stupid, I know what you're trying to do, provoke me, Pete, and you are doing a fine job!"

Pete looked out the window at the desolation of drought, dirt-covered fences, and the depression of it all. The La Salle was going down like the Titanic. Pete smiled.

Pete was in for a surprise, "Would ya look at thet wheat in them strips, Effie! I ain't bin out here fer, golly, guess nigh onto six months or so. I figured thet big blow we had smothered all the wheat. Why, thet wheat is even got a green color ta it. Must be a volunteer type of a crop."

There you have it, folks. Right there in a little county in western Kansas during the terrible drought and dust bowl, a county treasurer and farmer, former cattleman coined that word, "volunteer." A crop that came up from seed that was thought to be lost. Many a bushel of wheat was volunteer, and it was Pete Pisanmoan that first used that word along with "strip" farming.

Pete got out of the Terraplane, started to shut the door and then reached back and took out the ignition key.

Effie was not aware of what he was doing; she thought it was part of her driving lesson and it stuck. Effie never left a set of keys in a car again. She learned that in just one lesson.

Pete thought she just might double-clutch her way out of

there and leave him with the jackrabbits and prairie dogs. Pete walked over the ground, pulled a head or two off some wheat. He observed the wheat was in the milk stage. Then he observed the jackrabbits, "They must be 'bout fifty ta the acre."

Pete went back to the Terraplane and got his .22 rifle out of the back seat and began shooting jackrabbits. He shot a box of shells, .22 long rifle hollow points. He loved to shoot rabbits and watch the muscular reaction when they jumped up in the air about three feet and hit the ground dead. Meat for coyotes and magpies.

"What are you goin' to do with all them jackrabbits, Pete?"

"Leave 'em there fer the coyotes, but I got me an idee. I'm gonna write a letter on them jackrabbits. I think thet wheat'll make ten bushel. I'm gonna bring Lyle, the conservative, out here tomorry. He'll be powerful proud of this crop. We'd be the onliest ones thet has any wheat. Ya didn't see a spot of green comin' out here, did ya, Effie ol' girl?"

"All I saw was thistles, some sage brush and soap weeds. How's about me double-clutchin' home, Petey Pet, break in my new fawn driving gloves? You could shoot jackrabbits out the winder."

Pete didn't take the bait. "Naw, minimum of six lessons, one month apart. Ya got ta take yer time a-learnin' how ta operate an autymobile. When I have 'er parked out in the back yard, ya kin go out an' sit in 'er, pump the clutch, shift the gears, but don't press on the gas pedal, ya'd flood 'er." Pete exhibited a grand demonstration of double-clutchin' all the way back to town. Pete was thinking about jackrabbits and volunteer wheat. Pete prophesied profit on his property; he felt kind of perky. Effie was petulant and peeved.

When they got to Sharon Springs, Pete said, "Now when ya cross these here railroad tracks, always double-clutch 'er, Effie. Them La Salles have a tendency ta have the spare tire drop off when ya hit a bump." Pete slowed down, double-clutched across the tracks.

"I sure do thank you for the driving lesson, Pete. It was interestin' to see the difficulty of operatin' a autymobile. Are you sure I need six lessons before I can get m' hands on thet wheel?"

"Not sure, it may take seven, not sure when ya kin solo, Effie. Ya ain't very well coordinated an' all. I gotta go up to the courthouse, see Lyle. He'll want to go out an' see the wheat crop on the T.T.T. & T. ground."

Effie walked slowly toward the back door of the home she now called "The Dump." Pulling off her fawn driving gloves, Effie was downright dejected. Her Casa Del Sol was just sitting. Her La Salle was far into the future; things were kind of bleak for Effie Pisanmoan.

Pete backed out to the street, spun the rear tires and headed for the courthouse, a satisfied smile on his face. That driving lesson had given Effie a prolonged seizure of apprehension. The future saw little parturient for the suffering Effie. Pete smiled.

Pete parked, rushed into the Treasurer's Office; exuberance was part of Pete. "Otis, you should see the wheat crop I got out on the T.T.T. & T. ground! It ain't the greatest I've ever seen, but they's enough to combine. Here, let me rub ya good with some Ben-Gay, git some sparkle back in them eyes. How'd ya like ta ride out an' see thet wheat? They's 'bout a million jackitty rabbits on thet hunert an' sixty. I betcha if'n one was to sit out there at night an' pull the lights on the Terryplane ever so often, we could shoot them suckers at night, sit on the fenders, git us a mess."

"Thanks, Pete, but I'd just as soon go home and put m' feet up and take it kinda easy like. I sure would appreciate a ride home. Hobblin' home from the courthouse every evenin' is pure hell."

"I'm goin' downstairs ta see Lyle. We're goin' out ta the T.T.T. & T. ground an' view m' crop a wheat."

"He ain't in, Pete. He went out ta see Paul and Pansey Penrod, explain ta them how the new Agriculture Adjustment Act works; he stopped in the office on his way out."

"Otis, it ain't a-tall hard ta figure out thet Act. It's adjusted so's anyone in agriculture is jest 'bout adjusted offen the farm. I'll bet when they takes the census in '40 thet we got 'bout half the folks in Wallace County we had in '20. I'll wait till mornin'. Shut up the office; there won't be anyone in ta pay their taxes; we'll close early and I'll take ya home."

The next morning Lyle Lovelace walked around in the wheat field. It was the first field he had viewed that had something growing besides weeds. He hopped from furrow to furrow, pulled out several clumps of wheat, checked the root system. "Pete, you are correct; this wheat will make at least ten bushels to the acre. It's thin, but we needed the stubble. We've got to stop the wheat from re-seeding, must let the ground lay fallow. What was that new word you used for this type of wheat?"

"Volunteer, thet's the word, Lyle m' boy. Now I'm gonna let some idees go by ya, see if'n I got a strike er two. These idees come outta me like .22 long rifles. Ya ready, college boy?"

Lyle smiled, "Shoot, pistol Pete. I'll dunk 'em or dodge 'em."

"First, we need a combine. I got a good tractor ta pull 'er. Should I buy one or borry?"

"Difficult decision to make, Pete. You could depreciate the combine on your income tax, but I know you don't pay any tax, and that salary you make as Treasurer you use up in mileage and depreciation on your Terraplane. I do have a thought I'll throw back at you. Why don't I call up some of the conservation agents in Sherman, Greeley, Logan Counties? The agent over in Thomas County was a fraternity brother of mine. See what those boys are doing. If you'd buy a combine, Pete, we could maybe line up some work in those counties. If they have a little wheat to cut, charge for the work, say nickel a bushel plus mileage, we'd be custom wheat cutters."

There you have it, folks. Right there in a little county in western Kansas during the depression, the drought and the dust bowl, a conservation agent fresh out of Kansas State University came up with the idea of an entire new agricultural industry. The custom combine crews that one now sees moving from the wheat fields of Texas north to the Canadian provinces. Men and their families following the maturing wheat crop north, the custom cutter.

"Lyle, m' boy, I kinda like thet idee. Wish I had Otis here for some arithmetic, but I ain't too sure 'bout thet nickel a acre. We got us eighty right here, say ten bushel ta the acre. Thet's eight hunnert at a nickel. Why, thet's only forty dollar. Cost a gas, grease, tires, hire a tractor driver, tires on the truck ta haul the grain ta the elevator. Tain't worth it. Gotta have a minimum a twenty bushel ta the acre ta come out. Ya call them there brothers a yers. I'll cut wheat, be a custom cutter, but twenty bushel wheat or else the price goes up ta twenty cents a bushel. Now, I want ya ta take a look at all them there rabbits."

"What about them? There is certainly an abundance of them. Must be a couple of hundred right there within shooting range. I'll just get my .22, shoot a few; they'll eat that green wheat."

"You whoa-up there, boy!" said Pete. "Have I got plans fer them rabbits. You is lookin' at probably a couple thousand dollars worth o' rabbits right there a-fore yer very eyes, college boy. We's talkin' in the big buckeroos now. Nature runs in cycles; we is out of the wheat cycle and now in the rabbit cycle. Wheat is what we call incidental; we'll make a little money, but rabbits is the name of the game. Ya git thet one, college boy?" Pete gave Lyle a dig in the ribs with his elbow, smiled.

Lyle acknowledged that if it weren't for Pete, life would sure be dull in Sharon Springs and at the courthouse. It was Pete and that first grade teacher from Quinter that made life interesting for Lyle.

Lyle thought it time to explain something to Pete, "Do you realize that eight, just eight grown jackrabbits eat as much as one cow? I read that in an Agricultural Directive, came right out of Washington, D.C. Did you know that, Pete?"

"You is keerect, Lyle m' boy. I got a directive thet says one Congressman kin live better'n twenty-five ordinary families. Ya recollect when I was sleepin' out here in m' pup tent when I was plowin'? Ya never heard so much noise all night. Reproduction — thet's the secret. Rabbits is better'n wheat. An old cow brings four dollars; with calf by side, add 'nuther dollar. I had Sadie Sobles write me a letter this mornin', three of them as a matter a fact. When I gits some replies, we is in the big bucks, the really big bucks, Lyle m' boy!"

Lyle was skeptical. He said to Pete, "I need some assistance. As I stand here on these windswept plains of paradise in western Kansas, the thistles are blowing; dust devils all across the horizon. We're in a drought, depression, and there are millions of jackrabbits eating anything and everything that grows or moves, and you talk about big bucks. Just where are the big bucks?"

"Why, it's felt, ya ever heard o' felt? Ya know what felt is made of, college boy?"

"No, I sure don't know what felt is made of. You seem to always be talking about your Triple X Stetson, I thought beaver. Tell me all about felt and its ingredients, Pete."

Now it was Pete's turn to teach the college boy. "Felt is made o' fur; rabbits is covered with cheap fur; cheap fur makes cheap hats. We create a industry right here in Wallace County. We is the source of the raw materials, namely rabbits. You git us a governmint loan fer a felt plant; thet's your conservative duty. You an' me, we buy some cheap ammunition an' make a small profit, say we pay a penny a rabbit. Skin the rabbit, say we pay 'nuther penny fer the skinnin'. I kin skin a rabbit in fifteen seconds. H'm, thet's four a minute, four cents a minute times sixty. What's thet figure out to, college boy?"

"Two dollars and forty cents an hour; that is a pretty good wage, but it's not steady work, Pete."

"Ya ninny! A guy would only havta work two days a month ta make more than the W.P. and A's make a month. The women could work, too. Got ta make frames fer the hides ta stretch. We'll make 'em outta lath. Have a coupla guys making frames, the hides git dry and we send a carload a hides on the U.P. to the felt factory. Now, Lyle m' boy, I got m'self a kicker, a money-maker."

"What's your kicker, Pete? I do believe you are on a roll."

"We got the fur offen the rabbit, but we don't let nuthin' go ta waste. Rabbits' feet, we make good luck charms. Ever body an' soul in the U.S. of A. is a-needin' a heap o' luck in this here depression. We pervide the folks with thet luck. Economics is jest in the head anyways. They git one of our Jayhawker Lucky Rabbit's feet fer 'bout a quarter apiece. Why, it would change ever body's attitude. We'll pull outta this depression. Roosevelt 'll take all the credit, but me an' you'll know, we was the very ones thet did it. Ya jest look out yonder at them jackitty rabbits hoppin' around and figure this one out, college boy. Eight rabbits eat as much as a broken-mouth cow. She's worth four dollars. Them eight jacks are worth eight dollars on the hoof. I did think onct o' makin' powder puffs outta their tails, sell 'em fer fifty cents, but thought I'd wait till I heerd from the felt hat companies. Ya know somethin'? Otis said it was a-gonna rain. Look at them thunderheads a-buildin' up. Let's us slip inta town an' take out a dab o' hail insurance on this fine wheat crop. Ya'd make a fine witness in case thet Good and Bad News Insurance Co. don't pay off promptly, proper like."

Lyle was observing Pete and his driving on the way back to town. "What are you double-clutching this Terraplane for, Pete? This is not a truck; you are going through more motions than a Boy Scout with his semaphore signals."

Pete smirked. 'I bin givin' Effie lessons on drivin' a autymobile, teachin' her how ta double-clutch. We got us another problem with them rabbits. Guts, thet is our big problem, Lyle m' boy. We are gonna have us one powerful pile o' putrified guts with a coupla hunnert thousand rabbits. I thought once of a great big meat grinder. Git a guy er two with a number twelve scoop shovel. Shovel them guts into the grinder, grind 'em up. We might can 'em, make fine nutritious dog food. Why, the U.P. would havta put on 'nother freight jest ta ship out our hair, rabbits' feet an' Pride of the Prairie Dog Food. Thet's what I named the dog food. Why, Sharon Springs would become 'The Paradise and Pride on the Plains,' an' all this is promoted by Pete Pisanmoan an' Lyle Lovelace. I had me 'nother thought; git us a sculptor an' make a plaster a Paris jackrabbit. Make it nice an' light. Put him right up on the water tower; people could see him clear from Weskan and Wallace. Why, they'd stop in at our tourist trap up there on Highway 40, buy rabbits' feet by the hunnerts. We'd sell hats and feet. We'd need a coupla girls all dressed up like pretty little bunnies, sellin' them rabbits. We'd havta hire a girl jest to count the money, it would be rollin' in so fast, Lyle m' boy."

There you have it, folks, right there in a little county in western Kansas during the drought, dust bowl and the depression, a County Treasurer, farmer, rancher, an entrepreneur, a man of his time came up with the idea of the bunny costume for a pretty girl to peddle merchandise.

Pete was full of enthusiasm. "Boy, would we sell hats! Open

up a hat shop, Men's and Ladies' Hats. Put up a great big sign, have a sign painter write it in big red letters: 'CHEAP HATS.' When ya say cheap, folks will buy. Thet's always bin my philosophy, buy 'em cheap. Make the place a bus stop, little kids a-runnin' up and down at the U.P. depot, sellin' hats and rabbits' foots to the train passengers. We'd need a extry number eight scoop shovel fer all the money we'd be a-takin' in, Lyle m' boy." Pete jiggled the gold toothpick, grinned.

Lyle too was smiling. It was truly exciting to watch Pete Pisanmoan when he was on a roll, when he had and was full of — Lyle wondered just what was it? Why, it was enthusiasm. His eagerness and optimism — there was so little optimism in those depression days, the dust bowl; it was downright dismal. "How do you think we should finance this operation, Pete? You keep up this double-clutching and I'll get a neck ache."

"I've given considerable thought to the financial end of our endeavors, Lyle m' boy. One thought was we could establish us a co-op. Thet idee is no good; no one has any money ta invest. This should be a community project, everyone be in on the rise of the economy of our wonderful community and county. Jest think, take a Sunday drive out ta the country an' shoot jackitty-rabbits, jest a coupla hunnert. Folks could make money goin' fer a Sunday drive! Jest a minute whilst I go in an' take out m' hail insurance. I don't like the looks of them clouds. If Fondis F. ain't looked out the winder, I got the Good and Bad News Insurance Company nailed fer about eight hunnert bushels o' wheat. Might jest lop 'er off at a thousand."

Lyle Lovelace smiled; they didn't teach soil conservation that kind of lessons at K. State. Pete wasn't gone long. Fondis F. took his money, doubtful about any wheat growing, but he wrote out a receipt.

Pete came out, got in the Terraplane and asked Lyle, "Did ya ever wonder how many rabbit guts it would take ta fill a wash tub? A real tub-a-guts, I calculate a hunnert and fourteen rabbits would jest 'bout do it." Pete double-clutched it up to the courthouse. As they got out of the car, it began to rain. Not even a BB of a hail stone. Pete was now covered clear until harvest time on hail damage.

Pete brought up the subject again, "Back ta financin' this

operation. We could incorporate, git a bunch o' codicils in the corporation, but we is stopped again, no money ta buy our stock. Government grant ain't no account; yer 'bout all the government I kin stand. They'd send some college boy out here thet wouldn't know a jackrabbit from a jackass. We wait, yessiree, thet's what we'll do, Lyle m' boy. Wait till we hear from them hat companies on thet felt. We'll hit the People's State Bank right here in our wonderful paradise on the plains, our very own hometown bank. Prosperity is a-comin', the potential profit possibilities is practically unlimitless."

Lyle just smiled. He was well aware that Pete didn't use proper English, but he sure made a lot of sense. It just might be possible to sell those rabbits to a hat company; he was dubious about the dog food.

After the letters had been mailed a week, Pete began to become impatient. He had stopped by the post office every day. No mail from the hat companies, not an answer. He began to observe the men in town. They all wore hats. He went down to the depot and watched the men on the passenger trains; all wore hats. Pete was making a marketing survey; he didn't know it, but that's what it was. He did receive a letter; it was from Lester Pester, Sharon Springs City Clerk. Pete couldn't figure out what he could have on his mind this time:

April 21, 1935

Dear Mr. Pisanmoan:

You are hereby notified that we have intentions of filing a Lack-A-Action lawsuit against you as the sole owner of Lots 3, 4, 5, Block 3, Carter's Addition. One of your neighbors brought this to our attention, Mr. Pisanmoan. We were not aware of the State of Kansas State Code No. 477, Art. 44, Paragraph 21, Subsection C, regarding Lack-A-Action lawsuits. We need to see some building action on subject property p.d.q.

Sincerely,
s / Lester Pester
Sharon Springs, Kan. City Clerk

A steely glint came into Pete's eyes. His gold toothpick

quivered, and then he smiled. "It was Penelope Pinchlips, m' good neighbor, that put this here idee inta Lester's head. There ain't no sech thing as a lack-a-action lawsuit. She's bin pesterin' ol' Lester. He fell fer it. Time I played a little number an' I'll git me a lot-a-action." Pete headed for the courthouse. The timing on his number was perfect.

Otis greeted Pete, "Did you hear the news? Ol' Cletus Bemus stuck his .22 in his ear and pulled the trigger. Gawd, I'll bet that was loud!" (Pete knew now this was their very last term.) "He was too proud to go on welfare or work on the W.P.A. Rev. Cox called, and Cletus' sister, Dimples, from back in Missouri asked if'n you'd be a pallbearer. I told them ya would. Guess the drought and depression finally got to him. He batched all his life out there on that place he homesteaded. Just took the list of delinquent taxes down to the *Western Times* last week to be published. This was Cletus' first time on the list. We had a full page of tax delinquencies this year, Pete."

Pete's eyes puddled a little; he had liked Cletus Bemus. "Jest think, Otis. If'n Cletus had held off jest 'nother week or so an' I hear from thet hat company. Cletus was a dandy shot; he could have sat out there on his front porch in his rocky-chair an' pop them jackrabbits. Make hisself a coupla dollars a day. What a shame, I coulda saved a man's life with jest them rabbits. When is the funeral?"

"Day after tomorrow. Take that long for his sis to git here. Charlie Koons said it would be a closed casket service." (Pete glanced at Otis; there was no doubt this was their last term.)

"Otis, the day of the funeral I'll walk over ta the church, leave the Terraplane here fer ya ta drive. Ya kin take Effie, Penelope and Daphne ta the cemetery with you. Ya be sure an' double-clutch, thet's fer m' Effie." Pete smiled and winked; Otis winked back, rubbed his stocking feet together by the electric heater under his desk. Otis liked to work with Pete, admired him.

There was a good turnout for Cletus. He was one of the early homesteaders, kept a neat little place. Fences were three-wire, tight. Good fences make good neighbors. Cletus had only broken up a hundred and sixty acres, had a go-backers redemption on another quarter. Fair pasture for his few broken-mouth cows and a team of horses. When the cortege left the church, Pete glanced back from the pallbearers' car to see how Otis was handling the Terraplane. He could see he was doing a dandy job of double-clutching, car lurching, ladies holding their hats. He noted Effie was ridin' shotgun to give Otis instructions; she'd probably insisted on driving, but she forgot her fawn mittens.

Pete took a liking to Cletus' sister and her husband, Dink Dumas. They lived at Cliquot, Missouri, owned about a hundred acres of solid rock, had about an inch of topsoil. The Reverend Cox had thrown a fistful of dirt on Cletus' box; the mourners began to wander around the cemetery, check up on their departed loved ones. Wanted to see if the iris they had planted last year had survived. Rabbits had probably eaten them up.

Dink and Dimples were cozying up to Pete. They needed a friend, someone to handle the estate so they could get back to Cliquot. Pete was visiting but did not seem to be devoting his entire attention to the conversation; his interest lay elsewhere. Pete was observing Penelope Pinchlips and Daphne Damptowel leisurely strolling over toward the Pinchlips' sarcophagus.

Dimples inquired, "Why do you keep rolling your toothpick back and forth, Mr. Pisanmoan? That seems a lecherous grin on yer face!"

"Pardon me, folks. I gotta git just a mite closer. I think a 'Lack-A-Action' lawsuit is 'bout ta become a 'Lotta-Action.' Ya folks stay right here an' keep ol' Cletus company. I'll be back directly. I wouldn't miss this fer the world."

Some said it was the loudest shriek they had ever heard. One man said it came in a whooshy sound, a large gasp of breath and then that terrible shriek. Another said it was kind of like hearing the anchor man on the mile relay team trying to catch his breath after running the final quarter-mile. One of the members of the Literary Society said it reminded her of something right out of Edgar Allen Poe. It was Doc Carter who saved Penelope Pinchlips just as she fractured all five toes on her left foot kicking the Pisanmoan headstone; she kicked it right under where it was inscribed "Peter P."

Doc hit her in the right buttock with a double dose of morphine. One lady heard Penelope say as she was going down: "That dirty sonofabitch." Those were Penelope's last words for three days. Doc Carter put Penelope's jacket on backwards, tied the sleeves in a tight knot. They loaded her into the hearse, and Charlie Koons of the Koons Funeral Home drove Penelope to Goodland to the hospital. Charlie smiled, too; he had wondered about that headstone when he had it put up. Now he knew.

Pete was grinning ear to ear as he walked back to Dink and Dimples. "I thank ya fer waitin' fer me. I jest knew there was somethin' gonna happen over there. Sure, I'll handle the estate fer ya on this end. I'll git them cattle sold, ship them horses ta Denver the next time a horse buyer comes through. Horses ain't worth much now that most everyone's got a tractor. Maybe we outta let the governmint shoot them cows; they's payin' $12 a head; that'd be 'bout 'nuff ta pay off the funeral expenses. I bin thinkin' 'bout goin' inta real estate when m' term is up as County Treasurer. Workin' on a big deal right now, the felt business. I ain't felt so good since I don't know when. Golly, I feel good! Wonder what happened ta thet woman, shriekin' and carryin' on like thet. She went kinda loco like. Now, I wouldn't worry 'bout them taxes jest yit. They cain't sell the place fer 'nother coupla year. I'd sell the house an' buildin's, lower them taxes. All the farms is gittin' bigger. Lotta them blowed away."

"You do what you think is fair and proper-like, Mr. Pisanmoan. We know we can trust you. Pay Mr. Koons first when you get some cash money; we done gave the preacher a dollar."

Dink had taken a liking to Pete, talked like home folks.

"Ya go ahead an' drive the Terryplane, Otis. I'll jest ride back here with Miss Damptowel. Roll yer winder down, Otis, little fresh air would be nice. Miss Damptowel is sweating and kinda red in the face. Now don't fergit ta double-clutch, Otis. Effie is a-learnin' ta drive. She's got her heart set on a La Salle, and ya know them cars got soft clutches. Ya watch Otis there, Effie. He's almost as professional as me when it comes ta drivin'." Pete was nonchalanting it with Effie, trying to avoid the current and most popular subject, namely Penelope Pinchlips and her actions.

Effie turned around and asked Pete, "When did you purchase those lots and our headstone, Pete? You do the oddest things sometimes. It was really quite thoughtful. I do appreciate it, but how come ya put yerself next ta Penelope?"

"It has been m' experience thet the man goes on the left as yer lookin' at the headstone." Seemed reasonable except to Effie.

"Why, it don't make a whit of difference when one is dead," replied Effie.

Otis smiled; Pistol Pete was quick on the trigger. "Effie ol' girl, consider the grave digger. Most men is right-handed; they start at the foot of the grave, shovels the dirt to the right. It has been in many polls that women outlive men; man always goes first, now don't thet make sense? Double-clutch 'er, Otis!"

Effie pondered on the problem. Pete's explanation seemed logical; she watched Otis grind the Terraplane into high gear. She could have done better if she'd had her fawn driving gloves.

The next morning Pete hit the courthouse door and went up the steps to the Treasurer's Office two steps at a time. He had two letters in his hand, waving and hollering down the stairs to Lyle, upstairs to Otis. "I heered from 'em, boys! Come on up to the office, Lyle m' boy. We'll have a pan o' gravy comin' our way — number eight scoop shovel. One letter is from Worchester, the tuther is from Boston. They is hat companies, felt hat companies." First he opened the letter from the Dibbs Hat Company, "Home of the Permanent Crease."

"They's got a interest in our propysition; they want us ta sind them one hunnert hides as a sample, got a clinker in the deal. They want hides thet is with the winter fur, gotta be from November ta March."

"Looks like we're too late for this year, Pete," said Lyle.

"Nope, not-a-tall, Lyle. They say down here in 'nuther place they'll take a spring sample, since they is no money changin' hands. It'll give 'em an idee of the quality of our furs. If'n the furs is acceptable, they'll take 300,000 next year, pay us twelve cents apiece F.O.B. Worchester. Otis, how much is thet? I'll bet it's more than I ever found in the back seat of a autymobile."

Otis wet the end of his No. 2 pencil, "Pete it comes to $36,000 gross. You do understand gross over net, don't you?"

"Gawd, thet is a pile-a-plunder, partners! What's thet F.O.B. mean, Lyle m' boy? You bein' the college boy an' all. I know it costs, takes a portion o' the plunder; thet's the way business is done by them folks back east; they is experts at plunderin'."

"It merely means we pay the cost of the freight for the pelts delivered to Worchester. It is a fair deal, Pete. That is the way most business is conducted."

"Why, sure it's fair. I'd want the Union Pacific ta git a piece of the plunder. I'll contact the depot agent, John Ley, an' see if'n he can't git us a special rate fer all them railroad cars we'll be a-usin'."

Otis was curious, "When are we going to the bank and make our presentation, get a loan, get into production, Pete?"

"Hold 'er up a minute there, Otis. We're graspin' and gaspin'; let us see and observe this other letter from Boston. May have a better deal than those folks with the permanent crease." Pete read the letter, tossed it in the waste basket. "We'll jest forgit them folks. They is only offerin' us eight cents, and they ain't got no permanent crease. The way I see it is this-away. We go out an' shoot us a couple hunnert jackitty rabbits, skin 'em real nice and be sure and cut off their feet afore we sind them; that way they'll know we ship without feet. They accept them hides — we got the real money all locked up in the feet. Thet's where the money is, lucky rabbits' feet. When we git the big order, then is when we sit down at the bank. We got a contract in our fist, a rabbit's foot on our watch chains, and thet new banker will run back ta the vault an' wheel-barry out a load a money. Wallace County becomes the Paradise on the Plains. Prosperity reigns supreme. Why, when a new baby is borned in Wallace County, they'll name 'er Jackie or Bunny if'n it's a girl. A boy will be jest plain Jack, an' maybe" (Pete tongued his toothpick over to the other side of his mouth, smiled) "name him Pete; thet is, if they is real appreciative of m' doin's." Pete gave Lyle a dig in the ribs with his elbow.

The Conservation Agent was curious, "Just what are we going to haul all these rabbits to town in, Pete?"

"Lyle, you is a real educated boy; we git the Model A grain truck. We'll drive us a coupla nails in the side of the truck; ya stick their hind feet over them nails an' skin 'em. We'll throw the hides in the back a' the truck, cut off the feet an' throw 'em in a tub or a gunny sack, jest leave the guts out there for fertilizer. Come on, Otis, we'll let ya stand up in the back o' the truck an' shoot, box a shells apiece. See who gits the most outta fifty shots. Loser buys me an' Otis a bottle a pop. Me an' Lyle 'll skin, Otis kin use a hatchet and chop off them lucky rabbits' feet."

It would appear Lyle would be the loser since only his name was mentioned in the payoff on the most rabbits shot. They used Cletus Bemus' barn for their pelt-stretching and framing operation. They found an old piano box, perfect for shipping the stretched hides. Pete stuffed some newspapers down in the bottom, wanted to keep the hides fluffed up nicely for them permanent crease folks.

"Now, boys, let's keep this under our Triple X's till we hear from Warchester, spit an' shake on 'er."

They all spit and shook. Lyle was last. He got a kind of squishy handshake, went down to the men's room at the courthouse to wash up. He'd never heard of that western custom before. It sure sealed the deal for him.

Whenever Effie had pork chops for supper, Pete became suspicious. Effie had something on her mind and Pete knew it would be costly to him. "It would be very nice and neighborly if you would take Daphne and me over to Goodland to see Penelope at the hospital, Pete. You could give me a driving lesson on the way over and back. Why, that much distance would count for at least two lessons. The palms of my fawn driving gloves is just itching to get a grip on that wheel."

Pete's answer surprised Effie; she could have served biskits and gravy. "It has bin almost two week, ain't it, Effie ol' girl? Sure, I'll take ya over. Penelope probably is kinda pinin' fer me by now. Heard she had kind of a twitch ta the left side of her mouth. Doc Carter tole me he thought it would disappear with time. Quicker if'n she'd take a trip back east ta see Prunella, extended trip, he thought about six months. Now distance ain't considered when countin' drivin' lessons, Effie. The entire lesson is counted on the amount o' double-clutchin' one has ta do. Jest drivin' along in high gear and keepin' the autymobile between the fences don't hardly count a-tall."

Pete was sitting in the waiting room at the hospital, had his hat off and was writing the latest amount on the Casa account. It was sixty-six miles round-trip to Goodland at ten cents a mile.

Effie came tippy-toeing out to the waiting room and whispered to Pete. Pete wondered about that; Penelope was not in danger of dying, just had some broken toes. "Can you come and help us get Penelope in about three days? The doctor says she can come home then; she'll have a cast and need to use crutches for a while."

Pete had a hunch this was what was coming. "Nope, gotta start combinin' wheat day after tomorry." Then he said just a little louder so Penelope would be sure and hear, "Ya kin tell Penelope she kin take the Rock Island ta Limon, Colorady, then catch a U.P. down to Sharon Springs. Save us all thet drivin'. Ya didn't hear her say a thing 'bout givin' us a little gas money?"

Effie did not expect this turn of events. "Why, Pete, that's almost two hunnert miles of riding a train when she'd only have to ride about thirty-three in our Terryplane. It's hard for her to walk; she has a cast and then she's not used to crutches."

"Jest cain't make 'er, Effie. I'm jest too busy. Shame ta treat a neighbor thataway, particularly when they's cemetery plots is right next ta each other. When wheat's ready, it's ready. I'm pullin' a rented combine out ta the T.T.T. & T. ground tomorry."

It took three days to cut the wheat. Otis drove the Wallis, Pete was up on the combine, while Lyle drove the Model A to the elevator. They didn't get much wheat, took a lot of time, but they did get 876 bushels of wheat, and that was about twice as much as most of Wallace County had in 1935. The Union Pacific didn't run a Pete Pisanmoan Special; they didn't even spot a car at the elevator. The elevator sold the wheat for chicken feed. The wheat was in the bin.

Pete pulled up to "The Dump," needed a good bath. He had a bad case of grain rash, itched all over. He took down the wash tub on the back porch and asked Effie, "Where's the water?"

Without any hesitation, Effie said, "Don't have any water."

"Why?"

"Penelope took a double-bitted ax and chopped down the windmill. You had the Model A, I couldn't haul any water."

"How'd thet Penelope Pinchlips git home? Ya said she was on crutches, she musta bin plenty perturbed to chop down her own windmill." Pete was surprised at the malice shown by Penelope.

"Sylvester Beatum drove her home, that's her lawyer. Such a nice gentleman. I helped her sharpen the ax, used your whetstone. The hand pump still works, bucket's on the porch."

Pete had to take a trip up to the courthouse with the Model A and fill the water barrel. It gave Pete time to contemplate his next move. Pete was perpetuating the peremptory of Penelope. His plan resembled a bull fight. First the picadores, then the banderilleros. Pete decided his first picador would be a letter. This would take time to achieve just what he wanted. The timing and the detail of the thrust was important. He had Sadie Sobles type the letter on her L.C. Smith. It read:

Miss Penelope Pinchlips
City

Dear Miss Pinchlips:
You is what is known as in a heap of trouble! I am contacting my attorney, Mr. Simon Fixum, Esq., concerning a lawsuit, namely a "Lack-A-Water" suit. According to Kansas State Law and its said statutes, therein and thereon, if'n a party has used subterranean water fer a period of seven (7) years or more, that party has a vested interest in that there water. You done cut off my water. Next, I am contactin' a well-known mental institution concerning yer mental facilities. Not often does one see a woman kick a chunk of rock and then break all their toes on a foot. In all the annals of my owning propity, never has a person chopped down a windmill and felled it right on my propity. It is a dangerous menace to man and beast jest a-layin' there. Little children could git hurt playin' 'round it. You are therefore liable fer any accidents. The last item is one called defamation of character. You called me a fowl name up at that cemetery when you was bootin' our expensive headstone. I have obtained the names and depositions of witnesses to this here event. I have been called a number of names but never thet one and not in public. My bein' a elected public official makes it twice as expensive. You got jest five days ta reply.
Your Wallace County Treasurer and Neighbor
s / Pete Pisanmoan, Plaintiff

Pete rolled his toothpick over to the other side of his mouth when he put that letter in the local mail slot at the post office. It was his opinion that Sylvester Beatum would be driving over from Goodland for a little visit. Pete thought, "He kinda hung me out ta dry on thet last visit. Different this time around."

"Lyle, m'boy. I'm gonna run one by ya, college boy and all. It's bin mighty dry this summer an' fall. We got the wheat in the bin, what little they was of it. I'm a fixin' ta go out an' put in 'bout six hunnert acres o' winter wheat, Comanche. Thet seed had the best protein. Now I ain't agonna plow, disk, harry nor nothin'. I'm jest gonna put 'er in a drill an' commence ta drillin' wheat. No-till atall. Thet land has laid asleep fer over two year. I kicked 'er around a tad the other day. They's some sub-moisture. Cheap ta farm thataway. Yessiree, Lyle m' boy, I'm not agonna till atall."

There you have it, right there in a little county in western Kansas, during the depression, drought and dust bowl, a county treasurer and farmer became the first to use that word and develop a new method of farming: "No Till." It was Pete Pisanmoan who first used those words and method in modern day agriculture. A method to save the topsoil for future generations.

Lyle threw a little cold water on the idea. "The thistles will plug up the grain drill, bind it up, Pete."

"Nope, I don't reckon so. Those thistles is almost mature, main root is dried up, drill 'll jest loose 'em an' they'll blow clear ta Tribune; Greeley County gits all m' thistles."

Pete was hard to beat when it came to acting. Lawyers take thespian lessons in law school; it is part of the curriculum. Now Sylvester Beatum was good, mighty good. If a lawyer doesn't have a case, he assumes the air of victor. He becomes boisterous, more overbearing than usual, seems more important, taunt and flaunt. Sylvester Beatum hit the main door of the Wallace County Courthouse like he had the lease on it. Had on a linen suit, white Panama hat, white shoes with black wing tips, red silk tie and a pretty little red hanky in his breast pocket. A real danderoo. All he lacked was Claudette Colbert draped on his arm. Sly Syl was in town; that's what they called him over in Sherman County, Sly Syl, and he had a helluva practice, profitable, too. Syl went directly to the Treasurer's Office, tipped back his silver-bellied colored Panama hat and stuck out his hand. Fingernails were manicured; he gave Pete a limp one. Limp one always meant loser; hearty one meant he was considered a winner.

"How have you been, Mr. Pisanmoan? You are a hale and hearty one, aren't you! I just came from Miss Penelope Pinchlips' lovely home, and I wish to consult with you. It will take just a moment. I read your letter; it fell on quite deaf ears. Should you continue to pursue this farce, I shall have to counter-sue for a cool million dollars. You think on that rather large denomination; I shall motor back to Goodland. You have three days to consider this proposition, Mr. Pisanmoan."

Pete was still standing at the counter, tipped his Triple X back on his head, lock of grey hair fell across his forehead. He tongued his gold toothpick over to the other side of his mouth, looked a little bit like Will Rogers without his rope. He smiled; it was a friendly smile. "It's good to see ya agin, Sylvester. My, ya sure do look spiffy taday. Ya look like a big chunk a' alybaster, maybe a vanilly ice cream cone. Counter-suit, ya say? Why, thet sounds kinda like a threat. I'm gonna throw jest two words yer way and let ya think afore ya start motorin' back to Goodland. Them two words is Lis Pendens. Yessiree, everything I could find in all the county records, an' I got access ta all o' 'em. I done filed Lis Pendens suit on ever' propity yer lovely client owns. Bet ya ain't a bit deaf now, Sylvester."

Sylvester Beatum's complexion took a quicky turn to the color of his suit. He reached in his hip pocket for his hanky, a white one, wiped his face, removed the Panama hat and wiped his forehead. Otis burned his sock on the electric heater. It had the odor of burnt wool and Ben-Gay wafted through the Treasurer's Office.

"You realize what you have done to my client, don't you, Mr. Pisanmoan? You have clouded the title on every property she owns!"

"Why, Sylvester, ya did go to law school after all. Ya got 'er, Sylvester, yessiree, ya got 'er the very first time. Now I'm gonna head out ta some ground I own and git ta drillin' wheat. The country is comin' back, Sylvester. We are gonna see a turnaround in farmin'. Ya better go down ta the Sasnak Hotel an' git ya a room, stay over a coupla days. The way yer sweatin' ya better git one with a bath. We'll negotiate this problem and stay outta court if possible. Ya know thet ol' saw, 'A poor sittlimint is better'n a good lawsuit.' I'll be out on the T.T.T. & T. ground, Otis. See ya, Sylvester, give this problem some thought."

Sylvester Beatum just stood there waving his Panama, fanning his face. He had a formidable foe, not a fool. Sylvester looked over at Otis. "Ornery ol' cuss, isn't he?"

"Nope, you got it all wrong. He's a likeable ol' cuss, never knowed one quite like him. He'll do anything for you if'n he likes you. Just think, if he'd got an education he'd be downright dangerous. Why, you'd never know he only went to the fifth grade down at Wallace public school."

The next morning when Pete stopped in at the courthouse, there was Sylvester Beatum, Esq., sitting in Pete's chair having a cup of coffee with Otis.

Pete looked at the two, "Mornin', gentlemen. Why, ya don't look so spiffy this mornin' there, Sylvester, kinda wrinkled, look kinda sleazy. Git a good night's sleep? Are ya ready to palaver over some property?"

"I checked the records. You haven't filed a Lis Pendens, Pete. I realize you will if we can't settle this problem. Name your terms, I'll see what I can do with my client."

"You is one smart barrister. Hang on ta yer Panama hat. Ya want a pencil an' paper? This gits a tad complicated."

Sylvester declined the offer of paper and pencil.

"First off, give me a bill of sale on thet Dempster windmill head and the tower."

Sylvester smiled, "That is acceptable, proceed."

"Penelope pays the tap fees on m' present domicile."

Just a slight smile. "That seems reasonable, she will accept that. Proceed, Pete."

"She pays fer the labor fer the diggin' of the ditches fer both m' present domicile an' the Casa Del Sol. Sewer and water ditch diggin'."

No smile, but Sylvester was inquisitive. "Just exactly what is a Casa Del Sol? That is a new one on me."

"That name is some of m' wife's doin's. She reads magazines up at the Clip an' Curl. It jest means a hut in the sun."

"Is that all, Pete? Miss Pinchlips wishes to purchase your cemetery plots and have your headstone moved to another location. Would you consider selling?"

Now it was Pete's turn to smile. "Nope! Will trade though, an' she'll git some boot. Jest knew ya'd want them cemetery lots. Them's prime lots. Folks like ta be close ta the Pinchlips, fine family. Ol' Palmer was a provider.'

"Whatever would Miss Pinchlips have to give for boot?"

"I got a real zinger fer ya, Sylvester. Git yer white hanky ready fer this one. She deeds Sections 22 and 23 to the T.T.T. & T., and I'll give her five hunnert dollars and the deed to them two cemetery lots. Thet five hunnert dollars 'll jest 'bout pay yer bill an' git her back east fer a long visit with her sis, Prunella. She'll be gone fer at least six months. I'll git thet Casa Del Sol built an' have a little dab o' wheat land ta play with when we hit the wheat growin' cycle. Ya look jest a tad pale there, partner. Ya wanta spit an' shake on 'er?"

Sylvester declined the spit and shake. "You are a devious and deceptive individual. Would you have someone who could type some legal instruments for me, Pete?"

"Why sure, m' fine and politickin' friend, Sadie Sobles, is a whiz-bang on the ol' L.C. Smith. She typed thet letter I wrote ta Penelope; she takes dictation real good, too."

"I knew right away it was a secretarial expert that wrote that letter when I perused that piece of provocative blackmail." Sylvester had it all in his head, just what he needed. "I'll need a bill of sale for the Dempster, a warranty deed for the two sections of land, letter of intent to the city that Miss Pinchlips will pay the tap fees and the ditch diggers for both domiciles. Another letter that she will pay for the removal and erection of the Pisanmoan headstone in a far-off pair of plots. Oh yes, we'll need a deed from you to the City from you to Miss Pinchlips for your present cemetery plots. Then I have the dubious distinction and duty to present this proposal to Miss Pinchlips and hope she keeps her sanity. I shall possibly need another day."

Pete was quite sure he had won the day; he was in a jovial mood. Commented to Sylvester Beatum, "Sylvester, ya better git thet ice cream suit washed an' pressed or else go git yerself a pair a Osh-Goshers. Yer beginnin' ta look a little seedy. Man in yer perfession needs ta look tip-top, dress like a parasite."

(The purchase price of the two sections of land was not as cheap as it sounds. During the '30s it was not uncommon for western Kansas land that was blowing to sell for fifty cents to one dollar an acre, if it was for cash.)

Sadie Sobles typed all the letters and deeds Sylvester

Beatum required. He slid one by Pete; Pete missed it. Penelope kept the mineral rights on both Sections 22 and 23.

Volney Borst looked up from the newspaper when the door to the shop opened. "Where in the world have you been, Pete? I've sure missed you. I inquired from Otis one evening when he was hobbling home. He said you were out drilling wheat. When did you shave last, get a shampoo? You look like a bum that just got off a freight, not a County Treasurer."

"Volney, I have been one busy fella. I been batchin' out at Cletus Bemus place; it's close ta the T.T.T. & T. land. Lyle has been drivin' the grain truck out ever evenin' with seed wheat. He brings me gas, grease an' grub. I done drilled over fifteen hunnert acres o' Comanche. I went out there the day Penelope Pinchlips went on her sabbatical back east ta see Prunella. I do believe I've sold Cletus' place ta Lyle. He's saved a pittance, wants ta neighbor with me. We two is gonna farm m' ground tagether. Gawd, I own over four thousand acres o' Kansas blowdirt. I'm a-gonna put the marginal land back ta grass. Put a lotta soap in thet shampoo, Volney. I ain't had m' hair washed since Lyle an' thet first-grade teacher threw me in the stock tank."

Volney had the barber chair in the reclining position, Pete lying there — hot towel on his beard. The towel had a minty vapor rising up; Pete was relaxed. Volney looked out the window, "There goes Effie in the Terraplane, Pete. Jerking down Main Street."

"Is she a-double-clutchin', Volney?"

"She sure is, doing a good job of it, too."

Pete smiled under the warm and minty towel; he'd shot down one La Salle.

Social Security Enacted

Aug. 14 — Pres. Roosevelt signed into law the Social Security Act today, fulfilling a 1932 campaign promise. The Democrats had pledged "unemployment and old-age insurance under state laws." Now, America joins many other industrial nations in providing comprehensive care for its elderly, handicapped and unemployed. Payroll taxes will fund the legislation which has taken

more than 14 months to enact. Conservatives have fought the bill since FDR proposed it last June. One congressman believes the bill will "threaten the integrity of our institutions." But the majority of congressmen feel it will relieve the burden of many Americans.
—San Francisco Examiner
Aug. 14, 1935

The word "cheat" comes from the Middle English Escheater" — an officer of the king who collected dues and taxes from people assumed to be unentitled to inherited estates. Over the years, escheaters finagled so much money from people that their title became synonymous with swindling. In those days, the tax collectors, not the taxpayers, were the cheats.
—Joel Desang
Staff Writer, Gannett News Service

PLANS AWRY
1936-37

"IT'S A PURE SHAME you won't consent to one more term as our County Treasurer, Pete. Heard you attended the Republican caucus a couple of nights ago. Lots of pundits about your political purposes. You sure provoked a few of the plebeians." Borst was concerned.

" 'Scuse me, Volney. I warn't a-listenin' ta ya, I was sittin' here thinkin' 'bout war. There's a war a-comin', Volney. Sabers rattle most when they is held in tremblin' hands. Jest look at thet Mussolini over there in Italy. He jumps on thet little skinny guy over there in Ethiopia. Tanks, machine guns. The little skinny guy fights back with muskets and has his troops on saddle horses. Thet Hitler got them Germans goose-steppin' over the cobblestones. F.D.R. ain't preparin' us fer what's a-comin', Volney. It don't make a whit who gits the Wallace County Treasurer's position, Republican or Democrat. We are all jest home folks. Otis an' his bookkeeping was the key ta thet office. Otis said it was the double-entry. I never did know what he was a-talkin' 'bout. Ya notice how he's gotten better since I put him on the Wallis. He loves to run thet Wallis, likes to backfire 'er an' watch them jackrabbits jump straight up in the air. It come harvest time, Lyle is a-gonna resign outta the public trough, too. I finally sold him Cletus Bemus's place. He was too smart ta be a conservative agent anyways. Didja ever wonder what kind of a I.Q. test they give some of them government workers?"

Pete picked up the morning issue of the *Topeka Daily Capitol*. Volney thought it odd, Pete was pretty quiet this morning, must have a problem. Customer came in the shop, Pete perused the newspaper. Volney made another attempt at conversation. The customer in the chair was not responsive to the philosophical observations of a barber.

Volney said to Pete, "I see where the Supreme Court ruled

the Agriculture Adjustment Act is unconstitutional, Pete."

Pete didn't even look up from the paper. "Knew it was when the Congress passed 'er, kid in a eighth-grade civics class knowed thet was tomfoolery. Do ya know what a '36 La Salle is priced at, Volney? Costs $1,175, plus shippin' an' handlin'. Did ya ever wonder why they charge fer shippin' and handlin'? If the car warn't shipped, ya wouldn't drive 'er, would ya? Ya couldn't handle 'er now, could ya?"

Volney noticed that Pete wasn't rolling his toothpick forth and back, more from one side of his mouth to the other. He seemed to be tonguing it like a rattle. Volney knew Pete was perturbed, seemed to be under some sort of pressure, seemed disturbed.

Volney said, "You're next, Pete."

Pete hung his Triple X on the hat rack, sat in the barber chair, had a nice quiet shave. He sighed when Volney lowered the chair, the hot towel felt good. Pete relaxed. It was the first time he had relaxed in three days. Volney felt it kind of pitiful to see Pete in such a predicament.

When Volney tipped the chair up from Pete's shave, Pete asked a question. "How much money ya got in thet there bank up the street?"

"Why, Pete, I know exactly, ten dollars and forty-seven cents. I'm one of the largest depositors." Volney smiled, "How much do you have in that bank, penny-pincher Pete?"

"Not one cent, not one red, white nor blue cent, and thet ain't the half of it. I'll never put a dime in thet bank. Bankers is fools! No, I'll take 'er back. We is the fools ta let them manipulate us. Thet new boy up there at the bank, came from Ellis, he done emasculated three fine local citizens ta other day. We pranced in ta thet bank, we was all primed, looked like three old studs. Came outta thet bank like a bunch o' cur dogs; jest three ol' cobs. I ain't bin this mad since Penelope Pinchlips burnt m' fodder field. Thet was over sixteen, seventeen year ago."

Volney was curious, "I knew something was bothering you. Want to tell me about it, Pete? Maybe you need to tell someone. You are kinda peaked and pathetic looking, get your problem off your chest."

Pete pondered the problem, "Volney, a barber is 'bout the worst person in the world ta tell this here story to. Barber is the biggest gossip next ta the Clip an' Curl. I'll tell ya some of the highlights. Ya gotta spit an' shake on 'er though. Gotta promise not ta tell anyone jest yit. I might be able ta salvage this magnificent economic wonder yet. Spit!"

Volney complied, he spat, they shook, and then Volney washed his hands. Pete wiped his on the seat of his pants. "Hit was m' idee, jest mine alone. Not another body er soul in the whole wide world knew of this here idee. It would have solved the economic plight of our wonderful county. They'd bin no W.P. and A's. We wouldn't be sendin' our boys off ta them C.C.C. camps. No welfare; Paradise right here in western Kansas. Them boys in Washington, D.C., thet's the really big trough. They'd a been out here by the trainload ta observe our land-o-plenty. It wouldn't a hepped the Union Pacific though. Them congress boys must ride the passenger trains fer free. I know they's mail is free so's I guess them fellers ride the trains free."

"Quit your pussy-footing around, Pete. I am at the pinnacle of perturbation."

"Volney, it was kinda like providence had smiled down on Wallace County when I came up with this here idee. Perchance it was the Almighty hisself thet said it was Pete Pisanmoan thet was ta lead us outta this here mess a depression, drought an' despair. It was like the Divine that divulged this here idee, kinda like Moses scramblin' outta Egypt." Volney could tell Pete was coming around. Pete began to tongue his gold toothpick over to the side of his mouth. Why, he even smirked a little.

"Ya know anythin' 'bout hats, makin' hats, Volney?"

"Not a thing, don't throw one on a bed; that's bad luck. I keep a few things under my hat. As I recall, you keep all your financial books in your hat band. I think they do something with fur, that's about all I know. Your Triple X is made out of beaver belly, a fifteen-dollar hat; beaver belly is more expensive."

"Yer absolutely keerect, Volney. Hats is made a felt. Now right here in Wallace County we got the raw material fer cheap hats; depression means we gotta knock off the price a beaver, go fer a cheaper material. Now, Volney, kin ya think of anythin' we got right here in Wallace County thet might pervide cheap fur fer cheap hats?"

Volney pondered the question, looked out the window of the shop, watched a few people going to the post office. "I'm stumped, give me a clue."

"Jackrabbits, millions of 'em. Idees is what make money, I'm full of idees. Ya agree?" Pete was just getting warmed up.

"No doubt about it, you are definitely full of something."

"All right, are ya ready fer a kicker? Add to the wonderful idees I git. We need a big bundle of luck ta git us out of this here depression. I came up with the real winner, a by-product of jackrabbits, rabbits' feet, everyone have a lucky rabbit's foot, men, women an' all the little kids. Sell them foots fer two-bits apiece. Rabbits is worth more on the hoof than a old cow. Ain't them two danderoos of idees, Volney?"

"Seems to me it would be a prudent pattern to prosperity, pull us out of this poverty, Pete. Tell me what happened."

"I wrote a couple of hat companies back east, both showed a good deal o' interest. There was one outfit in Warchester, Mass., offered us — now get a-holt onta yer razor strop, good grip; twelve cents a hide delivered. They was the Home o' the Permanent Crease, a fine reputable outfit, made cheap hats."

"Gosh, that's a lot of money just for a jackrabbit. That is no paltry sum. Proceed, Pete." Volney was beginning to see just why Pete was peeved.

"Me, Otis and Lyle went out and shot a hunnert jackrabbits. We skinned 'em in Cletus Bemus's barn; we was keerful not ta knick the hides. We bought some plasterin' lath at the lumber yard and stretched and dried them hides. Why, we even took a whisk broom and had all the cockle-burs and sandburrs outta them hides; they looked real nice. We put the feets in a gallon a formaldahyde; thet was Lyle's idee. We soaked 'em, stirred 'em and then brushed 'em, too. Right away, our luck began to turn fer the better. Otis's arthritis seemed ta git better; he had two rabbit's feet; one in each shirt pocket. Then Lyle told me his relationship with thet school teacher began to improve a heap. And in my favor, thet Penelope

Pinchlips left town to go back east ta visit Prunella. Now there is practical and positive power of a Wallace County Lucky Rabbit's Foot. Say, jest a minute, I got one out in the Terryplane, give it ta ya, watch yer luck change. You is in fer a whopper of a surprise, Volney."

Volney shrugged his shoulders. After all, what did he have to lose; any improvement in his economic lifestyle was welcome.

Pete came hustling in the door, "Put 'er on yer watch chain. Now, with them rabbit's foots we jest knew we had 'er on the downhill with thet bank. Needed some financin' fer the project. We got a contract from this Dibbs Hat outfit. They was the home of the Permanent Crease; thet's what it said on their letterhead. Now, get another holt on yer razor strop; their very first order was fer 300,000 jackrabbit hides at twelve cents each. Thet's $36,000, Volney. Of course, they wanted them hides F.O.B. Warchester; ya understand thet meant we was to pay the freight, ya do understand thet, Volney. It weren't pure profit."

Volney was sitting up in the barber chair and listening to this delightful tale, "That was no paltry sum those Dibbs Hat people were talking about, 300,000 rabbits, that's a pile of rabbits."

"Pile o' guts, too. They was the one problem we had trouble with, them guts. I figured onct thet one hunnert fourteen rabbits made a tub-a-guts. We solved 'er though; it was 'nother of m' idees. I hadn't sold Cletus's team; they was jest a grazin', doin' nuthin'. I got a fresno and a slip; Lyle had trouble with the fresno but I showed him how. We dug us a ditch, threw in the guts and covered it up. I sint Cletus's sis, Dimples, a check fer $10 rent on the barn, and we used the house ta coffee up. We had 'er pretty well figured out. The hat people, the ones with the Permanent Crease, wanted a performance bond fer $50,000. Why, thet's no hill fer a stepper. Me and Simon has a bail bond shop in Denver over by the West Side Court, a real money-maker. Them Dibbs people wanted the bond as they was gonna hire some extry help. See how economics works, Volney. It stretches from our Paradise on the Plains, bond business in Denver, clear back ta Warchester; everyone has a piece of the action."

Volney studied the figures in his head, "Have I got this right? You get twelve cents in Warchester for a rabbit and then another dollar per rabbit for lucky rabbit's feet."

"You is one smart hombre. Didn't I say it was big buckaroos? Otis bein' a double-entry and all, sat down and commenced a figurin'. He called it a profit and loss projection sheet. I tole him ta toss out thet loss an' name it profit-projection. We had a production line set up out there in the barn. We was gonna hire some women ta yankee-drill the holes in the foots fer the little chains to slip through, salt the hides. We figured the ladies could all ride tagether out ta the place, save on 11 cent a gallon gasoline. Lyle called it car-pooling it."

There you have it, folks, right there in a little county in western Kansas, during the drought and the depression a conservation agent and a rabbit dealer for fur for a company with a Permanent Crease hat came up with that phrase, "carpool."

"It was our idee; it was ta be a county effort. People shootin' jackrabbits with cheap ammunition. Some were skinnin', others choppin' off foots, makin' frames, stretchin' hides, dippin' foots, slippin' chains in little holes, diggin' trenches fer guts, haulin' hides to the house track down by the depot. It was as if the Almighty had pervided fer the populace. We'd had our pride restored, heads held high, bin a purpose ta our lives; we was on our own. We was now producers, had our self-esteem."

"I certainly see no fault in your plan for prosperity, Pete. Seems like you and the boys had about every base covered. What happened?"

"We all put on our suits, I even had on a necktie. We got our contract with the Dibbs Hat Co., thet's the one with the Permanent Crease. Otis had Sadie Sobles type up our profit projection on her L.C. Smith, everything was very perfessional. Then we waltzed inta thet bank and got thet new boy cornered in his office. I was elected spokesman; it was all m' idee, and we hit him right atween the eyes. Why, we even gave him one of our Wallace County Lucky Rabbit's Foots. All we wanted was jest a $5,000 line o' credit. We'uns didn't want the whole shebang, jest a draw up ta $5,000. We'd pay the hep, skinners and haulers, the shooters and gutters. Ya know what thet banker did, Volney?"

Volney gave a curious look at Pete. "Why, he must have approved that kind of a loan. It is the finest idea I've heard in a long time. What happened, Pete?"

"I always understood thet banks made money by loanin' it at a higher interest rate than they paid the depositors. Jest makes sense, higher the risk, higher the interest. I was prepared ta pay say, eight percent, maybe even nine. Why, they's only payin' two percent on savin's. It was jest fer a short term. The way I had 'er figured we'd ship them 300,000 hides in 'bout three months. 'Tweren't like it was fer a twenty-year mortgage or a loan on a bunch of broken-mouth cows an' ya'd pay off with a calf crop. Thet banker leaned back in his leather chair an' commenced ta laugh, darned near choked. I never even got outta m' chair, 'cause if I did I'd a slapped him on the back an' broke his fool neck. Otis, he turned pale an' right away commenced hurtin'. Lyle had ta restrain him; Otis was reachin' fer his Buck knife. We three jest tucked our tails atween our legs and drug up ta the courthouse."

Volney was aghast, "You mean he turned you down flat! Why do you suppose he did that, Pete?"

"I've thunk on it, Volney. Tryin' ta see a flaw, bankers is nosey; he knows I don't bank there, bank in Denver. He cain't check on m' business ventures thetaway. Second thing, maybe our presentation was wrong. Shoulda had Simon Fixum there ta give him the treatment. They's only a few folks thet knows of the plan. Sadie, Lyle, thet pretty little school teacher, you'ns, the banker an' me. I'd like ta tell it ta the *Western Times,* have Swede write a editorial, but we've already had one bank go broke. Locals couldn't take it. We's not long on financial confidence as it is. Makes me plumb mad! Took a banker ta foul the nest a prosperity in our fine county. Remember now, Volney, we spit and shook on 'er. Not a word, ya understand!" Pete started to go out the door, turned back, rolled the toothpick over to the other side of his mouth, smiled. "One other thing, we got a telegram from the Dibbs Hat Company, the one with the Permanent Crease. They wanted ta know where the contract was and the bond. They upped the ante ta thirteen cents a rabbit. I stuck thet telegram in a envelope an' mailed 'er ta the banker. See ya, Volney."

Pete was never quite the same after the banker visit; brown lines of preoccupation became permanently etched into his care-worn face. Here he had had an idea, one that would have eased the depression for his friends and neighbors. He had failed; he wondered if he had picked up the wrong rabbit's foot. Every time Pete ran over a jackrabbit with the Terraplane or the Model A grain truck, he flinched. "A dollar thirteen gross." Pete had other projects. A house to build, wheat to cut and avoid the purchase of a La Salle. There was war on the horizon, and Pete knew people had to be fed. It was coming time to grow wheat.

Effie didn't help much when she said, "Well, penny-pincher, I got me a cozy little two-bedroom jobbie, brick front, and the rest of the place is slap sliding."

"Thet's lap sidin', Effie, rhymes with flap, like yer mouth thet's always a-flappin'."

Effie had put it off as long as she could, "I'm getting ready to furnish the Casa, Pete. How's the money? Can you let go of a nickel or two? Get some new furniture, toss out that old saddle blanket you been sitting on for God only knows how long."

"Glad ya asked. I got 'er all typed up and totaled. Sadie done made a complete financial accountin' on her L.C. Smith. I want ya ta take a good look at m' accountin' system; it's called the double-entry; it looks more perfessional that a-way. You jest take a notice of how nice it came out. Yer dealin' with a man thet had ever penny accounted fer when we was audited." Pete pulled the large envelope from under the cushion of his chair. He'd hid it there the day before; he could see Effie was getting yancy.

Effie looked. "Why, they is four full pages, little single-spaced! That double-entry system is very thorough. It doesn't look like you left off a single item; did you miss a nail or two? I'll look it over, see what you got on this list."

Pete smiled, compared this to when Penelope viewed the tombstone.

"My, that Sadie does play a merry little tune on that L.C.

I see where that Wallis tractor and plowin' the lots runs to ten dollars a hour — you was plenty high on that little dab of work, Pete."

"You just don't understand the charges for the use of fine machinery. Hit is customary ta charge what them fellers call a 'move in' charge. Part of thet is move-in, Effie ol' girl."

"What's this charge for driving gloves, eight dollars? Those fawn driving gloves don't have nuthin' to do with the Casa Del Sol. Why, look-a-here, here's driving lessons, ten dollars a lesson!"

"Thet's easy ta explain, Effie. Ya had a perfessional. Not many kin take a uncoordinated individual like you'ns an' teach 'em the fine art a double-clutchin'. Paticncc is the name of' thet game. Why, there ain't a pedestrian in this here town thet ain't familiar with yer approach. Down on Main Street ya is now known as ol' double-clutcher." Pete smiled, tongued his toothpick.

"Well, it's plain to see the La Salle done bit the dust. Looks like yer total is $3,721.41. Now anyone else would have kinda rounded it off, say $3,700. Nosiree, not penny-pincher Pete. Ya got another $21.41 tacked on. I get the difference to furnish the Casa?"

"Ya have now got the picture, Effie ol' girl. When ya hit five big ones, thet's it. If'n I was you, I'd kind of fergit goin' ta some fancy furniture store. I'd take the Model A an' start goin' ta farm sales, foreclosures, check on bankrupt stock up in Denver. Now, Effie, ya be keerful 'bout freight, if'n ya make a purchase up in Denver, the U.P. don't haul thet stuff down here fer nuthin'. Another thing, don't take a single item outta this fine domicile. I am a-rentin' this place out fully furnished. Price done went ta $22.50 a month since we put in them facilities. It was nice the way Penelope paid fer the ditch diggin'. I shoulda nailed her fer the plumbin' fixtures. Vitreous china is shure expensive fer whatcha do to it come a-mornin'.'"

Effie continued to peruse the sheets, going down the list with her finger. All at once she stopped, looked up at Pete. "Why didn't you tell me you where charging for driving lessons? Right here I see you have $6.60 just for me and Daphne to go to Goodland when Penelope was in the hospital, when she had that nervous breakdown. My, you are a pistol, Pete."

"Not m' fault she lost her foot in the stirrup of life for awhile; ya was the one thet wanted to see her. Thet Terryplane don't run on hot air. If'n it did, ya'd blow 'er all by yerself. Ya kin go over them figures fer ever an' a day. I'm agonna read 'bout a fellow Kansan, Alf Landon, got nominated fer Republican candidate for President. Says here, Roosevelt and his New Deal programs has usurped the powers of Congress, flouted the Supreme Court an' violated the rights an' liberties of the people. Pshaw and a pituey on politics! I had politicians ranked first on m' list a crooks; now local banker done reached the first notch. Alf's all right; he ain't got a chance. Jest 'bout like yer La Salle, never had a chance."

Effie glanced fondly at Pete's Winchester .22 leaning in the corner. He'd taken it out of the Model A grain truck, quit shooting rabbits.

"It's gittin' close ta harvest. I bought me a new Massey-Harris twelve-footer combine. I got fifteen hunnert acres o' wheat ta cut; then we boys is goin' out custom cuttin'. How'd ya like ta come along, Effie ol' girl? Drive a grain truck, scoop wheat and ya could do the cookin'. Be kinda like a picnic, drivin' down the road ta the elevator with a load o' wheat, elbow out the winder, have on yer fawn mittens, be a double-clutchin'. I think ya'd kinda like it, Effie ol' girl."

"Nope, I'm in the mood to commence to decorate the Casa Del Sol. When you are finished harvestin', you'll have a pretty new home, not what I wanted, mind you, but better than this old dump."

"Effie, jest a suggestion, minda ya. Watch the *Denver Post* classified section. Look fer freight salvage sales, fire sales, cheap merchandise. Onct in a while you kin hit on a bankruptcy."

The next day Pete was standing by his new combine. He and Otis had everything on the combine and tractor all greased, and they were ready to go to work. He looked at Lyle, "Lyle m' boy, I'm gonna start over yonder, nice stand there, but I got me another idee, might put a few dollars in our pockets and the screws ta thet idiot banker. Ya said ya had a brother over in Thomas County, didn't ya?"

"Yes, Pete, a fraternity brother, not any kin. He is the Soil

Conservation Agent, lives at Colby; that is the county seat. Why are you asking?"

"Here's m' proposition. We git thet contract thet the Dibbs hat folks, ya recall, they was the ones with the permanent crease?"

"Yes, Pete, I remember the Dibbs Hat Co. What's your idea?"

"Let's us go over ta Colby, see yer friend an' fraternal brother. Tell them all about them rabbits, lucky foots, the whole she-bang. I'll git Simon ta draw up a codicil, you an' me will tell yer fraternal friend we want a flat ten percent right offen the top. Thet ten percent is what ya call a commish. Worked on straight commish up in Denver sellin' used cars once. Made a pile a money. I'll git Sadie Sobles ta write Dibbs with the permanent crease, we done had a slight delay, will let 'em know pronto. We cain't kill us any jackrabbits till November anyhow. We'll take the commish money and pay off Cletus's place ta Dink an' Dimples. Ya and thet school teacher kin make 'er legal like." Pete smiled, he knew he had a danderoo of an idee.

"Her name is Lillian, Pete. I think that is a great idea. When do you want to drive over to Colby?"

"Any time. Been tryin' ta figure out some way fer the county ta pay us mileage. Must be some kind of business a politician can think up to put hit ta the taxpayer so's he don't feel hit. We should git ta harvestin'. Wait until we have a rainy day, hit fer Colby."

"Why, Pete, we don't have any problem. We merely charge it to the federal government. We'll drive your Terraplane, and I'll turn it in on my monthly expense account."

Pete was dumbfounded! "You'ns got a expense account! I didn't know thet. Why, we could have bin usin' thet all the time. Yer holdin' out on me, why ya got yer snout in the trough all the way; I jest take a little dip onct in awhile." Pete smiled.

Arthur S. Angle, the conservation agent, the Colby State Bank and the Thomas County Commissioners bought the idea with a great deal of enthusiasm. The Rock Island Railroad agreed to a reduced freight rate. A.S. Angle was "Man of the Year" for Thomas County. There was a large and interesting write-up about local ingenuity in the *Kansas City Star* and the *Topeka Daily Capitol*. *Capper's Farmer* gave Arthur S. a trophy; he was "Jayhawker of the Year."

Pete mailed each article, accompanied with a note, to the People's State Bank, added a nice note to each tear sheet, "I tole ya so."

People in Greeley, Sherman and Wallace Counties wondered why someone in their locale had not thought of the idea. Pete and Lyle later received a check for $3,103.44. Pete called it his "commish." Lyle called it a consultation fee. No income tax was paid on this type of income. Lyle was sure Pete was "keerect" in his reasoning. They split the money.

"Ordinary income is taxable, Lyle m' boy. This is what is called extry-ordinary income. Onct in a lifetime income; thet makes hit non-taxable. Thet's what Simon says."

Things were slow at the courthouse. "Otis, when did ya last have someone in this here office ta pay their taxes?"

"It's been all of a month, I haven't been a-tall rushed. Why?"

"I got me a idee. We'll hang a sign on the door knob, 'Gone harvestin'. See Sadie Sobles fer information ta pay yer taxes.' We are goin' harvestin', put you'ns on the Wallis, me on the Massey-Harris an' Lyle drivin' one truck, Lil on the other. We got us fifteen hunnert acres o' wheat ta git in the bin."

Otis reached down, pulled the plug on the electric heater, put on his high-top shoes, an old hat, got a pair of gloves out of his desk drawer, and he was ready to go a-harvestin'. His pain was gone!

While driving the grain truck back and forth to the elevator, Lyle came up with the idea for a brochure, a fee for consultants on the objectivity of strip farming and no-till. "Pete, I have a plan for some more of that extra ordinary income. Would you like to hear my idea?"

Pete smiled; he was augering a bin load of wheat into Lyle's truck. "Why, it must be m' Jayhawker's Lucky Rabbit's Foot. Hit me with yer idee, Lyle m' boy."

"Your bin is empty, Pete, shut off the auger so you can hear me. We get Swede to come out to the T.T.T. & T., observe our new methods of farming. He would bring his camera and take a number of pictures showing our strip-farming, describe your method of no-till. Then right after harvest we'll go around to various counties and make speeches to the conservation agents and the farmers. Give a brochure to all the folks that attend. We'll charge $100 a meeting, plus expenses, or the conservation agents can take the money out of their expense accounts. We'll take Otis and pay him $5 a day just to keep track of our expenses. It would be just as you say, 'extry-ordinary income.' Swede will make us up a thousand or so brochures to pass out to the farmers. There'd be free eats at the meetings, just drive around the country. We'd have time to do this before we drill wheat later."

"You is a wonder! Ya done hit me right where I like it when ya mentioned thet extra-ordinary income. I never heerd thet word, brochure. Sounds like somethin' ya'd shovel outta the end of the cow barn onta a spreader. I think Lil likes ta drive thet Diamond T. Ya got a guess on what the wheat crop is gonna make this year, college boy?"

"Might make fifteen bushel. What are we going to do with our extry-ordinary income money from our seminars, Pete?"

"No trouble a-tall, put 'er in thet bank up in Cheyenne Wells. We'll bank by mail."

There you have it, folks, right there in a little county in western Kansas, banker that had no confidence in loaning a small sum for a venture enterprise that would have been profitable to one and all caused the seeking of a financial institution elsewhere. It started an entire new method of banking, "banking by mail."

Pete drove home in the Model A grain truck. "Well, Effie ol' girl, we is commencin' ta harvest. I'll git m' grip, put in a coupla pair a overhauls, shirts, some underclothes. I bought me a new hay hat. I don't know when I'll be back. Jest as soon as we git through cuttin' our crop, we's gonna go custom cuttin'. Yer gonna havta walk; we need the Terryplane. Now ya have a good time furnishin' the hut in the sun. I think I got this here domicile rented ta a coupla school teachers, so clean 'er up nice an' tidy like. Pride of ownership — thet's the key ta ownin' income propity. Renters take better care of it thetaway."

"You betcha, Pete. Pride is what ya possess. Pshaw! I sure am ashamed of this place; it's a real dump. When you get back,

I'll have pansies, petunias, phlox and pelargoniums blooming down at the Casa. Then you'll be proud of our wonderful home, proud of your possessions. Pity you don't appreciate me, Pete, it's a real pity." Effie was too pathetic, not too convincing.

"Yep, probably gives ya pat right on the pastern. Keep track of yer purchases. Tell them merchants ya want two ten, net thirty. I should be back in thirty days or so. Now remember we is now on a water meter; watch how much water ya use. No income from the rental propity 'til school commences this fall. We might run a little short with me out there combinin'. Bye." Pete picked up his .22 Winchester and departed from the "dump."

"Shame ya cain't git started combinin' early of a mornin'." Pete was sitting on the running board of one of the grain trucks. "How can it be so dry and still have a dew on them wheat heads of a morning. It does give us time ta git everythin' all greased up, Lil do the dishes an' make us a picnic lunch. What'd she say she fried yistiday, six Leghorns? Mighty good potato salad, iced tea an' a chunk a devil's food. I coulda done with some home-made ice cream. It was nice she got thet ice at the ice house on her way back from the elevator. She gave me a funny look when I mentioned thet one. We'll git her trained proper-like, jest like m' Effie. She's a peach of a person; say there, Lyle m' boy, when ya gittin' married?" Lil was one busy girl.

"Why, Pete, you haven't given us time to even make any plans. You have so many ideas, hopping from Colby to the bank, out here with the harvest. Rabbits and hats. I've given some thought to this custom-cutter business. We're going to have to have Otis or Lil scout ahead for us, select the right roads for travel."

"Why, I don't see a lick a-trouble. Jest git on the road an' commence ta goin' north. Foller the maturin' wheat, talk to them farmers thet has a crop."

"Bridges, there is our problem, Pete. Do you want to pull off the header every time we come to a bridge? We're way too wide for most bridges."

Pete thought they just might knock off the railin's and proceed; he didn't say it though. "Thet tis a problem, ain't it?

Let me ponder on this one. Me an' Otis got almost eighty acres yistiday by m' reckonin'."

Otis popped the Wallis; they combined until as late as they could. Pete could tell when it was time to quit. "She commenced ta lug." That was the engine on the combine; it began pulling too hard, wheat was getting damp. He gave Otis the signal to stop; they augered the wheat out of the combine bin into the Diamond T.

It was past nine when they got to Cletus's place, now Lyle and Lil's. Lil didn't sign her teacher's contract for next year; she hoped they would be married, at least when Pete said they could.

"Jest two more days an' we got 'er in the bin. How much ya calculate we hauled, Otis? Ya been keepin' track in yer double-entry?"

Every time the bin was full on the combine, Pete gave a hand signal to Otis to stop the tractor. Otis would take out a small notebook from his overall bib pocket and make a note of the amount of wheat. They knew the Diamond T hauled one hundred and twenty bushels, the Model A just ninety. "I figure just about 11,440 bushels so far; it's doin' better than we thought, Pete."

"Tamorra' mornin', while Lil hauls a load ta town we'll board up thet chicken house. We need someplace fer our seed wheat fer next year. What's Spence say down at the elevator, Lyle? Any comments on our wonderful crop?"

"He says it's a bit weedy, moisture content is fine, protein is right up there. He did tell me something interesting; he said everyone that followed your advice and strip-farmed had a crop of wheat. Those that didn't summer fallow was done for."

"Weeds come from the no-till. I knowed thet was gonna happen." Life for the wheat farmer is fragile. One year it might be hail, another rust, then there were the grasshoppers. Drought!

"Nice article about you in the *Western Times,* Pete. Swede was quite impressed with our farming, he even had your picture on the front page." Lil handed Pete the newspaper. "See there you are up on the combine, there's Otis on the Wallis. See that belch of smoke coming out of the exhaust on the Wallis. Otis must have ker-powed about the time Swede took the picture."

"Thet was sure nice of ya, Lil, ta bring us thet paper. Gives me a idee. Ya recollect them brochures, we could use some of them pictures an' article as proof positive of our strip-farmin' an' no-till methods. When we hit the speakin' circuit, we got local publicity. People like proof, proven prosperity. Give me 'nother baloney sandwich, Lil. Otis is puttin' fuel in yer truck."

Some headlines in the newspapers in October of 1936, they could be the same as today:

October 4 — "U.S. Imports Exceed Exports for the First Time in Ten Years."

October 16 — "Philadelphia: Hoover Charges False Accounts Conceal Huge Government Expenses!"

November 3 — "Pres. Roosevelt Won Re-election Today by a Landslide, Defeating Alfred M. Landon. The President Had 523 Electoral Votes, While Landon Captured Just Eight."

Pete had the answer. "I'd tell ya what ta do, jest elope. No fancy marriage, go over ta Hoxie, git a cozy little cottage an' then git the judge ta give ya the nuptials. Here's a ten spot as a weddin' present. Take the Terryplane; soon's ya git back, we'll commence to hit the speakin' circuit. I'll git the Wallis ready, Otis kin start drillin' next year's crop. I'm goin' home an' see jest what Effie has done ta the hut in the sun."

Pete nearly fell out of the Model A truck. The Casa Del Sol had pansies, petunias, phlox and pelargoniums blooming, and right there in the front yard, grazing on a little dab of blue grass were three big pink birds. Two had their heads down, seemed to be grazing; the other one seemed to have something else on his mind; he sure was watching, had one leg up, feller never knows. Pete walked over and saw they were cast iron. He pulled one out of the ground. A big metal spike held the pink birds upright; he thought they might be pelicans. Never had seen a bird like that before; they were kind of pretty.

Effie opened the screen door, "Them is flamingos, dummy. There are a house-warming gift from our fine neighbor, Daphne Damptowel. Ain't they lovely? Creates quite a stir for the evenin' drivers. They stop and stare."

Pete walked around the new home, viewed every room. Effie had done a fine decorating job, far better than he had ever expected; maybe it was the magazines. "What's thet box over there, got a little gauge at the top an' them buttons?"

"Why, Pete, that is a Majestic Radio. I can get the KOA in Denver real easy. Listen to Amos and Andy. At night I can get Del Rio, Texas, comes in real loud and clear. Get the market reports every day at noon, wheat's up a penny today." Effie, I gotta take off m' Triple X ta ya. Ya did a real fine job. Ya saved yer hide when ya put m' Navajo saddle blanket on m' favorite easy chair. Make a feller feel right ta home."

Pete walked over and kissed Effie right on the lips, a real smacker type. A sparkle came to Effie's eyes, "Why, Petey Pet, you haven't kissed me on the lips since, gosh, I guess it was when we was puttin' up hay down on the bijou. Those were the days. I recollect that new three-tine fork you bought for me. It was a long time ago, Petey." Pete thought it was a short distance from dummy to pet.

"I'm kinda tired, I'll jest sit down here in m' easy chair an' read the *Western Times*. Ya see m' picture in the paper, ya got any coffee?" Pete settled down, wiggled around like a dog does, figuring out just exactly where and how. Picked up the paper and there was a headline that attracted his attention. It read:

"RABBIT DRIVE PLANNED
FOR LABOR DAY WEEKEND

The Gabby Spinks ranch will be the scene of the largest rabbit drives ever held in the world this Labor Day. A half mile of corn-cribbing fence has been obtained from our local conservation agent, Mr. Lyle Lovelace. The corn-crib fencing will be in a quarter-circle, and all interested citizens will spread out and drive the pesky jackrabbits into the enclosure. The enclosure will be gradually closed as the rabbits are driven in. Once closed off, the mayhem and slaughter will begin. No firearms will be allowed. The method of killing the rabbits will be clubbing them to death with whatever method the populace chooses. This writer plans to use his trusty Louisville Slugger. The Methodist Ladies Aid and the Sharon Springs Sensation and Sensibility Club will serve delicious refreshments at a modest charge during the slaughter."

Pete sat there on the ol' Navajo saddle blanket, smiled. He wouldn't miss this for ten acres of ten-bushel wheat. "Sind a special invite to thet banker. I'm gonna cozy up ta him an' ever time a rabbit gits his brains knocked out, I'll holler: 'There goes $1.13, Mr. Banker, friend of the people.' "

Pete attended the rabbit drive, took a broken scoop-shovel handle for his club. He gripped the handle like a ball bat. He used it like a mashie-niblick. Pete's method was different than the other slaughterers. They darted all over, chasing rabbits. Pete just stood in one spot, like he was facin' Ol' Diz or Daffy. Rabbit come zig-zagging by, Pete nailed him for a single. Pete was kind of enjoying the sport until he took a good hefty swing that knocked a jack's head off. It sailed out toward center field, ears still flopping. He walked back to the refreshment stand.

"Gimme a glass a lemonade. Ya girls sellin' anything?"

The answer was as he had expected, "Haven't sold a thing. Sickening sight, isn't it? Look at your shovel-handle, Pete. It's all covered with blood and rabbit hair. No wonder we can't sell anything!"

"Have ya ladies seen thet new banker boy? He out here observin' this here mess?"

One of the ladies pointed and said, "He's over there, kind of hunkered down. Got ahold of the spare tire on that Essex. He's been tossing his cookies. Got the drys now. Such a shame, delicate tummy, I suppose."

Pete strolled over to the retching banker who was gasping for air prior to another spasm. "Does the same thing ta me. Gags me ta think they's about $4,000 worth of fine fur an' feets bein' clubbed ta death."

The banker looked at Pete, eyes pleading.

"Yessiree, I figured 'er all out one time. Takes one hunnert fourteen of them rabbits ta make a tub-a-guts, counted 'em."

The banker went "Ahrrggg!"

Pete tongued his toothpick over to the other side of his mouth, smiled — threw his mashie-niblick in the back of the grain truck and headed for town. "What a waste," thought Pete.

Pete remarked to Effie, "Lyle an' Lil finally made 'er legal like. They done tied the nuptial knot over ta Colby. We are gonna start makin' speeches at seminars all around western Kansas. Say, hits time fer an accountin' on this here hut in the sun. Ya got them bills all totaled up, double-entry style?"

"Knew you would be asking, there you are, penny-pincher, there's your total. I got it all typed up for you, had Lester Pester do it. I got it to within fourteen cents, close as I could get, Pete."

Pete raised an eyebrow, "Which way, over or under on thet fourteen cents? Makes a heap o' difference."

"Under. You owe me fourteen cents."

Pete reached in his pocket and took out his coin purse. Leather type, two snaps, then a large rubber band was wrapped around the rolled-up purse. This was an extra safety factor. Pete was reluctant to lose even a penny; he continued to fumble around with the purse. Finally Effie became impatient, "One would think it was fourteen thousand dollars, not fourteen cents. Just forget it, Pete."

Pete smiled. That had been his intention all the time. Odd how frequently a small purchase or a debt was forgiven or forgotten while one watched Pete fumble with the rubber band and the snaps on his coin purse. Over the years, it came to a considerable sum. Quite a few meals and hundreds of cups of coffee were fumbled by Pete's proven pattern and policy of patience. Pete heard a sound, kind of a muffled sound, like a bell ringing. Pete rose from his chair, ramrod straight, nose on the point. The bell ringing seemed to come from the kitchen, from a kitchen drawer?

Effie knew the jig was up; Pete had found it. She thought he would be out on the T.T.T. & T. or custom combining for longer than she had anticipated.

"I know thet sound! Ya done got yerself a telephone!"

Pete found the telephone in the drawer where all the tea towels were stacked, black telephone, one of those new styles, had the headset all attached, sat in a kind a cradle. "Hello, this is Pete Pisanmoan, yer Wallace County Treasurer, at yer service. May I hep ya?" Pete listened, smiled, winked at Effie. "Yep, she's here, Daphne, I'll put 'er right on. Don't be too long whilst I go out and git the fence pliers outta the truck, make a permanent disconnection." Pete handed the receiver to Effie.

She hadn't talked long before the phone went dead. An old saying: "Secrets are like meat; they can be frozen or eaten but not kept." Effie remarked, "I guess modern conveniences like a telephone weren't in the plans for the Casa Del Sol?"

"Ya got 'er, Effie ol' girl. Runnin' water, electricity an' indoor vitreous china is 'bout all one can tolerate at one time. Thet Daphne lives jest two door down the street; she coulda walked up here and give ya a message; a little exercise would do her good. She's a gettin' kind a hippy anyways."

"Kind of an important message. You'll like this, Pete. Daphne just heard from Penelope; she has gotten married to a chiropractor; name is Pomeroy Primm. Ain't that real nice, Pete? Penelope Primm, got a nice sound to it, Pomeroy and Penelope Primm, positively precious, Pete."

THE REAL ESTATE BROKER
Late 1936 and 1937

A SUBSCRIPTION TO ONE DAILY PAPER was all Pete Pisanmoan felt was necessary to keep up on the unraveling world of the late 1930s. As had been his custom for almost twenty years, the morning paper, *The Topeka Daily Capitol,* was perused at Borst's Barber Shop. It was a good paper, conservative, and it was free.

"I knew hit, Volney, jest knew it. Thet F.D.R. is gittin' all his free financial advice from some Englishman. Says right here, John Maynard Keynes has writ a book, 'The General Theory of Employment, Interest and Money." Says the book is the answer ta the riddle of our times. Ya know what a riddle is, Volney?"

"Rattle off what you think a riddle is, Pete."

"Git out yer dictionary, I know ya got one. This is where the shakers an' movers meet ta solve Wallace County's riddles. Let me peruse yer Webster's."

Volney took the dictionary out of one of the barber drawers, handed it to Pete. "Look under R, Pete. Want me to hold it out for you, you got your arms stretched out about as far as they'll go."

"Didn't think I could spell it, did ya, hit's the small print. Yep, here she is; listen to this defynition: 'Something proposed to be solved by guessing or conjecture.' Now ain't thet some way ta run a country like the U.S. of A! Run 'er by guess an' conjecture; thet's the way they is runnin' 'er, too! This article goes on ta say, 'His solution is to increase the money supply, thus lowering interest rates and stimulating investment. He also favors an active government fiscal policy of deficit spending on public works and an unbalanced budget ta increase aggregate demand for goods.' Thet's exactly the way I run m' T.T.T. & T. farmin' operation. The Pisanmoan Real Estate Title and Trust Co. I runs a unbalanced budget, an' they ain't no deficits. When Otis writes up thet financing statement, there'd better be a profit down there at thet bottom line; thet's the line, the bottom one, Volney."

"Pete, you are full of prodigious wisdom. Please expound some more; this is an interesting conversation we're having."

"Awright, Volney. Jest look at this here headline, right here on page two. Ya ready? Blow ya right outta thet barber chair!"

"Let 'er go, Pete. Please pile it on."

"F.D.R. says a third of the nation is underprivileged. One third of our nation is ill-housed, ill-clad, ill-nourished. Now the way I see it he is really sayin' food, clothing and shelter and most of them is sick ta boot. Ya agree?"

"That's just what he said; that's the way fellas that went to Harvard express themselves. Read on, Pete."

"If I know aught of the spirit and purpose of our nation, we will not listen to comfort, opportunism and timidity. We will carry on." Pete removed his Woolworth reading glasses, looked at Volney and explained, "Now what he is really a-sayin', Volney, is one out of every three folks in our great land is runnin' around in their underwear, no roof over their heads, a dried-up cheese sandwich ta eat and is sick. F.D.R. is full o' pathos, look thet one up in yer Webster's. Now I kin tell ya I would be mighty timid runnin' around in m' underwear with a dried-up cheese sandwich a-lookin' fer opportunity ta knock. I read a dandy description of a politician ta-other day. Wished I had it with me for ya ta read. Kinda recollect some of it; I got sech a wonderful memory. Ya wanna hear it?"

Volney smiled; this was going to be one of Pete's doozies. "I'm listening intently to the fascinating elucidation of the details. Please proceed, Pete."

"I'm pretty good at memorizin', Volney. Read onct 'bout a photogenic memory. You'll git the gist of the description. Goes like this: 'It was miraculous, almost no trick a-tall fer a politician ta turn vice inta virtue, slander inta truth, arrogance inta humility, plunder inta philanthropy, thievery inta honor, blasphemy inta wisdom, brutality inta patriotism an' sadism inta justice. It required no brains a-tall, merely required no character.' "

Volney was surprised, "Say, that is pretty darned good, Pete. When you find a copy of that saying, I'd like to put it up here in the shop. Put it up there on the wall with some of those other philosophical items that the public ponders when on the premises."

"Yeah, I see a coupla a them danderoos up there now. I like that one by the hat rack: 'Credit makes enemies. I want to be your friend.' Kind of a gentle hint ta thet one. Then thet one ya got over there by thet ash tray is a whiz-bang: 'Ladies may smoke, but be careful where ya place yer butts.' " Both men smiled; humor did not altogether disappear during the depression.

"I hear Penelope and her new spouse have come back to Sharon Springs, Pete. Have you perchance met the new groom?"

"Saw a light over at the nuptial garden o' Prune-Face the last coupla o' nights, but Pomeroy hasn't made his appearance ta the populace yit. I bin gittin' down ta the office pretty early, had a guy in here from Texas lookin' at some land. Oil money — I tend ta like thet kind o' money. I showed him a couple thousand acres of m' T.T.T. & T. ground, prime blow-dirt. He says they got thet kind o' land down in Texas, too. Said they was askin' one hunnert dollars an acre down in Texas; he didn't say they was gettin' it, they was askin'. I kinda laughed, told him seemed odd; thet's jest what our blow-dirt was a sellin' fer, too. He said oil money does thet ta the price o' land. Most always seems ta increase the value. I told him mine was different; the crop was included. Ya know, he jest might fall fer it. If'n he does, I make a quickie trip ta Denver an' the Colorado National."

"Do you know where the good Dr. Primm is going to open his practice? Anyone mention that to Effie?"

"Volney, I got some plans fer the Doc. I got thet used-car lot up by the Township Hall. Got 'er back when I had ta foreclose on ol' Hubcap. Nice brick buildin' on the back of the lot, make a fine office. I kinda figured if'n the office was way out back by the alley people couldn't hear the screams and the bones crunchin' when they had what them chiropractors calls a adjustmint. Be nice ta put thet property back in the Pinchlips-Primm family, 'specially at a tidy little profit. Prime property on Main Street is hard ta find. Had in mind 'bout $3,000 fer thet piece."

Volney kind of smiled, "Seems to me you paid twenty-five dollars to Penelope for that property. What is the reasoning for such an increase in profitability? Is this vengeance or greed?"

"Yer keerect, but there are many things to consider in real estate. We all know about location, there's a good location. One now has ta consider parking, got 'er, right on Main Street. Next is the improvements; them is de-luxe accommodations. I am followin' jest what thet Englishman Keynes said we was ta do, increase the money supply. I'm increasin' the supply o' money, mainly mine." Pete smiled.

"I have been hearing your Pisanmoan Real Estate Title and Trust office is kind of on the austere side. You need to look that one up in the Webster's, Pete?"

"Naw, I heard thet word a number o' times. It merely means I done 'er on the cheap side. I am a firm believer in what I calls low overhead. I found an old double desk down in the basement o' the courthouse, gave the commissioners five dollars fer it. Got me four foldin' chairs from upstairs in the Township Hall an' took the back seat outta a '28 Chevy fer the ladies; it's low but cushions tender posteriors. Got Otis ta keep his electric heater, gave him a addin' machine an' a cheap set a books. He does them books all double-entry 'cept when he's out farmin'. Sadie Sobles does m' typewritin' on her L.C. There ain't 'nother real estate office thet I know of thet is outfitted so economical."

"How did you talk the County Commissioners into letting you rent that cubby hole down in the basement of the Township Hall?"

"Well, Volney, they was lettin' the American Legions have 'er fer a dollar a year. Me an' Otis partitioned off a space twelve by twelve, an' I told 'em we'd fire the furnace fer free for the rent. Them American Legions only meet onct a month, the Sons the same, we don't bother one another. The only overhead I got is Otis's salary an' m' telephone. I hate thet thing, but a feller needs a telephone when he's in business."

"Who answers your telephone when Otis is out farming?"

"Thet is one overhead problem thet gave me the skitters. I

was 'fraid I'd miss a important call. I solved 'er though."

"How did you do that?"

"Volney, when a feller is in business, he has ta learn ta cut them corners; it was easy-like. I jest give central a ring-up when we leave the office. She takes m' calls, tells folks I'm out showing properties an' I'll ring 'em up when I git back."

There you have it, folks. Right there in Sharon Springs, Kan. A small town on the western Kansas plains was the very first telephone answering service, a service that saved on office overhead and was an entire new industry and service to the small businessman, all over our great ill-housed, ill-clothed and ill-fed nation. It was a wonderful idea for the small businessman who could not afford a private full-time secretary.

Volney inquired, "What's the name of this Texan you have on the hook, the one with your potential possibilities of wealth?"

"Name's Poindexter P. Pudlik, said people down in Potter County, Texas, jest calls him Pud. Nice sort of a fella, make a real contribution ta our fine community. Cain't be nuthin' wrong with a guy named Pud. I better git ta the office. Pud may be comin' in an' make me an offer on some T.T.T. & T. ground. I sure wouldn't wanna miss thet!" Pete headed up Main Street to the office.

"Mornin', Otis. How ya feelin' taday? Got any calls fer me?"

"Feelin' right in the pink, Pete. Effie called from Daphne Damptowel's, said for you to stay away from home. She's havin' a tea for Penelope and her new husband this afternoon. Says she wants to make a good impression, and you was to get lost. Pud called, said he'd be in about ten, said he wants to look at Sections 22 and 23 again."

"Why, Otis, this jest might be m' lucky day. Let's you an' me rub each other's lucky Wallace County rabbits' foots. I don't have ta go home; thet's m' first piece a' luck. Ol' Pud is about ta unload some of thet there oil money. Call out ta Lyle. Tell him we want the Diamond T ta drive out in thet blow-dirt. If'n I put thet sucker in compound she jest kinda chugs along. Cain't git stuck thetaway. Tell Lyle ta throw in a shovel. See ya got a piller on yer chair, yer hemorrhoids botherin' with this office work?"

"Yep, the wife says it's from ridin' that Wallis. I'm gonna git me a bunch of gunny sacks and make a cushion for the tractor seat. I'd never give up driving a tractor. Here comes ol' Pud."

Nice-looking fellow entered the real estate office. "Mornin', ya'll. Pete, I been thinkin' about them two sections of prime blow-dirt. What if I was to load up about ten cars of purebred Mexican hide an' hair and we was to winter 'em on that green wheat. It's up pretty good. They wouldn't pull it out by the roots. If it gets wet, we could run 'em over on that ground ya'll call go-back. There's grass a-plenty on that to hold 'em over. I'll send my Mex, Estaban, you furnish a saddle horse, he'll ride herd. Maybe we kin make a few dineroos."

"Thet's a good idee, Pud. We could arrange ta have thet Estaban stay down on Lyle's place. Lil would be downright happy ta cook some freejoles an' tamales. She's gonna have a little one come late January or February. Why, it's no trouble a-tall; ya be shure and git them wobbly-kneed cattle a dab o' grain or cottonseed cake afore ya hit them boxcars. We git a cold wind outta the north, and those southern's drop from the pneumoni in no time a-tall." Pete rolled his toothpick over to the other side of his mouth, smiled. He knew one didn't sell if one didn't ask. "Ya want I should have Otis draw us up a contract on them two sections at $75 an acre whilst we're out there lookin' 'em over for our livestock operations?"

"Yep. I like that land. Ya'll go ahead, Otis, draw up them contracts. We'll close on this here deal right after the first of the year. I got some tax problems; ya'll be sure and include them mineral rights on them contracts. I always want them minerals."

"Thet was a cash deal, warn't hit, Pud?" Pete was quite fond of cash deals, and he meant the green stuff.

"Why, Pete, that's the onliest way we Texicans deal, cash. How much ya'll want for pasture rent, Pete?"

"Make ya a deal, Pud pal. I'll give ya the pasture rent fer free, providin' ya give me the job o' combinin' yer wheat crop next summer. I charges a nickel a bushel on twenty-bushel wheat. If she runs less, it's a straight dollar a acre. Ya oughta pay Lyle an' Lil thirty dollars a month fer Estaban. Let's us git in yer Cadillac an' drive out ta Lyle and Lil's. We'll git the

Diamond T an' look at the finest 7,280 acres o' blow-dirt an' strip farmin' in the state of Kansas. Now I gotta warn ya, you'll see a few jackrabbits on the wheat. I bought a little bunch of 'em ta keep the weeds down." Pete slapped Pud on the shoulder as they went out the door, glanced back at Otis, wiggled his toothpick. Poor Otis, he had a terrible time keeping a straight face. Pete buying jackrabbits!

"I'll git Sadie ta typerwrite up this contract. Be all ready fer yer signature when we git back. Need a deposit, jest for good faith an' all. How much ya want ta show on the deposit?"

Pud didn't hesitate, "That's just fine. Do 'er, Otis. Make the deposit $10,000."

Pete thought to himself, "This Pud, he don't piddle around."

That evening Pete was pleased as punch, sitting there on his Navajo saddle blanket, reading the *Denver Post*. It was just a small article that caught his eye:

"Buchenwald: Fourth Concentration Camp. This camp was built according to the criteria of functional unity and capacity for political prisoners and homosexuals."

Pete pondered on the article, sounded phoney to him. It wasn't phoney to those that were in the functional unit, seemed like a yawner to the rest of the world. History records different.

Effie just seemed quite jubilant, "Our Sharon Springs Sensation and Sensibility Club Tea was a real success, Pete. I was sure glad you weren't there. You should have seen that Pomeroy hold a little china cup and saucer on his knee and a slab o' angel food on the other. He had a black suit, rosy-colored bow tie. Why, he looked jest like a Methodist minister come a-calling. It was easy to see he was a real gentleman. He'll be prosperous, too, not like you and that real estate office. My, that is a real pitiful place."

"Yer sure right there, Effie ol' girl. Kinda like thet used car lot, not much on the money makin', but one gits ta palaver with the populace. Kinda odd, ain't it, ya got the only new house in town since about '28." Pete knew that would put a crimp in any further conversation from Effie. He scooched down in the saddle blanket. He had ten one-thousand-dollar bills in his kick, a signed contract up at the office for 1,280 acres of real western Kansas blow-dirt, a $96,000 deal. He was one pleased real estate man. "Did the Doc say anything 'bout a office fer his bone-crushin' an' muscle stretchin'?"

"I did tell him you was in real estate, kind of a dibbler and a dabbler. He said he'd heard so much about you, he was gonna drop by the real estate office tomorrow. Courtesy call was what he said. Now you be nice to him, Pete."

"Thet's too bad 'bout tamarrow. I'm gonna make me a quickie trip up ta Denver. Need ta see Simon on some business. Be back in a coupla o' days. Mention ta him them lots an' thet nice little brick buildin' right next door ta the Township Hall. Perfect fer him, only $3,500 cash. He kin git the key from Otis, peruse the property, make a perfect place fer his practice."

"Penelope made it quite clear Pomeroy was to be called Doctor and not Doc. Said she found the word Doc offensive. I told her I was pretty sure you'd call him Doc. She said you was about the most offensive person she knew, so guess it will be all right. Did you know the good Doctor makes house calls? Why, he went back to the house and got a foldin' table. He set it up right here in our living room. Penelope got right up on that table; he gave her an adjustment right before our very eyes. He threw a head-lock on her and grabbed one of her legs and gave a big grunt. Penelope said one of her garters came unhooked. She said that was how she met Pomeroy, had a house call. Sounded like she had quite a few of them."

Pete tongued his toothpick, flicked it a little, smiled. He could see some fun and games in the near future. "He sounds real perfessional. Where'd he go ta school ta learn how to unsnap them ladies' garters?"

"Somewhere's in Missouri. Why, he even sells medicine, too, and one doesn't even need a prescription. He gave some to all the ladies at the meeting. Gave out some Pennyroyal Pills, a real reliable monthly pill. Most of us don't need 'em any more, but some of the younger women grabbed 'em right up. I got me a small bottle of Piso's Remedy for catarrh. I got it for you, notice you been hawking up a wad now and then since we had them dust storms and you went to farmin'."

"Bet he had him a little black suitcase fer all his wares. Handy ta take along on them house calls when he uses thet foldin' table. Bet if'n a feller took a good slug of thet Piso's Remedy he'd fergit all about his catarrh."

"Now how'd ya know thet about the suitcase, Pete. He sure did, had some other stuff in it. I bought me a big jar of Malvina Lotion fer my liver spots. It says on the bottle it's for salt rheum, dandruff, scaly eruptions and all other diseases. A number of the ladies bought Dr. F.A. Sabin's Indian Vegetable Tea. It's a cathartic and blood purifier. The good doctor said this tea was mild and pleasant. Adapted to the different diseases of delicate females and little children. Such a professional personage, proud to have him and Penelope for our neighbors, kind of a feather in my social cap."

"The Doc didn't mention nuthin' 'bout snake oil, did he?"

"No, Pete. He just had that little suitcase full of various helpful remedies. He'll be a real boon to the community. Say, I heard you been ridin' around in a Cadillac with some Texican. Heard you even popped for his dinner up to Mollie's Cafe. You must have a hot one for you to be poppin' for some odd-wad's dinner. Did you perhaps sell him some blow-dirt?"

"Nope, but he's lookin' at thet prime property right next door ta the Township Hall, the piece I mentioned fer the Doc. This here Texican is a auctioneer, name's Pud, prince of a person. He's gone back ta Potter County. He'll probably make me an offer on them lots and thet nice brick buildin' in a week or two. He had him a big sale ta cry down in Texas, big foreclosure."

It was several days later when Pete walked in to the real estate office. "How was your trip to the Mile High City, Pete? Did ya see Simon, what'd he say?"

"Had a good trip, Otis. I got them ten big ones in the bank an' had me a visit with Simon. We talked a tad 'bout how to handle the tax problem on the sale o' them two sections. Good to have sound legal advice when ya got tax problems. We close thet deal after the first of the year. Simon says ta pay a commish ta Pisanmoan Real Estate o' five percent, then Pud writes a check ta T.T.T. & T., they's the seller. I give ya a $1,000 bonus outta Pisanmoan Real Estate Company, an' thet leaves T.T.T. & T. with a profit of jest a tad under $90,000. Jest 'nother one o' them extry-ordinary income deals, same as yer commish; it's all non-taxable. How's thet sound ta ya?"

Otis smiled, "Sure beats workin' at the courthouse."

"Did ya git them abstracts over ta the County Attorney? They need brought ta date an' git an opinion."

"I plumb forgot where they was, found 'em in the Treasurer's office safe. You got a whole bunch o' abstracts in that safe, Pete. I figured 'er out; after this sale ta Pud you still got about 6,000 acres in the T.T.T. & T."

"Yer close, Otis. Comes ta 6,240 acres, jest short a ten sections. Bought 'er all on back taxes. Did the Doc come in an' wanna look at Hubcap's old sales office while I was in Denver?"

"He sure did, liked 'er. He's a pretty nice sort of a guy fer hookin' up with Penelope. He tried to sell me some powder for m' arthritis. Said he'd give me a free adjustment, see if it would help. Said he'd be back, thought you a mite high on the price. He wanted a concrete sidewalk back to the office for his patients."

"I ain't a-tall keen on a concrete walk. I might slap a coupla two by twelves down fer the patients ta plod on. Glad ya liked him. Yer a good judge o' character. Bet he's got one of them snap-brim Dibbs hats, shoes polished ta a sheen. Delicate hands, a pompadour haircut all slicked down with some kind a grease, probably rose pomade. He got a little dab a moustache, jest a little tickler?" Pete flicked the toothpick, smiled.

Otis couldn't believe the description, "Golly, ya must have seen this guy somewhere, Pete. You got him right down pat!"

"Ya think he sings soprano, kind o' pansy-like, Otis?"

"Nope, he's no soprano. I got a hunch he's bin around a bit. Put the two of ya tagether and ya'd have a real pair, Pete. This Doc ain't no nit-wit."

Pete pondered Otis' appraisal. Seemed like Pomeroy might be a personality. The meeting of the two gentlemen was perhaps happenstance. Pete was coming out of the post office, and Doctor Primm was walking down the steps of the People's State Bank. He seemed rather preoccupied, perhaps petulant.

Pete walked right over and stuck out his hand. "Doc Pomeroy Primm, I presume. I'm yer neighbor an' local real estate broker, Pete Pisanmoan." Pete's smile was genuine, surprised the good doctor.

"Very pleased to meet you, Pete. I've heard a lot about you. Seems like you are quite a character. You appear to be a man I'd like for a friend. Might even do a little business with you. I looked at that lot with that pile of bricks out in back your man Otis described as an office."

"Otis tole me ya'd been in, had looked at thet prime piece o' property. Ya know the ol' rule o' real estate an' business. It's location an' location. Thet's exactly what a man new in practice of chiropractical medicine needs here in this here paradise on the plains. I don't know, ya might be jest a tad late. I got me a Texican auctioneer considerin' the property, cash deal."

"Let us walk up the street and look at that property. Penny, that is what I call dear Penelope, Penny informed me she owned that property at one time. Said her dear dead daddy, Palmer Pinchlips, gave it to her. She said you kind of snookered her out of it. I have a difficult time believing her after meeting you. Maybe perchance you merely stole it from her in some devious manner." Pomeroy smiled; it took the sting out of the word stole.

"Not a-tall, Doc. It was merely a series of circumstances thet prompted the purchase of this prime property. Thet's all in the past. Ya kinda seemed ta have yer dauber down when ya came outta the bank. Ya have a problem, Doc?"

"Why, yes, I do. I had some difficulty with the banker. I merely wished to borrow a small sum to tide me over until I could get my practice started. The man turned me down flat, said he needed considerable collateral. I mentioned this previously to Penny and inquired if she might perchance slap a small mortgage on her perky little bungalow. She said it is all in a trust and that some attorney over in Goodland doles out the dollars at his discretion. It's downright disturbing. I was given to understand she was a woman of considerable means."

Pete rolled his toothpick over to the other side of his mouth, smiled. His presumption of Pomeroy Primm was correct. The mere mention of the bank and the president of said institution could cause the gold toothpick to give the rattler's flick.

Pomeroy became disturbed. He'd never seen this type of oral action before.

"Some folks think of a bank as men, stockholders are their

friends an' neighbors. Not true a-tall. Every man in a bank hates what a bank does. A bank is somethin' more than men. It's a monster. Men make a bank. They jest cain't control it. Young fella came up ta me ta other day, borried a thousand. I knowed his family all m' life. Family is old-timers. His grandpa fought injuns, his pa fought rattlesnakes. This young feller is determined ta fight banks. He's gonna kill banks. Dynamite 'em or rob 'em. Thet's what he said, I think I talked him outta it. Otis says ya want a sidewalk back ta thet fine little buildin'. Why, it's perfect fer ya, Doc. Two by twelves would be the answer, put 'em down on thet bed a cinders, perfect fer yer pedestrian patient. I am well acquainted with thet attorney over ta Goodland. Name's Sylvester Beatum. Me an' him been matchin' wits fer years. Right now I'm one up on him. He's known as Sly Syl in these here parts. Imagine ya will have ta make his acquaintance right soon, Doc P. Now take a good gander at thet peach of a buildin'."

"Yes, Pete. I am partial to the location, but I have a problem. The building is not my immediate problem. I have a large C.O.D. coming rather soon, need a small pile for the purchase. A nominal sum, a mere pittance when one considers the profit potential that is involved. Two hundred dollars would cover the purchase quite nicely, Pete."

"Tell ya what I might do fer ya, Doc. I'll sell ya these lots an' thet prime brick buildin', put in a two-by-twelve walkway an' take back a first deed o' trust on these lots and Penny's pretty, perky little bungalow fer a mere $3,750. Charge ya a piddlin' ten percent per annum interest, an' she's all due an' payable in jest a year. Thet give ya time ta set up yer practice, peddle the patent remedies, an' ya will be sittin' right back there in thet brick buildin' watchin' the money roll in."

"Why, you are a real peach of a fellow, Pete. A prince, yessiree, a real prince. I shall go home and present this idea to my Penny."

"I thought ya'd like 'er, Doc. Soon's as ya decide, we'll spit and shake on 'er."

Doctor Primm gave Pete a questioning glance, the idea seemed both unsavory and unsanitary. "We shall get together in a day or two. Much obliged, Pete."

Pete went around on the north side of the Township Hall and downstairs to the Pisanmoan Realty and Trust. "Whatsa matter, Otis? Ya look kinda puny, pale-like complexion?"

"We got us a problem, Pete. Godalmighty, have we got us a problem."

"What kind of a problem, Otis?"

"You recollect how you bought them two sections from Penelope? You had that Sylvester Beatum draw up them warranty deeds; that was when she went berserk. You bought them two sections for only $500?"

"Thet's keerect, proceed with the problem."

"Well, Pete, ol' Sylvester put 'er to you. That Penelope and the Pinchlips Trust still owns all them mineral rights on them two sections. Sly Syl has been paying those mineral-right taxes every single year. The taxes are only two dollars and fourteen cents a year. They are paid right up to date. Here's the kicker; that contract with Pud says specifically the mineral rights was to be included. Attorney's opinion came in today."

Pete paled. "I gotta think on this a day 'er two. You is one hunnert percent keerect. We have done got us a prodigious problem. I'm gonna probe around a little. I'll git me a answer; now don't ya worry none, I'll git 'er figured out."

Pete decided he'd walk home, get the Model A grain truck and drive out and see Lyle and Lil. He'd buy a pile of pork chops for supper. Lil was a good cook. He needed to tell them about the new boarder and hired hand that was coming up from Texas to winter with them. Pete didn't waste much time with Effie; she was having two tables of bridge that afternoon. He merely told her he'd be gone a day or two. "Goin' out ta see Lyle an' Lil, check the wheat stand and get a decent meal."

It came to him on the drive out. Why, there was no problem, no problem a-tall. "I'll trade the Doc a sidewalk fer them mineral rights. "If'n I havta, I'll pick up thet C.O.D., git him ta peddlin' his potions to the populace, unsnap a few garters." Now that that problem was solved, he could enjoy his stay with Lyle and Lil.

It was really rather odd, but this young couple really did like Pistol Pete. That's what they called him.

"Didja git any calls whilst I was out ta Lyle an' Lil's, Otis?"

"Nothing much of importance. Pud called, has over four hunnert head of ratty-assed Mex steers on feed. Said he had 'em dehorned, dipped and was feedin''em ground corn cobs and a dab o' cottonseed cake. Said they was gainin' about six ounces a day. He's shippin' them around the first of the month. He ain't comin', jest Estaban. Said he'd be here around the 15th of January to close the deal. The Doc was in late yesterday, said he'd been over to Goodland with Penelope. Told me to tell you the news wasn't so hot. He'll be in today."

Pete smiled, tipped his Triple X back on his head. "I kinda figured Sylvester would find Pomeroy not ta his likin'. Sly Syl is a purty good jedge o' character, and thet Doc is a character. Takes one ta know one, I always said when I was dealin' in used autymobiles."

Otis smiled.

The good doctor came into the real estate office and plopped down on the '28 Chevy seat, seemed dejected.

"Ya look like ya need ta have yer pump primed, Pomeroy. Ya gotta git thet practice commenced, sell them potions and powders. Ya got a wife ta pervide fer now; it was a act a providence thet brought ya and Penelope the nuptials. Why, ya two was made fer each other."

Doc Primm smiled and looked wanly up at Pete, not much to say. "I heard you were the one that taught Effie how to drive that Terraplane, heard you charged her for the lessons, took the money out of her household building account."

"Thet's keerect, Doc. Ol' double-clutcher, we call her. Why ya askin'?"

"She drove Penny and me over to Goodland yesterday, said you were out on some land with a lot of T's in it. I never saw so much double-clutchin' in my entire life. I rode in back, precious Penny rode in front. We came to those Rock Island tracks over in Goodland, and Effie double-clutched over every track, said you had instructed. She said if she didn't the spare tire would fall off or some such ridiculous statement."

"Yessiree, I was her perfessional instructor, but I had me a reason. I thought if I made hit complicated 'nuff she'd give up the idee of drivin'. Hit didn't work; she have on her fawn drivin' gloves?"

"She certainly did. I noted the palms were damp. Pete, I may have to take you up on that loan to start my practice. That attorney was quite blunt on any advance on my pretty Penny's allowance. I fully explained she was receiving a mere pittance, but I got no pity from that posturing attorney."

"Well now, Doc ol' buddy, I got me a propyshishion thet I don't see how ya kin hardly pass up. Yer precious Penny has some mineral rights on Sections 22 and 23 down in Harrison Township. I bought them two sections from her long time ago. Now I'll jest loan ya the money fer them powders and potions thet's comin' in on the C.O.D., put in a concrete walk back to thet perfessional office and ya git her ta deed me them mineral rights. How's thet strike ya? I ain't bin this generous fer a long time." Pete smiled.

The good doctor kind of struggled to get up off the car seat. "Why, that sounds excellent to me. I'll just walk home and discuss this with pretty Penny, give you a call just as soon as I have her approval. Do you have the deeds ready for her to sign?"

Otis was quite quick to answer, "Yessiree, Doc. Right here on my desk. Had Sadie Sobels type 'em all up, everything's all legal like."

It was thirty minutes later when the telephone rang. Otis answered; he cupped his hand over the telephone. "It's Central says Penelope called Goodland on the long distance, talked to Sly Syl. Looks to me like the fat's in the fire. Seems he told Penelope not to sign anything until he could come over. She and Pomeroy are not to see or speak to you at all. That's all she heard when she had to disconnect from rubberin'. Whatcha plan ta do, Pete?"

"Nuthin', they's not a thing I kin do. All m' fault. I shoulda read them deeds afore Sylvester took 'em down fer Penelope ta sign an' git 'em recorded. Otis, never trust a lawyer. I knowed thet all m' life, lawyers and bankers. I jest gotta wait, thet's all I kin do is wait."

Patience and waiting were not two of Pete's finer attributes. He was a man of action. There had been exceptions, that delay in the installation of sewer and water on the rental property was an easy wait. This type of waiting was difficult. Pete was kinda dejected. It was three days before Sylvester

Beatum walked into the office of the Pisanmoan Real Estate Title and Trust. As always, Sylvester was nattily attired. Five X Stetson, gabardine suit, kind of a mauve color, pair of square-toed Justins. Pete thought he looked like a Congressman from the 7th District in Texas.

Sylvester extended his hand, friendly handshake. "Well, Pete Pisanmoan, good to see you again. It has been a while. I understand you have your ass back in that crack again. Just seems like I have to drive over from Goodland every year or so for an expensive extraction. It did take longer than I had anticipated for my small ploy to work. The omission of those mineral rights in that warranty deed was pure law, ethical law, prudent, too. Don't you think it quite proper, Pete?"

Pete agreed.

"Pete, I have been a busy man, law profession prospers when there are folks such as you around and about. Have everything right here in my briefcase; it won't hurt too bad after the initial shock wears off. It will tend to keep you on your toes in the future. First, I have a deed to the property right next door; note the deed is to Penelope Pinchlips Primm. I have a check for the sum of $25 as consideration. That's what you purchased the property for, and you were able to write off all those taxes you paid while you owned it, so there is no loss nor gain. Secondly, as a gesture of good will, you will see that a three-foot-wide concrete sidewalk is poured for Dr. Primm. I have the proper signed mineral rights deed from Penelope to T.T.T. & T. I had to look that up over at the courthouse; I wanted to make sure you didn't have some other name on the title by now. Never know which way you might jump, Pete. There is one last little item, my legal fee. I shall call it the Pisanmoan ass-removal-from-crack fee. It's just a mere $100, and I would prefer it in cash. That's just for old times sake. Sound all right, Pete?"

"Jest 'bout what I expected. Yer not worth what ya think ya are, but I do enjoy doin' business with ya, Sylvester. Thet cash is what I calls extry-ordinary income. Jest show me where ta sign. Otis, git a hunnert smackeroos fer ol' Syl, take these here deeds over ta the courthouse and git 'em recorded pronto. There's the phone; git it, Otis."

Otis answered the phone, looked up at Pete. "It's John Ley down at the depot. There's ten carloads o' cattle at the stockyards, says the way-bill has your name on it."

Kingfish Says FDR Policy Is Mishmash

July 25 — In another verbal assault on President Roosevelt, Senator Huey Long of Louisiana announced he would desert the Democratic Party in 1936 if FDR refused to drop his New Deal program.

"I won't hesitate to bolt the Roosevelt New Deal convention," the Kingfish said yesterday, "unless he stops deliberately perverting the course he promised the people to follow."

Long called the President a "faker" without a "sincere bone in his body." He continued to advocate his "Share-the-Wealth Plan" as he mixed drinks for members of the press behind the bar of the Hotel New Yorker.

(The senator assumed bartending responsibilities, claiming no one in the city knew how to mix a gin fizz.)

Predicting revolution if conditions did not change, Long characterized the New Deal as a "combination of Stalinism and Hitlerism, with a dash of Italian Facism."

The Louisiana dictator repudiated notions that his own program reeks of fascism.

— Washington Post, July 25, 1935

Huey Long Assassinated in Baton Route

Sept. 10 — Senator Huey Long died today after doctors conducted a third blood transfusion in a last ditch effort to prolong his life. The Louisiana dictator was gunned down Sunday night by Dr. Carl Weiss, a leader of an anti-Long faction and son-in-law of Judge B.H. Pavy, also an opponent of the senator. Weiss shot Long in the stomach just outside the chambers of the Louisiana House of Representatives.

—Globe Democrat, Sept. 10, 1935

ESTEBAN

THE CATTLE FEEDER

PETE PISANMOAN SAT in his easy chair, kind of snuggled down in his Navajo saddle blanket, cold evening. He only allowed one scoop of Hayden Lump coal an hour. He was reading the *Denver Post* and perusing the editorials. "Evenin' paper, Effie. Listen ta this: 'U.S. Census Shows Nearly 8 Million Jobless.' I see thet don't even count them's that's on the W.P. and A's. Why, thet's another two million, an' they's as close ta bein' unemployed as anyone I know. Now here's 'nother one. 'Hitler Promotes Himself to Military Chief.' Thet there is dictatorship. They's a war a-comin', Effie ol' girl. We done sint Piedmont over ta France, got rid of the Kaiser. Now it's gonna be Phillip and Portney. We got our grandkids in another war. Thet means wheat an' cattle is gonna go sky high. The Bar P jest might start makin' a profit an' we kin quit tailin' up Piedmont and Flo. Here's 'nother one. 'Mexico Takes All Oil. Mexico has seized 17 American and British oil companies, representing a $450 million investment.' Our dumb government don't do nuthin'. I'm a-gonna kick thet Estaban right in his oil can. I kin do somethin' ta hep the cause."

"I heard about them lively Mex cattle ya put out to pasture. Folks say they was so skinny they hardly cast a shadow. They your cattle, Pete?"

"Pshaw, Effie. They belongs ta m' friend down in Potter County, Texas, ol' Pud Pudlick. He's a auctioneer. He was gonna buy m' property up by the Township Hall, felt sorry fer Pomeroy. Now he's got him a practice, sellin' powders and potions, snappin' ladies garters. He needed to git away from thet Penelope; I sold him the Terryplane. He needed transportation fer his country calls, double his income if'n he'd make country calls. Bought me a new International truck, lotta power in a International. We needed hit fer the header on the combine when we git out custom cuttin', come harvest time."

Pete tongued his toothpick over to the other side of his mouth, smiled. He scooched down in his Navajo and hid behind the *Denver Post*. Waited.

"You done what!! You sold my transportation right out from under me so you could buy another truck! If you was successful at that real estate business, you could afford to get me a nice automobile. You are really a pistol, Pete!"

"You'll jest havta git ya a pair o' patent leather pumps and plod around like any other pedestrian. Plumb pitiful, ain't it?"

"You sure are good at them pithy phrases, Pete. Couldn't you just get me a little puddle-jumper, something I could putz around town in, go grocery shopping, visit my friends over on the south side?"

Pete was not overly enthusiastic, "Let me see how the wheat crop turns out. Maybe then I could put up a few bucks fer a used car. Say, lookie here at the sports section. Why, them crazy Cards done traded ol' Diz to the Cubbies. Ol' Diz, he's m' kind a guy, earthy sort of a fella."

The next morning at the barber shop, "Better have a shave, Volney. I gotta ton a work ta do, check on them Mex steers."

As Volney eased the chair down in the reclining position, he commented, "I heard you were now in the cattle feeding business. You must feel this a profitable venture. I never saw you do anything just for fun."

"I don't own them steers, they's Pud's. I done made m' nest egg, at least a part of it. I sure snookered the U.P. on some fine Flint Hills hay ta other day. Them bales was wire-tied. Musta weighed a hunnert pounds apiece. I asked the agent when them steers was fed and watered. He told me up at Kit Carson. I gave 'em twenty bales. Them steers ate that hay in five minutes, it jest kinda warmed 'em up. Thet Mexican, Estaban, he cain't speak a word a Kansas. I askt him a question, he smiles an' says 'Si.' I sint Otis down ta the section house an' got Manzanita Gonzalez. He was m' interpreter. Asked him why ol' Pud sint 'em early. He tole me they ran outta cobs; then I sint Otis up ta the depot. Asked John Ley if we could hold them steers fer a day 'er so. He said it was O.K. Hay was in a boxcar, spotted on the rip-track. We commenced ta haulin' thet Bluestem up ta them steers. We used m' Model A grain truck, hauled 'em four ton. I tole Manzanita ta tell Estaban ta sleep in the hay car. I took him down a peanut butter an' jelly sandwich along 'bout nine; he was squattin' in the hay car with a blanket over his shoulders. Them steers was all a-layin' down an' cuddin'."

Volney glanced out the front window. "I see you drove up in a new pickup, an International, pretty spiffy number. Did you trade in the Terraplane?"

"Naw, I peddled 'er, ya recollect I was in the used car business. I know m' autymobiles. I sold it ta m' new neighbor, Doc Primm. He needed some reliable transportation when he goes out ta the country ta make them adjustmints. Thet Terryplane was a problem, I knew the clutch was goin' out, them tires was bald from Effie double-clutchin' and spinnin' them wheels. It was usin' a quart a oil ta the hunnert. Had a bint drive shaft, thet car was kapoot."

"Seems kind of an odd way to treat a new neighbor. You did say reliable transportation, didn't you, Pete?'

Twinkle in his eye, Pete replied. "Reliability is an odd kind o' word, controversial. I am fully relyin' on thet Terryplane breakin' down most any time. I got a nice check from over ta Goodland fer thet automobile, $500, a good price. Pickup truck cost me $725 with them overloads. Built like a tank. I put twenty bales of thet U.P. hay in 'er when I took thet Tex Mex his sandwich. Them springs hardly bent a-tall. Took them bales out ta Lyle an' Lil's. It was kinda hard on m' herny."

"You getting even, Pete? Is there vengeance involved, bad blood?"

"Pshaw, Volney, not vengeance, let's us jest call hit perseverance. I shall persevere, need ta nail a barrister's hide ta a partition. We got a huckster playin' hocus-pocus with the public. He's a snappin' them garters. I plan ta warn the hoipoiloi. Got a odd-wad pillagin' the public, powders an' potions."

Volney thought it best to change the subject. "How did those steers adjust to the trail out to the ranch? Were they wild?"

"I had planned on a tub o' trouble. I had Otis git a ton o' cottonseed cake, drive ahead of the herd. He'd toss out a scoop o' cake ever now an' then. Them cattle jest grazed along in the bar-pit. Why, they was no trouble a-tall. Estaban rode drag with his riata and bull-whip. Godalmighty, kin thet Mex use thet bull-whip. I had Lyle an' Lil out ahead of us at the crossroads. Thet was ta keep the leaders from turnin' up the wrong road. No trouble, no siree, no trouble a-tall." Pete smiled, good cowman.

"How did those steers like that wheat pasture? Is it the first time to graze wheat? Did they settle down?"

Pete was proud of the progress. "Why, they nonchalanted 'er, Volney. Thet was m' plan when I filled them steers up with thet Blue Stem. They nibbled around on the wheat and began layin' down. They was tired Joses. I left Estaban with the herd, tol' Lil ta make him a peanut butter and jelly sandwich, an' me an' Lyle began buildin' feed bunks fer grain, git some weight on them."

Volney was curious, "What did you use for lumber? I didn't see you or Lyle haul any material out that way."

"Why, Volney, ya jest don't understand economics. First we tore out the stanchions outta the milk barn. Then we tore out the horse stalls. As fast as Lil could straighten them nails we'd git us a bunk built. I figured twenty head ta a bunk. We built us twenty-five. We gotta git some meat on them steers."

"What's your hurry? You have plenty of pasture, Pete."

"Pud tole me they was gainin' six ounces a day. Why, thet's downright pitiful, a mere pittance. At thet rate o' gain thet means they'd gain two and a half pounds a week or 'bout a hunnert and thirty pounds a year. A feller would havta keep them suckers 'til 'bout nineteen hundred and forty-six afore ya could butcher. Pud only paid two dollars a head fer them steers. I'm a-gonna build a feed lot outta some of them abandoned buildin's on the T.T.T. & T. ground. I hear they got a fair ta middlin' corn crop up at Cheyenne Wells, Colorady. When the critters come offen wheat pasture, they kin go right in the feed lot. I got in mind ground corn, maybe somethin' else fer fiber. Probably run some sunny-flowers through the hammermill, thet makes 'em ruminate better, slick 'em right up, ready fer slaughter."

There you have it, right there in a little county in western Kansas at the late stages of the drought and the depression and before the world decided to commence killing each other, a farmer, a former conservation agent and his pregnant wife started the very first feed lot in the entire state of Kansas. It was a prime idea, produced prime beef and was profitable.

Volney whipped the cloth off Pete, slapped his face with some witch hazel and tilted up the chair.

"Put a dab o' Lucky Tiger on m' locks, Volney. I gotta go over ta Toll's grocery, git a quart o' peanut butter, big jar o' jelly an' a couple loafs o' bread. Lil says thet Estaban jest 'bout wolfs them sandwiches down. He's one hungry cowpoke."

"I'll give you a little advice, Pete. I think you are feeding the Mex steers better than you are your Mex cowboy. You're liable to be leadin' ol' Paint and ridin' ol' Sam if you don't treat that Estaban better in the grub department."

"Volney, yer keerect, absolutely keerect. I gotta see Manzanita. I don't know what ta feed thet Estaban. I know they like goat meat; I might git him a goat ta butcher, cost 'bout fifty cents. See ya."

Volney watched Pete pace across the street for his provisions; he's a pistol.

Pete, Otis, Lyle and Lil were sitting at the supper table. Pete always brought three or four pounds of pork chops from town. "Yer a mighty fine cook, Lil. Gravy seems ta be yer specialty. Effie's always has the consistency o' wallpaper paste, includin' the lumps. When ya took thet peanut butter an' jelly sandwich out ta ol' Estaban, did ya notice them steers a-scourin' on thet green wheat, Lyle m' boy?"

Poor Lil, she jumped up, went out the back door.

"Guess them greasy pork chops got ta her. She got the mornin' sickness?"

"They seemed just fine, Pete. I'm beginning to be concerned with Estaban; he doesn't look very good. I think he's getting constipated on all that peanut butter. Perhaps we should send someone to town, talk to Manzanita regarding a proper diet."

"Volney mentioned thet. Yer probably right, Lyle. Spect he's plugged. He sure did like thet first sandwich I took him down ta the stockyards; I thought he was partial ta peanut butter an' jelly. Bet Doc Worminger would have somethin' to git him goosey-loosey."

Lil had just come in the door, heard the conversation and whirled around and went outside again. Pete had forgotten, been a long time since Effie was pregnant with Piedmont.

"Guess Lil's got a bad case of the skitters. I got me a idee, Otis. Ya take the Diamond T ta town tonight. Go over ta the section house and see Manzanita, tell him all about our dietary problem. I think thet Manzanita has a little sis, 'bout seventeen or eighteen. Git her ta come out an' cook fer ol' Estaban; she could perform various and extry sundry duties. We got us a contented Mex, them steers is gainin' weight. Thet girl kin hep Lil. Ol' Pud'll be mighty proud when he sees what we done with his ratty-assed steers. Then tamarraw, I want ya ta take the Diamond T up ta Cheyenne Wells, git a load o' ground corn. We'll commence jest a little light feedin'. I'll write ya a check on the Cheyenne Wells Bank. Bring the girl back with ya with the corn.

"I got it, Pete," Otis said. "We'll need us a tarp to cover the ground corn."

"Yer absolutely right, thet's a tax-deductible item. Git us a good one. Be sure an' git a receipt. If this works the way I got 'er figured, we'll be haulin' a heap o' ground corn this winter. Git a keg o' sixteen-penny nails fer the corrals. We kin pound 'em faster than Lil can straighten 'em. We commence ta build us a feedlot tamarraw. I even got a name fer our feedlots, the P.O.L.L. Livestock Feed and Cattle Company Inc. We'll incorporate 'er in Delaware. Simon'll take care of all the paperwork."

Otis looked at Pete, "What do the initials stand for, Pete?"

"Easy, P. is fer Pete, O. is fer Otis, L. is fer Lyle, and L. is fer Lil. Lil is president, Lyle is the vice, I'm secretary and Otis is the treasurer. Gotta have Otis fer treasurer, double-entry, ya know. Now, Mrs. President, why don't ya put a coupla o' them greasy pork chops in thet cast-iron skillit, make a dab o' yer good gravy. We'll throw a couple slices of bread on top and I'll run 'er out ta Estaban in m' new International. See what Estaban does with a different diet."

"Should I send a plate, some silverware and a napkin, Mr. Secretary?"

Naw, jest a fork. He kin eat outta the skillit, stay hot in the skillit. He's got thet pig-sticker on his belt; he kin use thet to cut them chops. We'll commence ta treatin' ol' Estaban better, give him a real Jayhawker welcome. Tamarraw we'll commence ta build us a wind-break, north side o' the feedlots. We bin lucky so far, but we're gonna git us a blizzard one o' these days, an' them ratty-assed steers got ta git outta the wind; otherwise they'd drift clear ta Oklahomy. Lyle, yer handy with a pencil, college boy an' all. Draw us up a plan fer a first-class feedlot. Make 'er big 'nuff fer a thousand head. We're jest 'xpermintin' with Pud's critters. If this works like I think it will, I'm headin' fer Texas an' we'll put a thousand head on feed. Mr. Treasurer, ya git home an' git some rest. Ya'll be drivin' thel Diamond T almost ever' day onct we git them steers on full feed. Need ta git a pair o' new post-hole diggers, git a good pair. Git a receipt as them diggers is a tax-deductible item." Pete tongued his toothpick over to the other side of his mouth, smiled. T.T.T. & T. and P.O.L.L. Inc. would do a wonderful job of feeding the U.S. of A., but they weren't going to support the follies of those fellows and fools back in Washington, D.C., with excessive taxes. This was New Deal time, and Pete was holding a pat hand.

"Otis, call up ta the telephony office. See if'n they's any calls fer the real estate office. Tell Central we is busy. She's ta call Lil. We kin bring the anvil in here in the kitchen, set 'er right up on the table. Lil kin straighten nails an' listen fer the telephony."

Lyle hid a smile and Lil wondered. She had her degree from Hays State, a Kansas State Teachers Certificate, she's pregnant, straightens nails for a crazy man. She is making gravy for a Mexican that can't speak a word of English, and now she's an officer in the corporate livestock feedlot feeding business. It did seem a long ways from Beloit.

Otis asked, "Do you want me to stop and tell Effie what we're doing, Pete?"

"Naw, she wouldn't care a-tall. You'd better hit the road with the Diamond T. Thet truck is powerful but slow. I floorboarded 'er ta other day; the speedyometer said I was only doin' thirty-five. Hit's thirty-three miles to Cheyenne Wells, take an hour ta git there, hour ta fill the truck, hour back, an' ya have done shot half a day."

Pete and Lyle were busy tearing down abandoned homestead barns, sheds and houses for corral lumber.

"Throw them bint nails in thet bucket. They keep Lil busy; she cain't think 'bout her condition thetaway. Didja notice all thet bailin' wire I brought out, Lyle m' boy?"

"Yes, I wondered where you got all that wire. What do you have in mind to use it for anyway, Pete?"

"When I put them extry twenty bales o' Blue Stem on the pickup, I saw all thet wire jest a-hangin' on a post at the stockyards. Why, it was jest a rustin' away. Lotsa uses fer balin' wire. Save us buyin' hinges an' latches fer our first-class feedlot."

Lyle smiled, said, "Pete, I need a car. I want to be prepared to get to town to the doctor when the baby is due."

"Ya is absolutely keerect, ya need reliable transportation. Tell ya what we'll do. Day afta tamarraw, ya and the President take the Diamond T an' go over ta Goodland, see m' friend Dismang. He's a Packard dealer; I used ta pick up his lemons, an' he had a tree full of 'em. I'll sign a check outta T.T.T. & T., make it a present ta the new high office of the presidency. Have Lil drive 'er home, ya git a load a ground corn, save Otis a trip. He kin straighten nails and listen fer the telephone. Thet Packard is a tax-deductible item, ya know." Pete and Lyle both smiled.

Pete pawed around in his overall bib pocket, dug out his coin purse, methodically took off the two large rubber bands and snapped open a seldom-used compartment. "Here's a coupla hunnert. Buy a bunch o' baby clothes, git a new Maytag gasoline engine washer; we'll put thet under office equipment. By golly, we'll all be mighty proud ta have the president drivin' around in a spiffy Packard. I was always kind a partial ta Packards, they don't need double-clutchin'."

It was just supper time when Otis came rumbling into the yard in the Diamond T, had a girl with him. She was pretty, skin kind of the color of Effie's fawn driving mittens. She did have a slight problem, buck-teeth. Pete tilted back his Triple X, tongued his toothpick over to the other side of his mouth, squinted in the window and asked, "Ya speak Kansas, girlie?"

It was Otis that answered Pete. "You bet she speaks Kansas. She ain't stopped since I left the grocery store; she spits words out like a machine gun. I ain't said a word. Them buck-teeth and that machine-gun talk has got the windshield all spattered up with spit. Her suitcase is in the back. The way I git it, her brother, Manzanita, was glad to git her outta the house. Her momma didn't say a word. This girl's name is Bonita; she's kinda a happy little thing."

"Lyle, you take the International, go out and bring in Estaban. Tell him ta ride his hoss. Bonita kin hep Lil. Why, we now got us a hired girl and a hired hand on the P.O.L.L." Then Pete leaned in the window of the Diamond T. "Bonita, ya keep yer trap shut when yer a-cookin', ya hear."

Bonita was afraid of Pete. Whenever he was around, she rarely spoke and that was just what Pete had planned.

Effie looked up when Pete came in the door. "I was wondering when you would come to town, Pete. You been gone four days. You let your real estate business go to pot. I'd get me a car if you'd just buckle down and make a few bucks. You never could stay with one thing that made us any money. It is odd though; I still know you got a wad squirreled away somewhere. That Federal Land Bank money, where you got it hid, Petey Pet?"

"Appears ta me ya is unfamiliar with the methods of' raisin' money, Effie. Right here on yer Casa, ya got the onliest new house built in this here town since '28. I want ya ta have whatever yer hard heart desires. Sorry I am sech a failure in yer eyes. The buyers a real estate ain't jest exactly knockin' down the door up at m' office. Here ya got all this fine new furniture, all these modern conveniences. Say, has them two school teachers paid the rent on our fine income property?"

"Yes, right on the first of the month. They paid in cash. Seems they are fine renters."

"What'd ya do with the money, Effie? Spint hit on somethin' useless thet the Doc is peddling ta the populace, perchance?"

"Jest groceries and a hair-do. Say, that brings up a problem on the good Doctor Primm. Penelope is quite perturbed about that Terraplane you peddled to poor Pomeroy. She said the good doctor was coming back from a perfessional call down on

Rose Creek and that automobile just up and collapsed and died. He had a farmer tow it in with his team of horses. Penelope said it was quite embarrassing sitting in the car and looking at the rear end of a team a horses. They told her the thing wasn't worth fixing. Said you sold them a lemon. Penelope said she was going to get Syl and sue. I told them you was flat broke, except for the Casa. She mentioned the rental property, thought that would cover the damages and get them better transportation."

"Is thet a fact? Thet's a pure shame 'bout thet Terryplane. Now let me tell ya something', Effie ol' girl. Ya drove them folks over ta Goodland, Pomeroy told me all about it. Ya double-clutched 'er all the way, ya didn't have a speck o' trouble, didja?"

"No, no trouble at all, Pete."

"There ya are, Effie ol' girl. Thet's what is called prima-facie evidince, hold up in any court. They done rode in the autymobile, they field-tested 'er. They was well acquainted with the autymobile; ya ever heerd of caveat emptor? Tell them two words ta ol' Penelope Prune Face Primm. Tell her ta put 'em right up there with them codicils and tell Sylvester what I said. He'll understand." Pete smiled.

"What was them two words again, I want to write 'em down, don't want Penelope to misunderstand and think you was using foul language."

"Caveat emptor, thet's Latin. I learned them two words when I was in the used car business. Feller learns 'em real quick up in Denver. They's folks up there just a-lookin' fer a feller's caveat." Pete settled back on the Navajo, shook out the evening *Denver Post* and prepared himself for an evening of news displeasure. One small article: "Minimum wage set at forty cents an hour." Pete became concerned. He wondered if he would have to pay Bonita forty cents an hour. Why, an eight-hour day would be three dollars and twenty cents. Then he read on: "The new regulations will apply only to those Ameri-can businesses engaged in interstate commerce." Pete felt quite relieved, no problem, no problem a-tall. He turned to the sports section: "Joe Louis floors Max Schmeling in the first round." Pete thought if they'd just send Joe over ta Germany an' floor thet Hitler permanent-like, there'd be no war.

Pete observed Effie putting on her hat. "Where ya goin', I kinda thought we'd sit here an' have us a little chin music. I'm kinda disappointed."

"Going to the Eastern Stars. I'm a Starpoint, you know. How about you driving me down in your new International pickup?"

"I don't know, kinda hate ta spind the money fer gas. I'll do 'er jest fer ya, Effie ol' girl." (And this was the same man who had purchased a new Packard for Lil, a new Maytag and gave them money for baby clothes. The word is priorities.)

"You are a real tight-wad, Pete. I notice you don't double-clutch this International, how come?"

"Ain't got thet tender clutch like the Terryplane. Has a tender carburetor, testy sucker. Notice when I shift the gears I push the gas pedal all the way ta the floor. Gun 'er real good?"

"Just why do you do that?"

"Feller tole me it cleans out the tender carburetor, gits the cobs out. This leaded gasoline kin cause problems, but otherwise she's a fine piece a machinery. Why, I might even let ya drive 'er around the block sometime. Now ya be keerful goin' up them stairs. I'd kinda hate ta catch me a fallin' star, 'specially one as big as you."

Effie got out and slammed the door. Pete rolled his toothpick over to the other side of his mouth, smiled. He decided to stop at the post office, get the mail. There was a letter from Pud.

Pete:

> *Guess you got them steers. I had them suckers gainin' real good. Oil wells is gushing, price of oil went up. My eighth is gittin' up there in the high numbers. See ya in January. We'll close the deal on them two sections. I may want sum more land.*

Love an' kisses, Pud

Pete considered the letter and thought thet's the kind a news a feller likes ta hear. He picked up the *Denver Post;* it was November 1938. This headline attracted his eye: "Crystal Night Horror Throughout Berlin Tonight. Anti-Semitism Exploded. Young Nazis went on a rampage, killing Jews at random, destroying stores owned by Jews and setting fire to the largest synagogue. Thousands of store windows were smashed in what is being called 'Crystal Night.' Hundreds of homes and Jewish places of worship were set on fire or ransacked."

Pete turned the page, on Page 4: "Kate Smith sings 'God Bless America,' for the first time." It was several days later when Pete was telling President Lil about the winders being smashed in Berlin that Pete learned about bigotry. There was not much bigotry in western Kansas at that time. However, they had hung a black feller on a Western Union pole in Sharon Springs many years ago. The father said the black man had raped his daughter. Maybe he did, maybe he didn't.

Pete was not familiar with that word. "Bigotry, I don't know thet word, Lil. Explain hit ta me."

"I read this in a book by Ernest Hemingway. Now listen carefully, Pete. Bigotry is an odd thing. To be bigoted you have to be absolutely sure that you are right, and nothing makes that surety and righteousness like continence. Continence is the foe of heresy. Do you understand that explanation, Pete?"

"Yep, thet's deep thinkin', Lil. Seems like them Germans kinda got their priorities all mixed up, don't hit? Positively perplexin'. Powerful problem fer the entire world. Ta think the onliest answer in this mess is war."

Lyle had the feedlot plan all laid out on the kitchen table. "I've drawn up a rough sketch of the P.O.L.L. Livestock Feedlot, Pete. Peruse this, see if you see any problems."

"Let's us look 'er over, college boy. I like thet, fifty head ta a corral, twenty corrals. Powerful bunch a gates; I see where ya got it so's we kin drive down on the south side and fill the bunks from the truck without opening gates. I never opened many gates down on the Bar P; Effie was m' official gate-opener. I see ya got a sick pen an' a hospital shed. Yer a good planner, Lyle. Ya got a crowdin' pen over there and some grain bins. Scales! Godalmighty, ya is now in the big buckeroos. Ya sure we need scales?"

"It's the only way we can check our weight gains. Sent away for some material from the Agricultural Extension Service. The article says we should weigh our feeders every twenty-eight days, Pete."

"Agents! This here country is fulla agents. F.B.I. agents, Secret Service agents. Postal agents. Depot agents. They got labor agents thet tells the workin' man how ta vote. Bank agents thet tells a banker how to run a bank and them folks couldn't run a hot dawg stand. They's folks that tell us how ta run our schools, and them folks has a lotta power and we're a losin' hit. We got ta git started on this here feedlot. Does thet Estaban know the business end of a post-hole digger, Lyle?"

"Sure, he is really a nice guy. The steers are all settled down. He can ride over there and check them twice a day. Put him to digging post holes. I'll mark them out for him."

"Lyle, what's this here word doin' on the feedlot, loadin' chute?"

"Pete, times are changing. We have to quit driving our cattle to the railhead; those days are gone forever. There's way too much shrink. They say in one of those pamphlets from the extension agent that cattle shrink five percent. Here's the way I have it planned. We load our fat cattle here on the feedlot onto a truck. Haul them to the stockyards; they go right onto a cattle car, straight to Denver via train and to the packing house."

"Sounds like a pipe dream. Give me some numbers, I ain't no good a-tall without numbers, an' then sometimes I need Otis."

"All right, hang on to your pockets. Thousand head, that's what you plan on feeding, isn't that right, Pete?"

"You'ns is keerect. Please proceed."

"Feed them to a thousand pounds or more, is that right?"

"Ya got 'er, college boy."

"A thousand head at a thousand pounds apiece is one million pounds of beef." Lyle waited for the reaction.

"I am quite sure. Five percent shrink is fifty thousand pounds of beef. That shrink comes right out of your pocket, Pete. That is the part that pinches, doesn't it?"

"Why, thet shrink could kill ya financially. They'd shrink a lot more if'n we was ta drive 'em ta the stockyards, wouldn't they?"

"Pete, you seem to catch on mighty quick when there are big bucks involved."

"What'd the fat cattle market close at yestiday, Mr. Vice?"

"Closed at nine cents a pound, nine dollars a hundred-weight. You want to know just how much that shrink would have come to, don't you, Pete?"

"Hit me with some kinda preposterous figure. We gotta prove this precarious problem of shrink!"

"How does about $4,500 strike you, Mr. Treasurer? That's what that little item called shrink costs. Now understand this, Pete, one must always figure five percent shrink; there's no way around it. Then there is another item called stress, that causes shrink. If we were to drive these fats to the stockyards horseback, they drop off another five percent. That is the reason I think we should figure out a way to put some type of racks on the grain trucks. Haul the steers to the U.P. stockyards; treat those steers nice and gentle, reduce the stress all we can."

Pete leaned back in his chair. "That sure be some kinda pitcher, wouldn't hit, Lyle m' boy? Ridin' a saddle horse an' watching' the fat fall off them steers walkin' down the road. We'd leave the place with a bunch o' critters an' see ten percent of 'em fall off right in the bar-pit. Why, thet is called invisible bankruptcy. Leave the T.T.T. & T. and the P.O.L.L. with a thousand-pound steer and watch him trot down the alley up ta the Denver Union Stockyards, an' thet sucker weighs nine hunnert. Let's us truck them powder puffs!"

(Now there you have it, folks, right there in a little county in western Kansas. While Hitler was goose-stepping all over Europe, prime ministers and heads of state were kissing him 'til they had chapped lips, there an innovator, a problem solver, a former county conservation agent and a man of many trades and talents came up with the idea of the livestock truck. Trucking livestock to market to reduce shrinkage. Truly, Wallace County, Kansas, was a wonderful paradise on the plains!)

"We have an additional and serious problem, Pete."

"What's thet? Why, there ain't nuthin' more serious than watchin' a steer drop off a hunnert pounds o' prime!"

"Water. We will need water to all the lots. All twenty-five of the lots, pipes to lay, water tanks. How do you plan to keep the water pipes from freezing? You have an answer for that one, Pistol Pete?"

Now some people are put in a box or they place themselves in a box. They spend a lifetime in that box and then they become afraid to leave the box; there is a familiarity to the box. Not Pete Pisanmoan, he could beat, gnaw or knife his way out.

"No problem, no problem a-tall, Lyle m' boy. We don't lay a foot a pipe. What with thet shrink and layin' pipe you is talkin' big buckeroos."

"Tell me how you plan to water a thousand head of cattle."

"Well, first we got two trucks, don't we? We ain't a-haulin' them powder puffs ta the stockyard ever' single day, are we? We slide a thousand-gallon tank on the bed of the stock haulin' outfit, put 'nother one on m' model A, a fifty-five gallon drum in the trunk a the Packard and commence ta haulin' water. See how easy I solved 'er, college boy." Pete wiggled his toothpick, smiled.

"I knew you would come up with some ridiculous answer; hang onto your Triple X, wise guy. Here's some more figures, you not being too good on solutions until you have the numbers. Ponder this problem. How much water does a steer drink a day?"

"Lyle, I ain't a-tall sure. A ol' cow drinks 'bout eight, maybe ten gallon when she comes ta water That reminds me, I got something' I need ta tell Effie." Cow, Effie, comparison?

"Let us figure six gallon twice a day; just figure twelve gallon times a thousand head. Now, how many gallon of water would that be, Pete?"

"Godalmighty, I don't know. Otis ain't here. Tell me, college boy." Pete had lost his smirk, toothpick didn't move.

"We'd need twelve thousand gallons of water a day, Pete."

"Why, thet's an easy one, Lyle m' boy. We jest cut down on the water if'n we cut down on the salt on them steers."

"Won't work, Pete. I put a pump jack on our well at the house. That well is a hand-dug well. I ran a test, six gallons a minute. We have a case of water shorts, Pete. We're short of water."

Pete pondered the water problem, Pete didn't give up easily. "Ya don't suppose we could put Estaban on the business end of a auger, run 'er down say, 'bout ninety foot, case 'er real good. I got me a extry windmill head, thet one Penelope felled on m' propity. Then we possibly could have two wells."

Lyle could tell Pete was dubious of the well; he was ready to accept reality.

"Nope, Pete, not possible. I think we got carried away when we went to a thousand-head lot. I think we should cut it in half."

"Yer a hunnert percent keerect. Ya got 'er, Lyle m' boy. We'll jest run these ratty-assed Mex steers o' Pud's through the lot, git us some valuable experience. Do it on a smaller scale." Pete had a rapid recovery in the enthusiasm department; he adapted well to the water problem.

"I have some other information I think you'll like, Pete. I have some information that would make the cost of our grain less for the feedlot."

"Lyle, if'n hit's cheaper than corn an' haulin' from Cheyenne Wells, I'm plenty pliable an' perked up. Deal me the dope on this dandy descriptive idee."

"Did you know milo has about the same protein content as corn?"

"Nope, I didn't know thet. Milo's a good crop here in this paradise on the plains; corn is good, too, hard ta raise. I raised me some sweet stalk Kaffir onct. It did real well, got drouthed out. If'n I jest got another rain I'd had a bountiful crop. Guess what yer tellin' me is thet milo makes meat, good as corn."

Lyle suggested, "I think we should drill in a couple hundred acres of milo this spring. We can combine it with the new Massey-Harris, same as wheat, cut down on overhead, not have to drive so far for corn. Otis is driving and spending too much time in the Diamond T."

"Ya hit me right in the solar-plexus when ya talk 'bout thet reducin' overhead. Didja ever wonder why they calls it overhead? We'll no-till 'er — git Otis ta poppin' the Wallis. By the time thet milo is up good, it'll be time fer wheat harvest. Remind me ta tell Otis ta keep proper tab on our feedlot buildin'. We'll charge ol' Pud fer all the material. We'll put the lumber an' used nails in at half the price of new. Thet's what ya always figure on used merchandise, half the cost o' new. Lil's time on straightening them nails an' her with a college degree, buck an hour. Now ya don't always count half the cost a new, not when ya sell used Terryplanes, thet's different." Pete smiled.

"What about Bonita, should Pud pay her wages, too?"

Pete became almost indignant, "Sure, ya some kinda ninny? Board an' room an' other various an' sundry duties. Why, she kept Estaban happy. Them two are mooney-eyed. I kinda figure we better plan on a priest pretty pronto. Ya seein' it m' way?"

"You are a perceptive man, Pete."

Pud didn't show up on January 15. Pete was not at all perturbed. It was Otis who was concerned about Pud. He was thinking about that $1,000 bonus of "extry-ordinary income" when they closed the deal. "It comes from dealin' with the public, Otis. Some folks says I am physic. Pud'll be here when he gits here. I know, no trouble a-tall, we spit and shook on it."

Pete was leaning against the inside of the windbreak, watching Estaban scoop ground corn into the feed bunks. Lyle was driving the Diamond T when Pete heard a car drive in the yard. He peered through a crack in the fence; that fence had a lot of cracks, saw it was Pud Pudlick from Potter County, Texas. There he was, a real live Texican. Deals only in cash. Pud didn't see Pete; Pud just stepped up on the middle rail of the fence, eyeballed his steers, smiled.

"Ya like what ya see, Pud?"

"Howdy, Pete. Didn't see ya. How y'all doin'? My, ya done wonders with them steers. That wheat pasture is good feed. I thought I sent 'em to you in tippity-top shape, but I see you boys done put the frosting on 'em. What's m' Mex feedin' them?"

"Pud, we done worked out the most economical feedin' deal a feller could make. They's ground corn, some cockle-burs and sunnyflowers mixed jest for rumination. We ran the whole mess through a hammermill; it sure did put the bloom on 'em. I wished they had a little more stretch. Whatcha think them steers weigh, Pud?" Pete was testing Pud on cattle weights, see if he knew diddly-squat about cattle.

"Hard to guess a steer's weight from up here on the fence. Feller has to see how even they are by their backs. They won't make seven; they'll go over six hundred though."

"Yer mighty perceptive, Pud. We got us a set o' expensive scales, ran a hunnert head over them scales jest last week ta git us an average. Otis did the figurin'; they hit 665 pounds. They is kinda rolly-polly, ain't they? Slicked up real good, mild winter so far, thet's bin a hep."

"Y'all think I oughta sell them wonders, Pete?"

"Pud, me an' Lyle has bin workin' out a sales program; he calls hit marketing. I want Lyle ta explain 'er. Soon's as them boys git through feedin', they'll come up ta coffee up. Lil 'll have the pot on, an' we'll put 'er ta ya. How'd ya know I was out here anyways?"

"Otis was in the office. He was so glad to see me. I was scairt he was gonna give me a kiss. Cuppa coffee sounds good."

Everyone was glad to see Pud. Estaban wasn't sure he wanted to go back to Texas, leave Bonita. Lyle laid out the plan.

"We are new at this feedlot business, Pud. We didn't have a soul we could talk to for assistance. First off, I think we all agree you bought some steers with a little too much age. I mouthed a couple, and they seem like two-year-olds. That is one reason we had trouble getting growth."

"Y'all may be absolutely correct. They do look a little agey, got meat on 'em though. You boys did wonders with them steers. What did those suckers gain a day?"

Lyle continued after he stirred his coffee; he intended to surprise Pud. "Weighed every twenty-eight days. We have only weighed twice, gained a little over two pounds a day. We have a proposal for you, Pud. We've developed a new method of transportation for livestock. You may have noticed our loading chute out in those first-class corrals, the ones with the baling wire hinges and gate latches. We have built wooden racks that fit on the Diamond T, working on a set for the Model A truck. With those two trucks, we can haul fourteen head to the stockyards in Sharon Springs. We developed this method of transportation instead of trailing the steers on horseback, save on shrink."

Pete made a fist and kind of pounded the table, "Ya better listen, Pud pal. Thet shrink 'll kill ya!"

"Pete's right. We don't think you should sell the entire herd

Poindexter P. Pudlick

at one time. We suggest you just average them out, say send a carload a day. We'll consign them to one commission house; we think Mann-Boyd-Mann is considered the best. We think we can get about forty head to a car. Take us three trips with the trucks to get a carload; it is called cost averaging, get a diversified market every day."

Pud made an inquiry, "What was y'all's death loss? I figured y'all would lose close to forty head, ten percent."

Beaming smiles all round the table, those Kansans were proud and pompous.

Pete said, "We lost jest two head. One got a bad case o' the scours, an' one broke his laig. We shot him and butchered us a beef."

Pud leaned back in his chair and laughed, "Now ain't that a wonder-a-wonders. I lost four dollars. Why, I'd lost more than that down in Potter County to my friends and neighbors that was short on meat. I like your ideas. Let's us commence to selling. You know something, I ain't never seen ol' Estaban have a gleam in his eye like he has today. I guess that Bonita's kinda got the answer to Estaban's problems. She talks kinda funny, spits a lot."

Pete was growing anxious to get some of that oil money.

"Are ya ready ta close the deal on them two sections of blow-dirt, Pud?"

"Ready, willin' an' able. That's what them lawyers say."

Pete was delighted, "I got me 'nother idee."

"Shoot, pistol Pete, you always got some kind of idee."

"Pud, let's me an' you ride with thet first carload. The U.P. 'll let us ride in the caboose fer free. We'll unload them cattle, git the commission house ta buy us dinner. Then we'll hop a streetcar, and I'll deposit the proceeds from our cash deal on them two sections a blow-dirt. I gotta git m' lawyer ta draw us up a corporation. We'll stay a coupla days, see some o' m' friends down on Lawrence St., git us some free lunches, and the commission house 'll pay our train fare back home. While we're gone, the crew here on the P.O.L.L. will git 'nother load 'er two on the way."

"That sounds fine to me, Pete, kind of a vacation. I brought y'all a present. Drove straight through from Amarillo. I got a pile o' tamales and burritos, few freejoles out in the car. We'll jest have us a Mex supper. Bonita, go out and get that big box outta the back seat of m' Cadillac."

"I believe I'll just have a small bowl of chicken soup." That was Lil; she wasn't into the Mex food epicurean delights just yet.

It was a little less than two weeks later when Pud got the P.O.L.L. together at headquarters. That's what Pete now called the house where Lyle and Lil lived, it was "headquarters."

"Y'all was correct on the method of selling them steers. That last load sold considerable higher than the first coupla of cars. Pete cozyin' up to that commission man helped. I now got what we call down in Texas some of that extry-ordinary income."

Pete gasped. "Pud, ya got thet down there, too. Why, we have some o' thet kind o' income up here in Kansas." Pete smiled.

"You folks bought a pile of grain, gas for your trucks, labor. You had a heap of expenses and overhead. All I had was freight and about $900 in them. A little bit for dippin' for ticks, labor for vaccinatin' and dehornin'. I got some cash money for each and every one of y'all. Pete, does $7,000 cover 'er for y'all?"

Pete tongued his toothpick over to the other side of his mouth and smiled. "Yesirree, ya blanketed it very nicely. I was gonna charge ya fer straightenin' them bint nails; ya done took m' plan outta existence."

Pud laid the hundreds on all the P.O.L.L. He was very generous, dealt those hundred dollar bills like a deck of Bicycles, even gave Bonita a century note; she'd never seen one. Pud was pleased, Estaban sat in the corner on his haunches, had on his poncho. He was quite fond of Pud, fonder of Bonita.

Pud went back to Texas, had a deal working. Pete headed for town, check out the Casa. He hated those flamingos; they didn't seem to be hurting the grass, but the dogs were taking the paint off the legs of the birds.

"Wipe your feet! You been going out to the T.T.T. & T., running up to Denver. I still think you got a floozy up there; that's where that Federal Land Bank money went; you spent it on a floozy. What have you been doin', Pete?

"Effie ol' girl, I got somethin' here in m' pocket that'll change yer tune. Got a little dab o' money, go buy ya a used autymobile. Here's four big ones. Pud made a pile o' profit on them Mex steers; he liked our ways o' feedin' his Mex cattle. Gave us all a bonus. I like ta share m' bounty with ya, m' helpmate and Starpoint. I'm a-gonna give ya m' entire bonus."

"You mean you actually made a profit on them ugly critters? Four hundred dollars is a tidy little sum for you to give me. You sure you're not bleeding just a little bit inside, Petey Pet. I will say this though, you are kind and considerate, better than that Pomeroy, what a pestiferous person!"

Pete was puzzled, "What happened to Pomeroy? I thought his practice was prosperin', sellin' all them powders an' potions. He got a problem?"

"Why, he's gone, skipped, he's missing! He took the car that Penelope had bought over at Goodland. Sylvester gave Penelope the money and a tidy sum to tide her for awhile. Her dear dead daddy's gold watch, it was an Illinois, it's gone. Her momma's ruby earrings, he cleaned her out. Odd thing, Daphne Damptowel is missing. We've looked all over for her, checked down at the depot, no luck. Pomeroy came home from out in the country couple of days ago, had a broken nose. Seems some fella punched him. We don't know for sure who done it. I kinda got a hunch."

"What's yer hunch, Effie ol' girl?"

"I think Pomeroy set a precedent unsnappin' them garters, had his paws in places that wasn't perfessional to the chiropractical process of manipulation. Maybe unethical in his promiscuous procedures, plausible hunch."

"Ya is keerect, absolutely keerect. Has Penelope fallen outta the saddle yet? Goin' back ta visit Prunella again? Take some treatments fer her mental condition?"

"No, she seems relieved. She isn't even gonna press charges against Pomeroy. I kinda think he snapped both of Daphne's garters a couple of times though; she's been smiling a lot lately."

"Effie ol' girl, I almost forgot ta tell ya. I done got a baby named after me. Now how ya like thet?"

"Now who would name a little child after the likes of you, I'd like to know?"

"Lyle an' Lil. They done had a baby girl; named her Petey Pat. Ain't thet nice? I sold two more sections o' blow dirt ta Pud an' gave 360 acres ta m' namesake, put 'er in a trust. Simon drawed it up fer me."

"You are a pistol, Pete. Giving away that no-good land. I know you got a pile hid somewheres. I'll find it someday, you just wait and see. I'll spend a bundle." Effie smiled.

"Always drink upstream from the herd."
— *Old Western Quote*

"Flakes, hacks and floozies come and go, but a good cigar is a smoke."
—*Rudyard Kipling*

"When a political system breaks down, history tells us the breakage is always thrown into the street."
—*Theo. White*
If you don't believe this, consider the depression.

Unknown to many, but consider this. The changes by Pete Pisanmoan reshaped the culture and economics of *western Kansas*.

Where Your Mail Went

The Postal Service may soon have to file environmental impact statements for all the mail it is dumping in America's trash boxes and dumpsters. For example, a Rhode Island carrier was arrested after 94,000 letters were found buried in his backyard. A 1987 survey by Doubleday and Company found that up to 14 percent of bulk business mail was either thrown away or lost. One Arlington, Virginia, postal clerk told a customer: "We don't have room for the junk mail, so we've been throwing it out." In 1987, 1,315 postal workers were fired for theft and/or mistreatment of mail. A Postal Inspection Service audit found properly addressed third-class mail vanished in the postal labyrinth. The throwing away of mail has become so pervasive that postal inspectors have notified employees that it is bad for the Postal Service's business.

— *James Bovard*
"The Slow Death of the U.S. Postal Service
Published by the Cato Institute

"Government, even in its best state, is but a necessary evil; in its worst state, an intolerable one."
— *Thomas Paine (1737-1809)*
The Freeman
Ideas on Liberty, April 1989

THE CUSTOM CUTTER

Pete WAS STANDING in the yard of a small wheat farmer. One must understand that, first, farmers are skeptical of strangers, and Pete's business was new; farmers resist new ways.

"Yessir, Mr. Platter, we kin blow through thet eighty acres of Kiowy in a day. We got us a sixteen-footer Massey-Harris, coupla a reliable trucks, perfessional drivers. Haul yer wheat, put 'er right in yer livin' room if thet's where ya want it. Got me reglar devils on the end of them scoop shovels. Ya want us to pull in here in the mornin'?" Pete chewed on several kernels of wheat, "She's ready ta cut right now."

"The name is Plate. Never heard of the likes of custom cutters. I agree that your price seems reasonable, Mr. Pisanmoan. I've got a little John Deere six-footer. Run it all by myself. The wife can drive the pickup to town. I dunno, guess I'll just think on it."

Pete smiled, kind of like that smile when the Union Pacific check came in for their real estate taxes when he was County Treasurer. "Why, thet's up ta ya, Mr. Platter. We call Denver ever' night on the long-distance, check on the weather. Last night they was a four-letter word thet kinda makes a wheat farmer sweat under the armpits, git a dose a jock-itch. When we pull by tonight, you and the missus come out ta the gate, look our outfit over. I'm ridin' the point; you change yer mind an' we'll pull right up here in the yard. See ya, much obliged fer ya listenin'."

Pete had the door to the International pickup open, one foot inside, had his Triple X tipped at an angle to keep the sun out of his eyes. He was eyeballing Mr. Platter, check his reaction.

"What was that word you heard on the weather? What was that four-letter word, Mr. Pisanmoan?"

"Hail, yessiree, now thet is a word for a wheat farmer ta ponder." Pete started the International, tongued his toothpick over to the other side of his mouth, smiled and waved at Mr. Platter; he knew he had another one on the hook. That word hail always got 'em. He'd get Mr. Saucer on the way by this evening.

In the various tales told about Pete Pisanmoan, there did seem to be considerable bombastic bamboozlement. However, Pete always delivered the goods; he did what he said he would do. Thus, when Mr. and Mrs. Plate heard the caravan coming down the road, a dusty procession, they were at their gate out by the mailbox. Pete was riding point as he had said. He was driving the Packard, which also included Lil and Petey Pat. They had a back seat full of supplies for the Lovelace family. Bonita was next in the International with the bedrolls, tents and other paraphernalia for the gypsies, the custom cutters. Estaban was driving the Model A truck with the combine header, spare tires, tools and spare parts, and Lyle drove the Diamond T. Otis was on the Wallis pulling the combine. Quite an impressive sight. As one may recall, Pete had a specialty when it came to advertising. One has only to recall his campaign when he ran for Wallace County Treasurer. On the sides of all the vehicles and on the bin of the combine he had had a sign painter letter professionally:

PETE PISANMOAN
CUSTOM WHEAT CUTTER
WE'RE NEAT ON WHEAT!
Sharon Springs, Kansas

The Packard slowed and stopped. Pete got out and held up his hand, stopped the caravan. "Mr. and Mrs. Saucer, m' girl is kinda tard this evenin', baby's been a-fussin' all day. Mind if we set up camp out here in yer yard right over there by thet box elder tree, close ta water an' facilities. 'Preciate hit." Pete scuffed his boot in the dust, took off his hat. A lock of grey hair fell down on his forehead. Pete was playing it pretty pitiful.

Mrs. Plate just couldn't stand it. "Why, a young woman with a little one, out here ridin' all over the country. Hot and tired! You just plan to spend the night, Mr. Pisanmoan. Pull over under the box elder." Mrs. Plate reached in and got Petey

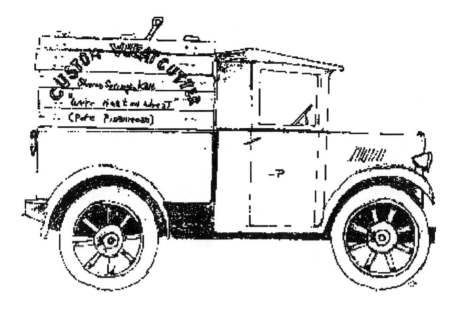

Pat, "Here now, honey, let me have that baby."

Pete had just a slight smile, "If'n hail don't git 'em, Petey Pat will."

Pete wasn't completed yet. "We're much obliged, ma'am. Lil, ya go over there under thet there tree, squat an' set a spell. Ya need the rest. We'll commence ta build us a fire, put the stew pot on." Pete stood up on the running board of the Packard and waved to the crew. They all knew Pete had conned another one. Otis popped the Wallis; Mrs. Plate was sure she had been shot! The "Neat on Wheat" boys and girls hadn't spent a single night in their bedrolls since they left Sharon Springs; that was three weeks ago.

"Don't you dare build a fire. I want you to come in and set at our supper table. I'll bet this little one needs a good warm bath. Why, it's been ages since I gave a baby a bath. Don't you unload them bedrolls neither. We got plenty of places for all of you folks to sleep. Now ain't that right, Herbert!"

"You bet, Mother. We'll show these folks some real Nebraska hospitality. Here, take m' arm, little lady, come on up to the house."

Lil had become a good actress, but she was reluctant to impose on people, didn't bother Pete a bit. He had told her to "kinda act like a half-wit." Teachers make good actors, too.

"I picked us up a pile o' pork chops back in McCook, Mrs. Plate. Bonita, git out ta the Packard, git them pork chops an' hep this nice lady git the supper on the table. Thet's a dandy stand o' wheat. Didja git the evenin' weather on the K O an' A? Be a pure pity ta see thet crop pounded inta the ground jest ta wait a couple days. Better fer the elevator to knock off a bit fer moisture than no wheat a-tall, Mr. Plate. You folks haven't met m' crew. This here's m' partner, Lyle Lovelace; he was the former conservative agent in Wallace County, he's the proud Papa o' Petey Pat. This here's Estaban, he don't speak no Kansas a-tall. Otis Armbuster, former County Treasurer o' Wallace County. Now ya folks have quite a distinguished bunch a-bellyin' up ta yer fine supper table. Now ain't thet Petey Pat jest 'bout the prettiest parcel a punkins ya ever laid yer pupils on?"

"How long have you been on the road harvesting wheat, Mr. Pisanmoan?"

"Let me see, Mr. Plate. First, we cut our own wheat down in Harrison Township, little over a thousand acres. Then we cut ol' Pud Pudlick's six hunnert, he's from Potter County Texas. Then we hit the road. Been out jest 'bout three weeks. Otis, how many acres we done cut as of taday? Otis, he's m' bookkeeper, he does it double-entry style. Auditors checked them books fer Wallace County. Checked right ta the penny, he's a goodun."

"Cut eleven hundred and forty, Pete."

"You boys have cut almost three thousand acres this harvest. That's a powerful lot of wheat. Makes my little eighty look pretty small, surprised you bothered to stop." Mr. Plate didn't know it, but Pete was looking for a nice place to spend the night. The eighty acres would pay for the gas and oil, some parts.

"Now we ain't partial, Mr. Plate. We cut little piddlin' pieces an' patches, no problem a-tall. People thet's got a crop want 'er in the bin. It's been a long time comin' what with depression, the dustbowl, grasshoppers, jackrabbits, government interference, them problems just seemed to keep heapin' up on the farmer an' rancher." Pete looked around the room, saw Bonita. "Bonita, tell Estaban ta change them sickles on the header. We want Mr. Plate to git a nice clean cut on his wheat." Mr. Plate had had the decision made for him, Pete was "neat with wheat."

"Say, it just came to me. You are the boys that developed that idea of strip farming, no-till as I recollect?"

Pete smiled. "Yer a-lookin' at 'em." Pete puffed up a little.

"Was your idea successful? What did your wheat down in Wallace County make this year, Mr. Pisanmoan?"

"Jest call me Pete, Mr. Plate. Piffle, we had jest a trifle. Otis, what's yer double-entry say on the T.T.T. & T? How much wheat did we put in the elevator at Sharon Springs?"

This was another part of the Pisanmoan plot. Otis was well rehearsed. He would dig into the bib pocket on his overalls, pull out a small spiral notebook, squint at the figures, quizzical look. He wanted to be exactly correct with his answer. All accountants have that look, like it would be a mortal sin to be off a bushel or two. "Seems like it was exactly twenty-two thousand five hundred and fifty-five bushels. Yep, that's right, Pete."

"My, that is a lot of wheat! You boys made about twenty bushel to the acre; your farming methods were successful."

"Yep, the Union Pacific ran a Pisanmoan Special. Course, I had Pud's on the special. War's a-comin', Mr. Plate. Got ta git this wheat in the bin. We is probably gonna feed the world, an' I figure ta feather m' nest on war. Shame hit takes a war to git a decent price fer our wheat. What kind of a world are we leavin' ta a little one like our Petey Pat?"

Mr. Plate said, "I'm curious, Mr. Pisanmoan, I mean Pete. Is Petey Pat a little boy or a little girl?"

"Little girl, prettiest little possum I ever played with, Mr. Plate. Hey, the ladies is a wavin' their aprons at us ta wash up. Let's eat, I hope thet Lil made us a big dose o' gravy. She makes the best gravy. Come on, Herbert, time fer supper." Seemed like Mr. Plate had just peddled the place, Pete had taken over. On the walk to the washstand on the back porch, Pete firmed up the custom cutting deal.

"We'll haul yer wheat ta McCook, put the first dump in yer pickup. Check the moisture content. Ya kin git lined up at the elevator; those boys at McCook knows us. Tamorrow night this time yer wheat's in the bin. We're down the road a piece, an' all y'all recollect o' us is a legend. Yep, a livin' legend, Pisanmoan Custom Cutters. Probably be back next year. Give ya piece o' advice. Buy more land. Next year, if'n ya git a crop ya'll pay fer it with just one crop. Let 'er rest, summer fallow, strip farm. Ya got ta let 'er lay fallow a year. Them dust storms was a sight ta behold. Never fergit 'em. My, Missus Plate, ya done wonders whilst we was visitin'. Ya made us some apple pie. Bonita, git out ta the Packard, I got some Long-Horn in the back seat. Ya know thet ol' sayin', 'apple pie without cheese is like tits without a squeeze.' If'n we was closer ta town, I'd git some vanilly ice cream, we'd have a dollop on yer pie. Thet is a mighty purty crust, bet ya used real lard. Thet's the way ta make crust."

Mrs. Plate smiled. Pie crust was her specialty; whenever there was a church social she always had to make the pies. The Plates didn't realize they were being had by a professional. If they did know, it was nice when Pisanmoan Custom Cutters came each year. Herbert would say, "Mom, that Pete Pisanmoan, he's a real piss-cutter, ain't he?" Mom would act properly embarrassed and nod in agreement, and then they would both wave good-bye.

"How far north you planning on combining, Mr. Pisanmoan?"

"We'll head fer Scottsbluff, then swing down towards Sterlin', Colorady. Thet section o' the state 'll probably be cut if'n they ain't already hailed out. Hope I jest make the fuel bill home an' I'd be happy. First year out custom cuttin', kinda a experimint."

"Must take a lot of money to just get set up in your custom cutting business, Pete."

"Ya kin bet yer Sunday suit and Panamy hat on thet, specially when ya got a banker like we got in Sharon Springs. Why, we had ta go to Cheyenne Wells ta git our financin'. Wonder if'n ya could do me a slight favor, Herb ol' boy. When we pull out of the field tamarrow an' ya are satisfied with our work, give me a coupla o' names o' your neighbors down the road. I'll kinda use ya fer a reference so's ta speak."

"Be glad to, Pete. I just don't understand you having any trouble with your local banker. All that wheat you put on that special. All that land you farm; you must have a pile of collateral?"

"All mortgaged up ta the hilt. Federal Land Bank has a firm grasp on m' pocketbook. They was a agent out ta the place; he counted ever' load o' wheat we delivered. Them's pathetic people. Lyle, m' boy, tell Herbert. Oh, m' goodness, Mrs. Plate, thet was wonderful pie, peach of a crust, real flaky-like. Lyle, tell these nice folks 'bout our felt hat business. Now, Otis, ya interrupt him any time ya want to. Ya got them figures we gave ta the banker the day we slid down them bank steps with our tails a-tween our laigs, whupped dogs, treated us like mongrels; thet's what we were, pure an' simple, jest cur dogs!"

The story of the Dibbs Hat Company fascinated the Plates and all the other farm families. All the farmers had had troubles with the abundance of jackrabbits. Lyle had told the story so many times Otis and Pete could interrupt right on cue. It was almost necessary to peel Mr. and Mrs. Plate right down off the ceiling, they were so perturbed with that pitiful banker. Lil got up and changed Petey Pat and started washing the dishes, that story had given her a "permanent crease."

"That's keerect, had a contract fer 300,000 jackityrabbits at thirteen cents a hide."

Herb couldn't believe it, "Is that right, there is one hundred fourteen rabbits to make a tub-a-guts? Interesting fact." Then he remarked, "Eight jackrabbits eat as much as one old cow?"

Herb was very interested in the table talk, "Rabbit's feet, why I never would have thought of that. Good one, you have any left over, Pete?"

Pete sent Bonita out to get one out of the Packard glove compartment. Pete said, "I'll jest give it ta ya, Herb. Ya jest watch, yer luck will change fer the better." Pete smiled and began picking the pork chop meat out of his teeth.

Farmer would bang his fist down on the supper table. The spoon bowl would jump up and rattle. The farmer and family's eyes would glaze over; they were angry at Pete's predicament. That Sunday at church they wouldn't even speak to their local banker. They had forgotten he was the one that had believed in them, their honesty and industry. That banker knew they were a good Christian family and would survive.

Harvest was over, it had been successful. "Here I am, Effie ol' girl. Betcha yer glad ta see me. It looks purty good aroun' here 'ceptin' them penguins rootin' around out there in the front yard. I got a gunny sack full o' dirty clothes fer yer laundry person 'er do ya call her yer maid? Ya got me workin' night n' day jest tryin' ta keep ya in the lap o' luxury. Notice ya got a sizable lap. Ya could take thet dress an' hang it on a hippo, fit jest perfect."

"I am kind of glad to see you, Penny Pincher Pete. You may think you is something special; I see that sign on your truck, says you're 'neat with wheat.' Your appearance ain't so neat. You look like one of them bums that camps out under Eagle Tail bridge. Been too quiet around here. You can liven up the atmosphere with that scroungy look and odorous smell. Good thing you pulled into town towards dark. Sheriff put your butt in the can for vagrancy. You do look kind of shiftless. Them is flamingos out in the front yard, not penguins."

"Yeah, them' penguins all right. Jack Larson's German Shepherd jest done a number on one of them bird's laigs. I see the paint is peelin'." Pete just smiled, nice to be ta home.

"You have a good trip? Were you financially successful? Make a buck or two for my livelihood? That twenty you left me didn't last long. I went to the bank to borrow a hundred, new banker, he just leaned back in that leather chair and laughed and laughed when I told him my name and intentions. You got some kind of problem with that guy, Pete?"

"Nope, no problem a-tall. Seems like thet new fella is a-gonna laugh hisself right outta his leather chair, need us a local ta polish the seat of his pants on thet leather. Out-a-towners don't ponder the problems of the plebeians, don't seem ta know how ta palavar, don't understand our parlance. Hilarity seems ta be a peccadillo o' his. It were a fairly successful trip. I think we made a tad o' profit. Met a world o' fine folks. We're havin' a business meetin' at headquarters tamarraw." Pete held up his hand, he knew what was coming. "Naw, ya ain't invited. Ya ain't no stockholder. Don't bother ta ask, fergit it."

"Pshaw, Pete, you are such a penny pincher, a real pitiful person. Say, who owns that green Packard? I see that Lil and little Petey Pat parading around town, pounding down Main Street. She something special, how come I don't get me a Packard?"

"Belongs ta the P.O.L.L. Corporation, jest a little company vehicle. Need thet Packard fer depreciation. Don't ask me 'bout P.O.L.L., real secret organization. It's kinda like them Easterner Stars, we is more into the secret monetary policy point o' view. Yer sure prolific with yer howdys and welcomes. Makes m' heart kinda go pitty-pat. Here's an extry sawbuck fer yer laundry person. Didja remember ta save all them *Denver Posts* like I askt ya ta? Lotta valuable information in a newspaper."

"I piled them right over there by your saddle blanket. Leave that hat out on the porch! You have grease, oil, sweat, and I don't know what all on that hat. You bunch of bums stay in a cottage court while on that nightmare you just got back from? Where'd you eat, take a bath? Did that baby cry all the time? Where'd you wash her diapers?"

"Effie, yer jest full o' questions, ain't ya? We stayed in a cottage court jes one night the entire trip, spint the rest of 'em with some mighty fine farm families, friendly and familiar folks. The farm women fed us fried chicken, baked chicken and chicken an' dumplin's. Why, them dumplin's was light as a feather, like bitin' inta a golden marshymellow. Not a-tall like yers. Yers hit the bottom of the kittle like a horseshoe. Stewed chicken, them ladies was powerful strong on feedin' us chicken. Why, we'd pull inta a farm yard ta git lined out ta cut wheat, an' Estaban would count the folks an' head fer the hen house. He'd hang them suckers up on the clothes line, git out his frog sticker and commence cuttin' off chicken heads. Them farm dawgs was standin' there lettin' the blood drip down their goozles. Hit was a sight ta behold. Petey Pat had a bath ever' night. Why, thet little piece a punkins kin gnaw on a drumstick like a growed-up. If I was goin' ta town fer parts 'er somethin', I'd get a pile o' pork chops. Pork's kinda scarce out on the farm since F.D.R. done shot a coupla million o' 'em. We boys would jest jump in the stock tank, git our clothes good an' wet, hang 'em on the fence ta dry an' then soap up. Otis and Lyle like ta drowned me one night. Now, if ya is through with all them questions, I'm gonna take a bath an' clean up, git me a shave come Monday mornin' up ta the barber shop. I know ever' barber clean ta Scottsbluff. What's fer supper, Effie ol' girl?"

"Chicken and dumplin's." Effie smiled; she just gave Pete a zinger. It was satisfying to give Pete a zinger.

Monday morning, Volney Borst smiled. "Boy howdy! I sure have missed you. This barber shop is mighty dull in the morning when Pete Pisanmoan doesn't show up professing the philosophy of these plentiful plains. How'd the custom cutting go? You make a pile a plunder?"

"Good ta be back, I missed ya, Volney. Fer the first time out on the custom trail I think we did all right. We got a meetin' out ta headquarters this mornin'. Otis is ta git all the figures tagether. Lil kept track o' the fuel, parts an' miscellaneous expenses. I'd jest give her a hunnert. When it was gone, she'd hit me up again. Didn't spind nothin' much fer grub, I bought some pork chops, little dab fer some boloney an' bread. Spent more fer ice cream fer the little farmers' kids than I did for anythin' else. Take the farmers' kids ta town with a load o' wheat, give the driver a dollar fer ice cream. Thet Estaban always bought them kids double dippers."

"How many acres did you combine, Pete? What was the total acreage?"

"Countin' the T.T. & T., Pud's patch, clear up ta Nebrasky, down ta eastern Colorady, Otis says 'bout five thousand acres. We dropped thet Massey-Harris off at Goodland, traded 'er in on a new one. I heard Otis come home on the Wallis last night. No lights on thet Wallis; he jest had a lantern a-hangin' on the front axle, guess he popped 'er 'bout nine. Ya couldn't guess what give me the most trouble on the entire trip, hit was flyin' ants. I wired me a long 2x4 and tied a gunny sack around thet board, and thet sack was jest covered with those ants. We did hit a hornet's nest onct, but I had Otis rev 'er up, and we each got jest one bite. Them ants was plumb pestiferous, didn't bite though."

Volney noticed Pete was kind of agitated. "Ya notice m' Effie lately, Volney. I was kinda snugglin' up ta her when Otis popped the Wallis. I got a heap more Effie now than when we was married. Next ta ice cream, I bought a pile o' pork chops. Needed thet grease ta keep m' scoopers in top condition. Wishst there was someways ta put a heist on a truck bid. Go easy 'round m' neck, I'm hottern' a two-dollar pistol!"

"I knew you were perturbed and perplexed about something, pray tell me what it is, Pete."

"I was readin' m' back issues o' the *Denver Post*. Roosevelt done changed the date o' Thanksgivin'. Now ain't thet one big crock? Ol' Abe named our date fer givin' thanks, F.D.R. up an' changes it. Next thing ya know the government 'll figure out a way ta change the time a day 'er some other fool thing! Ya know what I tol' ever' farmer I cut fer?"

"What preposterous presentation did you propose, Pete?"

"I tol' all my fine customers ta purchase more land. Wheat is goin' up. Pay fer their land with jest one crop. We is gonna feed the world. There's a war comin', I'm gonna git everythin' new. All m' equipment is gonna be in tippity-top shape. I need a ton o' depreciation, gonna feed the populace, but I ain't gonna support a bunch o' guys back at the big trough thet spends their time changin' holidays. Them boys 'll probably change Christmas to sometime in May. Feller don't need a weather vane ta see which way the wind is a-blowin'. War, and this 'un is gonna be a danderoo. Roosevelt says America is officially neutral in thet war in Europe, horse collars. He sounded exactly like Woody Wilson did in '14. Them politicians is liars, cheats, scoundrels, rascals, scalawags, and they is doin' a number on us, Volney."

"You missed a word, just one that comes to mind, despots."

"Good word, Volney, I'd a got ta 'er directly." They smiled at each other in the mirror.

"Did you have any breakdowns, mechanical problems with your machinery?"

"Little dab, got ta tell ya somethin'. Thet Estaban is a wonder a wonders. He's a natural borned mechanic, fix anything. Give him a crescent wrench, some balin' wire and a pair a pliers an' he kin fix anythin'. He fixed thet Bonita up pretty good. We had ta stop an' see a priest at Benkleman, Nebrasky. There's a little papoose a-comin'. Ya know what thet Estaban calls me, Volney?"

"I thought he couldn't speak English. I suspect he called you a lot of things but you couldn't understand him."

"Nope, he calls me Padrone, kinda makes me feel humble, makes a feller modest. Puts a heap o' responsibility on a man when yer called Padrone. Did ya notice m' new Triple X? Got m' old one out in the International, hatband full of information. I had so many receipts I couldn't git 'er on. I had me a hay hat, but it blew down into the header so I combined a hay hat. Slosh a tad o' Lucky Tiger on m' locks. We got a big meetin' ta attend. We got a powerful lot o' work ta do. Repair them feedlots. Otis has 'bout a thousand acres o' wheat ta drill and 'bout six hunnert o' milo. I gotta git ta Texas or else git Pud ta buy me five hunnert head o' ratty-assed Mex steers. Ya ever bin ta Amarilly, Texas, Volney?"

"Never have, why are you asking?"

"Pud says it's a wonderful place. They got palm trees, oranges and lemons. Grapefruit as big as watermelon. He says the wind never blows and they's got grass up ta a cow's udder. I think he's pullin' m' laig, the shape them steers came last year. I jest might take the Packard an' take a look at Texas. Couldn't be as good as our paradise o' the Kansas plains. If'n hit was, ol' Pud woulda spint his money down in Potter County." Pete headed for headquarters.

"By golly, Lil, them brownies are jest the ticket fer a board o' directors meetin'. I got a pile o' plans ta pronounce. Let's us proceed, Missus President. Where's thet Estaban an' Bonita? They out in the back seat o' the Packard agin? I never seen the likes o' them two, they's worse than jackityrabbits."

"I didn't call them in as they are not stockholders, Pete."

"Made 'em minority stockholders. They proved they was good hands on harvest. Go git 'em, Lyle m' boy. Be keerful, Estaban's got thet frogsticker."

Lil was now in charge, "The meeting will come to order. Mr. Secretary, please read the minutes of the last meeting." There seemed to be some confusion, when was the last meeting? Who was the Secretary? "That's you, Pete."

"No minutes from the Secretary, got 'em all in m' hat band or in m' head. Pass thet there plate a brownies, they's sure good." Pete smiled, big mouthful of brownie. He was pawing around in the sweat band on his old and dirty Triple X, new one tipped back on his head, lock of grey hair on his forehead. "Got me a wealth o' material in this here hat. Golly, here's the renewal on m' brand down on the Bar P, warranty on some tires fer the Terryplane. I shoulda give them ta Pomeroy. Say, ya know what thet Daphne did ta thet banker? I had me a hunch Pomeroy was snappin' her garters. She went up ta the bank, took out as big a loan on her house as she could git outta thet darn fool of a banker. Thet's when they both skipped town. Go ahead an' git the treasurer's report an' then I got a jimdanderoo of a idee."

"Mrs. President, before I commence ta give you my financial report, I wish to make a motion to all that is represented here in this fine group of citizens. I wish to make a motion to all to make sure that Pete don't purchase another pile of pork chops until at least New Year's. I am sick and tired of pork, and I got me some pimples and carbuncles in peculiar and uncomfortable places. Doc Nelson says I been eating too many fried foods and he especially inquired about pork. I've had to stand up to drive the Wallis the last two weeks."

"A motion has been made to put a restraining order on our secretary to refrain from purchasing any more pork chops. Do I hear a second to the motion?"

"Si!"

"I knowed it! Knowed it all the time, thet damned Estaban kin understand Kansas."

"A motion has been made and seconded to restrain the secretary from the purchase of any more pork chops until January 1, 1941. All in favor — the vote is unanimous. Did you get the message, Mr. Secretary?"

"I'll git m' own victuals, I like m' pork chops. I'll switch this here corporation ta liver, give Otis a pimple somewhere's else. I'd prefer it right on the end of his nose." Pete smiled.

"Otis, please proceed with your treasurer's report."

"I have it right down to the penny, people. We spent seven dollars for gas at Goodland. We cut 480 acres for Jethro Thomas, had to send Bonita to St. Francis fer thirty cents' worth of carriage bolts. Bought —"

"Godalmighty, Otis. Hold up, ya ox. We'uns don't need ever'

nickel an' dime we spint. We'll be here 'til day after tamarry. What's down there at the bottom line? Pronounce thet word profit. We gotta split the take, divvy up the pot. We're a talkin' 'bout extry-ordinary income here, all non-taxable. What's the net on yer double-entry? Give me 'nother one of them brownies."

Otis kind of smirked. Pete had come unglued quicker than he had anticipated. "$3,608.42 net. Mrs. President, what does it say in that book Roberts Rules of Orders 'bout the secretary interrupting the treasurer's important report, kind of rude-like? Pass the brownies, please."

"Fergit 'bout them rules. I make us a motion we accept thet fine report. Don't bother with all them seconds. We gotta split up the take, divvy up the plunder, split the profit by seven folks. What's thet come ta, Otis?"

"Where did you get seven? There's only six, Pete," said Lyle.

"Petey Pat, she gits a full share. She got us a bunch o' places fer a good supper an' a comfortable bid. Petey Pat gits a portion o' the plunder." Lyle and Lil smiled.

"Comes to $515.48 per person, Pete," said Otis.

"Make 'er $500 each. I need a dab fer seed money. Gonna go ta Goodland, see Sylvester. Thet blood-sucker 'll need a retainer fer what I got planned. I'd go ta Denver an' see Simon, but this is so simple I'll give Sly Syl a little shot at some blood money. Anybody want thet last brownie? Jest remember, liver is sure cheaper than pork chops, got a lot a iron. Thet Estaban sure don' need any iron in his rammer, pork chop dinner come New Year's!"

"I thought you didn't like Sly Syl, Pete. He's always getting to you on something."

"Why, I got no problem with Syl, Otis. In fact, after I unloaded thet lemon of a Terryplane on Penelope, made me one up on Sly Syl. Monetary problems don't count, not a-tall. Hit's the way we skin one another, thet's what counts."

"What kind of a preposterous plan do you have, Pete?"

"Otis, this plan 'll put ya right on yer pimpled posterior. We're gonna buy the bank. Git thet dimwit outta town. We'uns need locals ta run thet bank. People thet care, listen ta their problems. Help 'em. Thet banker is a pathetic personage, an' sides thet, we'll all make us a pile a plunder. Thet's where Sly Syl comes in. He's our negotiator fer the purchase, act as our fiduciary. I put up all the money, but no one knows I'm behind the bank deal. I'm what is called a secret and quiet partner. Thet's what I am, a hush-hush banker. Them kind is hard ta find, quiet bankers. Most of 'em is blow-hards."

"Pete, what you mean is you're a silent partner," Lil informed Pete.

"I ain't a-gonna keep m' mouth shet, jest so's no one knows I'm in the bank, the owner. Ya ll got thet? Now here's m' plan. Lyle is the president of the bank, Lil's the vice, and we'll put Penelope Pinchlips in as head cashier. We keep all the rest of the locals of the bank employed. This gonna be a home folks kind o' bank."

"Penelope Pinchlips! Godalmighty, Pete, ya must be possessed. You and Penelope haven't said a word since Pomeroy left."

"Otis, ya jest don't understand folks the way I do. Penelope has been here all her natural borned days. Palmer Pinchlips' daddy came to Fort Wallace, was a sutler with them folks. Now she got squirrely over Pomeroy. I knowed what he was an' nature done took its course. Besides thet, she needs the job an' money. Figure it thisaway. Penelope is m' decoy." Pete smiled.

"What is your plan for the rest of us, Pete?" Otis wanted that extra-ordinary income to continue.

"Otis, ya is now in charge of all farmin' operations. I done ordered a new WD9 McCormick diesel tractor. We'll keep the Wallis fer jobs around the feedlots. Ya got a thousand acres o' wheat ta drill, hunnert and sixty fer Petey Pat when the ground and the weather is jest perfect. Ya gotta keep the double-entry on this here operation. Thet includes the feedlot. Ya got a powerful pile o' responsibility, Otis."

"Do I still git ta pop the Wallis now and then, Pete?"

"Yep, now Estaban is in charge of the feedlots. We're gonna put in six hunnert acres o' milo fer them ratty-assed Mex cattle. As soon as I git rid of thet tickle-bone banker, we'll move Lyle an' Lil ta town. Put 'em in the banker's house, hit's fully furnished. Thet's the way I always purchase m' property, fully furnished. Estaban and Bonita, they git headquarters rent free. I don't want none of yer out-laws movin' in, this ain't no hideout fer Pancho Villa. Otis, ya think yer arthritis kin handle all thet tractor drivin'? Thet WD9 is a real smoothie; they say hit's the Packard o' tractors. Got a padded seat with a spring, easy on yer hemorrhoids. Jest like sittin' in a easy chair."

Otis inquired, "What about our custom combinin' business next year? We all like that extra-ordinary income."

"Glad ya asked. I got 'er all figured out. We'll leave Lil ta run the bank, she kin git along with Prune Face. Lyle 'll need ta git out fer some sunshine. He'll be soft as a baby's butt by then. We'll need ta hire us another hand, maybe git us some high school kid, maybe one o' my grandkids. Estaban an' Bonita's little papoose 'll take the place o' Petey Pat when we's lookin' fer food an' lodgin'."

"When are we going to Goodland to see Sylvester?"

"Lyle m' boy. Ya call him on the long-distance. Set up a appointment. Now don't say nuthin' 'bout a bank. Central's got both big ears and a big mouth even though I do slip 'er a ten-spot ever' month fer answerin' m' phone. We'll all drive over in the Packard. Otis kin drive the new WD9 home, pull thet new Massey-Harris combine. I bought us a new two-ton International, got duals on the back, already have 'er painted about us being 'Neat with Wheat.' We'll use the Model A fer a oiler an' spare parts. I'm tard o' buyin' piddlin' amounts o' fuel, we'll put a 300-gallon tank on the truck. Pull up ta the combine an' the tractor, fuel up and grease. Fuel, ice cream an' pork chops, them's our biggest overhead problem. When we git thet bank, I kin quit bankin' by mail up ta Cheyenne Wells. Them three-cent stamps are a financial killer. Now, how's them idees hit y'all?"

Otis asked, "Am I supposed ta drill six hundred acres for Pud, Pete?"

"Glad ya asked. I ain't heard a word from ol' Pud. We'll go ahead an' drill 'er, strip 'er jest like our own."

Lil just sat there and shook her head. Versatile was the word that came to her first. It seemed descriptive. First, Pete had wanted her to act like a half-wit; now she was going to be vice-president of a bank. She thought that man is crazy like a fox. He'll get that bank, too; then she asked Pete a question.

"I don't quite understand this sudden empathy for Penelope Pinchlips. You've been enemies since she torched your fodder field way back in the '20s."

"When a feller is standin' up on a combine platform all day, one has time ta think. Figure it this way, Lil. Bank sells ta new folks, locals. Thet's you, Lyle, and Penelope Pinchlips. Penelope is m' smokescreen. Not a soul an' body will ever figure Pete Pisanmoan is hooked up with thet bank, not with Penelope right there in the bank, cashier an' all. Perfect position fer m' principal participation."

"I thought all you did was fight flying ants, scratch grain rash." Lyle was dubious about being a bank president.

"Yes, m' man, yesirree, Lyle. Trust is what I need. Yer a good boy. Ya didn't know diddly 'bout feedin' cattle neither. Look at ya now, expert cattle feeder. Didn't know diddly-squat 'bout buildin' cheap corrals. I done showed ya how, economical like. Ya know the problems of the man in agriculture. Now thet humorous ho-ho up there at the bank, he's bin snuggin' up interest rates. That's legalized thievery. We're gonna slide them rates down on all the loans. They's bin 'nuff foreclosures in Wallace County ta last a hunnert years. I wanna increase the interest on savin's accounts; people save more, then we got more ta lend. Now, ya gotta be firm but ya gotta give the folks a chance. I done got me a motto fer our bank. Advertisin' has always bin my strong point. It's kind of a whiz-banger of a motto, "Thet's the Bank Fer My Money." We git thet bank opened, I kinda think I'll open me up a advertisin' agency. Seems jest like I have some sort of a gift fer words." Pete smiled, flipped his toothpick.

"Are you able to handle the purchase of the bank, financially speaking? May take a considerable sum." Lyle was concerned.

"Lyle m' boy, no problem, no problem a-tall. Why, thet little bail-bond business me an' Simon got up in Denver by the West Side Court is better'n a mint. Thet sucker pours out the bucks. We got another couple enterprises thet perculate right well. One's a industrial savin's bank, beats a hock shop ten ways from Monday. Thet twenty thousand bushel o' wheat kinda sweetens the pot, partner. Feller gits a good Jew attorney, make him a friend an' if ya got a little money, he does wonders with money."

Pete was looking Lyle over, made a comment. "Lyle, ya need ta commence ta look like a banker. When we git over ta Goodland, I want ya ta git a Five X'er, new gabardine suit, pair o' Justins; git square-toed, they look a heap nicer when ya got yer feet up on the desk. Sly Syl kin git us the bank; we need thet retainer figure in writin'. He's a slippery one; he don't deal on the up-an'-up like I do. Ya recollect them mineral rights. Cost me a pile on them fine lots up by the Township Hall. One other thing on the custom cuttin' business. While we're doin' the negotiatin' on thet bank, Lil needs ta write a letter, public relations type letter ta all them fine folks we combined wheat fer. Thank 'em fer their business, tell 'em we'll be back next year. We git us a nice list o' customers all built up, an' I'll sell thet sucker ta some cowboy someday fer a thousand er so, jest like I did thet list ta ol' Hubcap. I think they calls it blue-sky."

"But I thought you were the advertising man, had a gift for words. You should write that letter, Pete." Lil smirked.

"Lil, m' most prominent gift is idees. I admit I am gifted with the power o' speech. Spellin' an' punctuation is m' main problem, commas, them kind a things. Why, we kin whip out them letters in no time a-tall. I can't wait to shove thet banker on a east-bounder. Tell Sly Syl I'll personally pay his fare. Here's a five fer postage, Lil. Them folks 'll be lookin' fer us come next harvest; they was fond a' m' perky personality."

Pete went home, "Surprise fer ya, Effie ol' girl. We made us a profit on the custom combinin' trip. Give it all ta ya, ol' girl. Here's fifty buckeroos. Now ya squeeze 'em a little. I'm headin' fer Amarilly, Texas. Visit with ol' Pud. Buy me some Mex cattle."

"How did your secret meetin' go, Penny-Pincher? You sign your name in blood on them minutes?" Effie was curious.

"Meetin' went jest fine. Where's m' grip, the one with them wire handles? Probably be gone a month 'er so, have a good time."

Fonda Stars in 'The Grapes of Wrath'

Jan. 4, 1940 — John Steinbeck's novel, "The Grapes of Wrath," came to the screen tonight in a stunning production directed by John Ford. Some of the book's final chapter has been omitted from the screenplay. On the whole, however, it is a faithful re-telling of Steinbeck's novel of Okies pushing on toward California in search of a decent livelihood. Henry Fonda, who starred in "Young Mr. Lincoln" last year, is excellent as the fiery Tom Joad. Jan Darwell is sympathetic as his "Ma." John Ford is a visual story-teller. A few shots of tired, stained faces, abandoned farmhouses and rattling trucks, and we have seen the bottom of the Dust bowl.
— Chronicle of the 20th Century

Pete Pisanmoan attended the film at the Strand Theater in Sharon Springs, Kansas. Effie thought he would like it — said he needed some culture, Steinbeck was a fine author. "We have studied this novel at the Sensation and Sensibility Club."

Pete had to leave when Grandma Joad died and they were forced to bury her beside the road in a shallow grave. It reminded him too much of western Kansas. Pete knew, he had been right in the middle of the dust bowl; he needed no reminder.

THE BANKER
1941-1946

THE MANY HOURS PETE PISANMOAN HAD SPENT on the Massey-Harris combine platform custom cutting wheat, knocking off the flying ants and signaling to Otis to speed up or slow down, he was plotting; it paid dividends. Pete was not an impetuous or impulsive decision-maker. Pensive and perceptible, he perceived the goal of the departure of the then president of the People's State Bank. It was his plan to send him packin', sooner the better.

The purchase of the bank progressed as planned. Pete was down in Texas with Pud Pudlick in Potter County purchasing a passel of Mex steers. They took their time; both liked to visit and dicker when purchasing livestock. They had no reason to hurry, the two cattle buyers headquartered at Pampa. Fellow in Pampa ran a barber shop that was called Pop's Tonsorial Parlor. Pete liked Pop; he was partial to Pop's Place. The two strayed several times over around Dalhart and Dumas and picked up a few head from the destitute, delinquent and the desperate. Pete became quite fond of barbecue, mesquite style. He liked the pungent odor. The Texicans around Potter County thought there was only one Pud Pudlick; put Pud and Pete together and they were still telling stories about the two up to at least 1973 or was it '74? The fellows that sat in front of the pool hall swapping lies, the stories were like a rare wine, they became better each time they were told over the years.

Pete stayed with Pud and Prudence a little over a month. Prudence was peeved when Pud brought Pete home. But the more she got to know him, the more he became accepted. "He kinda grows on one, seems more of a gentleman than some of these geeks y'all bring home, but I can tell you one thing, Poindexter, I am really sick and tired of pork chops and the smell of mesquite!"

Pete and Pud had purchased about five hundred head. They drove in the driveway in Pud's Cadillac when he saw Prudence toss the welcome mat out in the spirea bushes.

Pete rolled his toothpick over to one side of his mouth. "Well, Pud ol' pal, guess I better hit the trail back to thet paradise o' the plains. Otis'll have yer wheat all drilled. I want ya ta sind them ratty-assed steers in 'bout a month. Vaccinate 'em fer blacklaig, dip 'em fer ticks and dehorn. Ya wanta go halvers? We'll run 'em on m' wheat an' yers. Too bad we had ta pay as high as five dollars a head fer some o' them jiraffs. Ya shure pulled a good 'un on me, tellin' me 'bout this pristine paradise with palm trees a-wavin', orange and lemon trees. Them Comanches was glad ta give ya this desert. Only thing good 'bout this country is the mesquite. Say, why don't ya come up fer harvest and bring a truck load o' mesquite; ya kin follow the harvest. We'd have us a peach of a time, mesquite fried chicken clear ta Nebrasky. I'll buy the pork chops; feller gits tard o' chicken, thought I growed feathers last year when we finally quit harvestin."

"We had a good time, Pete. Prudence is poundin' the walls and walkin' the axminster. Guess your welcome is runnin' thin. Them mesquite smoked pork chops was delicious. I'll ship this batch a critters; glad ya brought yer brandin' irons. We'll go halvers; I'll ship 'em in about a month. Fill 'em full of corn and cottonseed cake. Hope we make a pile. Adios, compadre."

On Pete's drive home he could see the country was slowly coming back from the drought; cattle seemed to be a little slicker, noticed the farmers were tearing out their fences that weren't covered with blow-dirt; big wheat crops were coming. Pete had a prince of a time in Potter County, but the good times kind of abdicated when he hit the Casa Del Sol.

"Here I am, Effie ol' girl, yer Petey Pet is home from his travels. I'm kinda weary. Here, let me see if I kin git m' arms around ya an' give ya a big hug. I shure did miss yer wonderful cookin'. Why, I haven't had a thing thet was burned 'er overdone since I left home. I see ya got yer hair all kinky-like. Ya think yer Shirley Temple?"

"You are sure not much on the end of a pen; not a word from you for over a month. You got thet Sheaffer's fountain pen; you could fill it at any post office for free, penny-pincher. I know, it was that one-cent stamp that stopped you. You waltzed outta here leaving me with just fifty dollars. I am not used to living below the poverty line, feeling like a pauper. I have my principles and pride. Lost m' transportation up at the bank. Do you know who bought that bank, Pete?"

"Really don't care a whit. I do what little bankin' I do up ta Cheyenne Wells an' Denver. Somethin' happen whilst I was gone down ta Amarilly, sittin' under the palm trees an' eatin' oranges? What's happened ta ya, Effie ol' girl? When I brought ya up from the Bar P, ya was nice an' quiet, kinda docile like. Now ya rip off a sentence jest a ratty-d-tat-tat. Reminds me o' Bonita. Give me the skinny on the People's State. It go broke agin?"

"Everybody's talking about the bank. That humorous banker had done left town. The new president is yer friend, that Lyle Lovelace!"

"Yer shure? M' partner out ta the P.O.L.L.? Thet conservative agent? Where'd he git the money? Made a little pile on the custom combinin' trip. I bet he inherited it. Where's m' little Petey Pat? She waitin' on customers up at the bank? Where's m' gravy-maker? Explain ta me how ya lost yer transportation. Why, yer the very first person I wanna be shure is properly taken keer of, m' Kansas sunnyflower of m' heart." Pete played the bank purchase quite proficiently and professionally.

"From what I hear from Penelope, this Lyle and Lil bought the People's State. They paid cash for it, cash right up front. Lyle is the president, Lil is the vice-president, and you would never guess in a million years who's the head cashier. This 'll give you a kick right in the patoot!"

"Why, I'm kinda flabbergasted. Who they got fer the cashier an' small loan officer?"

"Your fine friend and neighbor, Penelope Pinchlips. That Lyle ain't got nothing but praise for Penelope. Said she was a natural borned cashier, perfect for the position, positively a perfectionist. A 'Paragon of Parsimony,' those are his very words, Pete."

"Well, with thet ol' parsnip in the bank, I'll jest keep m' little pile up ta Cheyenne Wells an' Denver. What happened ta yer autymobile? Yer gittin' too heavy in the caboose ta do much walkin'?"

"You was down there in Texas sitting under them palm trees sipping orange juice; I needed money. I cozied up to my friend, Penelope. I just wanted a pittance, two hundred dollars to tide me over. She demanded collateral. I said what about the Casa Del Sol? She said I wasn't on the title; she said it is all yours! Why, I didn't know that. I thought we were halvers like on that dump rental property up the street. We sure were halvers on that outhouse. How come I am not halvers on the title to the Casa Del Sol, Penny-Pincher Pete?"

"Pshaw, purely a protective problem fer yer own personal well bein', Effie. I am being very keerful a' estate taxes. Simon says ta be keerful not ta put too much in yer name, plans ta leap-frog a generation. Hit's too complicated fer yer mentality. Why wouldn't Penelope take the investmint property, our fine income property, thet's collateral?"

"She said it warn't worth no two hundred dollars."

Pete kind of sat down on his Navajo. "She's a real estate appraiser, too. She's a person o' peculiar an' plentiful talents. So why aren't ya drivin' yer Model A? Hit's worth more than two hunnert smackers."

"She wanted insurance, wanted it to cover the bank in case I double-clutched it and killed a body. Then Fondis F. wanted to see my driver's license before he'd write me up on the insurance. I never got a license. He called the bank; they used some kind of word, indemnify. Wanted close to a million big ones. I was pretty darned mad by then. I just took that Model A up to Cowles Garage, had them put it up on blocks and picked up my two hundred. I thought that Penelope was going to take two pints a blood. Say, what's all that wood, sticks poking out of the Packard windows? See you have a trunk full, got the trunk lid tied down with a piece of baling wire. You look like you just left a Hooverville."

"Effie, thet's the best firewood in the world, 'bout the only good thing in Texas. Cheap cattle and mesquite. Thet's a odiferous wood thet makes m' pork chops delicious, a true delicacy. Me an' Pud is gonna start sellin' thet wood all around the country. Sell ta cafes, eatin' houses. Me an ol' Pud plan to make us a pile a' money in mesquite. Didja save m' *Denver Post?*"

Pete settled down in his favorite chair, picked up a back issue of the *Post,* looked up. "Ya bin sittin' in m' chair. Yer caboose has got the contours of my perfect posterior outta balance. Now hit's gonna take me a coupla months ta git it back ta normal."

"Ya sound just like the papa bear, Pete; just scooch your butt around, it will fit just fine."

"Yeah, and ya look like a hippo Goldie Locks with them kinky curls." Lovable couple, everything was normal in the Pisanmoan household.

Not a single person in Wallace County had the slightest inkling that Pete Pisanmoan was the owner, chairman of the board of the People's State. Pete's plan to be out of town when the purchase was completed had panned out. It is the careful preparation, the policy and the plot, purpose and ploy that results in the machination of success. Pete was sorry he'd missed the departure of the humorous banker. It really was a pity.

"Effie ol' girl, yer in fer a real treat this evenin'. I'm a-gonna barbecue yer pork chops, Texican style. Y'all have ta stand back when ya git a whiff of 'em, slobber all over m' far. I need yer oven rack. Git some bricks from out in back an' build us a little far in the back yard. Put some of thet mesquite on the far; thet's what makes 'em so delicious, hit's the smoke. Git a bid a coals."

"Why don't you go ahead and burn them, Pete? Make you seem more to home. Don't you ruin my new oven rack. I take pride in my possessions. Now if you should happen ta have a couple a hundred, I'd get my Model A out of the garage, get my license. Some folks say that Penelope has got interest figured out down to the minute. She don't go by days, slap a fifty or so extra on there for incidentals and interest."

Effie had to agree, the pork chops were really delicious. One problem, no gravy.

"I'm goin' out ta headquarters tamarrow — check on the feedlots. Got over five hunnert head a' ratty-assed Mex steers comin'. Otis better have coupla thousand acres o' wheat drilled.

Say, where is Lyle an' Lil livin'? They still out at headquarters? Bet thet Petey Pat has growed a foot; sure missed m' Petey Pat."

"They are living where the banker and his missus lived. I got to hand it to you, Pete. Them pork chops was delicious."

Pete smiled, picked a big chunk of pork chop out of his teeth.

There you have it, folks. Right there in a little county in western Kansas, out in the back yard of the Casa Del Sol, was the very first outdoor barbecue ever recorded, one that used imported mesquite from Texas. Now, if one were to be argumentative, create an imbroglio, dispute this statement, one might say the Comanches had done this out in west Texas for hundreds of years, perhaps thousands. That may be true, but only in the sense of necessity. There is no record that they used pork. Pete was the very first with pure pork! That's a fact, no disputing it, the creation of that wonderful American pastime, the backyard barbecue. The mention of pork may bring to mind the wild jablina (peccary), native to the southwestern United States. Doesn't count. Just doesn't taste like a Chester White or a Duroc.

Pete now had the People's State Bank in his possession; the pipsqueak banker was gone, but Pete had a problem. His officers at the bank knew he was back in town. Pete needed a meeting of the officers, excluding the cashier. He wanted to meet at headquarters; he needed to figure out a way to set up the meeting.

"By golly, it sure is good to see you, Pete. That Triple X hasn't hung up there on those elk antlers for, seems like a year. How'd things go down in that pristine paradise in Texas? You need a haircut, looks like you been out herding sheep, a tonsorial mess."

"Volney, most folks don't know it, but barbers is the smartest folks in the world. I had me a friend down in Pampa, Texas; thet's in Potter County. Name was Pop Plumber; thet man knew ever'thing. Ya kin see I didn't git no haircut, jest a shave. I tole him ya was m' personal tonsorial artist, an' with a fine head a hair like I got one has ta be particular. Me and Pud bought five hunnert an' twenty-four ratty-assed Mex steers.

Ol' Pud is putting a little bud on 'em, ship 'em up here fer wheat pasture an' I'll bloom them suckers out on milo an' sunnyflowers. Heard the bank sold; don't know where Lyle an' Lil got the money. He did mention one time he was due ta inherit a dab from some uncle back in Des Moines. Thet's in Iowy, Volney. I'll move a little batch I got up ta Cheyenne Wells — bank local now since thet tee-hee tenderfoot tippity-toed outta town. Ya recollect m' trouble with the jackity rabbits, don't ya, Volney?"

"How well I recall that disastrous decision. I've had my finger on the pulse of the populace since the bank purchase; folks seem pleased, especially with Penelope Pinchlips being employed."

"I was castin' m' eye on the *Topeka Daily Capitol.* Didja see that article on what F.D.R. done, Volney?"

"He does some fool thing most every day. Which one are you referring to, Pete?"

"This here one on page three, kinda down at the bottom — put 'er there so's people wouldn't pay no heed. Want me ta read 'er ta ya?"

"Proceed, Pete. I couldn't stop you if I tried."

FDR CREATES WAGE AND PRICE AGENCY

April 11, 1941 — Pres. Roosevelt has created the Office of Price Administration and Civilian Supply, and placed at its helm Leon Henderson. The initiative is necessary, according to the Pres., because the war is taxing the economy. It will enable the government to fix prices to prevent spiraling prices, profiteering and consumer hoarding; to stimulate provision of necessary civilian products to civilians after demands of the military.

—Topeka Daily Capitol

"All right, what did you find so profound and thought provoking, Pete?"

"Now if I was down ta Pop's Place, I wouldn't have to explain. Save my money fer a haircut so's I could do business at home, and now I got ta explain ta m' own personal barber.

This here's powerful economic panoply pervided fer the popu-lace. I shall pursue m' thoughts. First, we is facin' a shortage of all goods. Thet means some type of rationing. Next, I ain't goin' ta fast fer ya, am I? Then, if ya think 'bout it, he's sayin' price controls, no free market. If there's no free market, then there's a black market. Underground sales, barter system. I'll explain it simple-like fer yer mentality. I trade ya a bushel o' wheat fer three haircuts an' a pound a parsnips. No money changes hands, we done bartered. Next, folks will take ta hoardin', thet's jest another form a greed. Ya jest don't under-stand the problems of this here manifesto. They jest slid it by ya and ya didn't even feel it. We is at war — yep, at war, and the military comes first. Ya ever heard of the U.S. of A. declarin' war on Germany? Thet's what they call them Axis Powers. Not a word 'bout war; there's thet Lend-Lease. Ya know thet's just a giveaway, never pay it back, give Churchill fifty ol' rust bucket coal-fired destroyers. Why, we was gonna sink 'em anyway, use 'em fer skeet shootin'. I got me a idee. We're swappin' destroyers, tanks an' trucks fer time, maybe even some of our soldier boys' lives. Guess it's worth it. Ya seen Otis?"

"I sure haven't. I heard he was drilling wheat about sixteen hours a day. His arthritis has certainly improved. There, how's that bay rum feel? Now, you look like a Mex cattle buyer, a man of means, prosperous. Why, one might call you Pete Pisanmoan, Pride of the Prairie; still say you should run for Congress. Here, let me dust off your shoulders; I see a couple of grey hairs."

"Nope, Volney. I am now in a new business, messin' with mesquite farwood. Me an' ol' Pud 'll make us millions." Pete tongued his toothpick over to the other side of his mouth, smiled. "See ya, Volney. Got ta git out ta headquarters. Git Estaban workin' on them feedlots and corrals; steers are comin'."

In a small town it doesn't take long for news to travel. Lyle and Lil knew that Pete was back from Texas by dinner time, knew just how many Mex steers he'd purchased, was going into the mesquite wood business and had heard it was the smoke that flavored the meat, pork chops to Pete. They knew it was a smoke screen for Pete. They headed for headquarters just as soon as the bank closed.

"You check out the day's balance, Miss Penelope. We want to take Petey Pat for a little ride out in the country, give her some fresh air."

"Thank you, Mr. Lovelace. You have a nice drive; we'll balance out right to the penny or my name is not Pinchlips!"

After Lyle and Lil had left, Penelope made a comment to one of the local girls, a teller. "Lovely young couple, intelligent, but why they named that precious Petey Pat after such a despicable old man I'll never know. Did you know that wheat land Pete Pisanmoan gave that little Petey Pat put over $9,000 in her personal savings account just last year. Why, they'll probably send her to Colorado Women's College, maybe even send her to Bryn Mawr."

"By golly darn, ya brought m' little Petey Pat with ya. I sure have missed ya one an' all. Had a good trip down ta Amarilly. Me an' ol' Pud bought us a bunch of ratty-assed Mex steers. Got a new business for all of us; I'll git ta thet later. Tell me all 'bout the People's State; local folks didn't git a case a skitters?"

"You go ahead, Lyle. I have to wipe up Pete's shirt. Petey Pat spit up right in his pocket." Lil was a good mommy.

"You had it figured just right, pulled a good one, Pete. Sly Syl was the man to use for the pursuit of the purchase. He was the person that best personified perspicacity; he perused the problem and used craft and finesse. He explained the different banking regulations for a state bank than a national bank. There is a difference, you know, Pete."

"Godalmighty, Lyle, ya is already commenced ta talk like a banker! I don't care a whit 'bout regulations. I need me some figures. I work best with numbers; how much did thet sucker cost? What's down there on the bottom line?"

"Sly Syl got the stock for $50,000."

"A pittance, Lyle, a mere pittance. How much fer the improvements an' the blue sky. Gotta be blue sky with a bank?"

"Another $15,000, and you inherited a big bundle of foreclosures. We don't know what to do with those foreclosures; need your advice, Pete."

"Don't foreclose! Call ever' one of them folks in ta the bank.

Have a visit with 'em. Git a financial statement, check them assets. Lower the interest on their loans. If ya havta, loan 'em more ta tide 'em over fer another crop. They's war a-comin'; the price o' wheat and cattle is goin' up, even if F.D.R. slaps price controls on goods. How's 'bout the deposits? Any withdrawals since ya took over the store?"

"Not a dime; in fact, they have increased. We had a dandy just come in yesterday. A $100,000 deposit in our savings department. It came from Pampa, Texas. Wrote the check on the Potter County Bank and Trust." Lyle smiled.

Pete tongued the toothpick, and he smiled, too.

"Ol' Pud put a pile in 'er. Thet's what I calls a friend. How much was Sly Syl's fee? I'll bet he pasted us plenty. He knowed he had a patsy."

"Sylvester was quite pleasant to deal with; he had a couple of zingers for you — never said a word. They were down at the bottom of his statement. You now own your old Terraplane, cost you $500 and a pension for Penelope of $100 a month when she's sixty-five and a thousand in cash. He wanted it in tens and twenties."

"He done got me twict, a dead autymobile and a pension fer Pruneface. How old is thet Penelope anyways?"

"She was born in '89. She's fifty-two. All we did was have Simon write up an insurance annuity policy up in Denver. It is just a slight overhead problem, Pete."

"I got ol' Sly Syl this time, tens an' twenties. Thet means this deal was some of thet extry-ordinary income. Make a note of thet in the minutes; I'll nail his hide to the front door of the I.R.S. They's nuthin' worse than a unscrupulous an' unethical lawyer. I'll take keer o' thet autymobile. I'll see thet it's parked out in front of Penelope's house, right there on the city street. I got some advice fer ya, 'a ounce of keepin' yer mouth shut sure beats a ton a explanation.' I'll git John Craven ta pull thet Terryplane up in front o' her house late some night, no noise. Thet sucker'll sit there fer years, the City will make her move it, send the bill ta Sylvester. I'll loosen them headlights, tilt 'em up and make flower pots outta 'em. Plant some Golden Bantam Corn; thet sucker'll be a real eyesore. The city will have ta tow it away, sind the bill to Sylvester." Pete smiled. "I got another item, here's $200. Git Effie's Model A outta hock up at Cowles Garage, an' here's another twenty fer storage."

Lil could see the flaw in this Terraplane parking; it would be right next door to Pete's flamingos; Effie might have something to say about this caper. She remembered that warning about an ounce of keeping yer mouth shut, didn't say a thing.

"Give me thet Petey Pat. Let me hold her fer a coupla minutes. Did I tell ya me an' ol' Pud is gonna go in the wood business. May need a loan from the People's State; I'll make a loan application to ol' Pruneface." Petey Pat made a grab for Pete's gold toothpick, missed. Pete leaned back in his chair. He was playing horsey with Petey Pat on his foot, got a cramp.

"Here, take Petey Pat, will ya, Lil. I got some pronouncements ta make. Otis 'll recollect these words. Do ya remember this one, Otis? 'Drive a nail in the Kaiser's coffin'?"

Otis smiled.

"Yer too young, Lyle. You, too, Lil. Thet's loan talk, and it's war talk. Thet's the way the government takes excess money outta the economy, stops inflation thetaway. Thet's World War I; thet was the war ta end all wars; thet's what Woody Wilson said. I didn't believe a word of it neither."

Lyle was curious, "Why are you talking about loans and war, Pete?"

"Lyle, m' boy, we'll want the bank ta be the leader in the community, this paradise on the plains. World War I they sold them Liberty Bonds by the billions. Them smart politicians back in the big trough had slogans. I recollect one was 'Bond or Bondage.' "

Otis recalled several. " 'Keep freedom's lights burning,' you remember that one, Pete? Oh, I got another one, 'Build a monument ta Democracy.' "

The open air was helping Otis; Pete knew it would. In retrospect, it was all there in the *Topeka Daily Capitol* or the *Denver Post,* or any other newspaper for that matter. One just had to be observant and discerning, small articles, i.e.:

Oct. 11, 1941. Washington — It is reported that 2,000 Japanese will be evacuated from the West Coast."

"Nov. 3, 1941. Tokyo — U.S. Ambassador Joseph Crew cabled Washington, warning of a possible secret attack on U.S. positions.

November 26, 1941. Pacific-Japanese carrier force leaves base, moving east.

Washington Post

It was all the information the U.S.A. needed that there was an attack coming from the Japanese. It came, December 7, 1941, at Pearl Harbor. F.D.R. later said those famous lines: "A day that shall live in infamy." Then he later said: "Our enemies have performed a brilliant feat of deception, perfectly timed and executed with great skill." He let them come; he knew all about it.

Pete twitched his toothpick; he was kind in his statement. All he said after he read the article was, "Balderdash, Volney."

"Perspicacious" was a word often mentioned regarding Pete Pisanmoan. Yes, he was blessed with keen insight — always seemed just one step ahead of the crowd. He had lost his opportunity to lead Wallace countyites out of the land of depression when a banker refused to loan him the money for the rabbit enterprises; he would see that it would not occur a second time. "Them politicians 'll sell us a pig-in-a-poke an' the public 'll swaller it. A few in the know an' insiders 'll git rich. Most of 'em 'll jest work a lot harder. Some of our boys is gonna git kilt. Whey, Godalmighty! Bonita, ya is big as a house. Thet little 'un 'll git us a lot o' fried chicken an' clean bids next summer when we go custom cuttin'. Lyle, git ol' Estaban a good pickup truck, somethin' on a foreclosure. Git thet Bonita ta Doc Nelson when she's due. Them babies is wonderful meal tickets. Now thet ya got time ta work, ya got all them feed lots in tippity-top shape, Estaban? If they are in as good a shape as Bonita, they's O.K."

"Si, padrone."

Pete smiled, "Lookin' at thet Bonita seems his actions speak louder than his words. Ya got all thet wheat drilled includin' Pud's, Otis? Petey Pat's lookin' good?"

"We got a surprise fer ya, Pete. With that WD9 Estaban

rigged up a double-drill. Hooked two of them suckers together. I was drilling twenty-four-foot swath at a time. We drilled over four thousand acres. It's all up, be ready to graze steers when Pud sends them."

"How much milo we got in the bin?"

"Have about 5,000 bushels, it will be enough to bloom them steers out with sunflowers and thistles. Do it just like last year, Pete."

Pete was lucky to have a man such as Otis.

" 'Tain't nuff milo. I'll git out an' scout around fer some corn. I figure ta make a pile o' plunder on these steers. We got any more business ta come afore this meetin'? I'm gittin' hungry."

"You got messkeet, padrone!"

"By golly-darn, thet ol' Estaban done seen m' surprise. He knows farwood when he sees hit. Ya mix us up a batch o' freejoles an' burritos, Bonita. We'll have us a real Mex supper. Thet Petey Pat sure will like them burritos."

Lil smiled. Petey Pat was not about to have any such thing.

Pete was stuffing a burrito into his mouth when an idea hit him. As he had told Effie, "M' mind jest whirls around an' spits out these wonderful idees."

"We all been workin' too hard. We got the work all caught up until them ratty-assed steers git here. Me an' Otis 'll go scoutin' fer some corn, go up Nebrasky way. Estaban an' Bonita kin take the Diamond T an' drive down an' visit their kin folk. Estaban kin show off what a fine job he done on Bonita an' then bring back a big load a mesquite. While yer down there, I want ya ta look them steers over, Estaban. Probably hep git 'em loaded an' then ya hit the trail back fer the P.O.L.L. Lyle, Lil an' m' little Petey Pat need a vacation. Go back an' visit their folks — drive the Packard. Ol' Penelope, she kin run the bank; ya got her bonded, Lyle m' boy?"

"Yes, Pete, a cool million. Wrote it through your company, contacted Simon. He asked how much we were going to bond you for."

That was the last vacation any of them took that fall of 1941, and they weren't the only ones. Not another vacation until 1946. It was as Pete had predicted about the government messing around with the time. On February 9, 1942, all U.S.

clocks were turned ahead one hour for Daylight Savings Time. Few Americans understood where they saved an hour, but if it helped the war effort —

GAS IS RATIONED
NO JOY IN AUTOLAND

Dec. 1 — Gasoline rationing has gone into effect on a nationwide basis in the Untied States. The move affects 27 million passenger cars and five million buses and trucks and is an effort to conserve both gasoline and rubber tires. Some seven million auto owners in 13 eastern states have already had a taste of such restrictions, having been limited to three gallons of gas a week since last spring. Under the new plan, embracing the entire nation, car owners will get about four gallons each week. Pres. Roosevelt ordered the measure last week, and the rationing of coffee also took effect. A war Petroleum Administration is to be established.
— Kansas City Star, December 1941

Pete smiled, "I got me a idee to keep thet Penelope Pinchlips busy whilst yer on yer vacation back east. Lil, you cash a check fer Otis here an' give him an extry fiver outta the drawer. That'll keep ol' Pruneface busy lookin' fer thet fiver for a month 'er so."

"Pete, you do have a devious mind. Why do you pick on that poor woman so? She's a very good and conscientious employee."

"Now thet is an easy one ta answer, Lil. Hit's jealousy is the problem, pure an' simple, plain jealousy. I considered m'self the one an' onliest perfect person on this paradise o' the plains. Thet's the entire problem, competition. Penelope considered herself in the same condition, she was perfection. Now it cain't be, impossible fer two perfect persons ta survive in the same town. Then it came ta me the day she booted m' tombstone an' broke her toes. She was imperfect, they was a flaw, she knowed it. I was the winner. Thet's the reason she called me thet nasty name. It come ta her, I was the most perfect person an' she was jest the runner-up. I know hit's tough ta be a loser and a sore-footed loser ta boot." Pete just smiled.

Estaban summed the entire conversation up with three words, "Gringo bullsheet, padrone."

The Wallace County Commissioners were in session. They had a problem. They were accustomed to dealing with roads, the school districts, budgets and various complaints from the citizenry. This problem was different. It affected their very political lives; their future depended on their success. They had a directive from Washington, D.C. They were to appoint a person to head up the Wallace County Ration Board.

Henry Harper from Morton Township pretty well summed up the problem: "We need someone folks will respect. Someone that is uncorruptible and incompetent. The feller needs to have money; otherwise the public and populace would bribe him. We cannot let politics get mixed up in this job. Gimme one of them nickel King Edwards, think on this here problem awhile longer."

The three commissioners sat and contemplated. Cigar smoke filled the room; cigar smoke always fills a political room when a big decision is to be made.

Finally, Clem Clapper's eyes lit up; they weren't too bright what with all the cigar and the tears in his eyes from the smoke. "Pete Pisanmoan, that's our man! He pays his taxes; why, he even has paid other folks' delinquent taxes. He was a good politician, folks liked the way he was County Treasurer. He sure kept that Union Pacific on their toes, and he sure kept track of our mileage checks. How's ol' Pete strike you boys?"

The commissioners' vote was unanimous; Pete Pisanmoan was now the head of the Wallace County Ration Board.

"Why, he's just perfect for the job," said Marshall Finley. Apparently someone else considered Pete perfect. Pete was unaware of the commissioners' decision; he and Otis were on their scouting trip for corn. They renewed old acquaintances and cronies out on the custom combining trail. Pete handled the purchase of the corn diplomatically, really quite well, and during the course of the conversation he always used the word "cheep."

"Give ya a nickel a bushel more than the elevator in town.

F.O.B. my feedlots down in Wallace County, Kansas. Why, you and the missus haul a load down to the lots; I'll have ya up ta the house, an' we'll have a mess o' mesquite-smoked pork chops. M' missus would jest love ta have ya. Stay a coupla days, look at the paradise o' the plains. If'n I'm not ta home, we live over on the east side, couple o' ostriches out in front; two of 'em is bendin' over. The third one is a standin' on one foot. Effie, thet's the missus, she's a real peach of a person. Be sure an' tell her I sint ya. She jest loves company." Pete knew he couldn't haul corn that cheap; farmer needed a trip anyway after harvest.

When Pete got home, he was kind of reluctant to accept the job as head of the War Ration Board. It was all volunteer work, and some yahoo back in the trough was gonna tell him what ta do. He began to come round, "Need me some deputies, jest like I had when I was Wallace County Treasurer. Need Otis out on the implements. He git ta sittin' in a chair agin an' he'd git all stove up with arthritis. Give me Sadie Sobles part-time. Me an' Sadie bin through the political wars. She kin typerwrite m' correspondence. We need a woman on the board anyways. Now, I'm gonna be mean ta some of them folks, especially them railroaders. They don't git but their four gallons o' gas a month. They got them free railroad passes, ride the train free. Thet's m' first codicil. The farmer is m' first priority, an' I want an opinion on m' custom cuttin' business. I got farmers all the way ta Nebrasky dependin' on me ta cut their wheat. Them boys ain't got the means ta purchase a combine. I jest bought two new ones; I don't want nobody gittin' their tail in a knot 'cause I got gas ta run m' rigs."

Pete went on his custom combining tour during the harvests of 1942 through 1945. He always had gasoline coupons. Combining wheat was the only fun he had during the war, and the farmers were getting rich. Having Pete Pisanmoan, he's neat with wheat, was about all the fun they had, too. Farmers for miles down the road knew Pete and his crew were on the way; just don't hail.

It was the problems at home that gave Pete fits.

Here is an example of one of his problems:

CANNED FOOD, SHOES
RATIONED IN U.S.

Feb. 21, 1943 — At the expense of wearing out scarce shoe leather, Americans are flocking to grocery stores and buying up all the canned goods they can carry before rationing of food tins goes into effect March 1. Shoe rationing began several weeks ago, limiting each American to three pairs of shoes a year, due to a critical shortage of leather for soles. Americans purchased an estimated 450 million pairs of shoes last year. Now canned goods will join shoes, coffee and sugar on the list of rationed items, to be purchased only with stamps in ration books. Americans are stocking up. Mothers have wheeled away their canned goods purchases in perambulators. Young children are tugging toy wagons heaped high with the tins of food just purchased. "Talk about your gold rush," one New York grocer exclaimed. Canned fish and meat will not be rationed at this time, but will be included in a meat ration program to begin later this spring.

—New York Times, February 21, 1943

The war hit home when the draft board began sending out notices for the induction of the young men into military service. Pete molded the greedy, the diverse, the sometimes barbaric, and the restless into a platoon of patriotic paragons. He made Wallace Countyites proud. He plied them with platitudes, cajoled their consciences and conscripted their integrity. They cussed him and discussed him, but he was fair. On March 1, 1943, the U.S. coupon books were issued. School was dismissed, the faculty of the schools all assembled at the Township Hall for the dispersal of the ration books. Pete had his hands full.

Another headline: "March 21, Washington — Sale of butter, lard, fats, oils halted for one week." Pete made a pronouncement: "Don't pay a bit o' attention ta thet directive. How am I supposed ta stop Fred Frickle from comin' ta town Saturday an' sellin' his butter? Thet family has bin sellin' butter in town since '31. Pass thet directive ta the round file, Sadie."

"April 1, 1943. Washington — Meats, fats, cheese rationed in U.S." — *Washington Post*. That's the one that got Pete. "They done 'er now, Sadie! They done shut off m' pork chops, and the way I read this here directive, if'n they's any fat on the chops, we're in a heap o' trouble. Won't work here in Wallace County. It might work in the city. I got some fat heifers ready fer slaughter. Trade 'em fer a couple o' fat hogs an' a shoat 'er two. If'n we're gonna work like a bunch o' horses, we're gonna eat like 'em. Them railroaders is goin' sixteen hour a day. Farmers is, too. I saw a bunch o' kids in town last Saturday, ever' one was barefoot — savin' on shoes. Some rinky-dink up ta Denver drivin' a street car don't need as much grub as a guy out scoopin' wheat or coal in a U.P. locomotive. Ya notice all them locomotives? Ya notice all them troop trains headin' fer Denver?"

May 1944 — Meat rationing ends in the U.S."

— Rocky Mountain News

Meat rationing was not a large problem in the small towns of the west. The town butcher merely worked Sunday. Went out to a local ranch and butchered a beef; the best cut of beef went to the ration board. Pete's feedlot furnished quite a few.

November 19, 1944 — Washington. F.D.R. opens sixth war loan drive, seeking $14 billion.

—Washington Post

Pete received a letter from Washington informing him the Wallace Country contribution to this huge sum was $500,000. Pete remarked, "Why, thet's no hill fer a stepper, Lyle m' boy. Run 'er ta a cool million buckeroos. Our Wallace County farmers never had it so good; jest look at them deposits and cash on hand."

Wallace County continually oversubscribed and sold its war bonds. Children saved their quarters and bought the stamps. When their books totaled $18.75, they were issued a Series E bond. It was a $25 bond, payable in ten years. The People's State received an E Flag from the Secretary of the Treasury. That was a proud moment for Wallace County, that

E Flag flying out in front of the People's State Bank. The E stood for Effort, effort beyond the call of duty. Quite a crowd turned out for the presentation. Tuffy Lutz made the presentation; he was the State Rep. from that area. Lyle and Lil were there on the bank steps. Lyle was holding Petey Pat. Penelope actually smiled when Swede Lutz took the picture for the *Western Times*. Pete was back in the crowd; he tipped his Triple X back on his head, rolled his toothpick over to the other side of his mouth, smiled.

Headlines in various newspapers read:

February 20, 1945. Washington—War Labor Board orders the minimum wage of 55 cents an hour for textile workers.
— New York Times

February 26, 1945. Washington—Midnight curfew begins throughout the U.S.
— Washington Post

March 19, 1945. Washington — Office of Price Administration freezes prices on all clothing.
— Topeka Daily Capitol

April 12, 1945. Roosevelt dies on the eve of victory. Harry S. Truman assumes the presidency.

August 15, 1945. U.S. rationing of gas, fuel oil and food ends.
— Kansas City Star

The war was over! Pete Pisanmoan was out of a job. It took the atomic bomb on Hiroshima and Nagasaki to get his job. Pete was delighted. No one ever thanked Pete for his war efforts; no E Flag flew at the ration board; they were forgotten in the joy of victory. Pete had made no profit for his endeavors; he was not even paid the dollar a year some large corporate leaders received. He knew he'd done a good job; that was satisfaction enough.

There was a customer under the towel of the barber chair. Pete sat down and perused the morning issue of the *Topeka Daily Capitol,* tipped back his Triple X, commenced reading.

"You look kinda tired this morning. You have a tough night, Pete?"

"It's the years, Volney. Four tough years. We cut a powerful lot of wheat, fed a lot o' steers an' heifers. Boys are all comin' home; quite a few didn't make hit, makes a feller feel kinda blue. I done put m' grandson in charge of the P.O.L.L. Corporation. Thet Estaban and Bonita, they got four little ones now. Thet first one was m' favorite—little Pedro Pudcho Rodriquez. Named thet little sucker after me an' ol' Pud. Lyle an' Lil got the T.T.T. & T. ground in a trust. Estaban is kinda the foreman of the whole shebang. He's runnin' the custom cuttin' end of the business, knows all the folks from way back. Petey Pat is in the first grade next year. Thet little tyke has 'nuff money from a half section I give her ta git through college." Pete sighed, "Volney, ya know what thet Effie wants now?"

"Pete, I haven't the slightest idea."

"Effie wants wall-to-wall carpet. Didja ever hear o' sech a thing? They's number one oak floors in the Casa. Best thing I did fer the entire war effort was ta pitch them ugly pelicans onto a scrap iron drive. Thet really perturbed ol' Effie." Pete smiled.

"I'm really proud of you, Pete. That was a difficult position you had—performed it to perfection. The home folks did their share, too, didn't they?"

"Thet People's State was m' pride. Yesiree, proud of thet fine financial institution. Ever' time I got me a directive outta thet asylum on the Potomac, we raised 'nuther coupla hunnert thousand in bonds. Penelope Pinchlips deserves a pat on her pastern, along with Lyle and Lil. Say, I gotta tell ya 'bout a new business me an' ol' Pud got goin'. Fence posts, there's a real shortage a fence posts. I sint Otis an' Estaban down ta Potter County with the wheat trucks, bring back a couple loads a' posts."

"What kind of posts, Pete? I know the ranchers are sure in need of posts."

"Cedar, hard as nails, last a lifetime. Cheep, sell 'em fer a dime apiece. They's costin' me three cents F.O.B. Pud's place.

I figure we'll make 'bout fifty percent profit if the boys don't blow a tare. I got a method ta m' madness, keep Otis behind the wheel of a vehicle an' his arthritis don't act up. I keep Estaban away from Bonita an' he don't git ta actin' up, he's a randy one. I got ta build onta headquarters. Little Pancho Jesus done filled the last bidroom. Them's great kids. I'm goin' up ta the abstract office. See ya, Volney."

Pete tipped his Triple X at a jaunty angle. He felt like a post salesman. The war was over, he had a nice shave, a clean shirt and some new kangaroo boots, the first ones since the start of the war. He noticed Doris Dinwiddie, she was struggling up the steps to the People's State. Doris had come to Wallace County about the same time Pete's folks had settled up, she was a real old-timer. "Ya need some hep there, Doris? Them's tough steps."

"Godalmighty, Pete, I'm gittin' old. I got to deposit my old-age pension check. These steps are hard for us old folks."

Pete helped Doris up the steps, held her elbow, opened the brass door to the bank, saw Penelope Pinchlips at her desk. She looked up, and damned if she didn't smile at Pete. He wondered if Pomeroy was back in town, taken up residence. Pete told Doris to be "keerful" and left. Doris was right, those steps were hard for the old folks. Even Pete had to take a little blow when he got to the door. Then the idea hit him, a wonderful idea. Why, it was jest perfect for those people thet were in their wonderful Golden Years. He'd put a little window at the back of the bank, put plate glass in the window for safety. People could walk-up or drive-up to thet window; one of the tellers could shove a cigar box out on a track like on your kitchen drawers, make the transactions, drive down the alley to the cleaning shop and go out on Main Street by Joe Ward's drug store. Older folks wouldn't have to walk up those front steps, just walk on home and not out of puff.

There you have it, folks, right there in a little county and small town bank, out there on the paradise on the plains was the very first walk-up and drive-up window to a bank. *The Western Times* gave all the credit to the president of the bank, Lyle Lovelace. Pete thought it a nice photo and article; he just smiled. No one suspected that Pete owned the bank, that was, not until his obituary was printed years later; that was a real surprise! Pete read the following in the paper, economic news.

LORD KEYNES MEETS
HIS INEVITABLE FATE

April 21 — John Maynard Lord Keynes, whose efforts to restructure the theory and practice of economics won him worldwide fame, has died of a heart attack at age 63.

The Cambridge-educated British economist was married to Lydia Lopokova, the Russian ballerina, and was the center of the literary circle known as "Bloomsbury," which included Lytton Strachey, Virginia Woolf and their friends.

Keynes first achieved recognition as a brilliant thinker after publication in 1919 of his controversial book, "The Economic Consequences of the Peace," in which he warned that the harsh reparations imposed upon Germany after the First World War would prove harmful to both Germany and the victorious nations. He was subsequently proved correct, and the book has been translated in 11 languages.

In 1936, Keynes published his "General Theory of Employment, Interest and Money," in which he developed his idea that full employment should be the overriding goal of financial policy. This belief gradually took root as many nations adopted deficit-spending to overcome the ravages of depression.

When asked how to deal with the inflation resulting from such policies in the long run, Keynes replied, "In the long run, we are all dead."

—April 21, 1946 — London Times

Pete was well aware of Keynes; his finest pupil had been F.D.R. Sixty-five years later we are still pupils of Keynes and "We're a-spindin' money like we had it. Thet's deficit spindin'."

PETE THE PEDDLER

VOLNEY EASED THE NEW BARBER CHAIR UP; he'd finished the shave on a face he had shaved so many times that he almost felt it his own. "I'll bet I've shaved a mile of whiskers off that ugly puss of yours, Pete. Here, let me put a little styptic pencil on that little cut on your craggy chin. I ought to raise the price of my shave for an ugly face like yours. Say, how'd the post business go, you make a profit?"

"We done quit the post business, jest too good. Otis got a load a posts at Pud's, hit the trail. He got ta Lamar, Colorady, and sold the whole load, went back ta Pud's. Estaban made it ta Eads; he sold the load to Eads Livestock Co. He went back ta Pud's, but he met Otis on the way. Pud was about outta posts, an' they agreed ta raise the price ta fifteen cents a post. Guess we musta sold over two thousand posts, kept them boys busy." Pete fumbled around, "Where's m' gold toothpick? Ya done stole it so ya could pay fer this new barber chair. Bet this sucker don't have horsehair stuffin'. Didja see thet article in this mornin's paper 'bout folks back east eatin' horse meat?"

Volney looked quizzically at Pete. "Here's your toothpick; you put it right by your glasses with those little quarter circles at the bottom. I missed that article; what's it say about horse meat?"

Pete walked over to a chair, picked up the newspaper, sat down and began to look for the article. "Here it tis, page five. I'll read 'er ta ya." Pete glanced in the mirror. "I see ya got the bleedin' stopped; I think ya got a bad case o' the palsy; hit ain't m' craggy face, hit's yer shakin' with a razor. Ya better have yer liability insurance up ta date; about one more o' them serious cuts an' I'll call Simon. Ya ready?"

PRICES LEAD PEOPLE
TO EAT HORSE MEAT

Sept. 27, 1946 — New Yorkers are eating horse flesh in increasing amounts, it was learned yesterday as supplies of standard meats stayed at a record low, black marketing spread and poultry prices soared to one dollar a pound. Ceiling prices on choice cuts of horse meat are seventeen and twenty-one cents a pound. Former Mayor LaGuardia has called the eating of horses a sign of degeneration, while Health Commissioner Weinstein says horse meat is "as nutritious and as good as any other meat."

—New York Times

"Now I was always partial ta pork chops. I tried liver several times, beef's mighty good, and I don't think horse meat would be too bad," commented Pete.

"Was your custom combining profitable again this year, Pete? I heard something about lightning rods; what was that all about?" Volney thought he had something on Pete, didn't work. "You thinking of pursuing this lightning rod business, perhaps on a permanent basis?"

Pete just chuckled. "I am a borned peddler, Volney. Folks out there kinda put me up on a pedestal. I learned m' salesmanship and merchandisin' up in Denver. All ya have ta do is look 'em straight in the eye; I always wait fer 'em ta blink. Ya recollect m' used car business. Why, thet was pure peanuts compared ta what I done this year. Nuthin' permanent with them lightnin' rods. They's what I call a one-shotter; I never spint a day up on the combine platform this trip. I done put m' grandson Poke up there. I was makin' the big buckeroos sellin'. Thet's m' specialty. Why, I'm peerless at peddlin' — watermelons, autymobiles, wheat, fence posts. I bin thinkin' 'bout bein' a Fuller Brush salesman."

"Tell me how you flim-flammed the farmer, Pete."

"The first thing is ta have a machine-gun brain like I got. Ya gotta have idees poppin' all the time, constant flow of idees. I took Pedro, he's m' namesake, his little brother Jose Jesus, I jest call him J.J. He's a peach of a kid. Ya recollect the pony I bought fer them boys?"

"I sure do. What did those boys name that pony, I have forgotten?"

"Patches, fine name fer a pinto. He's kinda paint an' pinto. Thet Pedro, he's m' namesake, ya know. He rode Patches right up on the front porch. Patches' hoofs punched holes in the porch, ever' step he took. Otis like ta fell outta the Diamond T, he said he laughed so hard. Then Bonita came outta the kitchen door a spittin' Mex, made a grab fer Pedro, and danged if'n she didn't step in one of them hoof holes; she like ta broke her laig."

Volney asked, "Was she injured? She could have broken something. Is she all right?"

"She jest skinned up her shin. Otis got Pedro, he's m' namesake, ya know. He got Pedro and Patches offen the porch; then he pulled Bonita outta the hoof hole. Ever' one got ta laughin', so's no harm done. Ya wanna hear more 'bout m' wonderful idees?"

"We were on the subject of lightning rods. You had me positively electrified. Please proceed, Pete." Volney smirked.

Pete winced. Petulant glance at Volney, Pete realized he wasn't the only one to give zingers. "I got them two boys, Pedro an' J.J., ridin' with me. I know ever' farm from here ta Sidney, Nebrasky. I was out in front of the crew linin' up the custom cutters. Them two boys was with me ta line up our bid an' board. We'd git ta visitin' with a farmer; I'd commence ta look around at his buildin's, all the improvements so's ta speak. When I first started custom cuttin', I'd always mention hail to git the job. Now I have done changed m' sales pitch. I mention hail an' lightnin'. Ya live in western Kansas, eastern Colorady and up in Nebrasky an' ya know all 'bout lightnin'. I'd kinda eyeball the barn and the house, then disclose m' pyrotechnical intellect — like I do believe it would take jest four points on the barn — yep, jest three on the house. I could use plain cable, coppered, but zinc plate twist would be the best. It zaps thet lightnin' down in the ground faster. See, zinc plate twist was all I had, got it from an army surplus warehouse in Crete, Nebrasky. It was old cable they'd used on army radio towers, braces and lightnin' arresters. I paid a pittance fer it, bought me five rolls, thousand feet ta a roll. It was a good thing thet new International I bought had duals, them rolls a' zinc coat twist weighed a ton each."

"How'd you become knowledgeable about lightning rod and installation? You don't know anything about lightning except it doesn't strike twice in the same place." Volney was right in the question, how did Pete know anything about lightning?

"Ya doubtin' m' veracity, ain't ya? I saw an advertisement in *Capper's Farmer*. They sint one of them brochures. Thet's all I needed, jest a little information and imagination; the rest was jest sales pitch an' my idees, jest winged 'er."

"What you really mean is you're full of b.s., right, Pete?"

"Ya got 'er, Volney. Thet's all thet salesmanship is, but if yer presentation is good, folks jest loves it. I tole 'em their fire insurance rates would go down, they'd live a heap longer, git better reception on their radios and thet safety an' security of the family was priceless. I always talk ta the woman of the house; she's the buyer. She makes them important decisions."

"Farmers bought the lightning rods, didn't they, Pete?"

"Volney, it was like shootin' ducks on the set. I'd have the scoopers put up the points an' the cable, ground it with a piece o' pipe, clamp on the cable, and we was finished. Them boys would git the job done whilst we was a-waitin' fer the dew ta dry offen the wheat. M' labor costs was zilch. I'd slip the boys a fiver now an' agin come Saturday night."

"Did you charge by the foot or the point? How did you work out your overpriced lightning rods?"

"Charged by the point — twenty dollars a point. Them folks liked thet. They figured they was gittin' the zinc plate twist fer nuthin'. Ya wanna hear m' next idee? I made me a small commish on this one, jest 'nuff ta pay fer the fuel."

"You are, of course, still flim-flamming the farmer and his family, right? More ideas to make money, Pistol Pete?"

"I tole ya, jest like a machine gun. Otis's wife, Oscarina, wanted ta come on the tour this year. We could always use 'nuther woman on the crew fer hep in the kitchen, an' them boys was a handful fer Bonita. I got thet Oscarina ta become a Avon Lady. Why, she made a bundle o' money. She never got turned down onct. She had little Pasquale and Pablo ridin' with her. Them Mex kids is cute as bug's ear. I bought them four boys harmonicys. Ya oughta hear them boys play, sounded like a barn full a' cats."

Volney had no trouble imagining those four boys on their harmonicas. "How did you make your Avon deliveries? You were out in the country cutting wheat, installing lightning rods, zinc coated twist."

"No trouble, no trouble a-tall. Ya see, I had 'nuther one o' m' idees goin'. Tole ya, jest like a machine gun, spittin' out idees."

"Yes, Pete, you are sure full of something, guess it's knowing how to make money. Please proceed, Pete. Whom the gods will destroy, they first make mad. Tell me how you made your Avon deliveries?"

"It were m' grandson, Volney. I think ya know Plute, he's the one thet's kinda slow, inherited his genes from Effie's side of the family tree. His head kinda rattles, but I give him a job. I got him a used two-ton truck, a Mack. I drove down ta Pud's place in Potter County, Texas. Thet's over by Pampa. Got us a load o' posts; thet way Plute would know the way down ta git posts and deliver 'em back ta Sharon Springs. The Avon orders was shipped F.O.B.; Plute sells the posts, then delivers the Avon to Oscarina out on the trail. Back down to Pud's fer another load. Kind o' like a Rockyfeller, ain't I?" Pete smiled.

Volney was slightly confused. "Let me see if I have this scheme straight. First, you were in the lead hustling business for the custom cutters. If Plute didn't sell his posts in Sharon, he came on to where you were selling lightning rods with the zinc-coated twist, is that right? Then he'd sell the posts there."

"Ya got 'er, Volney."

"Let me take this a step further. In addition to all these schemes, you had Oscarina following up with her Avon sales — a real beauty consultant. You do realize she's about the homeliest woman in Wallace County. She's got a figure like a telephone pole, face resembles a chamber pot."

"Ya is one goofy guy; ya gotta use yer head. She had the perfect personality fer beauty. She is so homely thet it made them farm women look beautiful. Thet's why I thought she would make a wonder at sellin' Avon products. Even Plute or Patches would look better with lipstick than Oscarina. Ain't I a wonder o' wonders, Volney?"

Volney just sighed.

"Then I came up with 'nuther idee, leave each o' those customers a little gift. Lipstick fer the woman, a pomade with a good smell fer the menfolk. Then when she delivered the order, them folks sometimes bought some more. I knowed them women were on a party-line; leave a little gift an' the word sure did travel. When we showed up combinin', installin' lightnin' rods an' Oscarina taking beauty orders, it was kinda like a medicine show."

"How many posts did you finally sell, Pete?"

"I don't rightly know. I tried ta keep track, couldn't do 'er. Otis was keeping track o' acreage and bushels; posts were not in his double-entry book. Ol' Pud down in Potter County, he knows. He paid them tree cutters. He's comin' up pretty soon, bring me a load a' oranges from Potter County. He'll have a bill fer me. I'd guess we sold maybe seventy or eighty thousand posts."

"Pete, did you ever figure out what you are worth? You must be a millionaire. I recall the first time you ever came in the shop; you were just up from Wallace and looking for a home. First thing I recall you peddled was sweet corn. I recall I bought some. It was good sweet corn. Pete, you are truly a peddler."

"Yesiree, thet was Golden Bantam corn. Thet Penelope Pinchlips burnt m' fodder field, started the feud. Gawd, but I have had a heap o' fun with thet Penelope. Ya recall when I put thet belt dressin' on the windmill lever? Pulled all the skin offen her palms. I don't have any idee what I'm worth. Accordin' ta Effie, I ain't worth much, but she ain't no prize neither. We bin married forty-one year, had forty-one thousand fights, but we always made up. I'd jest git on the train an' go ta Denver. Ya ain't done so bad yerself. Ya got a new barber chair, an' look at all the friends ya got, not a enemy in the world. Ya got friends an' the respect of all the folks here in Sharon Springs. Money ain't no fun ta have if'n ya don't have fun makin' it. Friends is different. They's a heap harder to git than money. I count ya as m' best friend. They's a whole bunch thet are runnin' second. I love m' precious Petey Pat an' thet Pedro an'

J.J. Ya know what I ordered fer ol' Effie awhile back?"

"You are a real doozy, I couldn't guess, you bein' so generous and all, I'll guess a new toilet seat. Yep, that is my guess, Pete."

"Ya have no feelin' fer m' generosity; ya think I'm just a tightwad. I ordered her a new Lincoln autymobile, got a automatic transmission. She is done with the double-clutchin' ferever. Me teachin' thet hippo ta double-clutch has cost me 'bout $5,000 in tires, new clutches and fawn drivin' mittens, but it was worth ever' penny. It kept the town folks laughin' an' in a humorous mood when there was darned little humor or nuthin' ta laugh about during the depression an' the drought."

"I am truly surprised, how could you part with the moncy? That is a wonderful present, Pete. What color did you choose?"

"White, white leather upholstery. I ordered everythin' they had on thet entire list o' accessories. If'n I wanted ta go in the car business agin, I'd make me a pile on them accessories. Why, Volney, we bin so tight with our money fer so long, we jest don't know how ta live with no war an' no depression. Thet drought was a dandy, many a farmer showed the white feather ta the Almighty. I cain't hep it, I still look ta the west ever now an' then, eyeball fer a dust storm. Them storms blowed a lot o' good people outta western Kansas. Things 'll never be the same."

Pete didn't have his glasses on, looked out the window on Main Street. "Say, look at thet red Cadillac pullin' up in front o' the shop. Looks like a bucket o' blood. What's them license plates say, Volney? I cain't read 'em, haven't got m' glasses on."

"Texas, look at them horns on the hood, Pete."

"I jest knowed it was a Texican, only a Texican would order a Cadillac thet color and put a set a horns on it. I'm gonna go out an' look under the gas tank, bet there's a pair o' gonads. Peculiar people, them Texicans. Why, it's m' friend ol' Pud Pudlick pilin' outta the plush! I shoulda know'd it. Come on out, Volney, we'll git Pud ta take us fer a ride."

Everyone on Main Street was looking at the Cadillac. Somehow they knew it had to do with Pete Pisanmoan. Just as Pete and Volney got out the door, Pud pushed the horn button, and that Cadillac bellowed like a Hereford bull. Pete almost wet his pants from laughing so hard. Pud had to pull mighty hard on his puckerin' string to keep from doing the same, he got so amused at Pete.

Volney was so amused he just had to sit down on the steps of the shop. He noticed a slight pain in his chest; it seemed to go away.

There were the two friends, Pud and Pete, shaking hands like Pud's numerous oil wells pumped. He had a bunch of them down in Potter County, Texas, that is.

Pete was grinning, "I jest knowed ya was comin', wanted the money fer them posts. Yer out collectin', short on cash. Gawd, this is one ugly autymobile. Bet ya ordered hit special. Feller at the car agency put down the ugliest car he ever sold ta the ugliest man in Texas. Take us fer a ride, didja bring Pru? What's thet smell? I know, ya done brought some tamales, enchiladas an' some freejoles fer Estaban an' them younguns. Come on, Volney, we're goin' out ta headquarters, take all this here Mex food. Ya git in the back like Harry does back there at the big trough, peruse the pedestrians an' plebeians. Turn yer sign aroun' an' tell folks yer shut. Let's go, gawd, this here autymobile is like ridin' inside a cow." Pete just smiled.

"Pud, what's all this hair on the front seat? Pru ain't got white hair?"

Pud kinda squirmed around a little as he was backing out on Main Street; he knew he would have to tell Pete. "Pru's got a little French poodle. I cain't figure out how to kill the damned thing. She's up ta y'all's house with Effie. Them two women got along right well. Last time I seen thet poodle he was snugglin' down in a chair. That chair had a Navajo saddle blanket on it. Seems like that poodle done taken a likin' to that chair, seemed like his very own." Now it was Pud's turn to smile. He winked at Volney in the rear view mirror.

Volney didn't own a car; it was quite a treat for him to ride in a Cadillac.

Pete flicked thet toothpick; he jest knew he was gonna hate thet dawg.

On their way back to town it was Pud who spilled the beans. He didn't mean to. He didn't know about the secrecy of the bank ownership. "You paid my interest on my savings account right up to snuff, bank doing well, Pete?"

Pete tensed up. He seemed agitated at the question.

Volney leaned forward in the back seat, seemed anxious for the answer. He'd been suspicious for some time as to who really owned that bank. He observed the toothpick; that would tell him the answer. It flipped straight up.

Pete turned around and said to Volney, "Ya don't know nuthin' 'bout any bank, but ya do know what happens ta folks thet don't loan money fer felt hats, the ones with the permanent crease. Ya keep this under yer hat, Volney."

Volney knew what was expected; he spit on his palm, he and Pete shook hands, and Volney never told a soul about the bank.

It didn't take long for Pete to break that poodle from parking his fleas on his Navajo. The *Denver Post* carrier boy now had rubber bands for the paper, didn't have to fold them any more when he threw them in the nearest bush. Pete merely placed one of the rubber bands on his finger, formed a Y, pulled back with his thumb and snapped Pussykins on the nose. Pussykins howled out to the kitchen. Pru could not find the trouble with the howling little dog, what had happened? Pete put the *Post* up a little higher so Pru couldn't see his face; he smiled. So did Pud.

Pud was anxious to get on the road. "How long do y'all think it will take y'all to pack, Effie? We're gonna get in the Caddy and point them horns down the road, tour the country. Cain't leave until Pete pays me for them posts, then we'll take off."

Before Effie could answer, it was Pete who leaned back from gnawing a pork chop with a glow of satisfaction on his face; then a small scowl appeared.

"Folks, we have us a prodigious problem, and the name of thet problem is Pussykins!" Pete held up his hand when Pru opened her mouth to protest; she shut it. "Now, I was gonna be nice an' quiet an' not mention thet dawg, but I jest as well git it offen m' chest. I ain't gonna ride in thet ugly car with a dumb dog gittin' hair all over me, but I have done solved the problem. Effie will jest take thet mutt, Pussykins, over ta Penelope Pinchlips, an' she'll take care of the mutt 'til we get back. Why, we'd be a-stoppin' ever' hour fer thet mutt ta do his business on a post or someone's mailbox. Ya agree, Pud ol' pal?" Pete wasn't so dumb; he'd just volleyed the problem over to Pud.

"Why, yer a real peach, Pete. The care of the dog is of primary importance to Prudence." (Pud called her Prudence when he was in a tight spot.) "Penelope Pinchlips would take very good care of Pussykins, especially since she is employed at the bank. Does that meet with your approval, Prudence, dearie?"

"It seems acceptable to me, Poindexter."

Pru was sort of huffy and somewhat annoyed. Pete kicked Pud's leg under the table and winked. Pete smiled, leaned back in his chair and reached for his gold toothpick. He'd just foxed Penelope into taking care of Pussykins for about a month. What he really hoped was that German Shepherd that had worked them ostriches over would come along and eat Pussykins for breakfast.

"I plumb forgot yer name was Poindexter. I shoulda re-called it when we put yer name on them deeds. I'm agonna git ya a cap — shiny visor, pair o' black pants and jacket, little leather bow-tie an' some puttees. Me an' ol' Effie 'll ride in the back seat, Poindexter be the chauffeur. We'll put a Swift & Co. sign on them doors. Folks think I'm Mr. Swift out on a cattle buyin' trip. Looks like we butcher 'em right in the car, half a beef in the trunk."

Before Pud could come up with a snappy riposte, there was a knock on the front door; Effie went to the door.

"Hello, Mr. Cowles. Do come in, we just finished our supper. These folks is Mr. and Mrs. Poindexter P. Pudlick from Pampa, Texas. They's here for a visit."

"Nice to meet you folks. I just stopped by to tell you your new Lincoln arrived today, Pete. A wonderful looking automo-bile. The first Lincoln we've sold since the war. Wish you'd put in a telephone, long drive over here. Nice to meet you, Mr. and Mrs. Pudlick. Pete charging you room and board?" He shut the door just before Pete was going to sic Pussykins on Mr. Cowles.

Effie was extremely excited. She was still driving her Model A Ford, still double-clutchin'. "You purchased a new Lincoln just for me, now didn't you, Peter P.? You made all that money on those fence posts and bought me a Lincoln. What color is it, Petey Pet?"

Twinkle in his eye, Pete said, "I ain't gonna tell, but it sure ain't blood red. It's kinda homogenized. It is a delicate assemblage an' montage o' colors you'ns prefer, Effie. Has yer monogram on it; on the doors it has our brand, —P and the Pisanmoan family crest beside it. One kin tell them boys keered 'bout their work — what them advertisin' boys call a 'state of the art machine.' Not a body nor soul knows what thet means, but it sure does sound impressive." Pete wiggled his toothpick, smiled at ol' Pud.

There you have it, folks, right there in a little town in western Kansas, in 1946 the very first controversy over the merits of a Lincoln versus a Cadillac automobile. Right there in Pete Pisanmoan's dining room, and to make the controversy even more of a brouhaha, it included a Texican as one of the combatants. Of course, there would be other Texicans, but he met his match with Pete. The controversy continues to this very day.

"Y'all haven't told us what color that boat is, Pete. Y'all blow a lot o' hot air about montage and homogenized, what's the color? M' Caddy is known as Comanche Red."

Pete only smiled. "I ain't a-gonna tell ya neither, not tanight. We'll git in thet butcher shop on wheels an' drive up and see a real autymobile in the mornin'. Beautiful piece of automotive craftsmanship, be mighty proud ta have m' Effie patrolin' the byways of our paradise on the plains, cruisin' quietly in a Lincoln, listenin' ta Ma Perkins an' Stella Dallas on her very own radio, have her fawn driving mittens on. I was gonna offer ta drive on this trip, but I been thinkin' it would be right interestin' ta see if thet Cadillac will make it all the way ta Washington, D.C. I figure we'll spend most of our time in some Cadillac dealer's garage, minor repairs about ever' hunnert miles. Git back ta the nation's capitol, see the really big trough. Maybe we kin watch Harry take his mornin' constitutional, walk that is."

Pud sat straight up. "I done got it figured. Y'all bought a white Lincoln. Cain't be no other color, white covers up all them little imperfections. I think I'll just mosey uptown, take me a peek through the windows at the garage, see if I can see y'all's vestal virgin."

"Ya do thet, Pud, an' I'll sic Pussykins on ya, tear ya limb from limb. I'd like ta teach thet dawg ta sic 'em. I'd sic him on Penelope ever' time she prissed out the door ta go to work up at thet bank. I'll go down in the basemint an' git m' grip. Say, Pud, did I tell ya I got me a new Five X'er? New crease, bulldogger style. Folks back east 'll take notice when we blow inta town. We got us a horny Cadillac with a bull bellerin' horn an' me right up there in front in m' Five X'er and Kangaroo Justins. Let's leave long 'bout noon. We could git ta Oakley by sundown if'n the Caddy don't break down."

"Pete, please be patient. Prudence and I have to go to the Clip and Curl, have our hair done. It will take me at least a day to select my wardrobe. You'll need to get your good suit pressed. We'll plan on a departure day after tomorrow. Prudence and I are going to drive the Lincoln around town, not miss a street."

Pud smiled. Effie was queen of the Casa. Pete might be neat with wheat, but Effie ran the home front; this was her headquarters!

"Y'all owe me for 67,402 fence posts at three cents apiece. I prefer cash over a check; this is some of that extry-ordinary income, and I hear that bank is on the shaky side."

"How much thet come to, Pud? I ain't a-tall good with figures. Otis does all m' figurin' an' payin' the bills. He does everythin' on the double-entry. Mathematics was always m' weak spot; I made up fer it in salesmanship and merchandisin'. Pru, ya know how ta figure this one? I shure know hit's way over ol' Effie's head."

"I have not the slightest idea. Pud never had a dime until they hit the Prudence No. 1. After that we got us one of those C.P. and A's."

Pete was curious. "Jest how many Prudences ya got pumpin'?"

Pud smiled, "We got fourteen Prudences and eleven Puds. They are all pumpin', Pete. Price of oil went down after the war, but the checks jest keep comin', kind of like a bunch of geese, they lay them golden eggs."

The next morning after breakfast, they all four piled in on the plush of the Cadillac. Pud glanced over his shoulder at the back seat. "Y'all comfortable there on them cushy seats, ladies? Cadillacs is known for their comfort." Pete didn't take the bait.

Pete turned around and looked at the occupants in the back seat. "Why, them two looks like two ol' settin' hens. Didja notice how them rear springs went down a whole bunch when them two clambered in the back. You girls better take a tight grip when we see a bump a-comin'. This tub jest might bottom out, give ya a heckuva jolt. Why, looka there, they got the Lincoln parked right out there on Main Street. Look at 'er, Effie ol' girl. They calls thet color Seashells by the Seashore."

Pud said, "I was right. Y'all did pick white. Instead of that brand and that silly family crest, they shoulda put a red cross. That tub looks just like an ambulance. Y'all ever drive that sucker out to headquarters, git some hockey on your boots and then climb in that sanitized hearse, y'all be in for a bunch of trouble from Effie. Let's all get out and see if she'll start. Where do they keep the crank? Must be in the trunk. Sterile, that's what I'd call that car. It just ain't got any personality. It's just a white car, seashells by the seashore, that took a lotta guts. Watch those ol' boys come outta that garage when I gives 'em a real Texas-style honk."

Pud pushed the horn button; activity on Main Street came to a complete standstill. Pedestrians looked around, figured some rancher was moving his cattle to another range or else going to the stockyards. Pete was upset; he thought the color of his and Effie's Lincoln was clever, had a lot of prestige. Pud stood back and looked at the Pisanmoan crest on the door of the Lincoln. At the top was a small fleur-de-lis. Under that were three items: a cow, a pitchfork and two little stalks that looked like stems of some kind of grass or grain.

"Hey, Pete, tell me all about this crest. Down in Texas we are short on the nobility. What's all this stuff mean? See you have it on there in gold leaf; that'll last about a week."

"Pud, knew you'd ask, you bein' from the common folks. M' grandma, Phoebe Pisanmoan, held me on her lap and tole me all about thet crest. Now here's the skinny. The flower at the top signifies the Pisanmoans is from the nobility of Switzerland; it is Pink Phlox. Thet cow is a Brown Swiss. The pitchfork is for the hay on each side. The crest signifies our ancestors were nobility an' farmers, the yeomen of ancient Switzerland. I git in over yer head, Pud? Ya got any questions?"

"Now here's my interpretation of that crest. That sorry old cow ate the flowers and all the hay. That fork is a manure fork, fork out the window of the barn. Nobility, you're about as noble as Pussykins." Right away Pete began working on a zinger fer ol' Pud.

Effie and Pru had finally made it out of the rear seat without any assistance from the oil baron and the noble Swiss yeoman. They didn't even knock off their hats getting out.

"Effie ol' girl, I ain't a-gonna teach ya one thing 'bout this here autymobile. Ya an' Pru have one of them men from the garage take ya out fer a little spin. This fine machine has a automatic transmission; thet means no more double-clutchin'. Me an' Pud is goin' ta the bank. I gotta pay him fer the posts an' git us a coupla hunnert fer the trip. We won't need much money; we is guests of Prudence No. 1 and Poindexter No. 9. He'll jest write it off as a business trip." Pete smiled, there was his zinger.

On the walk to the bank Pete told Pud he thought they could make Kansas City in three days. "I wanna tour them stockyards, not much else in Kansas City. Then let's git on up ta Chicago, take a look at them stockyards. They is supposed ta be the biggest in the world; ladies will enjoy thet sight. Why, we might even go through Swift and Company's packin' plant. I always did wanna see how they make bologny. I guess ya already know yer so full of it."

The first person Pete encountered at the bank was Penelope Pinchlips. "Mornin', Penelope, see yer 'bout as prissy as always. This here is Mr. Poindexter P. Pudlick. She's m' neighbor, Pud."

"Nice to make your acquaintance, Mr. Pudlick. I will get our bank president, Mr. Lyle Lovelace, right away."

Pud kind of whispered, "She the one that is gonna take care of Pussykins?"

"She's the one. Slip her a fifty, git rid of thet mutt, Pud."

Pete explained the post transaction to Lyle and needed a figure. "You owe Pud $2,022.06 for the posts, Pete."

"Seems like a pile o' buckeroos. What'd I gross on them

posts at fifteen cents apiece, Lyle m' boy?"

"Figures out to $10,110, Pete. What did you pay Plute, by the load or was he on a salary? His compensation and your truck expenses would have to come off that figure to get your net profit."

While Pete, Pud and Lyle were discussing the fence post transactions, Penelope Pinchlips was telling the other employees that Mr. Pudlick was one of the larger depositors in the bank, and probably on the board of directors. Pete was probably borrowing some money from Mr. Pudlick. Maybe Mr. Pudlick was checking on Mr. Lovelace. Penelope said, "Mr. Pudlick, Texas oil money, you know."

Pete was explaining the deal he had with Plute. "I paid Plute ten dollars a load. He was drivin' night an' day tryin' ta make the big bucks. I give him a twenty each trip, jest fer his gas and grub. He went through one set o' six-ply Goodyears. Now, as ta Pud, pay him in cash; he's a little short, only got twenty-one oil wells pumpin'. Guess I'll need a coupla thousand, we're gonna take us a trip back east."

Lyle stepped to the door of his office and motioned to Penelope. He asked her to get $2,000 cash from Mr.. Pisanmoan's account; he was taking a vacation.

Wily Pete waited just as Penelope was leaving Lyle's office. "Now ya be sure, Lyle, have thet Penelope take good keer of thet dawg. Real valuable pedigree, a Frenchie poodle. Pud had thet Pussykins shipped all the way from Paris, needs a bath ever' day, eats nuthin' but top ground beef with a half a teaspoon o' cod-liver oil on the top, kinda spread it around."

That was the first Penelope knew she was going to be in charge of a dog. As she was counting out the cash at one of the teller's drawers, she stamped her foot and muttered to herself: "He did it to me again!"

"Where are you going on your trip, Pete?" inquired Lyle.

"Ol' Pud and I plan on viewin' the stockyards at Kansas City and toodle on up ta Chicago; thet's if his Cadillac ain't always in some shop fer repairs. We both want ta see them stockyards in Chicago; they say they is the biggest in the world. Goin' ta Swift and Co.'s, maybe over to Armour. Ya ever see a packin' plant, Lyle? I like ta git close ta the killin' floor, lotta blood an' gore, kinda like a rabbit drive. Me an' Pud watched 'em up at Denver when we shipped them ratty-assed steers."

Lyle was dubious, "Do you think the ladies will enjoy the killing floor in a slaughter house? You better give this some consideration in your vacation plans."

"Lyle, call up Cowles Garage and see what thet Lincoln cost. Sind 'em a check an' remind them folks, if they was ta sell another Lincoln I was ta git a commish. Write up the insurance on the Lincoln, put 'er under thet multiple policy we got thet covers all the trucks, tractors and combines. Now while I think of it, we're missin' the boat on some of this bank insurance. Now listen close, Lyle m' boy. Some cowboy comes in the bank, wants ta borry couple thousand fer some brood cows and a bull. We loan the money but insist he take out lightnin' insurance on the herd. Feller cain't use zinc-coat twist on an ol' cow."

It was not long after this suggestion of Pete's that Lyle and Lil began writing all kinds of insurance at the bank. As with most banks, when borrowing money there were unforeseen little charges. In later years they were called "points." Money makers.

It was Pete's idea to give away a fly swatter with every policy the bank wrote. "Give 'em somethin' free an' we'll make more on insurance than on loans." There was a piece of cardboard paper over the end of the swatter screen, a throw-away. It read: "Flies carry disease — People's State is here to please."

"If ya'd like ta see the ugliest autymobile in the world, jest step outside an' look up towards Cowles, Lyle. This is a pitiful sight. It looks like plain gore, good thing I don't have a puny tummy 'er I wouldn't be able ta ride in 'er. Say, thet reminds me, give Effie's Model A to Oscarina. She kin use it ta peddle her cosmetical products ta our beautiful Wallace County ladies in town an' out on the farm. Now, I'm goin' down ta the drug store, git me a camery an' a load o' film, some paregoric fer Effie's touchy tummy. I'm gonna take me some pitchers on this trip, record it fer posterity. *Western Times* jest may want a complete accountin' of m' opinions and observations of our post-war economy. Why, they might even pay fer m' expenses, be sort of a foreign correspondent."

Pud thought, "Why, he cain't even write."

Pete smiled, tipped his new Five-X over his left eye, kinda cocky-like. Why, he even looked like an economic correspondent and student of John M. Keynes, a seller of corn, cattle, wheat, fence posts and lightning rods. A giver of fly swatters. A master of the advertising slogan, he would have made a good Burma-Shave sign writer, a master of the one-liners.

CONTROLS REDUCED ON
WAGES AND PRICES

Nov. 9, 1946 — Pres. Truman tonight ended all wage, price and salary controls except the ceilings on rents, sugar and rice, thus cutting the nation's economy loose from the shaky moorings of a four-year-old program.

"In short," he said, "the law of supply and demand, operating in the marketplace will, from now on, serve the people better than would continued regulation of prices by the government.

The President said that the price control system had lost popular support, primarily because of the faulty control law passed by the Congress. While conceding that some prices would rise sharply, he predicted that buyer resistance to excessive costs would eventually reduce such charges.

— The Denver Post, 1946

The most popular book, "Spock's Baby Care."

A small headline went unnoticed by most newspaper readers. Their interest was to get the boys home, tired of war.

VIETNAM UPRISING
SPARKS WAR WITH FRENCH

Dec. 20, 1946. Hanoi — Viet Minh and French forces fight fiercely in Annamite section of the city.

— Washington Post, 1946

It was beautiful fall weather, a perfect time for a long and restful trip for the two couples who had worked hard and sacrificed during the war. The Pudlicks and the Pisanmoans left the next day.

Effie had remarked at the Clip and Curl, "Our venture back east to visit our relations." Pete had a cousin on a farm in Iowa. That was about all the relatives they had in the U.S. of A., maybe the rest were still in Switzerland. Effie and Pru had purchased several new hats, and each had purchased a pair of sunglasses at the drug store, couple of classy dames.

"Them two look like Jane Russell and Hedy Lamarr." Pete looked straight ahead — flipped his toothpick. The two women just beamed; they thought this was a compliment, it wasn't.

"Pud, take this gut bucket down Main Street, make a U-turn by the Sasnak Hotel, we'll wave everyone an' all a hearty good-bye. Honk thet bull horn." It was really a royal send-off, noisy one, too.

Everyone stood and waved; it was an event for the citizenry of Sharon Springs for people to go on a vacation. Many of those waving had never been out of the county except for a baseball game at Tribune or Goodland. Volney stood out in front of the barber shop, gave a hearty wave to his friend. Things would be dull at the barber shop. Pete had promised to send him a picture post card. Pete waved; that was the last time Pete was to see his best friend, Volney Borst.

It was a good day when the travelers made 200 miles. Pete had to visit with all the gas station attendants. He wrote what he called his "daily despatch" to the *Western Times,* to give his viewpoint on how the winter wheat crop was doing. They toured the State of Kansas Capitol at Topeka. The editor of the paper had to take the dispatches down to Lil so she could read them to him. Pete told them all about the Muleybach Hotel in Kansas City and how he had had to pay $12 a night "fer a suite an' thet's jest fer one night!" They enjoyed the Kansas City stockyards.

If it got a little dull and "them two settin' hens in the back" got to visiting too loud, Pud or Pete would break into song. They sounded like two old crows, but it was successful with the ladies; they quieted down. Pud's favorite was "Oh, That Beautiful, Beautiful Texas." It went like this, and Pete jest hated it!

"Oh, that beautiful, beautiful Texas,
The most beautiful place that I know.
The land of beautiful women,
Who didn't know the word 'no.'
You can live on the plains or the prairie
Or out where the blue bonnets grow,
But there's no place like Texas,
The most beautiful place that I know."

But Pete was no slouch at making up songs and the words. He might come up with a reply about Kansas:

"Oh, thet beautiful, beautiful Kansas,
The most beautiful place thet I know.
The land of beautiful sunnyflowers
An' wonderful wheat crops did grow.
Ya can live on the plains or the prairie,
Or you kin watch the dust storms blow,
But there's no place like Kansas,
The most beautiful place thet I know."

Pud and Pete vied to outdo one another on their wording, the song was the same, lyrics different. Pete had one, but he used it once. It had to do with Kansas women and "how their tits did grow." Effie slapped him alongside his Five-X'er.

They finally made it to Washington, D.C. Pete wanted to see the Smithsonian; he had recalled what Lyle had said about their way of life prior to the Casa Del Sol. "Lyle was kerrect; jest think, Effie ol' girl, we still own thet house and them artifacts."

The four of them were standing looking at the White House one day. As Pete had said, "We're really in the big trough now, folks."

They stood there and looked at that famous house. Finally Pud looked at Pete and noticed he was deep in thought, seemed to be figuring something in his head.

"What you thinking about, Pete?"

"I figure it would take eighteen points ta make thet house safe from lightnin' fer our President. Yesiree, eighteen points. I'd use m' zinc-coat twist." They both smiled.

Pete decided to use the long distance, call Lil and see if his dispatches had been getting through to the *Western Times*. It was then when Lil told him, "Volney died of a heart condition in Denver just last week." Pete didn't do much singing for several days, and Sharon Springs was never quite the Paradise on the Plains after that. It's tough to lose your best friend.

There is an old Western saying, goes like this:

"Go after life as if it's something that's got to be roped in a hurry before it gets away."

* * * * *

Could Pete's endeavors have really happened even with the adversity of Depression, Drought, Dust Bowl? Of course, it could happen. Could it happen later? No way.

"With the Great Depression came the rapid expansion of federal powers. The Smoot-Hawley Tariff, passed in 1930, was the most restrictive tariff in U.S. history. The Reconstruction Finance Corporation had the government financing banks, railroads and other industries. The Agricultural Adjustment Act regulated farm production, the National Industrial Recovery Act regulated most corporations, and later the Wagner Act shifted the balance of power from the entrepreneurs to the labor union bosses.

The tax revenues needed to pay for these and other programs were astonishing. The top federal income tax rate in 1930 was 24 percent. In 1932 under President Hoover, the rate was hiked to 63 percent. Under President Roosevelt the rate was first raised to 79 percent and later jumped to over 90 percent.

Who has the power now? It is labor unions, the academic elite, public employees, and big government. These groups have had the power for most of this century, and they will fight every attempt to wrest it from them. We must restore power to the individuals."

— Imprimis, a publication of Hillsdale College

EPILOGUE

THERE IS AN ELEMENT OF TRUTH to the times of Pete and Effie Pisanmoan in Kansas. Many of the characters were real. Pete and Effie, Penelope and Daphne were fictitious; some were not, but I changed their names for anonymity. The following are lists of social programs that have evolved during and since their time. All are expensive cultural experiments. To examine a few, you decide, one now works over one-third of a year just to pay for these social and cultural necessities. My sources are as follows:

RESTORING THE AMERICAN DREAM
By Robert Ringer

In the 1930s the U.S. government went off the gold standard, and in so doing allowed them to increase the supply of paper money more easily. People became confused, because there is no way to judge the value of paper money. But experts were not confused. As soon as we went off the gold standard, the price of gold in the open market zoomed upward. This is because financial experts realized that gold was far more valuable than paper money.

In less than 150 years, consider what had taken place. Government entered the money business, in competition with other minters and warehousers; government then outlawed all competitors and claimed a monopoly on the money system; government established a so-called Federal Reserve System which, among other things, gave it the power to hold everyone's gold in its vaults and issue receipts far in excess of the gold it had on deposit.

It was the most protracted THEFT in history, but it certainly made a case for advocates of the slow, sure approach. It had taken one hundred and fifty years for government to complete the theft of the American people's gold. It now had all the gold; it could print paper money at will. It was a total control of the nation's money system.

— *Pgs. 217-218*

THE PRESIDENCY OF JOHN F. KENNEDY

By James N. Giglio

Programs that were developed during his presidency:
- *Agency for International Development*
- *Alliance for Progress*
- *Area Redevelopment Act*
- *C.A.R.E.*
- *C.E.A.*
- *C.O.R.E.*
- *E.R.A.*
- *Equal Pay Act*
- *Fair Employment Practices Commission*
- *Food for Peace*
- *Inter-American Development Bank*
- *International Cooperation Administration*
- *The Trade Expansion Act*
- *Manpower Development and Training Act*
- *N.A.S.A.*
- *Organized Crime Control Act*
- *P.C.E.E.O. President's Committee on Equal Employment Opportunity*
- *Peace Corp.*
- *V.I.S.T.A.*
- *Dept. of Urban Affairs*
- *President's Committee on Juvenile Delinquency*
- *President's Council on Youth Fitness*
- *Revenue Act of 1964*
- *Rural Areas Development*
- *Senate Space Committee*
- *Urban Mass Transportation Act of 1966*

BIG DADDY FROM THE PEDERNALES

By Paul K. Conklin

Here is the economic list of Lyndon B. Johnson. As Pete would say, he was "A Real Doozy":

- *Aid for Families with Dependent Children*
- *Alliance for Progress*
- *Economic Opportunities Act*
- *Air Quality act of 1967*
  (He should have seen the air 1935 Kansas)

> *"The bills that fit the label of the Great Society numbered at least 200 and still defy easy classification."*
> — *Pgs. 208-209*

- *Community Action Program*
- *Comprehensive Health Planning and Services Act of 1966*
- *Council of the Arts*
- *Nurses Training Bill of 1964*
- *Allied Training Act of 1966*
- *Mental Health Centers Act of 1967*
- *Mass Transportation Act of 1966*
- *Model Cities Act of 1966*
- *Solid Waste Disposal Act of 1966*
- *Water Pollution Bill of 1968*
- *Fair Packaging and Labelling Act of 1966*
- *The Automobile Safety Act of 1966*
- *Meat Inspection Act of 1967*
- *The President's Committee on Consumer Interests 1964*
- *The National Museum Act and the Public Broadcasting Act of 1967*
- *Law Enforcement Assistance Act*
- Don't forget all the GRANTS.
- *Medicare and Medicaid*
- *National Endowment for the Arts*
- *Occupational Health and Safety Act (OSHA)*

The legislation enacted under Johnson did not fulfill, or has not yet fulfilled, the almost utopian vision of Johnson's 1964 speeches. This failure could indicate that the legislation was ill conceived from the beginning or that later politicians and bureaucrats betrayed its earlier promise.

And one must understand that all these programs, bureaucracies and huge debt were created when there were over 500,000 men fighting in Viet Nam. The above two presidents are not all to blame. We citizens had elected members of the Senate and the House. We are all to blame. We counted returning body bags, not social justice.

Had Pete Pisanmoan been alive, he'd have tried to derail some of these programs just as he did the La Salle "autymobile."

Seems like we "double-clutched" along life's highway, and we created a culture of greed.

Some have criticized the vocabulary of Pete in reviewing this book. Intelligence does not go hand in hand with proper English.

It is in vain to say the enlightened statesmen will be able to adjust these class interests and render them all subservient to the public good. Enlightened statesmen will not always be at the helm. Nor, in many cases, can such an adjustment be made at all without taking into view indirect and remote considerations, which will rarely prevail over the immediate interest which one party may find in disregarding the rights of another or the good of the whole."
— James Madison, Federalist Paper No. 10 (1787)

I wish to thank Mr. William H. Hull, M.A., for his assistance in some of my descriptions of the Dust Bowl. Mr. Hull is the author of the book, "The Dirty Thirties." Also the Kansas State Historical Society for furnishing photos of dust storms.

I thank you.

Keith A. Cook